THE crooked play STRAIGHT

Dear Marge,

Many thanks for your proofreading and your encouragement along the way —

All the best,

Jessie

THE crooked play STRAIGHT

A Tale of Medical Intrigue in the Inner City

Jessie Stanzel Goehner

CutLeaf
PUBLISHING

Library of Congress Control Number: 2013912997
ISBN 978-0-9895468-0-5 (trade pbk.)
ISBN 978-0-9895468-2-9 (electronic text, epub)

The Crooked Play Straight: A Tale of Medical Intrigue in the Inner City is a work of fiction. The names, characters, dialogue, incidents, businesses, events, and locales either are creations of the author's imagination or are used fictitiously. Any resemblance to actual events or persons, living or dead, is entirely coincidental and not intended by the author.

Readers should not construe anything in this book as medical advice, but should consult their own physicians regarding the diagnosis and treatment of any medical condition. Some of the scientific and medical information in this book is accurate (or was in its historical context), but much is purely fictitious.

Printed in the United States of America

Editor and project manager: Janet Frick
Design and layout: Saija Autrand
Cover photo: Philippe Kallagov
Author photo: Janet Frick

Published in the
United States of America by
CUTLEAF PUBLISHING COMPANY
P.O. Box 1398
Wayne, NJ 07474-1398
www.cutleafpublishing.com

In memory
of
my parents:
Janet Bain Stanzel, née McFarlane,
and
Rudolph Albert Stanzel, Sr.

The integrity of the upright guides them, but the crookedness of the treacherous destroys them.

—Proverbs 11:3

Contents

Prologue: A Forgotten Triangle

*I*T WAS A TRIANGULAR PIECE OF LAND carved long ago by the Leni-Lenape trails that led down from the mountain, skirting the chasms etched by the rivers. The trails had become roads paved with macadam, but their angled routes had never been straightened to ease traffic or square the walls of buildings constructed at peculiar angles on their perimeters.

That must have been why this patch of land was forgotten, cut off from the hospital parking lot beyond by a high chain-link fence. Passersby had taken a shortcut across the triangle, creating a dirt path now polka-dotted with bottle caps trampled into the soil. Weeds and clumps of grass subsisted on the rest of this gently sloping mound despite the litter of food wrappers, cigarette butts, soda cans, and liquor bottles. The more ambitious street people quickly collected all the aluminum and glass in huge plastic bags, then made a few dollars by pushing the bags to the recycling center in stolen supermarket carts.

The small plot did not exist on the city map. But it was home and marketplace for the homeless, the poor, and the not-so-poor who lived entrepreneurial lives at the bottom of the economic ladder, creating a subeconomy of survival while the hospital served as family physician and employer for them and others in the blocks nearby.

It was a culture for the immediate, since tomorrow never arrived.

part ONE

Research Below the Radar

Chapter 1

_I_T WAS ONLY MIDMORNING that July day in 2006, but Hughler
City had already hunkered down under a blanket of steamy smog.
Despite the heat wave, Ghanna Topallo was taking his daily walk
from his one-room apartment across the street to his plot of shabby
green shade. With his left arm thrust slightly to the side, he balanced the weight of his boom box despite his limping gait.

Ever since construction had begun on a new wing of Hughler
Hospital, three trailers—serving as offices for the supervisors—had
stood near the edges of the triangular plot, and another section
had become off-street parking for workers' trucks. Still, there was
plenty of space left for Ghanna and for the many people who took
the dirt-path shortcut from Hughler Street across to Woodhouse,
avoiding quite a few steps on the gritty sidewalk.

He sidled past a trailer office. No, he wouldn't sit in its ample
shade; the construction workers often sat there. _Ain't sure them
workers would like it. Me bein' poor and an ex-con an' all._ Instead he
sat in his favorite spot: the narrow shadow of a cracked utility pole
at the top of the park's little mound. There Ghanna had the best
possible view of both streets. Also, on the third side of the triangle,
he could see past the chain-link fence, ten feet high, that protected
the hospital parking lot beyond.

Ghanna smoked and waited. Head leaning back against the
utility pole, legs stretched out carefully within the stripe of shade,
he placed his boom box in the sun close beside him and listened

to some island music. He watched the heat-hushed neighborhood, occasionally hearing the usual car horn or angry voices drifting from the open window of a hot apartment. But Ghanna was not distracted. He focused like a vulture looking for road kill, watching for drug deals going down, moving with the shade until the shadow grew short and the sun beat down on his narrow-brimmed straw hat.

By two in the afternoon the wind was picking up, and gray-black clouds were darkening the sky. Then this wizened old man held on to his hat and boom box and struggled back across the street to sit again on the warm concrete steps outside his apartment house, letting the heat bake the ache out of his bones. That's when he saw a crooked flash of lightning and heard its vibration hum downward. Ghanna sped into the building as quickly as his limp would allow. He stood in the foyer to watch the storm through the front window. The thunderclaps crashed and the wind-slashed rain swept parallel to the street. *Shit, man,* he thought, *what we got here? A monsoon?*

Now Ghanna saw the smoke: billows of it curling up in the western part of the city. *The lightnin' strike a building? It still be rainin' hard, maybe put the fire out. Lightnin' move on. Thunder's softer.*

The honk of the alarm ripped through the usual city noise like chain saws tearing through a forest. Fire trucks zoomed by over the slick, wet roads, creating a cacophony of honking horns and squealing sirens in answer to Ghanna's question.

Ghanna knew the next step. Ambulances followed, adding the blare of their sirens to the chorus—rushing to return to the emergency room with the injured. The deluge continued as the wind whipped it on down the valley. When the wind let up and the pelting rain thinned into a drizzle, Ghanna shuffled through the puddles and over the stream that gushed down the gutter into the storm drain, back to his little park so he could see all the emergency rush more clearly.

"For God's sake, don't panic. Stop acting like the intern you are or I'll frog-march you out of here. Take this fireman and start him on

IV fluids for rehydration. He's suffering from smoke inhalation. Probably heat exhaustion too. Go, go, go. Josh, get more gurneys. Move those patients to be admitted over into the hall," Dr. Pannell barked. "Magahali, phone Admissions. Tell 'em I can't wait for them to saunter on down here for these new patients. They'll find them in the hall. Get rid of the ones in the waiting room unless they're critical."

Magahali sighed, then rapidly pressed the numbers with her pencil to protect her perfectly manicured nails.

"Étoile? Where's Étoile?"

"She's in the hallway checking on the patients there. You know, the ones being moved," Magahali told Dr. Pannell while she picked up the microphone. "This is Magahali Triestane speaking. Hughler Hospital's emergency room is at capacity. Please divert all emergency cases to other area hospitals and clinics." Magahali was radioing hospitals, rescue squads, emergency-management personnel, and police forces throughout the city and surrounding communities. She repeated the warning several times.

"At least those two ladies know what they're doing," Dr. Pannell announced as he eased a fireman onto a hospital bed. "No, pal. You can't go home. Let me just look you over for a minute." The fireman's eyes fluttered closed.

"Josh, bring in more linens," Étoile scolded. "We've got to get these beds made up. And get more hypodermics in here. I know you've been busy, but you're s'posed to keep this cart and tray supplied no matter what. A building just collapsed. Three more firemen are coming in, plus two brothers and their dog."

"Their dog! I'm not a veterinarian," Dr. Pannell yelled.

"He saved their lives, Doc. He led the firemen to them. The boys were trapped in the debris. That dog is a hero," Étoile yelled back, annoyed.

"Yeah? In that case, you and Josh here will have to treat him," Dr. Pannell said.

Josh raced to the supply cabinet, fumbling for the key as he went. "Worst I've seen in the two years I been workin' here," Josh mumbled. *Man, this place is like a drug war. The firemen are really sick. But it's my chance. Ghanna says, "Use the opportunity." Nobody'll notice if a few hypos get lost.* Josh bent down out of view and helped himself to twenty sterile hypodermic needles in protective plastic cases. He dropped them into the pocket of his jacket.

He lined the tray with twenty more needles, as well as packets of gauze, swabs, and sponges—tallying each item, including the twenty needles he took, on the inventory list. Josh signed the inventory with a flourish. Twenty needles just never made it onto the tray.

Worked hard for them to trust me—looks like today it's paying off. By the time General Stores gets around to checkin' this, they'll never notice. Ghanna says, "Don't get greedy. Keep it small and nobody'll notice. And never use the same routine twice." Now I gotta figure out how to get this stuff outta here come quittin' time.

Dr. Pannell saw Josh pat his jacket pocket.

"Supplies over here." Josh parked the cart between the bed area and the waiting room, which was rapidly becoming a treatment ward too. Doctors and nurses helped themselves as needed. Magahali tried to keep track of each patient's care, including the meds and supplies used. "Want me to check them patients up front for ya?" Josh interrupted her counting. "And maybe I can take a quick break? Get some fresh air. Storm's about over."

Magahali glanced up from her clipboard and nodded yes. She was a plump thirty-year-old with brown hair pulled back in a long ponytail. Her lipstick always matched the color of her bright nails. As he walked by her desk, Josh couldn't help noticing the drawer she had left open. Magahali had a wardrobe of nail polish and lipstick in it for emergency touch-ups.

Josh just chuckled to himself and continued on to the ambulance bays. The rain had settled into a drizzle now, but he could still hear the faint sound of thunder every so often as the storm moved away. Josh crossed the patients' emergency parking lot to the sidewalk so he could see down the street, jumping over puddles as he went. It was the only way since fencing had been installed all the way around the grounds. To his surprise, Ghanna was perched on the roof of a construction worker's pickup truck with a couple of newspapers for a dry seat and one folded over his hat. *He really wanted to see what's goin' down. Usually Ghanna never wants to bother them big construction workers.* Josh gave Ghanna two thumbs up. Ghanna grinned and waved in response.

Josh saw a golden retriever sitting near the emergency-room door. "You must be the rescue dog!" Josh patted the dog's head and scratched behind his ears. "You're not too wet. You must've been in the ambulance bays during the storm. Just drizzlin' now. You know you're a hero, fella. Yeah, a hero! Soon as I finish here, Hero, I'm gonna check up on ya again. I promise."

When Josh went back inside, the odor of smoke from the firemen's clothes and the acrid sweat from their bodies nearly stifled him. "You all right, Josh?" Étoile sounded worried.

"Yeah, yeah. Whew, the smell in here hit me like a punch in the belly."

"I'll never get used to it either. It's like Vietnam when I was a nurse there during the war," Étoile said.

Josh heard Dr. Pannell singing his nonsensical songs and knew the emergency had passed. "Why he gotta sing them stupid songs all the time?"

"Dr. Bob Pannell knows war too. He was in Desert Storm. He told me his brother does the same thing after he conquers a challenge. It runs in the family. Then he laughed and told me his dad's descended from a runaway slave who fled the bounty hunters before the Civil War."

Josh turned around and stared at Dr. Pannell in amazement. "Didn't know that," he said softly.

Étoile smiled. "You should ask him about it sometime. Apparently it's quite a story."

About four thirty that afternoon, medical research chemist Cory Maxwell, PhD, walked into the hospital office of his boss and closest colleague, eminent oncologist Dr. Frederick Truesort. "Why'd you call me up here, Fred? Thought I might get out of the lab early today. Never got out for a lunch break—the damn street level at the parking garage flooded. I put in enough time at this hospital. You should get an additional assistant. I can't do it all." Cory cleared the stack of papers and professional journals off the chair and sat down facing Fred across his desk. "Don't you ever clean up?"

"Of course not. The cleaning lady does that. I've got more important things to do with my time. I know where everything is."

Cory rolled his eyes. Yet despite their many arguments, he and Fred made a good team.

"Lost a patient," Fred said.

"And you didn't see it coming?"

"He had AIDS as well as cancer. It was inevitable, I guess. I'd just like to win a few." In his frustration, Fred's dark-brown eyes became slits.

"Trouble with you doctors is you all think you're God. Even you make mistakes, Fred," Cory retorted.

"You're wrong, Cory. We *know* we're God. Seriously, though, this patient would improve for a while, then get worse, then better, in an almost predictable pattern. There's got to be a reason why."

"So?" Cory stood up, hoping to leave.

"So-o, obviously I've got to learn more about the cancers HIV causes: Kaposi's sarcoma and possibly others. But I'd rather concentrate only on Kaposi's sarcoma. Easier that way."

"You know, Fred, we can talk more about this tomorrow," Cory said as he walked toward the office door. "I—"

But Fred continued, "Well, why can't I apply some of the techniques for diagnosing and treating other cancers to HIV/AIDS patients?" Cory turned with a sigh as Fred went on, "I could predict this patient's ups and downs almost to the minute, Cory. His cancer and HIV were in a battle. The cancer's attack on the HIV was right on target. Why? *Why* can't we take advantage of that? Hit that HIV with the cancer virus until we kill it."

"It's not that simple," Cory said, running his hand impatiently through his grayish-red hair. "The reverse could be true, too. The HIV could attack the cancer."

"Of course it's not simple, but something was going on. Why can't we use the equipment and knowledge we've got? Find some clues to this thing? Not just another medical cocktail like those used now, but a vaccine component, maybe. Something to prevent the HIV from mutating so fast that we can't combat it effectively."

"That won't be easy. You have extensive experience with treating cancer, Fred. You know the usual courses of cancers and their patterns. That's where you should start. The transition to HIV/AIDS will take time. And where will you get patients? Patients' DNA to study, I mean. DNA will supply the answer."

"Plenty of HIV/AIDS patients around this city don't even know they're sick yet. See them every day in the ER." Fred walked to his closet and carefully took his Armani suit off the hanger. With his upright bearing and white hair, he looked every bit the distinguished professional he was.

"How would you know? You never go there." Cory laughed.

"Okay, okay. I do avoid the place," Fred admitted as he changed out of his scrubs. "Our ER staff is the family doctor around here. At least that's what the staff tells me."

"Yeah, they're right about that. What do you want me for?" Cory crossed the room to the wide, rain-spattered window and stared down at the city, longing to be on his way home. The afternoon's thunderstorm had thinned to a drizzle, but the roads were still shiny, reflecting the lights of an ambulance as it wove through the rush-hour traffic below. He rifled through the medical journals spread across the conference table at the far end of the office.

"I'd like you to help with some of this research," Fred replied. "I know and respect your ability." He tied his tie, checking to see if it was straight in the full-length mirror that hung on the inside of the closet door. Satisfied with his appearance, he strode back to his desk, pushed his executive chair back, and thumped his feet up onto the desktop, sending papers flapping.

"Sure, sure you do." Cory shook his head and twirled his eyeglasses. *I'm never going to get out of here.* He walked back to the chair across from Fred's desk and sat down. Not even Fred could miss the gloomy expression on Cory's face.

Intuitively Fred said, "I know I don't often tell you how much I value your technical knowledge and skill. But work with me on this one. Believe me, it's worth a try—great opportunity. Gain prestige, even if we just scratch the surface of the problem. Can't lose. My private lab's the perfect place. Need your technical ability to photograph and work with cell cultures. Have to duplicate HIV many times over." Fred caught his breath and then plunged forward: "I want a geneticist and a good bioinformatics engineer who can analyze DNA sequences on the computer. Got a couple suited to the task. Figure we will attack this problem on several fronts. Look at bone marrow and—"

"Whoa, Fred. Like I said, why include me? Don't answer. I'll tell you why. You need somebody to do your scut work, your background work, and you and I both know I'm good. About the only thing I can't do is write prescriptions for you." Cory stood and leaned toward Fred. "You need me because I'm the only one who can do the work and I'm available." With his chin thrust forward, Cory continued, "I'll help you, not because you're a nice guy, but because I have a lot of interest in this topic. And I want my fair share of the glory and the money for once, understand? Understand?"

Abruptly he sat down again. He sighed, then after a moment said more calmly, "Well, Fred, you do come up with promising, creative ideas. I can help you research this one. How do we get started?"

Fred's demeanor softened. The wrinkles on his forehead had smoothed, and he leaned across his desk toward Cory. "I'm afraid much of what you say is true. However, during this original research our relationship will be different. I will be depending upon you to work with the geneticist and the bioinformatics expert."

"Yeah, I can do that."

"Good. I've kept tabs on Bob Pannell, the assist in the ER. He's that tall, black doctor who had the Desert Storm experience. Has the reputation of being very good at his job. But before his medical training, post-traumatic stress drove him into drug abuse. Pretty much common knowledge. He's been clean for several years, of course, but he still can't get a job anywhere else. He's stymied and anxious to move ahead. He also has easy access to the patients we need: ones with no next of kin."

"You have to give a guy credit who puts his broken life back together," said Cory. "Couldn't have been easy. How do you know about Pannell? Like I said, you never go to the ER."

"I have my informants," Fred admitted with a sly smile. "Initially I want another cancer/AIDS patient since that's closest to my experience. Generally they have Kaposi's sarcoma. To reduce the number of unknown variables, that'll be the only cancer we study. I'll just let you know when the patient is here. Needless to say, this is to be done outside hospital authority."

"What?" Cory snapped. "That's unethical. *Why* can't we get any goddamn hospital authority?"

"Don't get so agitated, Cory. Hear me out. I don't want to go the typical clinical-trial route for a number of reasons. This hospital is struggling financially. You know it and I know it. If we get a lot of the underclass in here, the hospital will have a slimmer profit margin because insured, paying patients will be scared away to suburban country-club hospitals. The only thing that brings many of them here is the fact that they can't find good specialized care like mine anyplace else."

Cory stood and began pacing around the office. "If the paying patients haven't been scared off by now, a few more homeless aren't going to do it. You've gotta give me more than that for a reason. Besides, why do you care if this hospital loses money? What's it to you? You've got hospital privileges all over this area."

"You know the kind of pressure they can put on doctors when they need hefty donations," Fred said. "Although we may be within the law, I think we may be considered unethical by the standards of Hughler Hospital or insurance companies. Oh, it's okay to do highly risky experimentation in developing countries, but in the United States, no way. Nobody wants to admit that some of our citizens are living as low as poverty-stricken people outside our borders."

"So just use any patients who are near death. If they're desperate enough, they'll try anything. Is that it?" Cory shook his head in disbelief and sat down. "Is that what you're saying?"

"Most of them have been on a lot of prescribed drugs—the AIDS cocktail—for years. I want untreated cases without the research complications previous meds can cause. I want a clean slate to work with. The homeless are the best source for that."

"Why not do both?"

"A vaccine or a simple single-dose medicine is where the money is. Something that's one-stop shopping . . . one visit to a clinic.

You don't have to worry about the patient returning to complete the treatment."

"I see. But tell me, Fred. It's where the glory is, too, isn't it?"

"You could say that. We get the prestige. We don't have other researchers looking over our shoulders. You've been around medical research a long time. You know the competition that exists in clinical-trial research. Everyone cheats, lies, and steals in the scramble to the top. You get some of those damn half-smart research chemists from one of the pharma houses with their half-baked theories, and you'll be at this thing for centuries. I'm not even taking the medical-journal, peer-review route. This stays strictly within my team until we're certain we have the answer."

"Well, you've got a point there. All right, I know how to be careful. But I don't plan to share in any of the expense. My expertise plus my ability to keep my mouth shut should be enough of a contribution. I pray to God it works."

"It will," Fred answered. "We agree, then. I'll take on the financial risk. I've been putting aside funds for about ten years now. There should be enough to provide us with money until we get a saleable product. You'll be well compensated; just send me quarterly invoices for your consulting fee. I'll probably pay the others monthly. About twenty-five thousand dollars per quarter all right with you?"

"I'll agree to twenty-five thousand for the first quarter. I may need to reevaluate my fee after that, once I see how much work is involved." Cory paused. "But please think again, Fred—you could lose your license. At least get the homeless to sign a permission/release-to-operate form."

"Cory. My oncology practice brings in a lot of money to this hospital. The administration here will cut me some slack. Those homeless people without any next of kin won't ask a lot of questions. I don't want any paperwork to come back to haunt us."

"I still don't see why you have to be so stubborn." Cory dropped his face into his hands. "I sure hope you're right."

Fred got up and tapped him on the shoulder. "You still with me?"

"Yeah, yeah."

"Bob Pannell usually parks in the parking garage near me, on the open top level. Lately he's been working days—arrives and leaves when I do. Other times it's nights. Never know. Really not a problem . . . always in the same spot. I'll probably talk to him within the next few days."

"You've been watching him?" Cory asked, incredulous.

"Of course I have. I've been planning this for a long time. I'd like to use the ER chief, but he's too honest. Have to see how Bob reacts to the idea."

Cory stood and shook Fred's hand. "You think of everything," he told Fred.

Fred held the office door open for Cory and patted his shoulder as he left. "Have to tie up some loose ends. See you tomorrow, Cory."

Fred watched Cory walk several yards to the elevator. After its door closed, the long hallway was empty. Fred took a deep breath.

"And so it begins," he announced to no one.

$$\sim\!\wedge\!\downarrow\!\frown\!o$$

By about six that evening, the emergency room was much calmer. "We had a real busy Monday," said Josh. "It's gettin' late—worked almost two hours overtime already. I'll help you clean up, Étoile. See some firemen already goin' home. They say how the fire started?"

"Maybe lightning, but they aren't sure. We had to admit a few. The kids have to stay. Their mom and dad are with them."

"Where were the parents when the fire broke out?"

"Working. The twelve-year-old was babysitting for his little brother. The deputy at the sheriff's office brought them over. The whole family's still pretty traumatized. Too bad we can't sneak the dog upstairs to them. It might help them feel better."

"I ain't sneaking any dog up there—could get fired. How'd the dog get here, anyways?"

"Rode with the firemen. They said he was upset when the brothers were put in the ambulance. You know, whimpering and sniffing the air, so they brought him over here."

"He the one outside the door? A golden retriever by himself?"

"That's the one," Étoile confirmed. "He's not tied up. He just won't move. I swear he knows the boys are here—been carefully trained—knows how to sniff the air to find people caught under collapsed buildings. He's a brave dog. A couple of the firemen told me they gave the dog to Matthew and Darian about a year ago after he was retired from duty as a rescue dog. The firemen couldn't believe it was the same dog, but he recognized them! Pretty amazing."

"Wow, that's somethin'. Were the kids hurt bad?" Josh asked.

"The fellas who cared for them in the ambulance said the older boy had a broken arm and the younger one probably had two broken ribs. A lot of bruises and scrapes too."

"Them brothers are damn lucky. Not everybody has a pet dog like that."

"Yeah, they are, but the firemen said the dog wants to be sure the boys are all right. And the brothers are probably just as worried about him."

Josh agreed. "Tell ya what. If you don't need me for ten minutes, I'll take some photos of the dog with my cell and bring 'em up to them brothers. Won't help the dog, but maybe the family will feel better."

Étoile walked over to the emergency-room door. "The drizzle hasn't stopped. He's still waiting, Josh."

Josh grabbed a towel. So he would have a dry place to sit outdoors, he pushed a wheelchair outside under an eave, then called the dog to him. Josh sat in the wheelchair and talked to the retriever while gently rubbing his wet fur. "So you use this nose to find them brothers? You a hero, you know that? You are golden."

The retriever whined softly, wagging his tail.

"Gonna take your picture with my cell. You gotta look good. Can't take ya into the hospital, but I figure this way your family will see you're okay. Hold still. Good dog! Whew, them paws look sore. Stay, now. I'll be right back." Josh returned to the emergency room for antiseptic ointment and supplies, then went outdoors again, where he deftly cleaned and bandaged the dog's feet.

On the way back in, he showed his photos to Étoile. "Nice pictures, Josh. You seem to have made friends with him quickly—"

"ÉTOILE CHANTEL, ÉTOILE CHANTEL."

"Oops, I'm being paged. The boys are in room 366."

Josh knocked softly on the door, then entered. "Good evenin', everybody. I'm Joshua King, an aide in the ER. The firemen brought your dog to us. He's waitin' for you outside the door to the ER. See, I just took photos of him on my cell." Josh sat in a chair and moved close to Matthew so the boy could see his pet's photo. "I been callin' him Hero. Whadda you all call him?"

"Sniffer. Maybe we should call him Hero now, though."

The boys' mom wiped her eyes. "Hero is good."

Then Josh slid over to Darian and showed him the photos. "You wanna call him Hero, too?"

Darian looked at Josh and said, "Yes. I love Hero." Josh passed him the cell phone, and Darian stroked Hero's picture.

"And Hero loves you both," Josh said. "His paws are sore, but I put medicine on them to help them heal."

The boys' dad had treated them to hamburgers and fries from White Castle. Their mom packed the remainder of the hamburgers into a bag for Hero to eat later. "Josh, he's been trained to carry food. He can carry this for you."

"The firemen teach him that too?" Josh asked.

"Yeah," she answered. "Just in case a victim needed something, I guess."

"What are we going to do with Hero for tonight?" Dad said. "I'm going to a motel; gotta get to work tomorrow in spite of all this. My wife's staying here with the boys. No dogs allowed here *or* there."

Mom added, "My brother from Virginia will be here to pick up Hero tomorrow morning. He's going to keep Hero until we get settled."

"Tell ya what," said Josh. "I know this EMT fella, Kevin, really good with dogs. Cared for 'em during 9/11. His shift's about over.

Lemme call him right now. He'll be glad to look after Hero tonight. You can call your brother, work everythin' out."

The arrangements were quickly made. With thanks from the boys and their parents, Josh quietly left the room. *Nice family. Trouble with workin' in a hospital is you only get to see most patients once.*

He took the elevator down to the employee locker room directly behind the ER. To his surprise, Hero was waiting next to his locker. "Hey, fella," Josh said softly. "How'd you sneak in here? You followed somebody in an' sniffed your way to me?"

Hero wagged his tail.

"Yeah, you're smart." Josh placed his bag of food on the top of the locker. Hero whined. He smelled the hamburgers.

"Quiet, Hero. You'll get your dinner in a few minutes." Josh changed into his street clothes. While hiding behind the locker door, he dropped the confiscated needles into the paper bag. He folded over the top of the bag twice and looked into Hero's eyes. "You can have this here dinner when we get outside. Understand?" Hero barked, stood up, and wagged his tail. Josh put the folded top of the bag into Hero's mouth.

Not concerned about a routine pat-down, he led Hero right up to the security guard.

"Thought I heard a dog bark. You know no animals allowed in here."

"Yeah, but this here's the dog that saved the two kids in the big house fire. I'm takin' him right on outside." The guard eyed the bag.

"He don't take kindly to anyone messin' with his supper," Josh told him, and walked out.

Outside, Josh knelt and patted Hero on his head, then rubbed his ears. Hero sat and allowed Josh to take the bag, whimpering and then pawing Josh's pant leg. Josh glanced around and then slipped the needles into his pocket. He stood and tossed the hamburgers to Hero, who caught and swallowed them in one gulp.

Josh and Hero walked over to the ambulance team. "G'night, guys. Glad the rain's over. Too bad it didn't cool off none."

"Heard you had to divert cases."

"Yeah. Pretty bad fire. The thunder and lightnin' sure didn't help neither. Firemen said the rain was heavy while it lasted, but them high winds just spread the fire more."

"Yeah, the roads were slick. Sewers backed up from debris flooded some of the streets," the driver told Josh.

"Hey, Kevin. Here's the dog I told ya about."

Kevin kneeled and scratched Hero behind the ears. "You really did a good job today, fella. I'll get you some water." Then, to Josh, "Did he eat anything?"

"Just a couple of half-eaten burgers is all."

"Okay, I'll get him some more food. Looks like his paws need fresh bandages. They're bleeding a little. Who put on these booties? You?"

"Yeah. Made 'em with gauze, cotton, and tape."

"Nice job. Reminds me of 9/11," Kevin said. "I'll get my kit."

Josh watched him expertly clean a burned paw and put soothing ointment on it.

Josh smiled. "Ya look like you're already friends. Thanks, thanks. I'll be goin'. You talked to that uncle comin' up from Virginia? Everything cool for tomorrow?"

"Yeah, that's all fine. You got a leash?"

"Nah. Never got time to make one. Don't matter. He just follows ya."

Kevin said with a smile, "My shift's about over. I'll take him home, bring him back in the morning. Maintenance must have something for a leash."

"Yeah, good idea." Josh knelt and patted Hero once more. "Nice to have met ya, fella. You be good, now." Josh stood and shook Kevin's hand. "Thanks again, Kevin." He turned and walked toward Ghanna's park. "Take good care of the kids' best friend," he called back.

Overtime and a little bit more. This is my lucky day. Josh grinned and patted his pocketful of hypodermics.

As it turned out, Fred spotted Bob Pannell in the parking garage that very evening. "You're Dr. Pannell?" he called across the parked cars. "Head of the ER?"

"I'm Dr. Pannell all right, but only the assist in the ER."

Fred smiled at his own deliberate mistake, then strode over to Bob and shook hands. "I'm Fred Truesort, chief of oncology. I know it's already six thirty, and that's late for a Monday. But can you spare a few minutes?"

"Sure. End of a long day. Had a bad fire in the west of the city. Several firemen injured. They'll be okay, though."

"Good, good, glad to hear it. Need to talk to you," Fred said.

"What about?"

"It's complicated. I just lost a patient. He had both AIDS and cancer . . . was into the drug scene at one time. I figure you must see a lot like him in your ER. Any suggestions? I must admit your fine reputation has preceded you."

"That's nice to hear. Wish I could help you, Dr. Truesort."

"Fred. Please call me Fred."

"Okay. Fred, I'm Bob. Well, as I say, I wish I could help you. Whenever I see those peculiar red to purple blotches and bumps, I'm certain those patients have cancer as well as AIDS. You know how it is when I tell them to see their own doctor: many say they don't have one. I offer to recommend one of our Hughler Hospital doctors, like you, but they just shake their heads and leave. They don't have any money or health insurance. Others go into denial, and—"

"Look, I'd like to discuss this further, but not in a parking garage," Fred interrupted him.

"You aren't really interested in any of these patients, are you?" Bob was suddenly wary. "If you want me to supply you with recreational drugs, you've come to the wrong doctor. Get out of my way!" he shouted, and pushed Fred Truesort backward.

"Hold on! You don't understand!" Fred protested, waving his hands above his shoulders to prove they were empty.

Bob stepped back. They glared at each other. Bob leaned his sinewy body slightly forward and slowly released his bent fingers from the tight fold of a fist. "You sure?" he asked.

"Of course I'm sure." Fred put down his hands. "Just because we work in an inner-city hospital doesn't mean we docs are looking for additional revenue or, worse, are users ourselves. Somebody must have approached you before."

"Yeah. You're right. Not here, though. Sorry," Bob said. "I overreacted. Very sorry." Bob shook his head and wiped perspiration off his face with his handkerchief. "I don't know how I could make such a mistake. I've been edgy lately. Really sorry. I apologize."

"Forget it. It's good to see somebody who is so alert and so honest," Fred yelled over the noise of the traffic. "Would you consider having dinner with me tomorrow, and my wife, Ingrid? We can meet here in the parking garage and drive over to my home. It's right here in the city. I'll lead the way. It's a little hard to find, but it's a quiet place to talk."

"That's a tough offer to refuse, but I really don't think my expertise is what you're looking for."

"Let me be the judge of that. You underestimate yourself."

"I could just refer patients to you."

"It's more complicated than that."

Bob stared at his key chain as though it could answer the real question on his mind—*Why?*—and without looking up said, "If you insist. I rarely get out of the ER at four when my shift is over. Five thirty should work unless tomorrow's as hectic as today."

"It will be worthwhile. I promise. Tomorrow evening, then. I'll meet you here at five thirty. Let me know if you get held up, and I'll tell Ingrid when to expect us." Fred marched back to his Porsche with his ramrod gait. Bob could see only his shock of white hair bobbing up and down as he threaded his way between the cars.

Chapter 2

*T*HE NEXT EVENING Fred led Bob to his home on Sherwood Boulevard, in a dignified, historic neighborhood near the edge of the city. A central median strip lined with blue spruces divided the boulevard. Bob slowed down his Camry as he saw Fred's Porsche turn toward a black wrought-iron gate in a twelve-foot-high wall of gray stone. *I might've known his house would be like this. Huge lot, stone wall, heavy gate. Looks isolated, too.*

Bob watched Fred push a button on his rearview mirror, and the gate rolled open. Once the two cars had entered the driveway, Fred closed the gate behind them with another push of the button. *Just like a garage door opener,* thought Bob. *Surveillance camera up there, too.*

Bob followed Fred around the circular drive, which sloped gently upward toward the house. At the top of the circle, Fred turned left to enter the three-car garage; Bob turned right toward the guest parking area. He then walked up the short pathway to the house.

While he waited for Fred to join him, Bob glanced back at the gate. He could see that the high stone wall continued along both sides of the property as well as the front. *This place is a fortress, all right, and the house is as big as a museum.*

"Glad you could come over, Bob," Fred said when he joined him at the front door. "We have to be pretty cautious here. Trust you understand."

"Sure," Bob said. "Quite an impressive piece of property you've got. What's beyond the two side walls?"

"The rocky field on the north side has a dirt path leading down to the river. By the way, some of the rocks from that field were used years ago to build the walls. On the south side, between the wall and the forest beyond, there's a dirt road going down to the water. Crazy daredevils occasionally launch rafts from there, but it's really dangerous so close to the rapids."

Fred held the collar of the Doberman that bounded toward him as soon as he stepped into the hallway. "Don't mind Chewy. Once he knows you're a guest, he's very friendly. Best for you to make friends in here. Ingrid didn't think you would like him barking at you when you arrived."

Bob scratched Chewy behind his ear and petted his back. "Good dog, good dog."

Fred sent Chewy down the long hallway back into the kitchen, then turned and pointed to the two windows in the living room. "I get a great view of the sunrise from the front of the house. We did add the three-car garage, but all the rest of the house is original."

"Beautiful view from this hilltop. You must enjoy your home," Bob said.

"The view out the back is even better," said Fred. "We'll watch the sunset after dinner. Now come meet Ingrid."

The dining-room table was spread with an embroidered linen cloth, and the glistening chandelier was turned down low. As they sat down to generous helpings of arugula salad, roast beef, garlic mashed potatoes, and fresh asparagus, Bob asked Ingrid, "Have you lived here long?"

"Oh, yes. About twenty years. We lived in a one-bedroom apartment when we were first married, then in a three-bedroom ranch before finding the house of our dreams."

"It's a lovely home," said Bob. "Lovely furniture, too."

"Thank you," said Ingrid. "That chandelier you are admiring

is from Venice. This carved oak dining-room set is Scottish. Our house contains many antiques and souvenirs from our trips. These high ceilings really set off our furnishings. Don't you think so?"

"Ingrid is a very talented interior decorator," Fred said.

Ingrid smiled. "The house itself has some interesting features, such as a walk-in pantry. That really comes in handy."

Later, as the plates were being cleared away, Fred said to his wife, "Please excuse us, sweetheart. We'll be in the library. Have Cook bring our coffee and dessert in there." Fred kissed Ingrid's hand, and she smiled, pushing a strand of blond hair off her face. Her classic pageboy was always neatly combed.

"It was delicious, Mrs. Truesort," Bob said. "I haven't had such tender roast beef in years."

"I'm glad you enjoyed it. We do have an excellent cook. And thank you for the bouquet."

"You are entirely welcome. Thank you again." Bob gave her a smile and followed Fred out of the dining room.

They walked down the broad hallway, past the spacious living room and den, to the library at the back of the house. Their footsteps resounded along the marble floor, and Bob admired the elegant mahogany staircase as they passed by.

"Our timing is just about perfect," said Fred, ushering Bob into the room. "The sun is ready to set." The two of them stood several minutes at the picture window, watching the clouds turn violet and apricot.

"Spectacular," said Bob. He noticed that the backyard swept downward quite steeply, in a series of terraced lawns and gardens, all the way to the river. "Are those rhododendrons way down the hill?"

"Yes, near the potting shed," answered Fred. "Too bad you missed them in bloom in the spring."

"Do I glimpse a pool down there too?"

"Yes, Ingrid and I like to swim."

"A healthy habit. I can't see from here—does the stone wall surround the property on all four sides?"

"No, just three. The river runs quite swiftly here because we're near the rapids. It's a natural barrier."

Once the sun had dipped into the river, Fred eased himself into his recliner with a wince. "Used to sit in a soft chair like the one you're sitting on. But my back won't let me anymore."

"I know what you mean."

"Ingrid hates this chair. It's not stylish enough, I guess. But after being in the OR for hours, I like to elevate my legs. You have a recliner too?"

"Right in front of my TV." Bob sat on the burgundy velvet sofa in front of the fireplace. "This must be stylish," he said, patting the sofa.

"That it is, with a price tag to match."

Bob gestured toward bookshelves that covered the longest wall. They were interrupted only by a handsome fireplace constructed of the same gray fieldstone as the walls outside. "Have you managed to find the time to read all those books?"

Fred laughed. "I still have a few to go. Now let me explain what I propose to do."

"Of course."

The Truesorts' cook stood at the door, dressed in a purple uniform and white apron. "Here is your coffee, gentlemen. Sorry to interrupt. I'll just put the tray on the table so you can help yourselves."

The large silver tray held a silver coffee service, silver spoons, and two Rosenthal china cups and saucers. Nestled beside these was a smaller silver tray covered with a doily and piled generously with dainty cookies and petits fours. Two luncheon-size linen napkins were tucked neatly beneath the smaller tray, their lace-edged corners peeking out.

"Let me know if you need anything else, Doctor."

"Thanks," Fred said. He waited until she closed the door behind her before he commenced with his proposal. "I have a plan that might interest you," he began. "A research idea . . . thought you might be a part of it. I won't kid you. I need access to a certain population of patients, and you seem to be right at the source."

"At the ER, you mean?"

"Yes. As I said, I lost a cancer/AIDS patient yesterday. Yet I gained a theory. While I was treating him for Kaposi's sarcoma,

I saw him rally for a while, then become more ill in an almost constant up-and-down pattern. I checked blood samples throughout his illness. The usual configurations developed first and then changed. The Kaposi's sarcoma tumor and the HIV were battling each other in their own private war, and they actually slowed each other down."

"How?"

"That's what I'd like to find out. We didn't have a fast-moving target anymore. It was sluggish. I think we can take advantage of that battle. Strike when the cancer virus slows down the HIV. Force the HIV to retreat."

"Amazing. How well equipped is Hughler Hospital's oncology lab?" Bob struck at the core of the matter.

"Not as well as I'd like. We'll need more equipment, including powerful computers. I may get them on my dime and put them in my private DNA lab. But that's my problem, not yours. Got a well-placed friend who might help us on that score."

"Didn't know you had a private lab," said Bob, stirring his coffee. "Anybody else involved? How about researchers?"

"Cory is the medical research chemist in charge of the hospital's oncology lab. PhD, worked for me fifteen years now. Meticulous. I just told him yesterday about my theory. He agreed to be part of the research." Fred selected two petits fours and continued talking. "To start, he'll probably be working at the hospital oncology lab some of the time and at my private DNA lab other times, wherever we need him. I plan on asking my colleague's daughter and her husband to join us. She's a geneticist. Her husband is a bioinformatics engineer. He's the one who will need the sophisticated computer equipment: a workstation with the most current components, like a motion-sensor camera attached to a high-powered microscope."

"And Hughler Hospital?" asked Bob. "What does that staff think?"

"I don't plan to detail any of this with them. No research company, no pharmaceutical company—this will be strictly our own operation."

"Ah. I get it. So that's why you don't want me to simply refer the patients to you. But why take such a risk? Hospital ethics are stringent at Hughler. You know that better than I do. How long have you had privileges there?"

"Thirty years," Fred said.

"Won't your ethics be questioned?" Bob asked.

"Probably. But Hughler Hospital needs me more than I need it. We'll be discreet, of course."

"Of course. But I still don't understand why. Why do this? You're comfortable: beautiful wife, magnificent home, the respect of your colleagues."

"I enjoy a challenge with the adrenaline rush that risk brings. My practice is at the point now that I can afford the time and dollars to strike out on a new course. 'Live your life so you have no regrets' is my motto."

"Sounds like a good motto. I guess you're not afraid of failure," Bob said.

"Failure is not an option," Fred corrected him. "Your only task is to get appropriate patients."

"By 'appropriate' I assume you mean the hopeless, homeless people living in a box on the street corner. I bet you take candy from babies."

"I resent—"

"Sure you do," Bob shot back sarcastically. "You'd better hope that cloak of professionalism is bulletproof."

"Let me take care of that. Will you do it?"

"I'm not sure. On one hand, you are helping needy patients, which certainly is our mission. But I feel this research should be conducted with the sanction of Hughler Hospital . . . maybe with other colleagues at pharmaceutical houses that become involved as we proceed. God, this could be the Salk-vaccine breakthrough of our generation! Frankly, I'd feel much more comfortable if this effort were approved by the hospital administrators at the least."

Bob took another sip of coffee, then continued, "I had a difficult time previously. Before I studied medicine, I mean. Medical school changed me. I enjoyed the challenges. Did my residency at Hughler for three years; went to General on a fellowship for a year and came back to Hughler in January 2003. I've worked as an MD in the ER three and a half years now. I must say, three and a half good years—and I don't want that to change. Will the propriety of your reputation protect me?"

"I doubt it will come to that," Fred answered, "but my professional reputation and the good we will be doing should provide a strong shield."

Bob nodded. "I appreciate your asking me to be part of your team. I need to sleep on this offer and consider the ramifications carefully. If you find someone else before I get back to you, that's fine. But as you were describing the research," he continued, "a thought came to me: you'll need savvy people from the hospital neighborhood to find you patients. That search will require cash, Fred. Lots of cash. That's the only thing they know. You can't meet with street people directly . . . well, maybe just to get started; you understand. I could find some competent people out there who have a lot of contacts," he offered.

"I don't want a lot of people involved in this," Fred objected.

"Of course not, but it would be too obvious for any docs to contact people from this neighborhood firsthand on a regular basis. You know that. They won't be interested in copying any of your scientific data. Like I say, it's money, just money, they want. I'm speaking from an ER doc's perspective," Bob explained. "I know these people."

"The fewer involved, the easier it'll be to keep the research quiet. Remember that. You will be well paid for your services. And you will be given credit for your assistance in the research, which shouldn't hurt your professional standing either," Fred said in his authoritative tone.

"Even so, I'm not sure I can afford to work with you. Too risky. It could kill my medical career. What kind of money are we talking about here? That, of course, might influence my decision."

"What do you think is fair?"

"For the risk of a lost license, at least fifty thou up front—in cash, small bills, hard to trace. Twenty percent of the profit when the research is sold, and named on any patents granted."

"You drive a tough bargain, Bob. Specific genes have already been patented. Today if you tweak a gene, you can get a patent. But I decided our aim would be analyzing *processes*. So a patent for a new process that leads to a cure would be more accurate for us. You wouldn't qualify for any patent rights anyhow. You have to actually do the experimentation and research." Fred grabbed a pad of paper near the phone and scribbled some figures. "How about forty thousand, in monthly cash installments of ten thousand dollars each, for the next four months?"

"No. If I accept, I'm sticking to my fifty thou in cash. I want *five* monthly cash installments of ten thousand dollars each, for the next five months," Bob countered.

"You've got it." Fred struggled out of his recliner. "I'll have my lawyer draw up a contract between us; I'm meeting with him in the morning. I'm forming an LLC just for this project."

Bob looked up at him. "Not so fast. You don't waste any time. Remember, I'd like at least twenty-four hours to think this over."

"If you don't feel comfortable with this arrangement and don't want to take this opportunity, I'm sure I can find another doctor. I was just going to see my lawyer on another matter, if that's what is bothering you. I didn't have this deal in mind when I made that appointment."

"Choose whomever you wish." Bob stood up. "As I said, I need to sleep on it. We can't meet in person. Tomorrow I'll be on the evening shift, four to midnight. We could meet briefly, but I'd rather call you from home with my decision, probably around ten on Thursday morning."

"You're a tough negotiator," Fred said, and then laughed. They shook hands.

Dr. Pannell arrived a half hour early for his evening shift on Thursday afternoon, anxious to speak with Josh. He parked his Camry in the hospital garage and walked quickly to the emergency room, his mind whirling: *Nice dinner Tuesday night at Truesort's. Glad I called him at his office this morning to confirm that I'll join the project. Easier to talk from home.*

But how do I approach that tall fellow, Josh? Hope he's still here. Saw him help himself to something Monday—hypodermics probably. Better not be using drugs again! ER aides are too vulnerable.

But no, he must be clean or he wouldn't have passed his latest employee six-month health exam. Checked it yesterday. So he must be selling the needles. If he's selling, he must know some people out there.

How do I ensure that the money's well spent? Trial run. Get one patient at a time. The less I give him, the more I keep. Old Doc Truesort doesn't need to know. No accountant here. Cash is hard to follow.

He looked around for Josh, hoping he'd still be working, then spotted him outside having a smoke. *Perfect,* Dr. Pannell thought, and went outside to join him.

"Working the evening shift now?" Bob asked.

"Nah. Étoile, she asked me to stay. Shorthanded or somethin'. I can use the overtime."

"Yeah. Can always use a little extra now and then. I'm covering for the chief for a few nights. He's attending a conference. Evening shift isn't bad during the week. Got a cigarette, Josh?"

"Didn't know you smoked, Doc." Josh handed him a cigarette and bent down from his six-feet-eight height to light it for him. When Josh's face was next to his, Dr. Pannell said quietly, "I don't, but I need to talk to you. Just walk along with me."

They walked past the ambulance bays out to the sidewalk. Dr. Pannell turned right, toward the trailer office where Ghanna was sitting, enjoying the slight breeze.

Damn. Uh-oh, here it is. I been snagged. Gonna be canned. Lose my supply. Frightened, Josh stopped and turned away from the doctor. He knew what happened to suppliers who could no longer deliver. Fear deafened him.

Then Dr. Pannell's voice punched through the scare barrier. Josh heard, "So, my friend, although I know a lot of medical supplies are going out the door in your pocket, maybe there's another way to earn some money without working overtime."

"You mean ya ain't gonna turn me in?" Josh turned and stared at the doctor.

"Let me start again. I don't think you listened to a word I said." Bob grabbed Josh by the elbow and propelled him around the corner, past Ghanna and the trailer office. "You see, Josh, we're trying to do some medical research. We need patients. Patients with AIDS . . . especially ones with Kaposi's sarcoma, the cancer they often get with AIDS. You've seen them occasionally in the ER. They need meds that allow the body to accept foreign cells that the immune system would normally kill off. And if you know anybody who's been HIV-positive for a long time without getting AIDS, that would be a bonus."

"So what's that have to do with me? I'm clean, man—quit drugs long ago. Maybe I make a few extra bucks because others are stupid, but that doesn't mean I do drugs. No more, man."

"Would you be willing to take a test to prove it?" Dr. Pannell looked up at Josh.

"Sure," Josh said without hesitation. "Especially if it helps me earn a few more bucks. Now I'm just out to have a good time, maybe have a few beers with my bros. I don't party like that any-more, not me." Josh shook his head and blew smoke in the air while checking around him. Like most streetwise people, he was never convinced he was safe.

"Okay, very glad to hear it. But you might still have some bros who do drugs, eh? You might know some people who have AIDS and are very sick. We want to help them, free of charge."

"Why don't you just take some of the patients you already got?" Josh pointed toward the hospital as he spoke.

"It's the usual medical red tape. We have to get all kinds of permission: okays for surgery, okays for meds, okays for risk factors and side effects. Look, let's face it: these people are going to die any-way. Maybe, just maybe, we can give some of them a chance—and with what we learn, help others later on." Dr. Pannell turned and looked up at Josh. "I would pay you per patient. The patient gets free treatment and free meds. Anyhow, what do you care why?"

"I'll think it over," Josh answered, looking down at the doctor.

"Think it over!" Bob scowled. "What do you mean, you'll think it over? It's a good deal all the way around."

"Look. I'm gonna talk to my friend, okay? You're right. I got some contacts out there." Josh nodded toward Ghanna's little park. Then Josh put his head down, turned on his heel, and loped back into the emergency room.

Dr. Pannell stood still. The creases of a smile spread across his face. *He'll do it,* he realized.

—ᐱᐟ⌐ₒ

After he got off work, Josh jogged back down the sidewalk to where Ghanna was still sitting. He was chatting with Sally McVeigh. "Gotta talk to ya, man, private," Josh said, slowing his pace. "Know it's dark. But I had a chance to earn five and a half hours of overtime."

"I can take a hint." Sally brushed her limp blond hair out of her eyes and picked up her trash bag of aluminum cans. "See ya," she said, easing her bulky body down one baby step at a time to the flat pavement of the sidewalk. She shuffled away.

Ghanna pushed himself up and ambled down the mound of grass, too. "Ain't no problem, Josh. You say private. C'mon over to my room. We be okay there." As they crossed the street, he added, "You shoulda been nicer to Sally even if she's a homeless woman. Just 'cause ya talkin' to a doc don't mean ya can't be nice to Sally. Anyhow, what he say to ya?"

"Sorry, I'll tell ya inside." Josh bounded up the steps to Ghanna's building three at a time and waited. Ghanna followed, unlocked the door of his room, and nodded for Josh to come in. Josh sat down on the top rung of an old step stool in the corner and waited while Ghanna shoved the window open to let the room cool down a bit.

Ghanna sat across from him on a wooden chair held together by layers of red enamel paint. He asked Josh at last, "What you want? I gave ya the money for them hypos. I told ya never to deliver 'em directly, just leave 'em by the pole in the garbage. The bottle of wine in the brown bag along with them hypos was perfect last time. Enjoyed the wine."

Now that he was face to face with Ghanna, Josh wondered how to tell the man about Dr. Pannell's offer. Ghanna stared at him, not saying a word. A shiver of fear shook Ghanna's body. *Maybe I shouldn't have let him in here.*

"Okay. I know I'm big, Ghanna. Used to run track and field. I ain't gonna hurt ya none. Just gonna sit here. Today I don't have no hypos in my pocket for ya, man. I came here for somethin' different. Remember that dude you saw walkin' with me? He said the docs at the hospital want AIDS patients to do some research on. They'll pay us for each one."

"Why don't they use the patients they got?"

"Ain't legal. What ya think it's worth? Ya think we can do it? The sicker the better," Josh said.

"Sure, we can do it. Them docs is wealthy. Thousand, maybe two thousand per patient. Toughest part will be gettin' them wasted fuckers to go in," Ghanna said.

"Let's make it three. Fifteen hundred for you and fifteen hundred for me. You get the patients. I take 'em to the doctor. Fair?"

"Yeah, but ya think the docs'll really pay us that much?" asked Ghanna.

"Sure. I can ne-go-ti-ate with Dr. Pannell," Josh said with pride. "We're important, Ghanna."

"You talk him into it, man," Ghanna said. "I got someone in mind already. This business could grow. Who knows? It's a deal." Ghanna got up, walked over to Josh, and shook his hand. "Soon as you're ready, just whistle when you walk by me. Let's take our time. Can't let them docs think this is easy. They won't wanna give us a lot of money then. We'll talk more."

"Knew you'd like it." Josh stood. "God, you is a short man. Next time, you sit on the step stool and I'll sit on that ole chair. Maybe we can even things out a little."

Ghanna laughed, more at the prospect of making money than at the strange picture the pair made. "Small but smart. That's me," he told Josh.

Josh just nodded agreement. He watched the back alley from the window for a moment, then opened the door and disappeared into another black, heat-soaked night.

Early Friday afternoon, with handshakes all around, Cory met the new members of Fred's research staff. They had gathered at Fred's private lab, Truesort Research, LLC. "Abby, Ian, this is Cory Maxwell, my lab assistant. He has a PhD in medical chemical research and will be a valued member of our team. Cory, Abby

Zelban-Lightfoot's a geneticist. Her husband, Ian Lightfoot, is an outstanding computer engineer specializing in bioinformatics: analyzing DNA protein sequences."

"Nice meeting you both," Cory greeted his new colleagues. "I hope you are as excited about this project as I am."

The group sat down at one of the lab benches while Fred reviewed the financial side of their research. "Since I'm paying all the start-up costs, and certain major ongoing expenses as well, I should get seventy-five percent of any deal once we have signed an agreement with a pharmaceutical house. You three will divide the remaining twenty-five percent of the payment among yourselves. I'll let you battle that out. But as you know, we won't be able to sign a contract until we can reproduce successful results many times—the final experimental confirmation. We have to prove the experiment is not a fluke. We must be able to demonstrate that our findings can be repeated and will provide positive results as we've claimed.

"Each of you will receive your consultant fee paid under the auspices of my private DNA lab. You are consultants for billing purposes, paid the regular stipend I discussed with each of you earlier. No benefits. You pay both sides of your social security. Just invoice me monthly. Basically, you get a big bonus when the process is sold. Any questions?"

"A consultant's fee's okay as far as it goes," Cory said. "I'll still be working at the hospital oncology lab for now. I need the pay-check and benefits. My work here will have to be on evenings and weekends."

"My dad will supply any health benefits Ian and I will need," Abby said.

"Your dad, *the* Dr. Zelban? The plastic surgeon who does all the charity medicine?" Cory was impressed.

Abby smiled. "Yes. We're very proud of him."

"Um," Cory continued, "well, we don't expect to gain wide recognition like your dad."

Ian laughed. "Don't worry. All Abby and I want to do is research. That's our contribution."

"Is it too early to decide in what order our names will appear on the patent applications and related professional papers for peer review?" Cory asked.

"*My* name is first," Fred snapped, remembering when he was placed third rather than first as he had expected. "*I* am the principal in this research. The chief researcher's name first is a well-established precedent. Cory's second, Abby's third, and Ian's fourth. Is that clear?"

He did not pause for an answer. "My work will also include some discreet marketing among the pharmaceutical houses, perhaps avoiding or circumventing a peer review. I've got a few friends out there, Charles Zelban among them. He might like to get a jump on the competition. The only problem I see is that just about every gene has been patented already, especially the ones that scientists have changed slightly. Don't ask me why a natural gene taken from the human body would need a patent. Our aim is researching processes such as how the virus mutates. Patenting the *process* is the best way for us. But we may also be able to patent a gene if we can deliberately modify it to gain a specific result."

"You'd better show us the proposed asking price in writing so we can have some input. We all need to be a part of that decision," Cory said. "And Abby, Ian, and I need to agree in writing how we will divide our twenty-five percent. Maybe your lawyer can help us with all that, Fred."

"Sure, I'll talk to him. All right with you, Abby? Ian?"

"Yes," Abby said. "Ian and I will also submit a copy of the proposed contract to Dad's lawyer before signing it," she warned.

"I will be recording all the data documenting every experiment we make," Ian said. "I'm going to need a more sophisticated computer than any I see here. I'll look online, research the options available that fit our needs."

"Give me your shopping list, including pricing. If I approve it, work with my secretary, Martha Antoine, on getting everything ordered and delivered," Fred replied.

"Now that business is out of the way," he continued, "let's get on to the challenge we've accepted. As you know, inhibitor drugs are being used with some success, but we still can't completely kill HIV and cure a patient with AIDS. The virus ruins one of our bodies' primary defenders, and it has an uncanny ability to change while still causing disease. As if that weren't enough, it creates different strains of the disease along the way. Unfortunately, the possibilities are almost infinite because the timing of the mutations varies. Recently, however, I watched cancer cells slow down these changes in HIV. I figure we can take advantage of this slowdown. It could be a breakthrough in the treatment and prevention of AIDS."

Ian asked, "Can you tell what causes this reaction? How do the cancer cells affect the HIV and cause it to mutate more slowly?"

"We haven't determined that yet," Fred acknowledged, "but Cory and I figure it's worth a full-scale investigation. The two of us do have experience working with bone marrow. That's where some of the defender cells begin, right in the marrow. Maybe we can get some ideas by following the development of these defender cells."

"Studying bone marrow," said Abby, "will also give me useful insight into the genetic reactions of various patients' immune systems. Of course, I'll need to analyze liver and hemoglobin samples as well. I want to examine infected cells from patients in early and later stages of the illness, and compare them with healthy, never-infected cells. And, as weird as it sounds, I want to look at some appendix tissue, too. An appendix has a lot of tissue that can produce immune cells; besides, with people having appendectomies, it should be readily available for study."

"Yes, studying all those types of tissue would be useful," said Fred. "We should be able to obtain those kinds of samples for you."

"Great," said Abby. "Your equipment is suitable for that. Glad to see you've already got a prep area and clean room set up, where we can keep everything sterile." Abby waved her arm in a sweep toward the light microscopes, slides, and other apparatus, and the entrance to the clean room. "That should save a few dollars."

"Yes," Fred answered. "I oversaw the installation of the clean room myself. It's got top-of-the-line HEPA filters and air ducts. And there's a large air shower right over there, so you can remove contaminants from clothing and other objects before entering."

"Looks good," said Ian.

"My ultimate goal," continued Fred, "is to use Kaposi's sarcoma to slow down the progress of the HIV. Abby, if you can find a way to target an HIV mutation, we could slow its rapid changes with an attack of cancer cells, causing the HIV to become sluggish, and, with further research, conquer its progression."

Abby added, "Another thing. As I'm sure all of you know, certain people test positive for HIV—they can even have it for years—but don't ever get AIDS. Do you know of anyone like that?"

Fred nodded. "I do know of a Caucasian woman who tested positive for HIV when she was twelve," he answered. "That was back in 1985, and she's still doing fine. We aren't sure when she became infected. Possibly she was raped, or perhaps she was born with HIV."

"Do you think she would give us a DNA sample?" asked Abby.

"Maybe," said Fred. "We have some old samples from her in the lab freezer. I can look into getting some current ones, even though she's out of the country at the moment."

"Why did you test her? Did she appear ill?" Ian asked.

"No. We had an HIV/AIDS medical task force at Hughler, which I initiated. Confidential testing was offered free to everyone who came to the hospital for treatment of any kind. The girl's mother simply wanted her checked. I did not ask why."

Abby nodded. "I think the mom was wise, if she suspected for any reason that her daughter might have HIV. According to what I've read, by 1982 the Centers for Disease Control received its first report of mothers with AIDS having babies with the disease. By 1983 the CDC knew that women with no other risk factors might get AIDS passed through heterosexual sex."

"That's true, Abby," answered Fred. "In fact, you may have read that experts now believe HIV reached the United States in the late 1970s. Generally, the medical community and the public weren't aware of its deadly effects until 1981. We've continued checking this patient periodically, but AIDS has never manifested itself. Even now she continues to have her checkups despite traveling in the U.S. and Europe. I hope her HIV remains dormant. Louella is a fine young lady. Martha keeps in touch with her. In fact, they've become friends."

"If she was twelve in 1985, she must be in her early thirties now," said Cory.

"Right," Fred confirmed. "The Hughler Hospital AIDS Database is a confidential file. Martha is one of the few nonmedical personnel to have access to it. That file will help you track down this patient, Abby, I'm sure. Martha will have all the contact information and the results of her checkups."

"Martha must be very trustworthy," Ian commented.

"Absolutely. In addition, she tries to keep current on AIDS research and often asks me about the many forms of cancer I treat. She claims that it helps her understand my patients. She makes my job easier because my patients are less tense and fearful after they've chatted with Martha."

"She's self-taught," Cory added. "And nothing short of amazing. She immigrated from Haiti, right, Fred?"

"Yes, about twenty years ago now. She's been working for me for the past fifteen."

"I look forward to meeting her," Abby said. "Where is Louella now?"

"A few months back Martha showed me photos Louella had emailed her from Paris."

"Do you think she could send us some fresh specimens?" asked Abby.

"You'll have to ask Martha."

"Okay. Since they're friends, she may be persuaded," Abby said hopefully.

"We can always play our ace: she will be part of a lifesaving research project," Fred answered. "As for the other samples Cory mentioned, I'll probably get you those in a few days if possible, Abby. No rush. You can use the time to get set up. Once we start, I'll want a progress report every week from you and Ian. If you get a breakthrough, tell me immediately. And I'll keep you informed of Cory's and my experimentation. All of us will function as a team. We'll be approaching this problem from different angles, so our insights will complement one another's, for the maximum chance of mutual success."

"Sounds fine to me," said Ian.

"I'm the only one who will hold the password to the main computer network," Fred continued. "All files will be dumped into it daily, or more often if necessary. Ian, you'll need to track all the experiment results and provide programming for each experiment. You and I will discuss how to secure all our computerized work: other passwords and so on. The record keeping can make or break a project like this. We'll start Monday." Fred glanced at his watch. "Now I've got to get back to the hospital. If anything comes up, you know how to reach me."

The nine-to-five workers were circling down the parking garage levels to the exit. There always were more people leaving on time on Fridays with the weekend ahead.

"Glad you found someone," a man said.

William, who worked on the hospital maintenance crew, looked up when he heard the man's voice.

"Yeah, it looks like he'll do it," he heard another man reply.

"Good. Just came from a meeting with my research people. Looks like we're making progress. This should get you started," answered the first one.

William inched out of the parking-garage stairwell where he had taken refuge from the hot summer day. A tall, dignified man with white hair thrust an interoffice envelope into the hand of a robust younger man. *That's Doc Pannell from the ER and Doc Truesort, head of the cancer department. What the hell are they doin'?* William watched as Dr. Pannell unwound the red thread that bound the brown envelope flap closed. He puckered the sides of the envelope and stared inside. William saw Dr. Pannell's eyebrows arch and his lips tweak up. Then Dr. Pannell grinned. "Nice. Very nice. Yes, this definitely will get us started, Fred."

"Get me some patients and there will be more where that's coming from. For now you keep whatever you don't use." Dr. Truesort walked to his black Porsche. "Keep me up to date," he called back over the screech of brakes.

William was the only person close enough to hear Dr. Pannell counting the cash out loud. "One thou, two thou . . ." He crept closer, hiding behind the cars, and watched Dr. Pannell cram some of the bills into his inside pocket. Then the doctor shoved the rest behind the torn lining of his briefcase, walked over to his red Camry, and locked the briefcase in the trunk.

With a final nod and good-bye wave to Dr. Truesort, Dr. Pannell hurried toward the side entrance of the hospital, patting his inside pocket as he went. His tie billowed out behind him as though it had trouble keeping up with his fast pace.

"G-good evening, Doctor," William called. "Remember me? William Meddlebach, the stubborn German," he said, limping across the parking garage. "You on evening shift again?"

"Yes." Dr. Pannell turned. "Thought you worked nine to five."

"Yeah, but s-sometimes I stay a little longer. Maybe pick up some extra change helpin' people havin' trouble with their car."

"I see."

"How come that other doctor's leavin' now?" William asked.

"Don't know. Weekend, probably. How're you feeling, William? That medicine I gave you helps? Leg less painful?"

"Yeah. It's okay.

"Let me know if the pain gets worse. You may have a little arthritis in your good leg now."

"I'll keep an eye on y-your car for you, Doc."

"Don't bother about it, William. But thanks. No thief wants to be bothered with an old Camry. That's why I drive it, especially here in the inner city. Besides, this open top level is generally safer from vandals."

"Yeah. Yesterday the g-guard and I caught a g-guy tryin' to steal hubcaps down below."

After Dr. Pannell passed, William limped around in time to see Dr. Truesort loop down the lower parking levels and wave to the guard as usual before he merged into the traffic.

William had been a surgical patient at Hughler Hospital twenty years before. His leg had been crushed in a motorcycle accident on the Garden State Parkway, and he was fitted with a prosthesis from the knee down. The hospital policy was to offer employment to disabled patients if at all possible, so William had been hired to help maintain the buildings, grounds, and parking lots. He was a conscientious worker who reveled in watching the hospital personnel, almost living their lives vicariously.

After Fred left for the hospital at about four forty-five, Cory drove Abby and Ian to a local pub so they could get better acquainted. The pub could have been on the Thames. It featured dark and light ales served in heavy glass mugs at room temperature. There were hard-boiled eggs stuffed with sausage meat, small shrimps, or small sardines. Cory, Abby, and Ian helped themselves and, with a barman's assistance, carried their food to a picnic table overlooking the Sandy River. They watched a crew sculling, singing as they rowed to keep all the oarsmen in rhythm, so one oar wouldn't hit against another.

When they were comfortably settled, Abby asked Ian, "Did you ever think you'd find a charming waterfront pub like this so close to Hughler Hospital? Just one more attraction the East Coast has to offer! Complete with warm ale!"

"Never drank warm ale before. It's okay. As for the East Coast, the people here have such diverse backgrounds and homelands! That's great to see."

"It's true. We do have a rich culture," Cory agreed. "My daughter has learned Polish by cleaning houses with some friendly Polish women. She laughs and tells me she didn't have to pay for the course. Earns a little toward incidentals." He took a gulp of ale. "A number of teams use this river for practice and for races. It's a tributary of the Stormy River—joins it a couple of miles from here. Even though we're several miles upstream from the Stormy's rapids, boaters should always be careful," he continued. "As for the warm ale, the barman might throw you out if you asked for it chilled. If he's in a good mood, he would give you the name of another bar."

Ian gave a hearty laugh. "I get the picture." He was dressed in his usual jeans, with a short-sleeved shirt and sandals. "Never saw a scull before either. Now I won't have to go to England. Thanks for saving me some money, Cory. But tell me, does Fred always wear a suit and tie?"

"When he's not in his scrubs, yeah, he does. But don't worry about what you wear, Ian. It's results he wants."

"I see. How long have you been working for Fred?"

"Too long. But he's an easy boss," Cory lied. "I get to explore new ideas. I manage the bone-marrow bank for him. We store the marrow in the oncology lab. Actually, I was the one who suggested it. Altogether we've had a good working relationship, as the human-resource people would say. I've been working with him fifteen years. Not on his Truesort Research payroll, but at the hospital. And how did Fred find you both?"

Abby explained, "When I finally got my PhD, I worked for a small California research lab. Good experience, but no future, so I began looking. Dad knew Fred from Harvard, and they've stayed in touch over the years. Dad suggested I contact him. The rest is history."

"It wasn't quite that easy," Ian said, glancing at Abby through his wire-rimmed glasses. "If we were going to relocate, we needed two jobs close together. This is a perfect fit."

"One coast to another," Cory said. "That's a pretty big move."

"Yeah," admitted Ian. "Lived most of my life in Southern California, except when I went north to study at Stanford. Loved my graduate work there."

"He also loved surfing and riding his motorcycle up and down Route 1," added Abby with a playful smirk at him.

"Beautiful, rugged scenery out there," said Cory.

"As for Abby," said Ian, "she was born and raised in Boston. Went to Tufts and then west to seek her fortune. She found me instead. I'm a lucky guy." Ian smiled at his wife, and her brown eyes glimmered with tenderness. She patted his black ponytail.

"I'll admit I was homesick for the East Coast," said Abby. "I knew it wouldn't be the same now that my mom is gone"—she sighed almost imperceptibly—"but even so, I wanted to come back. We've bought a condo for the time being. The plan is to live in it until we get to know the area, then buy a home and rent out the condo."

"You certainly are organized," Cory said. "My alimony payments keep me poor. I'm hoping this extra cash will help ease the burden. And maybe I can retire."

"We're happy to actually be helping humanity with something so vital, like my dad does," Abby said.

"Cory, if you don't mind my asking, why is Fred doing this?" Ian asked. "Is it altruism, like Abby's? He certainly doesn't need the money. I guess I'd like to know a little more about the guy. Might make working with him easier."

"He's odd. You know, when you've got everything, you should be content. My guess is the one thing he craves is professional recognition, even though he's Hugher's oncology chief and widely considered one of the most talented, experienced experts in his field. I'm his assistant chief in the oncology lab; usually it's just the two of us who use it. Most of the laboratory work for the hospital is done in the large lab next to ours, but Fred and I rarely need to go over there."

Cory glanced back and forth between Ian's face and Abby's, then continued. "To answer your question, he thrives on praise. I don't mean that's-a-sharp-jacket-you're-wearing kind of praise. It's got to be genuine. It's got to be big. A difficult case he's cured or his name on a cornerstone. Big always, something hugely significant."

"You mean he'd like to become surgeon general or have a disease named after him?" Abby kidded.

"Don't laugh. That's how he thinks," Cory said.

"That's why he cut you off when you asked who would be named first on the research publications?" Ian asked.

"Yep, that's it," Cory said. "He's got a good bedside manner, but it's all an act. He's compassionless. Everyone thinks he's all broken up when a patient dies. Not so. He just hates to lose, the way a football player hates to fumble a pass or a chess player hates to hear an opponent say checkmate. No matter who you are, if you're of no use to him, he ignores you."

"And you still like working for him?" Abby wanted to be reassured. "I mean, he is a little intimidating."

"You can learn from a guy like that," Cory said. "And the work is never routine." Then he stood and asked, "Speaking of work, would you like to go back to Fred's private lab? I could show you around. See more than workbenches. I realize it's almost six thirty, after normal working hours. We could discuss this project a little more."

"Sure, we have to go back there to pick up our car anyway," said Ian.

"Yes. We're anxious to get started," Abby agreed, shoving her sunglasses into her purse.

As she stood up next to her husband, Cory realized that Abby had style; despite her jeans and floppy safari hat, her posture signaled someone with pride and self-confidence, a graceful Yves Saint Laurent type. *Her oval face and high cheekbones might give her a haughty look if it weren't for her warm smile,* he thought.

"Thanks for bringing us here, Cory. It was relaxing to sit and chat, and I'm glad we could eat outside. The breeze off the river was cool and comfortable after all the heat we've been having."

"It's quieter during the week—not as crowded," Cory said, opening the door to his car.

Watching Cory unlock the door to Fred's private lab fifteen minutes later, Ian observed, "Fred obviously trusts you with the access codes. You work here a lot?"

"It depends on the project," Cory said. "The AIDS research will probably keep me at the hospital oncology lab most of the time, since that's where the patients will be." He stopped at a doorway near the front of the building. "Here's Martha's office. She stays in the hospital office most of the time, but she'll be coming over here to help get you set up. There's a coffeemaker in the kitchen, over there. Help yourselves if you ever want a cup of coffee. There's also an under-the-counter refrigerator for your use." Then Cory pointed toward the far end of the hallway. "My office and Fred's office/lab suite are behind the main lab. I rarely use mine, but that might change with this new project. We may need to put your offices in the main lab. It's big enough."

Next they walked into the main lab, where Cory unlocked the door to the lab freezer on one side of the room. After he explained where samples were kept, they returned to the main lab.

"Once I've got the right equipment," said Ian, "I'll disinfect it and bring it into the clean room. Then I'll be able to build a phenomenal database. We'll be able to analyze DNA, watch cells in action, find genes and tRNA, all thanks to some very sophisticated software."

Abby asked, "When do we get to see all this in action, Ian? It's got to be amazing to watch."

"I may need some technical help setting it up. I'll check to see what the manufacturers offer, maybe do some comparison shopping while I'm at it. Setting this up will be a first for me. The company I worked for in California already had a complete installation."

"I can't wait to see it," said Abby. "Meanwhile, I've been doing some research to bring myself up to date, starting with the anti-retroviral drugs used in the 1980s and 1990s. AZT wasn't effective over the long term; nor were there good medicines to deal with the opportunistic diseases that took advantage of the patients' immunity breakdown. The cocktail approach that uses a mix of medicines is good. Frankly, there doesn't seem to be much that experts haven't thought of—yet still there's no cure. No wonder everyone's stymied."

"Yeah, it's not going to be easy," said Cory. "We really need a fresh approach. That's what Fred's looking for. What I'd like to study is precisely *how* and *when* the HIV attacks."

"Your idea is good but will take a lot of time, Cory. The drugs that have been developed so far are the result of careful research of HIV's RNA cycle. That's when mutations may appear. I'd like to study that further."

Cory answered, "It's worth a try, Abby."

Ian added, "I understand the hows and whys of DNA sequence. I can construct a messenger RNA by using a DNA molecule as a template to transfer genetic information to the messenger RNA with the equipment I have in mind. You could use that in addition to Fred's idea: add cancer cells to slow down the mutations of the HIV."

"Great. No way could we track all of the changes without good, sophisticated programming." Pleased, Cory clapped Ian on the shoulder.

"And if we can take HIV's new messenger RNA and twist it a tiny bit, it may get lost on its journey," Abby said. "If you change a gene that causes mutations, for example, so that the code it carries no longer pairs up with its partner, you could render both partners useless, so that they can no longer invade their host's DNA. But when can we get some samples to experiment with?"

"Soon, soon," Cory put her off. He did not tell her that street people would be the source, or that Fred didn't want to bother with consent forms. "Meanwhile, you're welcome to work with some of the samples we have here in the freezer. They're labeled, but check with me first."

Chapter 3

*T*HE NEXT DAY, SATURDAY, Josh hung around the emergency room even after his day shift was over, waiting for Dr. Pannell, who was still on the evening shift. When the doctor arrived a few minutes late, he just looked at Josh, raised his eyebrows, and asked, "Well?"

Josh nodded yes.

Dr. Pannell picked up a chart and signaled for Josh to follow him into his office, then closed the door quickly and leaned against it. "Five hundred now, as a retainer. Five hundred when you bring each patient in. Make sure it's when we're busy. Saturday nights are usually good. Let me know the name beforehand."

"One thousand now, three thousand when each patient arrives," Josh countered.

"Five hundred now, two thousand when each patient arrives. I'm the one taking the risks, not you," Dr. Pannell said.

"Not good enough, Doc. You got your jungle to work in and I got mine. Besides, who else are ya gonna get to do this for ya? No one with my special knowledge applied for this here job," Josh said.

Dr. Pannell realized Josh was right; besides, it was Truesort's money, not his. *So I pocket a little less.* "Okay," he said, "you get your three thousand bucks per patient on delivery, plus a one-time retainer of a thousand bucks now. Agreed?"

"Yeah, agreed. Maybe we have somebody in a couple weeks. Tough to get some of them sickies to try. They're scared, ya know," Josh said.

"All right, I understand."

"So, where's the money?" Josh asked.

Dr. Pannell held up the chart he had just picked up. "If you don't deliver a patient, you're out of a job. Bed four. It'll be in here. Ten one-hundred-dollar bills. Make sure you get to this chart before anyone else does."

And Josh did.

Ghanna grinned when Josh slapped five one-hundred-dollar bills into his hand. "Figured you wouldn't mind my stoppin' by your room this time."

"This be good, Josh. Real good," Ghanna said, staring at the bills in his palm.

"There's more, Ghanna," Josh told him. "Doc Pannell wants the patients on Saturday nights, when the ER is busy."

"Yeah? How soon you wanna start?"

"You got someone *already*?"

"I don't waste no time," said Ghanna. "Lee Ribbentrop, he ready to go to the emergency room anytime now. You know, that white guy, he sleep in the basement. I talked to him. He wants to go soon."

Josh whistled. "Man, you is one slick operator!"

Ghanna smiled. "Yeah, that's me. Like I told ya, small but smart." They slapped five.

"Not tonight, though. Remember, we decided to go slow. Looks harder that way. I even told Doc Pannell a lot of them sickies are scared."

"Yeah, we should go slow," Ghanna relented. "Anyways, Lee say he don't have no AIDS. A test he took said he was okay. He ain't. He's too sick to even deliver them hypos over to the farmers' market. No more. He'd be jumped. No use to nobody. Never saw a white guy so sick."

"Uh-huh, maybe he got AIDS. The doc say those early tests not much good. Told me they got wrong answers. Doc call it a false negative. Anyways, it look like the kinda patient they want. We can take him next Saturday. I'll get on the midnight shift. Start at midnight, get off at eight in the mornin'. Doc Pannell can arrange it. He won't change his evenin' four-to-midnight shift, just stay a little longer. He usually does anyhow. I'll just go a little early. You can bring Lee over. I'll be waitin' on ya. You okay with that, Ghanna?"

"Yeah, sure. I'll bring him over 'round midnight. I ain't gonna stay till no eight in the mornin'."

At nine o'clock Monday morning, Abby looked up from her microscope as Cory walked into Fred's private lab. "Hi, Cory. Thanks for your help Friday night. Enjoyed the pub."

"My pleasure, Abby. Nice getting to know you and Ian."

"Glad you thought to give us a lab key and the access code. Ian dropped me off a little early, so no one else was here when I arrived." Abby's jet-black hair was pulled back into a ponytail. Her jeans showed beneath her white lab coat, which was embroidered with her name and *Truesort Research, LLC*. Fred had supplied Abby, Ian, and Cory with these coats.

"No problem," said Cory. "Martha will be here soon."

"She'll be at this lab today?" Abby asked. "That's great. I need to speak with her."

When Martha arrived at nine thirty, she went into the main lab where Abby and Cory were working. "Good morning, everyone," she said with a bright smile. "Sorry I'm late. Something urgent came up at Dr. Fred's hospital office." Unlike Abby, Martha wore an attractive gray suit and brilliant purple blouse.

"I'm just glad you're here. I'm Abby Zelban-Lightfoot. My husband, Ian Lightfoot, and I are working with Fred and Cory on a research project. Fred and Cory spoke very highly of you."

Martha put down her briefcase to shake Abby's hand. "That's very nice to hear. And Dr. Fred asked me to give you the contact information and file for a certain patient. A technician will be changing some of the building access codes today. Once I get him started, we can get together and discuss what you need, okay? Say, around eleven?"

"Fine with me," Abby agreed.

As Martha walked down the hallway, Abby turned back to Cory. "I'm trying to isolate some HIV," she told him.

"That's such a good specimen, it's dangerous: you might get sick. Seriously, be careful when you work with this stuff. A prick on your finger can become a major problem. I'm glad to see you're wearing surgical gloves."

Abby held up her gloved hands. "Of course. I found them over there on the other bench."

"Good. I'd better leave my coffee over there too," Cory said. "I worked in a biological-warfare lab during the Vietnam War with Agent Orange and nerve gas, among other stuff. That was decades ago, and I'm still scared. Are you onto anything?"

"Maybe. I want to see how the HIV mutates," Abby said. "If we can halt the virus before it gets into the patient's cells—shunt it off onto a dead end—maybe we could stop it before it shifts gears and starts up again."

"Once we have the right computer equipment," said Cory, "we should be able to observe the activity of cells—well enough, at least, to formulate a plausible theory."

"Exactly. Later on, once we're in the home stretch, we'll need time on an expensive electron microscope, with its superior technology, to confirm that our theory is viable."

"I know you want to work with the HIV's RNA, Abby. So first maybe we should explore the DNA properties of a person who defies the norm. I've been thinking about what you said the other day: it's strange that certain people test positive for HIV but don't ever get AIDS. How do you get that unlucky and that lucky at the same time?"

"Good question," said Abby. "It reminds me of the city kids in Boston who tested positive for tuberculosis but never succumbed to the disease. Of course, TB is a bacterial disease, not a viral one, but the principle is somewhat the same."

"True. Why don't we start by allowing HIV RNA to attack a DNA sample from that patient of Fred's? We have frozen samples on hand to start with."

"Good idea," said Abby. "When I meet with Martha at eleven, I'll explain that we need a fresh supply of samples. We might find out if anything in the patient's DNA has changed."

Cory nodded. "I think this patient's HIV history will be very informative."

Martha was talking to herself as she went through the correspondence, sorting bills from junk mail.

"You always talk to yourself?"

Startled, Martha jumped.

"I'm Tim from the security company. Let myself in. What's the problem?"

"You wait for *me* to let you in! Do you want me to call your supervisor and Dr. Truesort, your client?"

"Sorry, lady, sorry. I wasn't gonna hurt nothin'. Whaddya need me to do?"

"We have new staff. Dr. Truesort wants new codes."

"Why don't he just give them the ones you're usin' now?"

"He's keeping his suite the same. He's the only one with that code. Just the common area is changing." Martha handed him the work order and explained, "That's just the locks to the exterior doors and the interior doors to my office and the main laboratory. We do not use any keys."

"This here is gonna take a while. Company'll send you the bill." Tim helped himself to a cup of coffee. "If you need an alarm system at home, let me know." He winked.

"Don't worry about me. My boyfriend's a big guy—over six feet; weighs around a hundred eighty pounds. . . ."

"Okay. Sorry. I'll do a good job."

"You'd better. A lousy job I could do myself," Martha said without looking up from her computer. She was setting up a new account: HIV/AIDS RESEARCH PROJECT. She created classes and categories so each disbursement was traceable.

"By the way," Cory asked Abby half an hour later, "where is Ian?"

"Buying a workstation—a really powerful microcomputer designed especially for bioinformatics. For example, we'll be able to watch the changes of the RNA messenger protein."

"He's a talented guy, Abby, but you already know that."

Abby smiled. "After Ian looked at some workstations when we were shopping on Saturday, he discussed it with Fred on the phone, and Fred gave the go-ahead to purchase it."

"Sounds great! I'll be interested to see it. I knew he wanted something like this, but I wasn't sure Fred would go for it." Cory walked over to the workbench, took a sip of his coffee, and picked up some surgical gloves. "You should've seen the clean room we had in Vietnam. Used an old operating room. It was simple to scrub down—easy for us to keep foreign particles from contaminating our specimens."

"Wow, practically ideal." Abby looked at her watch. "Wonder why Ian isn't back yet. Cory, tell him I'm meeting with Martha in her office."

"Sure."

"You just missed Abby, Ian. She's in a meeting with Martha, down the hall."

"Okay."

"See you've been shopping! Here, let me help you with that equipment."

"Thanks, Cory. These are just the smaller pieces; the big stuff will be delivered and installed tomorrow."

Using a dolly, the two brought in several large boxes from Ian's car. Ian explained with boyish delight, "This will let me magnify images enough to show and automatically record the changes in CD4+ T cells. And I have global access to gene sequences!"

"Wow," said Cory. "This is cool, really cool!"

"We'll be able to monitor and store everything. Can't wait to get started!"

Ian and Cory meticulously cleaned all the new equipment with isopropyl alcohol wipes, then carried each piece into the air shower in the vestibule of the clean room, where high-pressure jets of filtered air blew off and removed any remaining particles of dust or contamination. Then, before they entered the clean room itself, they put on sterile nylon hats, sterile booties over their shoes, and sterile lab coats. This was standard procedure whenever they entered the clean room.

$$\sim\!\!\wedge\!\!\!\downarrow\!\!\sim_{o}$$

"Hi, Ian!" said Abby as she returned to the main lab an hour later and gave him a kiss. "I see you found a workstation. When will the rest of it be delivered?"

"Tomorrow."

"Great!" she answered, smiling at Ian and Cory. "I'm eager to see it in action."

"How was your meeting with Martha?" Ian asked.

"Superb! She showed me the detailed medical file on the patient Fred mentioned. Her name is Louella Parkman. Believe me, Martha lived up to Fred's description: smart, efficient, easy to work with."

Ian smiled. "I like Martha already, and I haven't even met her."

"And guess what?" continued Abby. "Louella's in Paris now, but she's coming home soon for a visit! Isn't that fantastic? We'll be able to get current DNA samples!"

Cory whistled. "How'd Martha manage *that* so quickly? I know Louella and Martha have been friends for years, but that's still pretty amazing."

"Well," Abby began, "Martha emailed Louella and explained why we need her DNA—how important this project is. As it turned out, Louella had been thinking about coming back to the States sometime soon anyway. Martha planned all the logistics of flights and lodging."

"Impressive!" said Ian. "Remind me to hire her as a travel agent for our next trip."

"Good idea," said Abby with a grin.

Ghanna and Lee limped across the street from Ghanna's apartment house at eleven thirty the following Saturday night. It was now late July and as hot as ever. With his right hand, Ghanna grabbed Lee's belt as if it were his boom box. His left arm was thrust out waist high as usual for balance. "Steady, man. You is doin' just fine. I get ya close to the ER. I ain't goin' in with ya. Can't."

Lee stared at his feet. He had to. His back was hunched over, and his head sagged and swayed downward with each pause and shove of his feet.

"Go up this here driveway. Better than goin' over a curb." Ghanna let go of the belt. "Easy now. Easy. Nobody in the way. Go on in. Josh be there. He the big, tall black guy. Just look for him."

Lee swung his head toward Ghanna. "Bye. Thanks, Ghanna." His voice sounded cracked and gruff. He carefully slid his feet on the driveway as he approached the hospital entrance, rocking left and right. When he reached the door, he saw the round steel button that opened it automatically. Placing his hands on either side of it to steady himself, he tried to press the door opener with his head.

Josh ran a wheelchair through the exit door, turned toward Lee, and said, "Get into this wheelchair, man. It's easier. I'm Josh."

Lee flopped into the wheelchair, and Josh brought him inside. "Yeah, I know. Ghanna told me. What's that noise?"

"Woman in labor. Ain't you heard that screamin' before?"

"Uh-huh."

"Josh, help me with this patient. He's got a stab wound and lacerations on his hand," Étoile called. "Push that patient over to the admittance desk. Magahali will take care of him. He's gonna have to wait."

Josh shoved the wheelchair over to the desk. "Sorry, man. This here's Magahali Triestane. She'll take care of you."

"Get scrubbed so you can help me clean this wound. I need an irrigation kit and some Betadine so I can disinfect the wounds," Étoile said.

"I'll take over, Étoile." Dr. Pannell stepped in. He looked at the knife wound. "Good clean cut. Knife must have been pretty sharp. Easy wound to close. Just put your arm on this table." Josh handed the Betadine and irrigation kit to Dr. Pannell. "Who did this to you, my friend?" Dr. Pannell asked.

"Who ya think?"

"One of The Oxman's boys?" Dr. Pannell guessed.

"Yeah, how'd you know?"

"Mended a lot of his work. You a dealer?"

"Not after tonight."

"Get me some sutures, Josh. Oh, never mind. Étoile already put some right here."

Josh leaned over and said softly to Dr. Pannell, "Got another special patient over at the counter for ya."

Without looking up, Bob sutured the wound's edges and asked, "Our Saturday-night special?" He then neatly bandaged the patient's hand.

"The very one. Magahali's checkin' him in."

"Okay, you're good as new, sir," Dr. Pannell said. He and Josh helped the patient to a sitting position on the bed. "The sutures should be removed in ten days," he continued. "Make sure to keep the wound clean so it doesn't get infected. Call us if you have any questions. Make an appointment with your own doctor to remove the sutures. If you'd like to, feel free to sit in one of the chairs over by the door and rest before you go home."

Dr. Pannell and Josh watched their patient take a seat.

"Distract Magahali, Josh," Dr. Pannell said quietly as he walked to another patient. "The Saturday-night special has to stay below the radar."

Josh asked Magahali to print out instructions for the care of a wound and the signs of infection. He gave it to the former drug dealer. To keep her distracted, he propped a druggie up against the counter. "Take this guy, Magahali. Cops brought him in hours ago. I'll take the wheelchair patient."

"I haven't finished with him yet."

"That's okay. I'll get him."

"You sure?"

"Yeah. I'm sure."

Magahali shrugged. "Okay."

Josh overheard her robotic voice, "Name . . . social . . . insurance. . . ." Ignoring the hospital's entrance-form file, he pushed Lee past the admittance desk to the bed closest to the hall. "I'm gonna take off your shoes and socks, hear? And you're gonna get into this bed. Soon we'll take ya upstairs. Ya may have to wait in the hall some. Whatever ya do, don't talk to nobody. Don't say nothin' to nobody. Doctor'll be here soon."

"Help me with this drunk, Josh," called Étoile. "Dr. Pannell said to just let him sleep it off. I can't get him into the bed."

"How much he weigh? A ton?"

"Maybe two. I get his legs up, his head falls over. I get his head up, his legs fall over."

"Grab his legs, Étoile. I got his head. One, two, three. He's in."

Étoile pulled up the side rails. "That should hold him until his family comes. I know them. He's a Saturday-night regular."

"Maybe we should call the counselor. He 'round?"

"Don't think so. Get Magahali to page him. Family's usually here pretty quick. I can introduce them. You getting to be a do-gooder, Josh?"

"Hardly. Just don't want us to break our backs every Saturday night. You're okay, but this guy is still too much."

Dr. Pannell strode up the annex steps two at a time to the pay phone, yanking coins out of his pocket as he went. *Pay phone better work. My cell doesn't in here. Gotta get a prepaid untraceable mobile. Glad I memorized Fred's private number.*

Ingrid answered. Fred told her, "I've got it, Ingrid. You can hang up." Bob waited for the click.

"Lee Ribbentrop, he's here, Fred. He's exactly what you want. No family. I found a file on him in the archives. He tested negative for AIDS in 1988. Back then, of course, the tests were not as accurate. But a later test countered the earlier one. He has AIDS."

"Okay. Sounds promising," Fred said. "Glad you waited for my wife to hang up. She is not to know anything. Anything at all."

"Don't worry. I'll be careful about that. Anyhow," Bob continued, "Lee doesn't believe he has the disease, which will help keep our research quiet. He's got the bumps and blotches typical of Kaposi's sarcoma in an AIDS/cancer patient. He may even have thought it was just a skin disease. I'll run the necessary tests to verify our diagnosis."

"Good. Does sound like a promising patient."

"But where shall I put him?"

"Keep him in the ER. I'll be over to see him myself."

"I could move him into the hospital for you. But you know we should at least have him sign a consent form," said Bob.

"I'll be there in fifteen minutes. Get your aide to help me take him upstairs. I'll call Cory to open the oncology lab. And don't worry about any goddamn consent form," Dr. Truesort said, rather than "Good-bye."

Dr. Pannell shrugged and walked past the front desk to see if Magahali had noticed anything unusual. She hadn't; she was too busy keeping up with the latest influx of Saturday-night revelers. Lee Ribbentrop was just one more homeless sick man without health insurance.

Bob picked up a consent form and walked over to Josh. "Get a gurney, Josh. Keep it by Lee. Be ready to take him upstairs when the doctor arrives—but this time it'll be Dr. Truesort. I doubt you've ever seen him in the ER. Here's the chart. While you're waiting, explain this consent form to Lee and have him sign it. When he's finished, bring it back to me."

Josh took the chart folder along with the consent form and drew the privacy curtains around the bed. He looked out into the emergency room. No one was approaching. He opened the folder and nodded to himself. His payment was there, as promised. Josh counted the bills as he stuffed each one into his trouser pocket. "Got a gurney for ya, Lee. Can ya slide onto it?" Lee coughed and nodded his head in response. "That's the way." Josh helped Lee onto the gurney. "I ain't hurtin' ya none?"

Lee just smiled. His "I'm okay" was punctuated by another coughing spell.

"Now I gotta wash down your bed for the next patient. Probably should've put ya on the gurney right away. Later I'll wheel ya to the hallway. We'll wait for the doc here." Josh pulled open the squeaky privacy curtains along the rod.

"Sure hope they can help me," Lee said. "You know Ghanna, don't ya? He said all this is going to be free. Somethin', huh?"

"Shut up, man. Or you ain't gonna get nothin'," Josh told him.

Dr. Truesort saw them as soon as he walked in.

Now who's being obvious, he thought as he briefly examined Lee. *The whole staff is watching me.*

"Lee, do you have any family who've looked after you?" he asked quietly. "Any close friends in this area?"

"Nah," said Lee. "If I did, I might've"—he broke off, coughing—"not gotten this sick."

The staff had never seen this doctor in the emergency room before. "He the doc with the black Porsche?" an intern whispered. "Arrogant as hell?"

"Yeah, and the minked and diamonded wife. Saw her at the Christmas party," a resident whispered back. "How the mighty have fallen. You know, you are judged by the company you keep." They both laughed.

Hiding his involvement, Dr. Pannell spoke for them all as he watched Dr. Truesort disappear down the hallway with Josh and Lee. "I don't believe my eyes."

"Neither do I, Doctor." Étoile laughed and rubbed her eyes as if she were trying to clear them.

$$\sim\!\!\Lambda\!\!\int\!\!\sim\!\circ$$

As he held the elevator door open so Josh could wheel in the gurney, Dr. Truesort saw Lee's dirty feet dotted with red flea bites. He saw lice crawling onto the pillow from Lee's tangled mat of long, steel-gray hair. Stifling the impulse to hold his nose, he ordered, "Josh, take him to the fourth floor. Put him in room 424 next to the back stairway. It's a private room I've had decontaminated, and I can get there quickly from my office. Nurses' station's around the corner, out of sight. We can slip in and out without being noticed if we need to. Call me when he's cleaned up." Dr. Truesort thrust his business card into Josh's hand. "Phone number's on there. I'm getting off here on the third floor. I'll be in my office."

Josh got a clean gown, paper slippers, and the usual personal-care articles, along with delousing shampoo for Lee's hair and salve for his feet. He led him to the shower room and after ten minutes yelled, "Hurry up, man. Ain't you had no shower before?"

Lee got into the hospital gown and looked at Josh. "Not in a long time, a long time. For me it was a luxury."

"Now what're ya doin'?" Josh thought he'd never get this guy ready for the doctor.

"Shavin', man." He laughed. "Ain't you seen nobody shave before?" Lee was able to see only the top half of his face in the small mirror.

"Want me to help?

"No."

"Maybe we can find a doc here to help ya," Josh suggested sympathetically.

—ᴧᴧᴧᴦᴧᴦᴧᴀ—

Dr. Truesort stared at Lee when he returned, to be sure it was the same patient he'd just admitted. "Here's the official ID I had made up for you. It probably won't be checked, since I'll give orders directly most of the time. You look better already. You mind if we continue the disguise?"

"If bein' clean and comfortable is a disguise, it's okay with me." Lee sat down on the edge of the bed and coughed, putting his hand over his mouth.

Dr. Truesort said, "I'd like to cut your hair. Put a business suit and briefcase in your closet. You know, make you look like an upper-middle-class patient."

"Why? Do I embarrass you, Doctor?" Lee laughed.

"No. Would just lessen the questions from others treating you."

"Sure. Go ahead. And I just shampooed my hair." Lee laughed again.

Ten minutes later, most of Lee's damp hair lay on the floor. Dr. Truesort smiled. "I never thought my surgical skill with scissors would be used to such advantage. It's not too bad a job."

Lee held on to the bed as he walked over to the mirror on the nightstand. "Damn, I do look different. Thanks, Doc."

After the metamorphosis, Dr. Truesort took some blood and tissue samples. He put the vials into his medical satchel and started Lee on the monitor for his vital signs and heart rhythm.

"What happened to your back, Lee?" he asked.

"Born this way. Worse now. Docs are afraid of messing up my spinal cord."

"Can ya help him, Doc?" Josh asked.

"Mmm . . . not me. There are other doctors that do treat spines. Once we get you feeling better, maybe we can work on caring for your back," Dr. Truesort said without any hopeful enthusiasm.

"Had a brace once. Did help a little."

"I'll check you again tomorrow. Call the nurses' station if you need anything. It's this button here."

Josh swept up the hair into a dustpan and carried it to a large disposal bin in the porters' closet down the hall.

Dr. Truesort stopped at the nurses' station to let them know he had a patient in room 424. It was one of the few single rooms in the hospital. "I will take full responsibility for his care. No one but me will be treating him. Is that understood? Just bring him his meals and soda, juice, or water, as well as any incidentals he might need such as soap or a toothbrush. You get what I mean. If any medical staff ask about him, refer them to me."

The charge nurse nodded. "All right, Doctor."

Josh followed him along the hallway to the elevator bank. "Doc," he asked quietly, "what'd you do that for? He ain't in the computer."

"I know. That's why I'm going to help keep things quiet. Understand?"

"You talkin' to a pro, Doc. Of course I understand." Josh was insulted. "ER busy, a clerical error—I know what to do."

"Good. If you have any problem, call me immediately. I know a per diem nurse I can call on once we get started. For now we will just have to help Lee ourselves." Josh nodded his agreement. "Going to the oncology lab now. If anything comes up, that's where I'll be."

Dr. Truesort got into the elevator and quickly back out. "Josh, another thought. If anyone questions you, say he's got TB."

Josh laughed. "That'll scare 'em off."

—ᴧᝰᴧ∘

"Glad I got right over here. What took you so long?" Cory complained.

Ignoring the question, Fred began putting vials on the lab bench. "Most emergency lab work's done at the hospital lab annex adjacent to the ER during weekends. Seems a good time to work in my hospital oncology lab. Nobody will notice, and I can check on Lee as we go along."

"Yeah. Only you could find two o'clock Sunday morning a good time to work."

They began examining the samples and preparing the cultures. The intense silence was occasionally punctuated by a sigh, an expletive, or an excited "You gotta look at this." They concentrated with an enthusiasm driven by the expectancy of finding a new phenomenon—the excitement of the chase.

The sun shone through a hole in one of the opaque window shades, spotlighting a microscope slide on the lab bench, when Cory finally said, "I'm too tired to do any more. I'll come in sometime this evening and continue, Fred. That ray of sunshine is the sun's way of telling me it's dawn."

"Yeah, I'm leaving too," Dr. Truesort agreed. "This culture has to grow anyhow. Call me at home when you know anything, but use the pay phone like Pannell did. It can't be traced."

—ᴧᝰᴧ∘

Cory returned early Sunday evening and analyzed the samples. The improved test for AIDS came out positive; Lee had the disease. Cory watched it multiply all night. He photographed reactions and changes, jotting down his observations in his computer notebook, along with the time and date, and occasionally drawing important patterns in a pad of art paper. "Got pneumonia too . . . easy to treat with antibiotics," he murmured.

Next Cory watched a familiar telltale pattern. It confirmed that Lee had contracted the cancer peculiar to AIDS patients.

He left his research for a few minutes and called Fred from the lobby pay phone. "Your guinea pig tested positive on both counts," Cory told him, and hung up.

Cory was setting up his camera to photograph more slides through the microscope when Dr. Truesort arrived early Monday morning. He had a garment bag slung over his shoulder.

"Photos, good; let me see what you found. I guess you got reactions at all stages. I'll prescribe some antibiotics for that pneumonia. That should make him feel a little better in a couple of weeks. Where are the other images? I have to plan the cure for his cancer and AIDS. I'd like to start the chemotherapy as soon as possible."

"Only have diagrams in my pad and some photos. Happened too fast. Could use a better camera."

"Fuck, I knew I should have been here."

"We can run it again. Got to anyhow for verification," Cory said. "What's with the garment bag? Taking a trip?"

"No. Business suit, shoes, shirt, tie, and an old briefcase. Ingrid was going to throw them out. Thought I'd have Josh put them in Lee's closet to improve his image." Fred laughed as he placed the clothing bag on the edge of a lab bench crowded with unwashed beakers. "Tell Josh to take these clothes up to him. People will wonder if I carry them to the patient."

"Yeah. They might get the idea that you're a nice guy," Cory told him.

Fred smiled. "Lee wasn't half bad after we started cleaning him up. A shower, a shave, and I cut his hair. I'd better go check on him . . . get the antibiotic started. Then I'll be in surgery. Oh— Cory, take a picture of Lee when you get a chance so we can show his progress. Didn't think of it when he first arrived. He probably still looks gaunt. Give us some comparison anyway."

"Will do," Cory said.

"Cory, you could use a shave too. You look like hell."

"Been here all night watching these experiments."

"Didn't you realize I never showed up Sunday evening? Didn't you notice it's daylight out?"

"Yeah, because the sun began shining through the hole in that shade. But I was in the middle of the experiment and intent on the outcome," Cory said.

Fred shook his head in disbelief. "It's six thirty Monday morning." He paused at the door and looked back at Cory. "Never knew you worked that hard. Sorry." Fred left, still shaking his head.

God, he can be human, Cory thought. *With nobody interrupting, I was completely absorbed in the work.*

Josh had asked to switch to the evening shift, from four to midnight weekdays and some weekends, to match Dr. Pannell's hours as much as possible. He liked the guy. Dr. Pannell found that the ER worked best when the personnel knew one another well enough to work as a team. This particular day, Josh went to room 424 before reporting for his ER shift.

"Lee, Doc Truesort told me to go to his oncology lab and bring ya these clothes before my shift starts. Doc Maxwell was working all night, doin' tests on your blood. Later he's comin' up to take your picture. You can wear these here clothes when ya leave." Josh opened the clothing bag, hung the suit, white shirt, and tie in the closet, and put the shoes and a briefcase on the closet floor.

"Thanks, man," Lee managed to say between coughs.

"You been takin' any medicine?" Josh asked.

"This morning I took some pills the doc gave me 'cause he said I have pneumonia," Lee said. "I'm getting chemotherapy soon 'cause he also says I got cancer. Chemo can be rough for some people. Doc Truesort said if I had someone to help me, I could go home. But I ain't got a home. Have to stay here and get stronger."

"Ya look a little better. How ya feel?" Josh asked.

"Still like crap."

"You only got here late Saturday night," Josh reminded him.

"Well, at least now I got a good bed, some peace and quiet. This is the life, ain't it? Pretty nurses bring me my meals. I order what I want. Read. Watch TV. I was in this hospital once before. They're good to me, Josh, real good, but I miss bein' with people. You know what I mean? I used to help out at the city food bank, mow lawns, wash dishes. Stuff like that till I got too weak . . . couldn't do nothin'."

"Maybe I come up sometime and watch TV with ya. Keep ya company and see them pretty nurses."

"I was kiddin' about nurses. If you would come up, that'd be good, real good. You like to play cards, read or anything?"

Josh waited until Lee stopped coughing. "I like to draw buildings and stuff; play rummy, but never was much good at readin', just enough to get by."

"Next time bring some cards and a newspaper. We'll play rummy, and you can read the paper out loud to me," Lee said. "Practice your readin' that way."

"Nobody ever much interested in teachin' me 'cept a couple of my vo-tech teachers," Josh said. "Most show ya somethin' only if they could get somethin' outta it."

"You helped me. Least I can do." Lee leaned back on the pillows, tired from all the conversation.

Josh nodded. "I'll be back. I'll be back with the newspaper and them cards," he promised. "When you get tired, I just sketch somethin'."

"That'll be fine."

"I'm on the evening shift now with Doc Pannell," Josh explained. "We work from four in the afternoon to midnight. I better go—don't wanna be late for my shift. See ya."

Josh arrived in time for the Monday-evening shift. "How's Lee doing, Josh?" Dr. Pannell asked.

"Too soon to know. He said he took some pills for pneumonia. Will have to get stronger because he's gonna get chemotherapy. Doc Truesort asked me to bring Lee some clothes. They were in his lab."

"Nice of him," mused Dr. Pannell.

A couple of hours later, Bob handed Josh a medical journal. "Slow tonight, Josh. You want to read this? Help time pass?"

"Nah, I just read the easy stuff. I do know the meds we got here, though. Like you say, it's slow tonight. Just one stabbin', two births, and a kid with croup. Positively a quiet night for an inner-city ER."

"Yeah. Monday nights usually are pretty calm. We have time for cocktails and canapés."

"What the hell are canapés?" Josh asked.

"Fancy sandwiches. High-society cocktail party, upmarket food for snobs," Dr. Pannell said. "Me, I'm a pretzel-and-beer guy. But I'd settle for a cheeseburger, fries, and a Coke. You mind going down to the cafeteria and bringing it back here?"

"No, I don't mind."

Bob gave him some money. "You know what to get me. Get whatever you want. We'll have our own party."

Josh went to the cafeteria and back in record time. The two spread their food out on an empty bed and chewed on their cheeseburgers in thoughtful silence for a while. "So, Josh, you like working in the ER at night?" Dr. Pannell asked, squeezing a packet of ketchup over his fries.

"It's okay."

"What would you like to do if you had the chance?"

"Architecture. I was good at mechanical drawin' at the vocational high school. I always liked to sketch and stuff. Liked physics too. We used to build models."

"You'd probably be good. I notice you're good with math, have a good memory, and seem reliable. What kind of architecture?"

"I ain't worked that out, maybe freelance. My drawin' teacher told me about it. But he say I don't talk too good. Gotta clean up my English first and improve my readin'."

"He's right. Architecture school is tough, even for students who love to read. You've also got to lose that street slang if you want to become an architect. Whether it's fair or not, employers and clients will judge you by the way you speak. If they hear good English, they'll treat you with more respect."

Josh nodded.

"In most fields, to succeed in your own business, first you need experience working for someone else. A lot of risk, going into business for yourself. Why do you want to do that?"

"Like to be my own boss. Don't like takin' orders." Josh looked Dr. Pannell straight in the eye when he spoke.

"I don't blame you. Sometimes orders can be unreasonable," Bob agreed. "And I speak from experience."

"You referrin' to Desert Storm?"

"Yeah."

"But the docs don't get ordered around."

"They do, but I wasn't a doctor then."

"No?" Josh was surprised.

"Went behind enemy lines into Iraq. Then, for a change of pace a few years later, in 1993 I went on to college and then med school with the help of my dad and my brother. Members of my family have been fortunate to be able to get the education we wanted. My dad's a lawyer. My brother's a mechanical engineer. He builds bridges. They were able to help me. If I'd used the GI bill to finance my education, I would've been required to work for the military for ten years. I wanted to help my own people. This ER is where I belong. Had an accelerated program—took six years combined college and med school instead of eight."

"So you were just a soldier in Desert Storm?"

"Don't ever, ever say 'just a soldier' to me. And that's an order."

"You're right. Sorry. But what did you do?"

"I'm a Green Beret—Special Forces."

"You? You are? That's one tough outfit, man. I didn't figure you for no Green Beret. I mean, you musta done some amazin' stuff. You ever get scared?"

"Of course."

"I bet ya got lotsa medals?"

"A few. I don't like to talk about it that much, Josh. But I will tell you this: my mission during Desert Storm is what convinced me to become a doctor."

"You're a damn good one, too. Patients that know you wait until you're in. That is, if they ain't feelin' too poorly to wait. Some almost as sick as Lee. Ya know, Doc, I like Lee. I'd like to stop by and visit him now and then. Should I be usin' more protection around him than I do in the ER?"

"You wear gloves and change them after you take care of him? How about a mask? Do you wear that?"

"Do all that stuff, but I feel like I'm hurtin' his feelin's. Ya know. It's kinda embarassin'."

"Blame it on me. Tell him your boss insists that you change your gloves often and wash your hands a lot so you don't infect him or yourself. The same with the mask. Of course it's very important to be careful with HIV/AIDS patients. As you probably know, HIV is a virus that attacks the defense system of the body. If it wins the attack, the patient's own defense system turns against him. Then the patient progresses to acquired immunodeficiency syndrome. Without antiretroviral therapy the patient could die in a year."

"Yeah, I know. Basically, the body beats itself up." Josh shook his head.

"When you go to visit Lee, keep gloves on. Change to clean ones when you leave. The same with the mask."

"Okay, I hear ya, Doc. Hmm, maybe I'll give architecture a try instead."

They fell silent again as they finished their canapé-less supper. When they were through, Josh pushed the paper plates, plastic forks, soiled napkins, and crumbs to the center of the bed; gathered up the four corners of the bedspread and spilled what he could into the trash; then threw the bedspread into the soiled-linen bin.

part TWO

Room 424

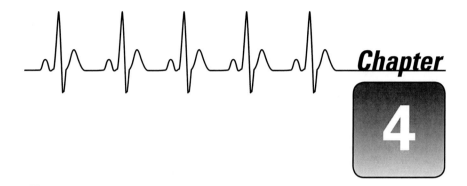

Chapter

4

IT WAS ALREADY THE BEGINNING OF OCTOBER. Abby enjoyed the colors of the autumn trees as she drove to work. Ian was going separately on his motorcycle because he had an errand to do in the evening.

Since they'd started working for Fred in July, Abby and Ian had been analyzing and comparing samples of DNA from Lee as his treatment progressed, as well as other patients' DNA samples from the lab freezer. They knew nothing about Lee as a person—just what his cells looked like.

Abby was particularly fascinated by DNA from Louella, who had indeed returned briefly from Paris and donated some fresh samples. *Exactly how does her immune system keep repelling the deadly virus?* Abby wondered as she drove. *That's the $64,000 question. Is she really immune, or is the HIV just hiding out in her system, ready to attack again when she's vulnerable? Does she have a DNA sequence that thwarts the virus? Once we find out, I wonder if it could be isolated, then replicated artificially in other patients.*

Fred hung his suit jacket on the padded hanger in the closet of the hospital oncology lab. He buttoned the woolen jacket closed to be sure it maintained its shape. The jacket had a faint smell of mothballs since the colder weather was late in coming this fall. Many people still had summer garments in their closets, in case the oppressive heat returned.

"Clean lab coats are in the box back there, Fred, in case you've forgotten," said Cory.

"Why can't they hang these things up for me? They get all creased and crushed in here."

"Guess they figure we aren't going to be on the cover of *Vogue* escorting some gorgeous model."

"What did you say?"

"Nothing."

Fred began examining some of the slides he had prepared the night before. During the preceding two and a half months, he and Cory had made preliminary progress in studying the interaction between cancer cells and HIV. "Hey, Cory, take a look at these samples from Lee! Just as I thought, his HIV and cancer have been battling each other, and it's slowed both of them down. The four low-dose chemotherapy treatments I've given him over the past nine weeks have almost finished off the cancer cells. But the re-maining ones are *still* helping us by slowing down the HIV. The HIV virus has become sluggish, and it's stopped changing rapidly! Looks like Lee's HIV is weakening almost naturally. Cory, I've got something! My theory can work!" Fred looked up from the micro-scope with a big smile.

Cory dashed over to look at Fred's slides. "Well, I'll be damned. You know, Fred, I doubted it would work, but this may be the answer! Lee is a good candidate for your study."

"Within a week or so I'll transplant fresh bone marrow into Lee's body, which will replace all his dead stem cells. The chemo-therapy has served two other purposes besides fighting cancer: along with the HIV, it has further weakened Lee's old immune sys-tem, and it's cleared out his dead stem cells. Thanks to the chemo, his body will now be far more likely to accept the stem cells from a bone-marrow transplant, even if those new cells aren't a perfect match for his own. If all goes well, the transplanted cells will mul-tiply and form a brand-new immune system for him."

"I sure hope it works," said Cory. "Good thing we knocked out the pneumonia first. Lee would never be able to fight it off now; his immune system is really shot."

"Right. Ironic, isn't it, that his weak immune system is now actually an *advantage*? If he were healthy, of course, a strong immune system would fight off disease by attacking any foreign bacteria or viruses that tried to invade his body. But now he actually needs a *weak* immune system—one too feeble to fight the new bone marrow. I wish I could have given him a higher dose of chemo just to make sure, but he couldn't have handled it. Too sick already."

"You think he's strong enough to cope with a bone-marrow transplant?" asked Cory. "Reactions to them can be debilitating— vomiting and so on—even if the patient eventually accepts the donor's cells."

"I know the risks involved. That's why I'd like to give him a few days to rest. I want to gather some more data, see if maybe I can find a better donor match. But cancer can go into remission. We have to act while it's still attacking the HIV. It's a battle for territory."

"He's very vulnerable to infection at this point," said Cory.

"That's right. Lee will have to be in isolation. I had his room thoroughly decontaminated in July by hospital staff on the same Saturday night he arrived. That was over two months ago. The daily aides do clean as thoroughly as they can, but we need someone who can take care of the vents. His room needs to be decontaminated again because he'll be so susceptible to infection. Cory, do you know anyone who can do decontamination? I can't use hospital staff. They might question what's going on."

"I've done it before. I know a guy who can put an air filter in the HVAC vent as well as decontaminate the room. His kid has a lot of allergies," Cory explained.

"How long does it take?" Fred asked.

"One workday with two men. But where do we put Lee while we're preparing the room, Fred?"

"I'll keep him in the operating room until you call me. I'll rig a tent over the gurney when we take him there. First decontaminate the bathroom and the area around the bed. Put a tent over the bed, then go ahead and work on the other parts of the room. Afterward, just be sure to remove the tent and put a fresh one on. Call me when the room is ready, and we can bring him back up there. I'll pay your friend whatever you think is fair. Consider your role part of the overall project."

Cory laughed. "You think of everything." He already had his cell phone out of his pocket and gave his friend a call. "Fred, tomorrow okay?"

"A Thursday—sure."

"Okay, good. He'll be here." Cory closed his cell phone.

"Now, before we get sidetracked again," Fred continued, "I want you to know I checked the blood and tissue types you have listed in the bone-marrow bank. Mark Calhoun, who died in a car accident, is probably our best candidate. He was a charitable donor and has no next of kin we would need to contact for permission to use his bone marrow. No red tape to go through."

"Yes, I recall his parents died in that accident as well," Cory added. "Really tragic."

"His marrow isn't a perfect match to Lee's, but it's almost as close as you'd get from the national bone-marrow registry. I'll double-check it again to make absolutely certain the match is close enough. A transplant is always a risk, though. Even with a weak immune system, Lee's body may try to fight off the donor's stem cells. Wish I could be sure."

"If he does fight it, immunosuppressant drugs should help. You'll have to calibrate them carefully to suppress the old immune system without threatening the new one—but the risk is probably worth it in a case like this. He's certainly not going to make it without a transplant."

"Yes, and I can adjust the dosage of the immunosuppressant if necessary," Fred mused out loud. "With healthy bone marrow on the battlefield and a decrease in the strength of the damn HIV and cancer, sooner or later Lee's new, healthy bone marrow will force that HIV into a full retreat."

"Hold on a minute, Fred. When did you draw the blood for the slides you just showed me?"

"Yesterday, around four in the afternoon."

"I just prepared some from blood I drew this morning. I was about to check them when you walked in. Let me take a look."

A minute later Cory clenched his fists. "Damn it! Look at this."

Cory pulled Fred over to two microscopes. "Look—look at these slides. We're late. His body is swimming in HIV, even if it is changing more slowly. See, there's more HIV than there was yesterday afternoon. The cancer virus isn't the conqueror you thought it was. What was left of his immune system's being wiped out. You don't have much time to get the HIV under control. He needs a transplant, and he needs it soon!" Cory insisted. "At least you have to try to help him."

"Yes, of course, but I don't want to rush into a transplant headlong. It's a crucial step. Need just a bit more time to—"

"You have no time! You can see for yourself in these slides. Just make sure it's a good enough donor match and move! You have to act *now* or he'll die!"

"Don't panic, Cory. We will have enough time. Even if we don't, we will still learn something. Remember, I graduated from Harvard Medical School. My research with dogs was some of the most original work they had ever seen."

"Jesus. That was with dogs, not people—and cancer, not HIV. Face reality, Fred," Cory yelled.

"This research is under control, Cory. Under control," Fred yelled back.

"No, Fred, no. HIV is biting at your heels. Believe me, damn it! You may lose."

"And if I win?"

—ᴧᴧₒ

Fred marched back to his office in his rumpled lab coat. The slides Cory had shown him repeated in his imagination like faulty videotape blinking the same scene to an exasperated viewer.

"My suit jacket, Martha. Left it in the lab. Go get it," he barked.

Seeing his clenched lips and scowl, Martha shoved her chair back and rushed for the door in one swift motion.

Fred was Martha's icon. She was devoted to him; he could do no wrong. When he was upset, she was also.

Fred plunged into the stack of folders on his desk. Fortunately Cory and Martha had organized them according to blood types. *Here it is:* CALHOUN, MARK. *Exactly as I remembered. Charitable donor, good health. At least the tissue type is in the same category as Lee's.* Fred studied Mark's blood-test reports one more time, tapping a pencil as he read, then pulled out Lee's file. Just as he recalled, Lee's blood-test report had a number of tissue markers that matched Mark's. Fred made up his mind to give Lee the transplant sooner than he'd planned. As Cory had said, it was a risk worth taking.

On Thursday afternoon, after Lee's room had been decontaminated, Fred and Cory brought him to room 424 on the express elevator using a gurney covered with a sterilized transparent tent held in place at the foot and head bars. As soon as they were in the room, both of them carefully washed their hands and quickly changed into sterile gowns, masks, and gloves. Together they removed the gurney tent and deftly shifted Lee onto the bed under its own transparent tent. The tent was supported by removable dowels strapped in place at the head of the bed, halfway down the sides, and at the foot.

Cory pushed the gurney into the hall for the aide to pick up. He told Lee to take it easy and went down the back stairs to the oncology lab. The fewer people near an isolation patient, the better.

The next morning Cory delivered the sterile, defrosted bag of bone marrow to Fred. He changed into sterile scrubs, mask, and gloves. "Looks like you're ready to go, Fred. How about you, Lee?"

"The sooner the better," Lee responded in a croaky voice.

"How are you feeling, Lee?" Dr. Truesort asked.

"Real weak and tired, Doc."

"That's because your body's defenses are down. It's why Dr. Maxwell and I are dressing up like this: don't want you to get an infection." Fred moved an IV pole over to the bed, hung the bag of marrow on it, and leaned under the tent. "This infusion will help you feel stronger. I'm going to start it in your chest, Lee."

Dr. Truesort infused the bone-marrow stem cells through a central line, which was a small, flexible tube inserted into a large vein near Lee's heart. "Now, these new cells are smart. They know their destination and will swim through your bloodstream till they find their new home inside your bones. There they'll multiply till they completely replace your old bone marrow and make healthy new blood cells for you. Finally, you'll have a new immune system to take over altogether."

"Okay, Doc. I trust you," murmured Lee.

"I'll stay a couple of hours, Lee, to be sure you are okay. Go to sleep if you can."

Cory stayed awhile to be sure the marrow was flowing properly and then told Dr. Truesort, "Everything looks good, Fred. I'll be in the lab if you need me."

"Thanks, Cory. A lot is riding on this."

Cory just nodded and left quietly.

Dr. Truesort phoned his hospital office. "Martha, I'm in room 424 if anybody needs me. Yeah, I'm with a patient. No, I don't know how long. Several hours, I guess. Just tell Ingrid I'll be very late. Oh, and can you get some per diem nurses specializing in bone-marrow-transplant patients? We need them ASAP. Thanks."

At the knock on the door, Dr. Truesort seethed and called, "Don't disturb us."

"Got Lee's lunch here. It's late. Almost two o'clock" was the aide's muffled response.

"He's asleep. Eat it yourself if you can," Dr. Truesort bellowed at the closed door. "Don't come in here. This room has been decontaminated. The patient's immune system is compromised. Keep out. He will be given nutritional supplements."

"Your yellin' better'n alarm clock. He prob'ly be awake now."

"He's learned to sleep through noise at this hospital. He wouldn't even turn over with the roar of a million howitzers." Dr. Truesort heard the slap of the aide's feet and the clanking of her cart fade away.

Despite Fred's claims, Lee woke up. "You're doing well, Lee," the doctor told him. "Got to be on my way."

But then it started. *Oh hell, hope it's just the usual reaction to a transplant.* Dr. Truesort grabbed a small emesis basin to catch the vomit. When Lee stopped vomiting for a few minutes, Fred took Lee's temperature, which was slightly elevated at 100 degrees. *Glad I still have on my sterile scrubs. These side effects are rough and may last three to four weeks. But he doesn't seem to be rejecting the transplant: pulse still normal, only a low fever—both good signs. Looks like he may still accept the new bone marrow.* Fred washed Lee's face, rinsed his mouth, and settled him more comfortably in bed, while continually checking his vital signs.

"Thanks, Doc," Lee managed to whisper.

Lee remained quite weak and nauseous. Dr. Truesort raised the head of the bed so that Lee could vomit into the basin easily; the central line was firmly taped into place on his chest. Fred carried the basin to the bathroom every time Lee vomited, rinsing it thoroughly, and then rinsed Lee's mouth—a humbling experience for an elite oncologist. But if Lee fell walking to the bathroom, Fred was afraid he might not be able to help him up.

Exasperated, Dr. Truesort phoned Martha. "Get Josh from the ER and tell him to come see his friend. He'll know whom I mean. He works evenings now? Tell Pannell to send him up as soon as he arrives. Okay, four o'clock. Thanks."

At last Josh arrived and knocked on the door. Dr. Truesort stepped into the hallway. "I'll be right back, Lee," he called. He led Josh by the elbow to the stairwell. "Don't want Lee to overhear us. Listen, Josh, this is an emergency. Lee's reacting poorly to the transplant. The side effects are pretty severe, especially since he's weak already. It's like having a bad case of the flu: vomiting and so on. I need you or someone like you to tend to him for now; he cannot be alone. Would Dr. Pannell be willing to spare you?"

"You gotta discuss that with Doc Pannell. I'm happy to do it."

"Very good, I'll page him right now. I'll pay you the same wage as a per diem nurse. You can work out a schedule with Dr. Pannell. It's only temporary, and completely hush-hush. I asked Martha, my secretary, to contact some per diem nurses experienced with bone-marrow transplants and who can scrupulously maintain patients' privacy. Should have one within a couple of days."

"Okay, I follow ya, Doc."

"Keep a close eye on Lee's monitor, which tracks his vital signs and heart rhythm. And remember, always wash your hands very thoroughly before approaching Lee, understand? Wear a mask, gown, and gloves. Lee cannot fight infection since his immune system is compromised. I'll probably give him parenteral nutri-tion—usually these patients' mouths get very sore.

"Here's the key to my office in case Martha is gone. There are some extra sterile gowns, masks, and gloves wrapped in plastic bags in my closet. Put them on up here so you don't carry any unnecessary bacteria getting here or raise any suspicions. Change in the back of the room, and again, be sure to wash your hands frequently. I'll stay with Lee until you get back."

While waiting for Josh, Dr. Truesort stood near the window, away from Lee, to avoid transmitting any germs. But he still watched all the monitors closely. Lee's vital signs remained steady.

Josh returned ten minutes later carrying a gown, mask, and gloves in their plastic packages. "You're back. Good." Dr. Truesort waited while Josh washed his hands and changed. "Let me explain to you how this transplant is working, Josh." Fred remained at the window, pointing as he explained: "Bone marrow is in the blood-collection bag and travels through the filter to the central line. Keep an eye on the flow rate. Just make sure the fluid moves through at a constant pace. It will take a while. You can adjust it with that valve if necessary."

"Okay."

"Give him a urinal if he needs it. I don't want him out of bed."

"I can read to him."

"You have the idea, Josh."

"How you doin', Lee?" Josh sat on a chair next to the bed.

"Sick worse than a week-long-binge hangover."

"Doc Truesort told me to stay with ya for a while. I'll help ya with this here urinal. Get ya some cool water and anythin' else ya want. Can't play no rummy. You gotta rest. Just as well, 'cause you always win anyways," Josh kidded him.

Dr. Truesort explained from the doorway, "Lee, I asked Josh to stay here as long as he can. Later I'm going to ask a nurse to help you also. Josh, you can phone me if you have any concerns. Just dial O for the operator. I'll be in the hospital probably for the next forty-five minutes. If all else fails, have the operator call Security. They will know whether I'm still in the building when I swipe my ID card. If not, they know how to find me."

"Thanks, Doc," Lee said hoarsely to Dr. Truesort's quick good-bye wave.

"Yeah, thanks, Doc," Josh echoed, but he thought, *I'll call Doc Pannell if I need help. He already knows what's goin' on, and he's right downstairs.*

Cory knocked as he entered Fred's office. "How's Lee doing?"

Fred leaned back in his desk chair and looked up at Cory. "Vomiting. It'll take a while for the nausea to subside—three weeks, maybe four. Didn't plan on a transplant so soon; had hoped to gather more data before this stage. Also hoped to give Lee a little time to recuperate from the chemo first, but the resurgence of HIV left us no choice. Fortunately, Martha has compiled a list of per diem nurses who specialize in treatment of bone-marrow-transplant patients. She's emailing the nurses now. We didn't think we would need anybody this soon for Lee."

"Good. Martha's terrific; she'll take care of it. All right if I get some blood samples from Lee? Maybe take a photo of him?"

"No blood samples; I just took some a little while ago and will analyze them myself. I'm anxious to see how his body is reacting. If you want a photo, okay, but don't let anyone see you," answered Fred. "Use the back stairs. Josh is with him now. Take some gowns, masks, and gloves with you. Remember, Lee is open to infection at this early stage. Wash your hands. Take your photo and leave promptly."

"Okay. You coming back?" asked Cory.

"Yeah. Got to see some other patients and get some immuno-suppressant drugs to have on hand in case Lee needs them."

Josh devoted himself to his new task of nursing Lee, doing whatever he could to keep Lee's spirits up as well as tend to his physical needs. By the third week after Lee's transplant, Lee began to feel a little better. He wasn't vomiting quite so often and had a bit more energy between his bouts of intense nausea.

"You like workin' here, Josh?" Lee asked.

"It's all right. Really wanna be an architect, though. Design and build, that's what I wanna do. How about you, Lee? What you wanna do when you get outta here?"

"Have an Internet café. All kinds of fancy coffees and technical help too."

"I tell ya what. I'll design your buildin' for you. Maybe renovate an empty buildin' over at the farmers' market. You find the tech support."

"Okay, and add a little bakery so customers can have cupcakes and Danish with their coffee."

"Lee, you got any family to help ya with this?"

"Nah. My parents passed on. My brother I haven't heard from in five years. We were in foster care growing up . . . didn't stay with the same families."

"That's rough. My mom and dad worked full-time. They had a corner store in Newark. Sold newspapers, magazines, ice cream, deli stuff. During the summers I went to South Carolina and stayed with my grandparents. They were tenant farmers. I'd help with the chores, play with their dog, and swim in the stream out back. I never wanted to go home when summer was over. But now I ain't got no family either."

"You have family now, Josh. Funny, we don't look alike at all, that's for sure, but we get along so well, we might as well be brothers. We could form a company, you and me."

Josh grinned. "Adopted brothers, huh? One white and one black?" They both burst out laughing. "Okay, brother, fine with me. We can dream on. Maybe forget the tech support and just have Wi-Fi so folks could use their laptops. Later, when we're rich, we can hire us some computer geeks."

Dr. Truesort walked briskly up the back stairway and entered room 424, not even noticing the cheerful Halloween decorations the nurses had taped up in the hallway. He had established a routine. Lee watched him wash his hands and put on gloves, a gown, and a mask. Then Fred turned to him and asked, "How are you feeling, Lee? Most of the nausea gone?"

"Yeah."

"How is our patient doing, Josh?"

"Better, but it's been a lousy three weeks."

"Yes, I know."

"The nurse told me the nausea isn't as bad," Josh continued. "She's gone to get lunch as long as I'm here. Normally they've been bringin' her lunch to her so she doesn't have to leave Lee. She eats in the patients' lounge right across the hall, but today she went out 'cause I could stay."

"Well, we appreciate all you've done for Lee, Josh."

"Lee and me, we're friends now, Doc. I come up from the ER when I get a break, and before my shift too. Lee even taught me how to play chess. He tells me where to move his pieces."

"So I see." Dr. Truesort smiled and walked over to Lee's table, where he studied the pieces. "Who's got black?"

Lee smiled. "Me."

Dr. Truesort laughed and turned to Josh. "You are in trouble."

Josh stared at the board. "I don't see. . . ."

Lee laughed. "Don't tell him anything, Doc."

"Before night?" Fred asked.

"Maybe. Sooner or later he'll figure out my strategy," Lee added, and winked at Dr. Truesort.

Josh looked puzzled. He sat down in front of the chessboard. "I just don't see . . . Oh, damn, I get it. If I move the knight over here . . . it's safe. Your turn, Lee."

Dr. Truesort nodded. "Nice move. Any news for me, Josh?"

"Workin' on it for ya, Doc. Soon, soon.

"Stop by my office. I have something for you."

"Okay." Josh smiled. He knew Doc Truesort was going to pay him for helping with Lee's care.

"He's a good reader, Doc," Lee added. "He visits often. Fact is, he's probably the only friend I got, outsida you. He brought me a warm-up suit, some cool T-shirts, and jeans to wear once I'm discharged."

Fred just nodded in acknowledgment. He took a blood sample and felt Lee's pulse. It was rapid. He listened to Lee's heart and lungs, checked his blood pressure, and saw that the nurse had recorded elevated temperatures. *Oh-oh, may be the first stages of rejection. Better get this sample to Cory; his earlier findings weren't good. Goddamn it, we need this bone marrow to work!*

"Lee, I'll be downstairs in the oncology lab for a little while, but I'll be back soon."

Dr. Truesort saw the per diem nurse hurrying down the hall toward him. He interrupted her as she tried to give him the caught-in-traffic excuse. "Get to your patient. Keep monitoring his vital signs. Call me instantly if there is any change."

Worried, Fred didn't wait for Cory but started the analyses himself. He compared past samples of Lee's blood with the new sample. The new, stronger immune system was there next to the old, weaker one. But the new system wasn't as effective as he'd hoped. Also, the AIDS virus was lurking in the background. *He needs more immunosuppressant. Got to adjust the dosage again; his old immune system is still strong enough to reject the new one.*

Dr. Truesort returned at once and gave Lee an injection of the immunosuppressant drug from the hospital pharmacy supply. He checked Lee's pulse, blood pressure, and lungs every fifteen minutes. Lee's pulse became a little stronger.

Josh returned with two dinner trays. He stood at the door. "Hi, Doc. Thought I'd dine in tonight and see how the patient's doin'."

"He's being fed intravenously. He won't need one of those trays."

"I know, Doc. I'm gonna eat 'em both. Got a friend in the kitchen."

Fred laughed. "Always have friends in the right places, Josh."

"Yeah, I just go into the patients' lounge to eat. I peek in occasionally to make sure Lee is okay."

"Keep checking Lee's pulse. Give me a call downstairs in the oncology lab if there's any change. In any case, call me when you leave."

"Sure."

Josh stacked his trays on a corner table to return to the cafeteria when his break was over. "How ya feelin', man?" Josh asked Lee from the visitor's chair once he had washed his hands and changed into sterile scrubs, mask, and gloves.

"Like crap. Read to me, Josh. Read the paper to me."

The sound of Josh's voice soon lulled Lee to sleep. Josh called Dr. Truesort. "Just fell asleep. I'm goin'."

"Okay. I'll be right up, Josh. The AIDS may flare up again. I may not have eliminated all the cancer, but I got as much as I safely could."

"Whatever that means. He ain't gonna die, Doc. Not now. He's doin' good," Josh said.

But before he left the room, Josh felt Lee's pulse. It was weaker. The pulse monitor was showing smaller and smaller peaks in the moving line tracing across the screen. He looked at his watch. *Per diem nurse is late again.*

Josh phoned Dr. Truesort, and then sat down on the chair next to Lee's tented bed.

—∿⌇o

"Cory," Dr. Truesort yelled across the lab.

"Yeah?"

"Josh called. Says Lee's bad. We've got to get up there. This is it. Lee's body will either accept or reject the fresh bone marrow. After all, it wasn't a next-of-kin match. Those are the risks you take. His outlook wasn't that good at the start."

"Okay, okay. Lee's failing. You scram. I'll finish here. Be up in a few minutes."

As October turned to November, Lee's condition wobbled from good to fair. The nausea had abated. His body began accepting the fresh bone marrow and fighting off the AIDS virus. But the cancer was rebounding.

"Soon as I get stronger, the doc says I gotta have more chemotherapy for my cancer, so maybe I should start workin' out or somethin'," Lee joked with Josh, who had stopped in for another visit.

"Yeah. Be a superstar and make millions of bucks. Football season's already started. Thanksgiving's comin', with all them games on TV. You may have to wait till next year to try out," Josh advised, not even looking up from the newspaper. He began to read the sports section out loud.

"What would ya do with a million bucks anyways?" Josh asked. He looked up when Lee didn't answer. Lee was blinking and clutching his chest with both hands.

Josh jumped up. "Answer me. Goddamn it, answer me!" he yelled.

Josh grabbed the phone and dialed Dr. Truesort's direct line. "Room 424. Get up here! Ya gotta do somethin'!" he yelled, cutting off the doctor's hello.

"Don't die. Jeezus, don't die, Lee. Who's gonna teach me stuff?" Josh shoved the tent onto the floor, moved the pillow to the side, and began compressing Lee's chest, but he did not respond. Josh was afraid to give him mouth-to-mouth resuscitation since Lee had AIDS. Instead he held Lee's wrist. There was no pulse.

Josh gently placed Lee's head back on the pillow, crossing his hands over his chest. Crumpling in dejection, he sat beside Lee on the bed, his head bowed. Josh was surprised to see wet splotches on his green scrub pants. He could never remember crying since he was grown. But he'd never had a brother before. Now that brother was dead.

Chapter

5

*F*RED STUFFED HIS EYEGLASSES into his lab-coat pocket and bent over the microscope, gently moving the lens into focus. Still staring at some of Lee's final blood and tissue samples, he said in a hushed voice, "Cory, we're onto something! Lee's new immune system was working. The AIDS virus is dormant. Look, look for yourself." Fred stepped away from the microscope.

Cory studied the cell pattern. "Cool."

Fred complained, "If his heart hadn't given out—"

"Yeah. At least we got this far," Cory said, still looking at the samples. "I did a pretty good job of preparing these slides, if I do say so myself."

"If that's the case, you shouldn't have any trouble replicating them. We'll need them down the line to show that Lee's new immune system did work. I did an autopsy, took the organs Abby asked for. Got good specimens before the cells started to decompose."

"Fred, you know sometimes you disgust me. Don't you feel anything? No remorse? Nothing?" Cory shook his head in revulsion. "Pannell was telling me about his aide—you know, Josh, the one who cared for Lee?"

"Yeah. What about him?"

"He's grieving for his friend. Pannell said they were like brothers."

"Josh will get over it. It's only been ten days since Lee's death. I guess they were pretty close. I saw Josh in Lee's room quite a few times. Didn't think much about it—it's how I stay in control," Fred said, continuing to look through the microscope.

"How are you going to get rid of the body—while staying in control, that is?"

"I've signed a death certificate. The immediate cause of death was heart failure. Never thought that would happen. Hate to include the cardiology boys in this. Just send the body to the morgue, Cory. Have Josh wheel it down. I've spoken to them. They'll use the two-in-a-casket trick soon as they can. I've paid them to be cautious."

"You must be kidding. Wish I could be that casual about death. This research thing's become an obsession with you. And *no*, I'll wheel it down myself."

"Relax. Way I figure, he'd have been dead anyway. In fact, we extended his life. Pannell's got to get a couple more research candidates. Like I say, Cory, I think this idea is going to work . . . definitely going to work."

"Don't get your hopes up too high, Fred. Don't start to celebrate yet. You'd better get more bone marrow and immunosuppressant drugs before we get anyone else in here," Cory warned. "If the HIV comes out of hibernation with the next patient, you're going to be in bigger trouble than with Lee. Talk to Pannell about that also."

The Friday afternoon before Thanksgiving was cold and windy. Miano Tse Liu, who had immigrated from China seven years before, had ridden her bicycle to meet with her friend Ghanna in his one-room apartment. She wore her favorite item of clothing: a Communist-style blue denim jacket with a mandarin collar. Because of the chilly wind, she was bundled in additional layers beneath, including a woolen sweater. "Hi, Ghanna. Cold out today," she greeted him.

"Sure is. I just been outside too. C'mon in, Miano Tse. Better bring your bike inside my apartment. Not safe even in the foyer 'round here."

She wheeled her bike in, took off her scarf and mittens, and rubbed her hands together. Miano Tse noticed that Ghanna had left on his hat. She smiled. *He is forgetful sometimes.*

Ghanna moved the red chair farther from the window. "Sit down here, Miano Tse. It's too drafty by that window. Almost Thanksgiving time. You have Thanksgiving in China?"

"No. I learned about it in my English class in Shanghai. We read about Pilgrims and Indians having this big harvest feast. We wondered what they were going to eat through the winter if they ate up their food all at once. I thought it was just another odd American idea. I must have been at least sixteen . . . that's twenty years ago."

Ghanna chuckled. "Yeah, I think they did go hungry. Your English is real good, Miano Tse. You still got a bit of an accent, but I can always understand you. How long did ya study in Shanghai?"

"About seven years. I knew for a long time I wanted to come to America someday. Once I settled down over here, I took English classes at the community center for another two years."

"Maybe I could do that, but I reckon I'm too old to change. Now, what's on your mind, Miano Tse?"

"Doc Pannell spoke to Josh a couple days ago," she told him. "Said now that Lee is gone, they need new patients. The doc told Josh to get on it right away."

"How Josh really doin'? Ain't seen him too much lately."

"He's quiet. He doesn't have any patience. Says things never work out for him. He misses Lee, keeps saying Lee was the best friend he ever had. I'm worried about him, really worried, Ghanna. Maybe now that Lee's gone I should help Josh with his reading or play chess with him. He's helping me all the time, like if anything breaks in my apartment. I'm saving up to get him a good camera for his birthday. He's very artistic."

"You and him been together how long, Miano Tse? 'Bout six months now?"

"Yeah, since May, on and off. He's always been cheerful. Usually he's restless, not ready to settle down. But I've never seen him so sad before." Miano Tse sighed. "At first we were concerned that people would laugh at a Chinese lady dating an African American man. Sometimes we get long stares, but so far that's been all."

Ghanna nodded. "Around the city it ain't uncommon to see

stuff like that. We still got a lot of problems between different groups, but many of us learnin' to get along with each other. You just keep on bein' his girlfriend, Miano Tse, and I'll keep on bein' his friend. Time will help him heal his heart. It just take time," Ghanna counseled. "It's only been a couple weeks."

"Thanks, Ghanna, thanks. I'll be patient. Give him time to heal. I promise."

Ghanna nodded.

"Meanwhile," continued Miano Tse, "I have my junkyard crew helping us find sick people for the doctor. I already talked to them about it. They'll give us extra eyes and ears, you know?"

"That's fine, Miano Tse. You got some real dependable guys in that crew, like Carlos, and they listen to ya. People see 'em searchin' in that mound of junk at the yard. They see 'em carryin' it to the recycling center on their bikes to sell for a few bucks. Them junk-yard guys won't look outta place ridin' their bikes all over the city, keepin' an eye out for sickies while they look for the junk. They know a lot of people. And they like workin' for ya."

Miano Tse was a leader. She assigned each man a territory. If anyone disregarded this arrangement, Miano Tse would take his territory away and give it to one of the more loyal workers. She kept arguments among the crew at a minimum.

The workers discovered that they made more money with her as their leader. They spent less time arguing and more time collecting discarded metal and selling it for a profit. In addition, Miano Tse often found recent demolition sites where used metal could be found.

"I try to be fair. I find a lot of waste metal down by the abandoned warehouses too," Miano Tse said. "The scrap-metal dealer on the north side of the city accepts all kinds of metal. The bigger stuff is hard to carry, but my crew found an old pickup truck in the junkyard and rebuilt it with used parts. Francisco, one of my crew, is an auto mechanic. Brings us junk from car wrecks. Now, with the truck, we can haul heavier discarded machinery and pipes."

"You already expandin'. You a smart businesswoman."

"We get good money for it. My crew and I all collect the junk.

Then I negotiate a price with the dealer, and I give each guy on the crew twenty percent of the price of whatever he brought in that week. When somebody's territory no longer has any good junk, I divide the territories differently to keep things as fair as possible for my crew."

"This all sound good, Miano Tse."

"Now there's finding patients, too. That's three thousand dollars to split, every time: a thousand apiece for you, me, and Josh. If one of the junkyard guys gives me a lead that works out, he gets half my share, or five hundred. That'll motivate them to keep on looking."

"You keep track of all the math in your head?"

"I'm Chinese. We all got an abacus up here," Miano Tse said, pointing to her black hair with a laugh.

"This gonna really add up!" said Ghanna with a grin. "I told Josh I'm helpin' him find patients too. I know lotsa people 'round here, see 'em when I'm sittin' outside in my park."

"But Ghanna, we have to be careful. We don't want The Oxman finding out about this."

"That's for damn sure."

"I'll pay my junkyard crew one at a time, just like I pay them for collecting junk. If you find sick people, be sure to handle it discreetly. Talk to them casually . . . one at a time. No groups. And don't let people overhear."

"Course not, Miano Tse. Don't worry, I know how to be careful. That's how come Josh picked me for a business partner."

"I have to watch out for The Oxman all the time. The other day, Josh brought me a computer from the hospital. They were selling old ones cheap. He brought it over to my apartment. Had to come in the back way, from the alley."

"Why?"

"The Oxman's always watching me. One time I went into his cloth shop for fabric to send to my mom in Shanghai. Everybody stopped talking and just fastened their eyes on me. The Oxman always thinks I'm up to something. I can see his shop and the parking lot from my front window. He's right across the square."

"Huh, huh. Didn't know that."

"I'll stop by in a few days, see how you're doing. Ghanna, you should get a cell phone. Can't keep coming over to your room all the time. No good. Somebody's gonna wonder."

"Ain't they expensive?"

"Yeah, but you're in business now. Ask Josh. Maybe he can find you one. Maybe even a computer too."

"Did you discuss all this with him, usin' the junkyard crew to find patients and all?"

"Yeah. When he brought the computer over, he was so quiet. As soon as I explained everything I was going to do to find more patients, he stayed a few minutes, set up the computer on my desk, and left. Usually he stays and visits for a while."

Ghanna took off his tan, broad-brimmed hat and twirled it in his hand. "I don't know nothin' about them cell phones and computers . . . but like you say, we in business. Guess I could learn."

"Ramiero could help you. Kids know what to do." Ramiero was the six-year-old son of Alvarez and Asunta Delgado, who lived in a larger apartment on the second floor, directly above Ghanna.

Ghanna laughed. "Yeah, he's a smart kid."

Ramiero's dad worked for the company that provided security services to the hospital. Alvarez had recently been promoted from guard to shift supervisor and had spent part of his raise on a used computer and printer for his family. He knew that computer skills would soon give Ramiero an advantage with his schoolwork.

"Gotta go now," said Miano Tse. "But we've set up a good deal here, good for us and those doctors too. Who else could do this but us? Right, Ghanna?"

"Yeah. We got an exclusive."

"I just hope the next patient will do better than poor Lee," she added as she put on her scarf and mittens again.

Ghanna put his hat back on and opened the door for Miano Tse, who rolled her bike out through the foyer and down the front steps of the building.

"See ya," she said.

"Ride home safe, Miano Tse. Have a good weekend, and a happy Thanksgiving. Funny American custom." Ghanna grinned and tipped his hat with a bow.

But Miano Tse didn't go straight home. She headed to an abandoned warehouse to follow up on a tip from one of her junkyard crew.

The following Monday afternoon, Ghanna put on his tan, broad-brimmed hat and shabby jacket, then limped back across the street to his park to watch, sit, and smoke. One of the hospital people from the administration building hurried by, never noticing him. The man's head was down, butting the brisk wind. Ghanna chuckled, watching him try to straighten his tie underneath his coat as he rushed along toward the hospital rear door. *Glad I'm too unimportant to have to worry about no tie.*

"Hi, Mr. Wimpler." William held the door open for him. Mr. Wimpler's only response was a curt nod as he strode down the hall. William watched this short wisp of a man stop to run a comb through his brown hair, then disappear into the meeting room.

Harry Wimpler was late for his two o'clock meeting. Lunch with the chairman of the Hughler Hospital board of directors in the prestigious conference room had taken longer than he'd thought. Now Harry had to run from the administration building to the main one across the street. Yet a quick smile flashed across his face as he thought about the luncheon meeting: the chairman had confirmed the board's unanimous vote to promote Harry to chief executive officer. Though he had plotted and parried for years to achieve this goal, in the midst of his triumph he found himself uncertain and maybe a little frightened about this new responsibility. Not the deep-down fear he had felt in his gut when he'd admitted to his parents that he had left the priesthood, but close to it.

As head of Human Resources, he had listened to employees' complaints. His quiet reserve and "tell them what they want to hear" adeptness had fooled everyone. Through that strategy he had learned who could be trusted and who had a selfish agenda. He'd discovered only a few idealists searching for the better health care of humankind. He recognized the techniques of subterfuge and half-truth. After all, he should: he did the same thing himself.

Now he simply had to continue to stay well informed. With his promotion, this might become difficult.

Will have to develop new liaisons, he thought. *Strike up a rapport with some of the people down in the trenches. . . . Must be careful what I say at this next meeting. Let the others do the talking; learn more that way. Got to work out a new power plan. This place is like a minefield.* He arrived at the meeting room, opened the door with a flourish, and strode in.

That evening when the ER was quiet, Josh met Dr. Pannell in the supply room. "May have another patient for ya soon," Josh told him. "Heard about a guy been shelterin' over at one of them old warehouses near the railroad tracks."

"Glad to hear it. Thanks for moving on it so promptly."

"I got some good people workin' on this, real professionals. Maybe sometime I'll introduce you. How soon you want this next patient? You got enough meds now?"

"We're ready anytime. Dr. Truesort set up a pharmacy account through his private lab. He's impatient to get moving again. Think you can get this guy here this Saturday night, even though it'll be Thanksgiving weekend?"

"We'll do the best we can, Doc. But ya gotta realize, some of these guys afraid to come, need a lot of persuasion." Josh couldn't quite meet the doctor's eyes. "Lot of persuasion."

"I understand," Dr. Pannell said. "Just see what you can do, and keep me posted."

Josh nodded.

"And—Josh? Don't let Lee's death weigh heavy on your conscience. He was a very sick man. Probably would've died weeks sooner if he hadn't been here at Hughler. You know that, right? And your friendship meant so much to him. Hopefully we can help the next guy even more." He patted Josh's shoulder in reassurance.

Josh cleared his throat. "Thanks, Doc," he mumbled.

The two men returned to the emergency room several minutes apart. No one noticed that they had been in the supply room simultaneously.

William put his TEMPORARILY OUT OF ORDER sign on the exterior elevator door and rode to the top level of the parking garage. It was about 5:30 the next evening, the Tuesday before Thanksgiving. There was the usual traffic as the nine-to-five employees left for the day. He waved and nodded to the folks he knew and received a hearty "Hi, William" from most. As the drivers reached the ground level, no voices could be heard. The cars were now out of sight.

William emptied a nearby garbage pail into his large, wheeled trash bin, then used the empty pail to prop open the elevator door so he could sweep the elevator floor. After sweeping some wind-blown leaves and litter into a short-handled snow shovel, he threw the mess into his wheeled bin. He had started pushing it over to another garbage pail when he heard a screech of brakes. He smiled. William saw Dr. Pannell drive his red Camry to a whiplash halt directly behind Dr. Truesort's black Porsche just as he was backing it out. The Camry rocked from the sudden stop.

"What the hell do you think you're doing?" William heard Dr. Truesort yell.

"Was afraid I'd miss you," Dr. Pannell said, getting out of his car. He strode over to the Porsche, where Dr. Truesort handed him a brown interoffice envelope through the driver-side window. "It's all in here," William heard Dr. Truesort say. "Second installment we talked about."

Dr. Truesort scowled and looked downward, muttering something to himself that William could not hear. Dr. Pannell just turned away and undid the red string around the envelope while he strolled to his Camry.

William dumped his shovel and broom into his wheeled bin and stared straight ahead in studied nonchalance. Leaning on the handles for support, he wheeled his trash bin past the doctors and stopped at the next row of cars for a better view. The doctors heard William but ignored him; he was only a maintenance man. They had more important matters on their minds.

Those two must be into some deal, thought William. *They're in different departments. No reason for them to talk otherwise.* William swept and watched, watched and swept. Dr. Truesort's voice was muffled by the echoing noises from the garage's lower levels. Only William could hear.

Just a few rows of cars remained. William wheeled his trash bin behind the first car in a row to keep both doctors in sight. Dr. Truesort revved his engine, but Dr. Pannell made no effort to move his car. He pulled a wad of cash from the envelope and counted it, occasionally moistening his fingers in order to separate the bills. Dr. Truesort tapped his fingers on his steering wheel and yelled at Dr. Pannell, "Let's go, damn it."

Dr. Pannell nodded in response while continuing to gaze at the cash he was counting. Finally he shoved the bills back into the envelope and tossed it onto the passenger seat. He gave Dr. Truesort two thumbs up and turned into a space reserved for another doctor so Dr. Truesort could pass. Impatient, the older doctor raced to the exit, ignored the toll collector, and sped through the gate an instant before it blocked the exit onto Woodhouse Street.

William wheeled his trash bin to the elevator, mulling over what he had seen and heard. *Cool . . . Doc Pannell keepin' Doc Truesort trapped like that. Wonder if there were prescriptions in with that money? It's one way to deal drugs. Maybe that's what they're doing.*

When his shift was over on Tuesday night, Josh went out the front door and down the walkway to the street. Not feeling ready to go to the one room he called home, he began walking aimlessly down the cracked sidewalk, kicking an empty beer can along, when he saw Miano Tse walking toward him, pushing her bike by the handlebars. She was wearing her usual jeans and denim jacket, but she'd added a white scarf, knit cap, and mittens to keep warm.

Somebody was holding on to the back of her bike, stumbling along behind her. Occasionally the bike tipped with the force of the gusty cold wind. The man hanging on would cry out in pain when the wind swept across his face. Miano Tse just kept pushing the heavy bike up the street, staring straight ahead.

That guy in sorry shape. Gotta be that warehouse druggie Miano Tse told me about. He got no family, just like Doc Truesort wanted. She sure didn't waste no time! I better give her a hand.

Josh ran down the street to help.

"That warehouse druggie," as Josh had just thought of him, had once been the hope of the neighborhood. Abandoned by his drug-addicted parents as a boy, raised by his gospel-singing grandmother, he soon sang at church every Sunday too. As an adult he had done one-man stand-up comedy, sung ballads, and strummed a hot guitar; he'd been well known in the local club circuit for a while. Bright and witty, he wrote most of his own material and was consistently employed. But Vincent Monique had advanced from smoking marijuana to sniffing cocaine and mainlining heroin. At first he had been able to support his expensive taste and buy the best, but drugs began to absorb more and more of his life and his resources.

His slip was gradual: first the car, then the apartment, along with fewer and fewer gigs. Finally he'd had nothing but a warehouse with a broken door. That had been okay till the weather got cold. Then some Chinese woman showed up on a bike, reminding him that he had to go on.

That night as he lurched unsteadily along behind her, Vincent remembered thinking in the warehouse, *Maybe she'll come back. She asked if I could move outta here. She wants me to move. Damn that freezing wind!*

He had walked through the doorway and into the next room of the warehouse, holding on to the wall as he went. The outside door was still open. He had put up his hand to shield his eyes from the brilliant lone streetlight, then blinked and staggered forward. *God, I'm stiff. Can hardly even bend my knees.* He stood at the doorway a long time; he realized he had no choice. *If that Chinese woman comes back, I better go.*

And then he saw her.

She gave him a chocolate bar. He told her he was known as the famous Rafferty Court musician, actor, and comedian. She didn't believe him, but it didn't matter. "So your name is Vincent Monique?" she asked. He merely nodded his head.

"You sure they're gonna take me at the hospital? Got nothin'. No money, no insurance."

"Come with me, Vincent. Keep walking. Yeah, they'll take you at the hospital. No-o-oh questions. You go to the hospital, get well," she insisted. And so they walked all the way to Ghanna's building.

—ᜆᜆᜄ

"Hey, Miano Tse," Josh called, "lemme help you. I'll push the bike. You go tell Ghanna you got a guy here needs shelter. Go to the back door . . . no stairs."

Miano Tse nodded her thanks, ran through the alley, and knocked on Ghanna's back door. "It's Miano Tse, Ghanna. We have a patient. Josh is helping me."

Ghanna opened the door a crack, looked at Miano Tse, then at Josh and a white man stumbling behind him. Josh leaned the bike against the wall and grabbed the man's arm. "This is Vincent Monique," Miano Tse explained. "He needs help, Ghanna. He's been living in a warehouse."

"Come in. Come in. That wind too cold. Yeah, man, you can stay here. There's a bunk downstairs near the furnace room. You can stay down there. Landlord ain't hardly never around. Ain't glamorous but should be warm."

"Thanks, man! Thanks! That's real good of ya." Vincent shook Ghanna's warm hand with his own cold one. Ghanna didn't wince, just said good night to Josh and Miano Tse, then helped Vincent down the basement stairs. Once Vincent was settled, Ghanna brought his boom box to Vincent so he could listen to some guitar music.

—ᜆᜆᜄ

Back outside in the alley, Josh went to Miano Tse's bike. "Come on, Miano Tse. Sit on this here crossbar. I'll pedal you home."

Miano Tse smiled and hopped on. She looked up at Josh. "How will you get back to your place?"

He laughed as he hugged her. "I figure I can stay with you tonight."

Miano Tse looked at him and paused before she laughed too and said, "Okay, it's a cold night."

Josh gave her a kiss. "You know I love you, Miano Tse."

By the Saturday night of Thanksgiving weekend, there had already been freezing rain that hardened into ice, and a light snow was falling. Because Ghanna's footing was insecure, it was Miano Tse who brought Vincent across the street to Josh in the emergency room. *Don't she look adorable with snow sticking to her black hair!* thought Josh. He gave her a smile and a quick good-bye kiss, then turned to help Vincent into a wheelchair and through the door.

Inside the emergency room, Josh lifted Vincent onto a gurney and covered him with a sheet, neck to feet. (Later Josh would throw the sheet in the incinerator and disinfect the gurney's plastic-covered pads and the wheelchair.)

Josh winced when he removed Vincent's shoes and socks and saw the red dots of flea bites on his bare feet, along with pus-filled blisters. *He worse than Lee. These Saturday-night specials are really bad.* Afraid Vincent might infect other emergency-room patients, Josh moved him out to the hallway on the gurney.

He put Vincent's socks and shoes into a plastic bag. *I'll just throw it in the furnace.* Josh took them outside. "William! Hey, William!" he yelled. William just kept on salting the ice. "Hey, William, I need ya." Josh used the ice and slid down the sidewalk. "Hey, man, don't you hear nothin'? Get rid of this here bag before the fleas multiply and hop away. As long as you're still here with nothin' better to do on the Saturday night of Thanksgiving weekend." *And my girlfriend gotta spend tonight alone,* Josh thought.

William limped over to Josh. "'Nother street person, huh?"

"Left my patient. I gotta get back. Talk to ya later." Josh hurried up the slick walkway as best he could, back into the emergency room, then on to the adjacent hallway with his long-legged stride. "Sorry I left ya, man," he told Vincent. But Vincent lay asleep in the fetal position despite the noise in the hallway.

Josh shook Vincent awake. "We're goin' partway up on the elevator. Then you're gonna have to walk to a shower and get cleaned up."

Vincent rasped, "I can do it if we go slow."

When they got off the elevator, Josh helped Vincent off the gurney and nodded toward the shower-room door. "The shower room's in here. C'mon. Here's a couple of gowns. Once you're clean, put 'em on. Make one go 'round one way and the other opposite-like till I find you pajamas. Put all your clothes in this here bag and close it up tight. Oh, and I found you some flip-flops. Put them on, too. You need help or you wanna be on your own?"

"On my own."

"Okay. Here's a plastic chair if ya get tired. I be right outside if ya need me. After that we take the stairs to your room. Think ya can do that?"

"Yeah, but like I say, we gotta go slow."

"He's settled, Doc. . . . Same private room. His feet are a mess of flea bites like Lee's . . . had to give him lice-killing shampoo. No, nobody knows he's here. Brought him up the back stairs one step at a time like a kid."

After hanging up the phone in room 424, Josh turned back to Vincent. "Doc Truesort's comin' right up to examine you, Vincent. I told him to bring somethin' for your feet. Gotta get back to the emergency room. See ya."

"Thanks, Josh, thanks."

"Hi, Vincent, I'm Cory Maxwell. I work with Dr. Truesort. Okay if I take your picture? We're doing a research project. It's just for our records."

"Sure. Go ahead."

"Can you stand up?"

"Of course." Vincent twisted his scrawny body out of the bed and leaned against it for support.

"Turn to the side, Vincent. I need a profile. That's good. Thanks. Now to the front. Your blue eyes and brown hair make a good contrast."

"Lemme know when they get on the cover of *GQ* so I can buy a copy."

"I like your sense of humor, Vincent. Don't know about *Gentlemen's Quarterly*. I'll give you a copy of these photos for your scrapbook, though. Dr. Truesort should be here soon."

Fred stopped at the nurses' station to arrange for Vincent's care.

"Another charity case, Doctor?"

"Yes. Room 424. Send any billing to my attention. Do what you did with the previous patient in this room. You know, meals, water pitcher . . . I'll have private per diem nurses on duty around the clock as well."

"You sure? Can't you get any assistance with the medical bills?"

"Maybe."

"I know you paid for the previous patient in room 424. See what you can do, Doctor. If you have a problem, let us know."

"I should be okay." *Not going to let you know why I'm paying this patient's bill.*

But the nurse wondered, *Wow, that's a switch. What's caused his change of heart? He never bothered before.*

Fred knocked at the door of room 424 and went in. "You must be Dr. Truesort," Vincent greeted him with outstretched hand. "Nice to meet you."

"Strong handshake. That's good, Vincent."

"Comes from playin' guitar. . . . Josh said you can fix my feet."

"Maybe I can do more than that. First, let's see those feet." Dr. Truesort pulled on examining gloves. He lanced the blistered areas, spread analgesic antibiotic ointment on them, and wrapped them in gauze. Vincent grimaced only once. Next Dr. Truesort spread another cream over the flea bites. "Here, keep this cream handy. Just put it on these bites when they burn or feel itchy."

"Okay. Thanks, Doc. I've been living in one of those old warehouses. Better than nothing, but doesn't stop the bugs."

"I figured something like that. Are you a drug user, Vincent?"

"Been clean for two years. I had some good counseling. And then I had no money. I stole when and where I could. I finally realized I was killing myself. It was just a long, slow way to die."

"You're sure right about that. I'd like to take some blood to analyze. It will help me figure out how I can help you. Just put your arm up here. Make a fist for me. That's it."

Vincent turned his head away as Dr. Truesort filled two vials with his blood. "It ain't blue, is it, Doc?"

"No. Look for yourself. It's just plain old red. Let me swab your mouth to get your DNA. . . . That's done. Get some rest. It's late, but I've ordered dinner for you. It should be here shortly. I'll see you tomorrow."

"Take a look at these blood samples, Cory. Physically he looks like he's got AIDS." Fred and Cory were working in the hospital oncology lab. It was convenient to be near the patients.

"Just been up to his room. Took his picture. Cheerful fellow." Cory began preparing a slide. "I hope you're wrong about the AIDS. You going, Fred?"

Fred looked at his watch. "You better go home soon, too. No more all-night stints for me. I'll be in late. Ingrid has some charity brunch I have to attend."

"Do you know his blood type?"

"No. Type it while you're at it. And check his DNA. Call me on my cell when you know anything. It'll save me from a boring Monday morning."

"I've already started; think I'll stay and get our analyses done. Maybe just come in a little later Monday." Cory picked up an empty slide.

"Suit yourself."

Monday morning Cory called Fred's cell. "Fred, think we've—What the hell is that noise? What kind of party are you at, anyhow?"

"Some drunk went for a swim in the punch bowl. I'll call you right back."

A minute later Cory's phone rang. "Sorry, Cory. Can you hear me now?"

"Yeah. Looks like Vincent's a good candidate for your study. He's got Kaposi's sarcoma—not as advanced as Lee's was—and AIDS."

"Don't go. I'm coming over. I'll tell Ingrid it's an emergency. She can get a ride home from our neighbor. See you in twenty minutes."

Fred studied Cory's slides. Cory had Vincent's blood type and tissue markers, and Fred could see the pattern of cancer cells. He looked up at Cory. "Yes, Vincent will be an excellent subject for our study—*if* we can find a good bone-marrow match for him after his chemo. Let's start looking right now."

Cory brought up the Excel spreadsheet of the hospital's bone-marrow bank on his computer and searched for a match, but none even came close. "Looks like we'll have to go through the national bone-marrow registry for this one, Fred."

"We can't. They'd ask too many questions. Frankly, I don't think they'd accept our application anyway since we don't have the proper paperwork for Vincent. Got to keep this below the radar, Cory. Come on up to my office; we'll look over some other data there. My oncology patients may be a good source for us."

Cory raised his eyebrows. "Do you really think that's safe, Fred? Would *you* want to receive marrow from a former cancer patient, even one in remission?"

"Cory, relax. Remember, I'm a leading oncologist," Fred snarled. "I know what I'm doing. If a patient is now in remission and we cleanse the marrow, it'll be almost as good as new. Besides, what chance would this patient have if he didn't receive our treatment? You know perfectly well he'd be dead in a few months."

"Perhaps so, Fred, but Christ! If you give him marrow from *any* cancer patient, you'd better cleanse that marrow very thoroughly. *Very* thoroughly, do you hear me? And I insist on examining it after it's cleansed, to make damn sure it's pure enough!"

"All right, all right! No need to be so offended. Besides, his HIV will be fighting any few remaining cancer cells he receives."

The two of them walked in tense silence to Fred's office, where a pile of file folders was strewn on his desk. "Not even Martha can keep you organized," Cory commented.

Fred ignored the sarcasm in his assistant's voice. "Let's look at my oncology patients' blood and DNA records. I have the data in my private computer. For years now I've been recording all my patients' blood types and HLA just in case I might need the information in the future," Fred said. "You look through those files on the desk; they're too new to be on the computer yet."

For the next two hours Cory and Fred sifted through data about many hundreds of patients: blood type, age, gender, HLA (human leukocyte antigens—proteins that determine tissue type), overall health, outcome of case. It was easier to eliminate the hopelessly inappropriate matches than to find promising ones. A few were marginally acceptable.

Then Fred checked out another one that looked possible. "Willington, Patsy. Here she is. . . . Oh my God, look at this, Cory! They are an unbelievably close match! I've checked and rechecked both Vincent and Patsy. Maybe I'm missing something. I've never seen so close a match for people who don't claim any kinship. I'll print it out. Maybe I'm seeing things."

Cory stared at the printout. "It's almost as good as an immediate family member! Is this possible, Fred? You sure about Patsy?"

"We'd better check both of them again. You check Vincent, and I'll have Martha call Patsy and make an appointment immediately so I can double-check her too," Fred said.

Three days later, Patsy Willington's mother was already pacing in the hallway of Hughler Hospital's same-day-surgery ward when Fred arrived at 8:30 a.m. "We just checked in, Dr. Truesort. I want to speak with you out here about Patsy. We are so upset. Does she really have to go through this?" *What a fidgety sparrow of a woman,* thought Fred. But his manner was professional as he answered her.

"You don't need to be, Mrs. Willington. All we are going to do is harvest some of your daughter's bone marrow to have on hand. Think of it as savings for a rainy day. It is simply a precaution."

"I see. I was afraid it meant her cancer had returned and that maybe you were not ready to break the news. Sometimes I can't accept the fact that she has fought off cancer. Other times I'm okay. A precaution. That's good, Dr. Truesort—very good."

Dr. Truesort followed Mrs. Willington into the same-day-surgery ward to Patsy's bed. Picking up her chart, he said, "Your vital signs are good, Patsy." He looked at her carefully. "You look healthy. How do you feel?"

"Great. This place is boring. My cancer has been in remission for four and a half years. How long does it take to recuperate from this bone-marrow-harvest thing? As you know, I've returned to work. What do I tell my boss?"

"So you know what to expect, let me review the procedure with you both in case you have more questions since we spoke in my office on Tuesday. We took blood and DNA samples to be analyzed then, to be certain we could proceed with the harvest," Dr. Truesort began. "Now, this is same-day surgery. After it is done, we will monitor you carefully until the anesthesia wears off. Then, depending on how you feel, you can go home today or stay over-night and go home tomorrow. Once you're home, I'll call to see how you feel. You may have some soreness in your back. If your condition worsens at any time, give me a call. Generally patients return to their normal routines in a week."

"My boyfriend and I plan to go scuba diving in three weeks." In frustration Patsy fluffed and punched the bed pillows and leaned back with a heavy sigh, her single braid of brown hair jouncing in rhythm. Her sturdy arms and shoulders certainly looked like those of a strong swimmer.

"Don't cancel those scuba-diving plans, Patsy. In three weeks you should be recovered. Today we'll remove marrow from the rear of your pelvic bone. You will lie on your stomach, and the anesthesiologist will put you to sleep. You won't feel any pain during the procedure. I will simply make about four tiny incisions in the skin over the back of your pelvic bone. These incisions are so small that no stitches are needed. Then I will put in a hollow needle with a syringe attached to draw out enough of the liquid bone marrow.

"The incisions will heal up quickly. Your body will replace the marrow we take today in four to eight weeks, and you'll have fresh bone marrow on hand in case you need it later. So I'll see you in about an hour, say about nine thirty, in the operating room."

Dr. Truesort saw Patsy's mother's lips quiver and tears slip from her eyes. "Mrs. Willington, if you have any questions, just give me a call." He patted her hand.

"Thank you. Thank you, Doctor."

But Dr. Truesort never heard the second thank-you. He rushed from the ward to his office, unlocked the door, and grabbed his phone. "Cory, I've got it: a source of bone marrow. Yeah, it's a go! Our experiment can continue."

In the operating room, Dr. Truesort and an intern chatted about their golf scores as they harvested the bone marrow. After Patsy was wheeled from the operating room, Dr. Truesort picked up the sterile bag of marrow and held it under the bright lights shining on the operating table. "Pack this lightly in ice right away," he told the intern. "Give it to Cory Maxwell as soon as you've finished. He's in charge of our bone-marrow bank, as you may know."

"She a donor?" the intern asked.

"No. It's for her—just a precaution in case she needs it later," Fred said. "I certainly hope she doesn't. Nice girl," he added, feigning compassion.

part THREE

A Fortune Walking

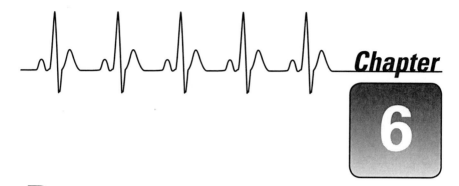

Chapter

6

DURING THE NEXT FEW MONTHS, Miano Tse's junkyard crew developed a steady routine looking for possible patients whom Dr. Truesort could help. Miano Tse insisted that her crew had to look like they were going about business as usual with junk lashed to their bikes. No outsider must find out their latest way of making money. "They take business away," she warned. Meanwhile, she spoke with managers of recycling centers and city engineers. She searched on her bike and online for demolition sites where her workers could collect scrap metal.

Some of her crew lashed junk to their bicycles and rode across the city, checking out alleyways, bridge overpasses, and other places where the homeless might seek shelter. Others filled shopping carts packed with recyclables and walked to the recycling center nearby. Occasionally high school kids used a skateboard to search.

To add to the research record and documentation, Cory videotaped Vincent as he progressed over five months. Winter dragged on, then turned to spring. During that time it was amazing to watch Vincent rally. Like Lee, he had received chemotherapy first, then bone marrow, which Fred had cleansed and Cory had carefully checked before the transfusion. His body had accepted Patsy's marrow with only a low dose of immunosuppressant drugs. By late February, Vincent's blood work had shown remarkable recovery from both AIDS and cancer. A few weeks later, his six-foot body had become strong and muscular again. His appetite was good, his blue eyes shone, and his brown hair had become thick and wavy.

One mid-April afternoon at a team meeting in Fred's private lab, Fred and Cory brought the videos, along with the microscope slides, to show Abby and Ian. They watched Vincent doing calisthenics in his small hospital room. He even performed a soft-shoe number and sang some ballads he had written. "He's had physical therapy during his stay," Fred pointed out.

Abby laughed. "I've never seen such entertaining research before."

Ignoring her, Fred continued, "I hope Vincent's enthusiasm is contagious and you catch the spirit of success, too," he told them.

"Is he still getting chemotherapy, Fred?" Abby asked.

"No. We're monitoring him closely, of course. Both his AIDS and his Kaposi's sarcoma seem to be in complete remission. He will continue to need immunosuppressants to ensure that his body doesn't reject the new bone marrow. If we find that he needs additional meds or treatment, we'll provide them through the research budget."

"Should we let him go home, Fred?" Cory asked. "Other patients don't stay hospitalized once they're this well. He has been here nearly five months. He could just come back for checkups on an outpatient basis."

"You know how these people are," Fred reminded Cory with a frown. "You'd never get him back for a test, and I still want more tests. He needs careful monitoring for his own safety. Besides, he doesn't have a home to go to. Remember?"

"But you can't keep him prisoner here indefinitely," said Cory drily.

"If you paid him, I bet he would come back," Ian suggested.

"No. You know how much his chemotherapy treatments cost alone? I've already spent thousands. And I convinced Wimpler it was a charity case, so he reduced the cost."

"Why don't you complain to the American Medical Association about the high cost of health care while you're at it?" Cory snickered at him. "As for Vincent, scare him. Tell him if he doesn't come back, he certainly won't make it."

So Vincent was discharged with the warning to return weekly for a checkup because his condition had been life threatening.

On a warm, cloudless morning near the end of April, Vincent left the hospital, wearing the warm-up suit and sneakers that Cory had bought him for his physical therapy. He strode across the parking lot, leaned against the fence, and stared at the people walking by: the mother and her son waiting for the bus, the truck driver asking directions, the construction worker flirting with a hospital office clerk. Then he walked to the corner, dazed with the feeling that it was great simply to be alive. "Ghanna," he called.

Ghanna was sitting on the concrete steps, enjoying the warmth of the April sun. Looking up, wondering who had called, he saw a tall white man walking straight toward him. *How come he know my name?* Ghanna wondered. Then a smile of recognition spread across his face. He limped to Vincent, faster than he had in years, and slapped him on the back. "You look new. You almost new," he told Vincent over and over again. "Go tell Miano Tse. You remember her, right? The Chinese lady with the bike. She's by the junkyard. You go. Show her you all better."

Vincent found Miano Tse down by the junkyard with some of her crew just where Ghanna said she'd be. Finding a purple crocus struggling to grow in the sparse grass near the curb, Vincent plucked it to give to her. "Hey, Miano Tse, it's me, Vincent. You know. The guy you sent to the hospital. I came to say thanks."

Miano Tse climbed down the embankment and looked at the man shouting at her. "What? What are you talking about?"

"I'm tellin' you, thank you. You saved my life. It's Vincent. Remember, you dragged me up the street from the warehouse? You said I was sick." Vincent, standing tall with his shoulders back, declared, "I'm better. Here, this purple crocus is for you."

"Thanks." Miano Tse took the flower, but she continued her studied look at Vincent. "It hardly looks like you. You're better, huh? It worked, huh? Stay right there. Don't move," she ordered, backing away from him in awe. "Hey, fellas!" she yelled as she continued to stare at this stranger in front of her. "Look who's here! Vincent! He's all better. Look," she called to the men, "look. He made it! He's standing! He's standing straight up."

They scrambled down to see this reincarnation. Some touched Vincent's arm to be sure it was so. Others walked all around him and stared.

"This should make gettin' more junkies easier," Miano Tse said quietly to the group, recovering from her amazement. "Any doubt, just show 'em Vincent here." They nodded in agreement.

Miano Tse invited Vincent into the junkyard. "Give us a hand hauling this stuff if you're so healthy now," she kidded, but Vincent surprised her and began hauling away debris with the rest of the men, laughing and singing joyfully with his wonderful vitality.

With Vincent as a walking advertisement, it became easier to find destitute applicants for Dr. Truesort's experiment. Those who thought they might have AIDS and wanted medical help soon learned to talk to Ghanna in his park or stop by the parking lot in back of Lefty's Bar, where many of Miano Tse's junkyard crew had been hanging out lately.

And with their new wealth, the crew was able to spend money. "Not on crack, no drugs," Miano Tse warned. "You get cut out if you do drugs, even if you start dealing in 'em, whether it's for The Oxman or anybody else. You guys got that?"

"You sound like the board of health," they kidded her, but they knew she never wanted to confront The Oxman or even hint that she was taking a business opportunity away from him. So now they spent more time in Lefty's and less time searching for good junk, auto parts, or homeless people with HIV/AIDS.

Earlier Josh had told Dr. Pannell about another possible patient found by one of the crew. Her name was Camilla. When interviewing her, Miano Tse noticed Camilla's many telltale bruises: signs of physical abuse. Camilla told Miano Tse that her husband had HIV, which he had passed on to her.

Another one of Miano Tse's crew had found Midgin, a young man who had once made good money in real estate. When the housing market started going downhill, he had lost his job and never quite managed to get back on his feet. He had been turned down for dozens of jobs and had worn out his welcome with friends. Finally he had sought refuge in the train station: walking the interior mall lined with shops to beg for bread and other foods whose sell-by date had expired, napping on a wooden bench until a guard shooed him away, and using the men's restroom as a place to sell his body. That's how he had been infected with HIV, he'd explained to Ghanna.

Their ability to handle these cases convinced Dr. Pannell that Miano Tse, Josh, and Ghanna were ready to begin their own screening practice. He had taught them what to look for and what questions to ask. People were not good candidates for the experiment if they were suffering from malnutrition or had cancers other than Kaposi's sarcoma. If a patient was accepted but was ultimately found not to benefit from the treatment or was not cooperating, that person would be discharged.

From then on there had been three patients at a time, in private rooms 424, 425, and 426. Initially it was difficult to care for three patients simultaneously and keep the experiment secret, especially after Vincent left. Dr. Truesort had hired per diem nurses to care for his special patients, covering all shifts. He had warned them not to discuss his patients' cases with anyone, not even with their own families. And he paid them well.

Josh and Ghanna continued to control the number of patients allowed through now-friendly Security into the three private rooms. They had a policy of no more than three at a time, which aroused less suspicion, kept the price up, and kept Dr. Pannell believing it was no easy task to find the right kind of patients and persuade them to come in.

Later that same month, Fred began thorough medical screenings in his hospital office, checking new patients recommended by Bob. Once Fred had determined that the patients were good candidates for the clinical trial—and that Hughler's bone-marrow bank had marrow compatible enough with theirs—he admitted them into the hospital. He consulted with twenty-eight patients in this process, but only eleven qualified for the research project; many of those rejected had AIDS that was too far advanced to be helped by his treatment. At Cory's insistence, Fred sent them on to a local clinic for care. Several other people chose not to participate at all because they didn't think it would work.

By now, Miano Tse had bought herself a new wardrobe, abandoning her Communist-style mandarin-collar jacket with matching blue jeans and replacing it with embroidered jeans and matching jacket. But she kept her broad straw hat, which had protected her from sun and rain years ago in China. Her mom had given her that. She could not part with it, even though she would feel ridiculous wearing it on the city streets.

Now she had a large-screen HDTV and a new refrigerator—even had them delivered to her second-floor apartment, but to the back of the building out of her fear of The Oxman. She put her aging television on the curb out back and gave her old under-the-counter refrigerator to Ghanna for free—much to his amazement. He told his homeless friend Sally McVeigh about it.

One cold, windy morning at the end of April, Sally lurched down the street, dragging her heavy body to the garbage bins as she did every day. She dug through them with her bare hands in search of aluminum cans. Sometimes friends and neighbors donated cans for her to recycle—even William at the hospital. Her faded blue warm-up suit and torn sneakers were all she could fit over her large body and misshapen feet.

After making her collections, she wearily rocked to and fro down the block to sit for a minute on the concrete steps of Ghanna's apartment building. For her it was a resting place before she trudged on to the recycling center.

On her way back she always stopped in at Lefty's for a glass of wine, paying for it with the money she'd earned from her aluminum-can collection. Smiling her gap-tooth grin, she bragged to everyone, "I'm doin' somethin' for the environment."

That was what she was saying when The Oxman barged in, squeezing his huge, muscular form past the men seated at the bar, who studied their drinks or blew smoke at the nicotine-stained tin ceiling.

"Josh here?" he asked, cracking their silence.

No one answered him. No one looked at him.

His green eyes became slits. "You'll answer me when I come back," he shouted, and slammed out the back door.

Sally slid off her bar stool and edged toward the window, where she used a paper napkin to rub a clear spot. Peering through it, she watched The Oxman swagger across the street in his leather jacket. "He's gone," she announced, and the chatter began again. "Chinese lady gave Ghanna a little refrigerator. How about that?" she asked the group, proud of her tidbit of gossip.

When Sally left, she lumbered toward Ghanna's park and called to him. Ghanna abandoned his wine bottle and cigarettes to cross the street and talk to her. "The Oxman is, uh . . . lookin' for your friend Josh," she warned.

"Thanks, Sally. I seen The Oxman go into Lefty's. You get on to the shelter—too cool an' damp to be hangin' out in no street even if it's supposed to be April. I gotta watch from out here. Can't see nothin' from my window or this here trailer. Trailer's good most of the time, though. The construction workers left it. One of 'em said wasn't no room for it at the other site."

"But Ghanna, ain't you cold out here?"

"Don't worry, I be goin' in shortly, but The Oxman walkin' toward William right now. Gotta keep an eye on things, figure out what The Oxman up to. Don't like his askin' for Josh, neither."

As Sally shuffled away, Ghanna returned to his park. He casually propped himself against the utility pole, made an elaborate show of lighting a cigarette, and watched the other two men out of the corner of his eye.

A block away, William was sweeping up the trash in the parking lot. The Oxman picked up a wine bottle he found on the curb, strode right up to William, and smashed it at his feet. "Make sure you do a good job cleanin' up that broken glass," he sneered. "Be glad I didn't break it over your head."

Despite his fear, William glared at this six-foot-five, two-hundred-eighty-pound hulk of a man. "What's on your mind? You didn't come over here for nothin'."

"Think you're smart. Then you tell me what's goin' on here." The Oxman took a step toward William, gesturing toward the hospital. His wide-open leather jacket flapped away from his torso, defying the cold wind.

William hoped his own jacket hid the fact that his body was trembling. He backed away from The Oxman. "They c-come to the hospital sick. We make 'em well."

The Oxman spat. "Wise-ass! Don't you mess with me!" He watched William sweep the jagged neck of the bottle, along with smaller chunks and slivers of glass, into the old snow shovel and turn away to dump it into the garbage barrel. "And don't turn your back on me!" he yelled. "You little stutterin' idiot."

"Why not? I ain't afraid of you." William suddenly turned, grasping the neck of the jagged-edged bottle.

Again The Oxman stepped forward. "Somethin's goin' on. Ya know that Chinese woman? Suddenly her and them junkyard guys got money to spend. She musta got a new TV. Saw her old one on the curb at the back of her building. They say she gave her little refrigerator to old Ghanna. Guess she couldn't sell it for junk. Assam drove it over to Ghanna's in his pickup truck."

"So what?" asked William. "What's that got to d-do with the hospital, or with me?"

"Because the hospital's the only place within a mile of here where anybody makes money. That, or dealing drugs. I know the Chinese woman and her junkyard guys ain't interfered with my space. I still get the same dough from that. Ya know what I mean?

But the city's givin' away free sterile hypos these days. Cuttin' in on my business. Damn fuckin' social concern." He stopped abruptly, worried he might have said too much. "You work at the hospital. What's Miano Tse doin' with them junkyard men? She just didn't find a new TV there."

"I don't know any Chinese l-lady," said William.

"Yeah? Well, ya know Josh, don't ya? Somethin' fishy's goin' on, somethin' to do with the hospital. Think Josh is in on it too. He used to supply me with good needles. Now he says he's too busy to bother. He even told me he don't need extra money no more," The Oxman said. "Somethin's up, man. Ain't you seen anything? You keep your eyes open, don't ya?"

"Wha-what's it worth to ya?" William looked straight at The Oxman, holding his broom in front of him with the brush side up and the jagged bottle in his other hand. Although ten inches shorter than The Oxman and many pounds of muscle lighter, William was ready to shove the bottle and broom into The Oxman's face if he came any closer. If that didn't work, William planned to drop the broom and surprise The Oxman with his "sucker punch," which had never failed.

"I gotta give ya credit. Most guys woulda run by now." The Oxman pulled a roll of bills from his front pocket and held them out. William looked at the money—looked at The Oxman—then dropped the broom, grabbed the money, and pivoted backward on his good leg in one motion. He stuffed the bills into the pocket of his jacket and stammered, "Uh, a hearse w-went out sometime last fall. T-two bodies in it, not one. None I know of since."

"How ya know that?"

"I, uh . . . d-drive when they n-need me. Helped get the bodies in. G-get a little on the side."

"Some doctor mess up or what?"

"Maybe. One . . . one doctor is passin' money to another. S-saw them in the parking garage. Positive it ain't . . . it ain't drugs."

"How ya know?"

"Uh . . . one doctor, emergency-room doc, he got real mad when he thought the other doc offered him a lot of cash for a drug deal. S-started to walk away," William said. His head was beginning to jerk spasmodically, so he reached up and put his eyeglasses in his pocket.

"Emergency room involved, huh? What they doin'?"

"Why don'tcha check in? F-find out," William joked.

"That wouldn't be a bad idea, except they know me too well."

"Yeah. Maybe you should ask Josh's friend. He's s-sittin' right over by the trailer." William pointed around The Oxman to Ghanna.

The Oxman turned and looked at Ghanna leaning against the broken utility pole. "My dealers smarter than him. They'll find out what's goin' on. That wimp. He makes more sense drunk than sober. Once or twice he tried helpin' me, but he's stupid, man, stupid."

"Don't b-be too sure. He pretends to be st-stupid to save his hide."

"Maybe, but I need somebody who knows what the hell they're doin'. As far as I'm concerned, he ain't it. I'll be around to see ya again." The Oxman strode back to Lefty's.

William dropped the broken bottle into his garbage bin and wheeled the bin in the opposite direction.

—√\─○

Ghanna watched them move out of sight. He hadn't been close enough to hear their conversation, but he hadn't needed to. *Don't like it one bit, them two talkin'. William's a squealer, that's what he is.*

Then Ghanna saw Josh come out of the emergency room. Ghanna limped over to meet him at the edge of the park and said, "Sally say The Oxman's lookin' for you."

"Maybe he wants more hypos," Josh told him.

"Maybe only a few. City's givin' 'em away now. He was talkin' to William. Be careful. We don't want him musclin' in on our trade. Watch out for William. He gave The Oxman a mean time, and The Oxman didn't do nothin'. Fact is, he done give William a few bills."

"Don't worry, old man. I'm over at Lefty's havin' a beer if The Oxman still lookin' for me."

"That's where he at. Remember where the money for them beers come from," Ghanna yelled at Josh as he crossed the street.

"I can take care of myself. Stop your fuckin' worryin'," Josh yelled, not bothering to look back.

∿

Josh blinked in the smoky gloom of the bar, trying to adapt to the dim light.

"Don't be so surprised to see me," The Oxman said, misinterpreting Josh's blinks. "You ain't goin' blind. It's me, The Oxman." He laughed.

"How ya doin'?" Josh said. He ordered a beer and sat down next to him.

"Hear ya been pretty busy," The Oxman said.

"Yeah. Been workin' a lot of overtime."

"Sure. Sure. I wanna talk to ya. Lefty, we gonna use your office," The Oxman stated, assuming compliance. Lefty nodded his balding head and drew a beer for Josh. Josh picked up his mug and followed The Oxman into a tiny storeroom overflowing with crates and stacks of old wooden pallets.

"What's goin' on?" The Oxman asked him. "First you don't need my business no more. The Chinese woman is givin' stuff away. And me and my boys is hungry. Didn't I give you enough for them needles?"

"Look, man, if you want my needles, I'll get you a couple. What do they say? 'For old time's sake.' No big deal. Just been workin' overtime. My job started payin' real good. Real good. I'm finished takin' a lot of chances," Josh told him. "I ain't doin' nothin' like that no more."

"It don't pay *that* good. Gotta be somethin' else," The Oxman insisted.

"Okay, I get you a few hypos when the ER gets real busy. Everythin' been quiet lately."

"Josh, you don't understand me. You dense or somethin'? I want a piece of the action. I know somethin's goin' on. I know those guys sellin' stuff they steal from the junkyard ain't on my payroll. The Chinese woman, she come snoopin' our way, and my business is fallin' off. You ain't helpin' yourself to any business that's rightly mine. You wouldn't be that stupid, or would ya?" The Oxman pushed Josh's mug out of his hand, spilling the beer, and grabbed the front of his shirt. He lifted Josh up with one hand so that Josh's face was now high above his own.

"We ain't interested in any of your business," Josh wheezed. "None, just your homeless, used-up junkies is all."

The Oxman threw him against the crates. "Whaddya mean, used up?"

Josh struggled to his feet. "Just that. They ain't buyin' nothin' from you anyways." Josh put his fists into his pockets, resisting the impulse to try and break The Oxman's face. He knew he'd lose. Instead he said quietly, "You owe me a beer."

The Oxman couldn't figure it out. He scratched his head. "Yeah. Come on."

But now he was certain he was missing a chance for more money. As he drank another beer, he reasoned, *William said one of the ER doctors was gettin' cash from another doctor. Josh works in the ER too. What does he mean, "used-up junkies"? Josh knows. Bet Ghanna knows. William knows. Probably I can find out from William. Then eliminate Josh and Ghanna before they know what hit 'em, or maybe just move 'em out.* "See ya around, Josh," The Oxman said, and left to find William.

That didn't take him long. William was picking up branches that had blown down onto the sidewalk along Ghanna's triangular park. "Funny, I thought nobody used this here walk. Hospital make you do this?" he said to William.

"Whaddya w-want?" William watched The Oxman warily.

Ghanna, gazing around the corner of the trailer, watched both of them. This time The Oxman's back was toward him, blocking his view of William.

"What are the names of the doctors? You know, the ones ya saw with money." The Oxman threw some bills into William's trash barrel.

"Whaddya wanna know that for? Won't h-help ya get no money," William told him.

"Don't be so certain. Somethin' goin' down. You and me, maybe we could help ourselves to a few of those hundreds."

"What makes ya think it's h-hundreds?"

"People spendin' like it is."

William paused for a moment, then decided that forking over the information would do no harm. "It's every man for himself. Figure what I tell ya is worth a hundred up front."

The Oxman threw two fifty-dollar bills into the trash barrel.

William began, "Dr. Pannell is the ER doc. Strong black guy, jumpy, nervous, singin' to himself, laughin' at nothin'. Ya know he's scared of somethin'. The other guy, he . . . he's real smart, real smart. Head of cancer medicine, Dr. Truesort. He's the one p-payin' out the money."

"What's he look like?"

"'B-bout six feet. White hair. Standard d-doctor type. Drives a Porsche," William said.

"They live near here?"

"Dr. Truesort lives in the fancy section of the city. Pannell has a condo near the h-hospital. What d-does it matter where they live?"

"Know anythin' else?"

"Yeah. Dr. Pannell don't l-like ya. He don't know what ya look like, but he's the d-doc who patches up your temper-tantrum victims. Heard him tell the c-cops to take ya down. He's tired of his ER being overrun with your deadbeat dealers and druggies. Last time a . . . a thirteen-year-old kid. Owed ya some bucks. Ya . . . uh . . . fractured his arm."

"So I'll put 'em all on the installment plan." The Oxman laughed.

William began to move away. "T-told ya just about all I wanna tell ya."

"Ya sure ya don't know nothin' more? Like what is this Dr. Truesort payin' Dr. Pannell for?" The Oxman asked, walking along with William as he broke up fallen branches and threw them into the barrel.

William didn't want to admit he didn't know something, especially if he could find it out and make a few dollars from his knowledge, so he said bravely, "Stop walking with m-me. Wanna get me in trouble? If anything happens to me, ya l-lose your pipeline, so get the fuck outta here."

The Oxman shoved past him. "I'll be back. I'll be back for some firewood." He laughed and dropped a few more bills into William's barrel.

William grabbed them out, stuffed the money into his pocket, and continued his patrol, progressing around the corner along the sidewalk closer and closer to Ghanna, who had casually strolled out from behind the trailer. *Sure he saw us, but he couldn't hear us,* William realized. *Wonder what he knows? Probably should talk to him.*

"Nice day," he said to Ghanna.

"Kinda cold. You sure do work hard," Ghanna said.

"It's a livin'. Ya know that big guy? The one I was just talkin' to? Know anything about him?" William asked, wiping his glasses on a torn handkerchief he pulled from his pocket. One of the bills spilled out at the same time. Quickly he stuffed it back in.

Ghanna noticed his haste and realized The Oxman must have been buying information again. "Yeah, course I know him. The Oxman. Everywhere he go be trouble. Nobody with any sense do business with him," Ghanna told him.

"Yeah, yeah, I figured he was mean. See ya." William walked away.

"Don't work too hard," Ghanna said derisively. Then he limped into the abandoned trailer out of the cold wind. "He can't say nobody warned him," he muttered to himself as he turned the electric heater on. *This make a good meetin' place for Josh and me. Maybe I clean it up, and we get Miano Tse to meet here too.* Soon Ghanna turned off the heater and left the cleanup for another day. It was his supper time.

That evening was even colder. Bob, who had the night off, slowed down his Camry as he approached the twelve-foot stone wall that surrounded the Truesorts' property. His headlights shone on the wrought-iron gate. *I'm here just about when I told Fred I would be.* Then the gate rolled open and he drove through, hearing a sharp click as it automatically locked behind him. *Great electronics. Fred probably checks the surveillance camera himself.* Bob circled around and left his Camry at the top of the driveway by the front door.

"Thanks for coming over tonight, Bob," Fred greeted him.

"Sure, no problem. Impractical to meet in the parking garage today."

"I put Chewy in the kitchen when you phoned that you were coming."

Bob grinned. "Thanks, Fred. But I think he actually likes me now that I've been here a few times." Bob could hear Chewy whining behind the kitchen door.

Once they were settled in the library, Bob said, "Josh has screened another patient for you. Ready for your own medical screening anytime now."

"Great. I'll have Martha set something up this week. We've got to keep at it till we duplicate Vincent's successful results with more patients."

"Vincent's made quite a sensation in the neighborhood, Josh tells me. Practically raised from the dead."

"My private charitable cause, eh?" Fred chuckled. "But one patient's not enough. The treatment has to be more reliable before we can sell it."

"Of course," said Bob. "Well, let's hope our current patients will be successful."

"The per diem nurse says one of them's an odd sort," said Fred. "Sure hates chemo, she says; whines about it all day. But he must realize he'll die without it."

"Hopefully he'll recover as well as Vincent," responded Bob. "Meanwhile, I owe Josh another three thousand. Plus I'm due for my next installment."

"I have the cash for you." Fred got up out of his recliner. "I must say," he added, "I never thought the expenses would pile up so fast. . . . But we're so close to a breakthrough. I can feel it."

"I hope you're right."

Fred sighed, then opened the heavy oak door and walked out of the library.

While he waited for Fred to return with the cash, Bob wandered around the library, humming to himself and rocking back and forth on his heels as he admired the exquisite Chinese vase on the shelf, the highly polished mahogany furniture, and the heavy drapes of burgundy damask held open with twisted golden metallic tiebacks. All signaled wealth and position. *Why didn't I notice all the details of this room before? Guess I was too focused on the conversations with Fred. Yeah, and the sunset that first evening.* Bob returned to the picture window. The river was a black swatch of crinkled silk sliding along in the moonlight.

He heard footsteps approaching on the marble floor and turned toward the doorway. "Would you like a cup of coffee or glass of wine before you go?" Ingrid asked, interrupting his casual tour. Chewy followed close at her heels and went straight to the window.

"That's okay, Ingrid, nothing for me. Thanks anyway, but I've got to get going."

"Chewy usually guards the gate, but I thought it would be too cold out there tonight. Fred thinks I spoil him," Ingrid said. She looked lovely in a gold lamé lounging robe.

"Here, Chewy," coaxed Bob, but the Doberman, still at the window, suddenly growled and began to bark.

"Hush, Chewy! Calm down, boy," said Ingrid. "There've been raccoons in the backyard lately," she explained, "and they get him all upset."

"That would explain it."

"I think it's wonderful the way you and Fred are helping the poor people. I really do," she gushed.

"It's the least we can do," answered Bob, stifling a laugh at her innocence as Fred returned and handed him an envelope.

"This should help," Fred said with a broad smile and a nod toward his wife.

Bob, catching on to Fred's ruse that the envelope supposedly held money for a charity, thanked Fred for his overwhelming generosity.

Fred grinned, relieved that Bob had been discreet and not divulged any information about the project to Ingrid. He responded simply, "You are very welcome."

As Bob put the envelope into his inside jacket pocket, something outside the window suddenly caught his eye. *Could have sworn I saw a shadow move out there. That dog senses it too. Or maybe it's just my old Desert Storm nerves again.* The Truesorts had their backs to the window, and Bob realized they had seen nothing.

"Fred and Ingrid," Bob said casually, "it's getting late. Don't bother to see me out."

"All right," said Fred. "I'll put the front gate on automatic. It'll open to let you out, then close right behind you."

They said their good-nights in the library. Then Bob quietly slipped out the front door and closed it softly behind him. *If there's somebody out here, I don't want to be noticed.* He crept to his car, eased himself in, and locked it with one hand as he put the key in the ignition with the other.

I could swear someone just darted into the bushes near the garage. Bob didn't start the car but sat humming softly, waiting and peering into the darkness. *Call Fred on his cell to warn him? NO. Discover it for yourself. Try to get a good look at this guy.*

Bob sat in the car for ten minutes, staring into the darkness, but all was still. *Maybe he went around the back. Following on foot would be asking for trouble. Better drive out to the street, see if I can catch him off guard when he leaves.*

He started the car and drove to the gate, which opened automatically. He steered the car parallel to the curb. No one followed or slipped through to the street while the gate was closing.

Bob looked at his watch as he drove around the tree-lined median to the other side of the deserted street. *Nine fifteen.* He parked directly across from the gate, where he could watch Fred's circular driveway and some of the area at the front of the mansion. The trees on the median hid part of his view, but then the intruder couldn't see much of him either. *Only someone very strong and agile could get over that stone wall. Whoever it was probably wouldn't come over the gate. It would be harder.*

The wait seemed interminable. Bob kept cracking his knuckles and humming a nonsensical tune, checking his watch and rearview mirror constantly. *Maybe he slipped away while I went around the median. But that drive only took thirty seconds, no more. If the guy got over one of the side walls, I may be out of luck. He couldn't swim down the river; current's too strong. Maybe I should call Fred.*

Suddenly he saw a figure on the sidewalk, leaning on the north end of the front wall. It was a big man who began trotting purposefully across the deserted intersection onto a side street, heading west toward the center of the city.

That's got to be him. With a little boost that guy could get over the wall, avoid the surveillance camera. Sure doesn't look like he'd have business so late in this neighborhood, either. Bob's hands trembled as if he had the DTs again. He gave the envelope in his pocket several quick pats and started the car. When the intruder was half a block ahead of him, Bob followed at a safe distance, hoping to see his face. Unable to get a good look, he finally drove around the block, put on his high beams, and let his headlights shine on the man's face, temporarily blinding him. In an instant Bob got a clear view of his face and physique.

Rarely had he seen such a giant boulder of a man. He looked powerful. His light-brown hair hung loose to his shoulders. A dark leather jacket rode up at his waist—too small to cover his huge frame. A torn T-shirt scrunched into his jeans provided scant warmth to the strip of flesh not covered by his jacket. His arms were so muscular that they bulged away from his sides.

Bob hit the gas and sped off as though catapulted before he himself could be recognized.

—∿—∘

The Oxman studied the red Camry that raced past, got a glimpse of the driver, shrugged, and quickened his pace. *Hey, is that the same Camry that was parked at the doc's house? Shit, maybe that dude saw me there, followed me. How much does he know?*

He jogged back to his pickup truck, which he had parked on a busy thoroughfare a few blocks away. *My old truck would look suspicious in the doc's neighborhood. Maybe I better get dressed up if I come back.* The Oxman smiled at the thought.

He had decided to look over Dr. Truesort's house to see if he could learn anything. It had been easy to find the address: he'd given one of his dealers a fifty to follow Dr. Truesort home one evening.

Bet the house is layered with alarms once you try to get inside. Probably has a surveillance camera, The Oxman reasoned. *Anyhow, the stone wall wasn't too tough to climb. I could get into the place from the river, but the current's swift here just above the rapids. The blonde must be his wife. The doctor seems to be like William said. Didn't get a good look at the other guy, but that could've been him in the Camry. Gotta track down that dude.*

The next evening The Oxman drove into the visitors' area on the second level of the hospital parking garage, then took the elevator to the open top level. *If I'm lucky, the two docs might park up here. Anyways, I got a great view of the garage entrance gate, the elevator door, and a door to the main building.* Prowling around the top level, he spotted the black Porsche, but no red Camry.

When The Oxman finally saw a red Camry arrive at the entrance gate, he hid behind an SUV. *Sure enough, here it comes all the way to the top level.*

As the driver stepped out of the car, The Oxman took a good, clear look at him: a well-built black man carrying a briefcase, walking quickly toward the elevator. *Uh-huh, he does look like that guy I saw through the doc's window last night.* When the elevator door closed, The Oxman hurried to the railing overlooking the doorway into the hospital. A minute later he saw the man again, striding so swiftly to the hospital door that his tan trench coat flapped around his knees. The man pushed an access card into the electronic monitor, the door swung open, and he disappeared.

That's gotta be the ER doc for sure, The Oxman knew. *He's the one who booked past me last night. Looks just like William said. At least the little twerp was straight with me.*

The Oxman was heading for the elevator down to the second level when he saw a tall, slim, white-haired man getting into the black Porsche. *Well, ain't this lucky? Both docs at once.*

There was a lot of traffic leaving the garage. By taking the elevator, The Oxman arrived at the second level before the black Porsche and followed the doctor out of the garage, driving a few car lengths behind him until he turned toward the mansions along the river. *He's gotta be the other one. He sure looks like the guy I saw through the window last night. Now that I'm certain who they are, I gotta figure out what they're doin'. Blackmailin' docs could be tricky stuff.*

─∿╫~∘

A couple of weeks later, Miano Tse kicked down the stand on her bike and joined Ghanna on the grass. "I like being outside. Great to have warm weather again. May is my favorite month. How's your refrigerator working? Keeping your wine cool these days, Ghanna?"

"My fridge is fine. Business ain't. Now that we screenin' the patients, too many of 'em get rejected, like that last guy. Nobody's been accepted since Camilla and Midgin."

"Yeah, I know. They've been in the hospital awhile now. I hope they're getting healthier like Vincent."

"Hope so too," said Ghanna, "but I ain't bettin' on it."

"Hey, are you going to stop by Lefty's tonight? I want to ask Vincent to come meet some of the regulars. He still looks so good after all this time: stands up straight, has a cheerful smile."

"Yeah, he looks great," Ghanna agreed.

"Maybe if he tells his story again and it gets around more, we won't have to work so hard lookin' for people. The doctors have enough patients for now, but we should have a waiting list of screened patients ready to go. What do you think, Ghanna?"

"I dunno. The Oxman, he's snoopin'. Don't like it. He done paid William to talk, remember? William don't know much, so that ain't bad. But I don't like him nosin' in our business. He always messes things up," Ghanna said, and then he was quiet for a moment before he spoke again. "Be careful. Be careful who Vincent talk to. That's what I'm thinkin'. Maybe Vincent should just keep quiet."

Miano Tse laughed. "You know why you're so tired? You worry too much." Then she asked, "How are Ramiero and his mom and dad? They still live upstairs from you?"

"Uh-huh. Ramiero, he fine. Seven years old now. Noisy as a horse when he clatters down the stairs."

"I bet."

"Alvarez doin' fine," continued Ghanna. "Real busy workin' security at the hospital. But the missus, she always poorly now. Coughin', tired. Pale, too. You don't think . . . ?" Ghanna said as he stumbled onto a new thought.

"Maybe." Miano Tse nodded her head.

"I didn't figure her for no AIDS," Ghanna said. "That mean Alvarez and Ramiero got it?"

"Could be," Miano Tse said, "could be. She used to be so pretty, remember? Now she's skinny and drawn."

"Yeah, Asunta look bad all right," said Ghanna, struggling to his feet. "But I ain't sendin' them for no goddamn experiment. You hear me? I'll tell Alvarez what you say, but they smart. They can figure out what to do for themselves. You and me, we ain't no doctors. Just leave it be. None of our business."

"Okay, okay. I know they're your friends. Thought I'd better say something, that's all." Miano Tse got up to escape Ghanna's anger and rode off on her bike.

Ghanna held on to the utility pole until he got his balance, then tottered back across the street to his room.

—⋀⎮⌐o

Miano Tse rode her bicycle to the junkyard and found Vincent, as she had hoped. He was lashing two boxes of scrap metal to the rear rack of a bicycle. "What are you doing, Vincent?" she called.

"Helpin' my man here. He needs to get this stuff onto his bike."

"When are you gonna get your own bike?" Miano Tse asked.

"Don't figure on goin' into the junk business permanent. Got me a guitar. I gonna start singin' again and tellin' a few jokes," he told her.

"Where'd you get a guitar?"

"I seen one, just itchin' to be played. Got it on loan. Kinda permanent like, if ya know what I mean. People careless with their stuff," he told her as he pulled the guitar from the backseat of a junked car.

"You stole it. That's what you mean," she accused him.

"Look who's talkin'. Whaddya think you doin' here?" he said, pointing to the mounds of junk around them.

"A guitar is valuable. My junk is just junk. Besides, if you steal something, you should say so."

"Yeah. At least be honest 'bout that." Vincent sat on the backseat to tune the guitar, humming softly, tightening the strings and strumming some more.

"Play, Vincent. Play somethin'," the men said. They pulled some wooden boxes and a few cinder blocks into a semicircle facing him and sat waiting for a song. Their jeans were frayed at the ankles and worn through at the knees. Their sweat-stained baseball caps were on backward, defying the glare of the sun. Vincent smiled at them all, climbed onto the car's hood, and sat facing his audience with his feet dangling.

He leaned his head back and began to sing a ballad, tapping his heels in rhythm against the car. He improvised the words and rhymes as he sang, describing the men and Miano Tse. They laughed; they clapped; they began humming and singing along—all but Miano Tse. So Vincent sang:

> *Ain't got no rhythm, but she got brains.*
> *If ya don't mind her, she'll put ya in chains.*
> *That Miano Sigh, little woman from Shanghai,*
> *Knows about rice, never ate no apple pie.*

The men drifted back to their work, but Miano Tse stayed. "Vincent," she said, "I'm going to stop by Lefty's for a beer tonight. Why don't you join me? You could always sing. Maybe tell them the story about how you got well. Beer's on me."

"Sure. I'll go with ya."

At Lefty's that night, one of the junkyard gang stuffed a dollar into Vincent's beer mug. "Sing another, man. You is lookin' good." Vincent was wearing a fringed jacket, clean black jeans, and a broad, black cowboy hat.

Lefty's patrons enjoyed Vincent's music. Some even laughed at his jokes. Others who knew him when he was sick asked how he got well. Lefty found they stayed longer and spent more money, so he enjoyed Vincent's songs too. His blue eyes lit up as he smiled and told his customers, "I've got the best beer on draft in the city."

It wasn't long before Vincent's story reached The Oxman. *So that's what's happenin',* he thought as he walked into his cloth shop. *Those doctors curin' people of AIDS. Maybe that's what William meant: "They come to the hospital sick. We make 'em well."* The Oxman unlocked a door to the back room and descended the stairs to the basement, where he unlocked the hidden drug-storage room. *I gotta talk to this Vincent. They say he's usually down by the junkyard. I'll tell one of my boys to fetch him over here to the cloth shop. Rather talk to him private.* He stood in front of the shelves stacked with his illegal supply. *We got too much inventory,* he realized.

A few days later, one of The Oxman's dealers went to the junkyard to find Vincent. "The Oxman wants to talk to ya, man," he said. "Over at the cloth shop. C'mon, I'll drive ya."

Vincent knew he had no choice. He was scared but also curious: *What could The Oxman want from me now? Sure hope he don't want to hire me. He's one tough dude.*

"Just so you understand," Vincent told the dealer, "I ain't buyin' no drugs. No way—I'm done usin'. I ain't The Oxman's customer anymore. Nobody else's, either."

The dealer only laughed.

Vincent closed the car door behind him and stared at the huge man waiting at the back door of the cloth shop. *Damn, he's even bigger than I thought. How could I ever stand up to this guy?* He instinctively stepped back.

The Oxman looked at Vincent's face and grinned at the fear he saw there. "You used to be one of my customers, right? Indirectly, I mean."

"Yeah. I'm Vincent. Vincent Monique. But I'm finished usin' anything. Whaddya want me for anyways?"

"Just wanna talk. Private. You c'mon in, Vincent Monique. Okay, Joe, you can scram now," The Oxman called to the dealer, who promptly sped away.

"Hear ya use to be real sick, real sick," The Oxman said, opening the door to the shop.

"Uh-huh. Still have to go back for checkups." Vincent followed The Oxman inside. They both stood near the door.

"Who made you well?" The Oxman asked.

"Dr. Truesort at the hospital. He's the one who still checks me. They say one guy they tried to help died. They told me I'm important. Somethin' about me provin' what they do, provin' it works. Dr. Truesort calls me his successful experiment," Vincent bragged.

"You have AIDS?" The Oxman asked.

"Yep, but they quieted it down so as I can live. That's why I ain't takin' chances. I'm not your customer," Vincent told him. "And I ain't sellin' no drugs for you, man. Hear what I'm sayin'? I know what that stuff can do."

"No problem," The Oxman said. "Don't worry about it. But how much was your hospital bill? You were there for *months*, man! Whaddya owe them? You ain't got no money left to be a customer."

"I ain't had no money before, and I ain't got no money after. Miano Tse and Ghanna and Josh, they made me go to the hospital. I was too weak to do anythin' but what they said," Vincent explained.

"But who paid your bills? Miano Tse, she didn't. Ghanna, he didn't. Who did?" The Oxman asked.

"The doc, he done ask me not to talk about it, but I guess he did," Vincent said. "The doc did it for free."

"Why? Why the doc do a thing like that for free?" The Oxman asked.

"What do I care why? Maybe he's a nice guy. I'm better, ain't I? What do you care about this anyhow? Why all these questions, man?" Vincent asked. "You got AIDS?"

"Hell, no. Done heard a lot about ya. The fact is, we been losin' a lot of customers. Thought you might know somethin' about that," The Oxman said.

"You sell lousy stuff. That's why you lost customers," Vincent told him. "This all you ask me down here for? I got an important gig to do."

Vincent abruptly turned and marched out into the spring day with its sharp blue sky.

The Oxman sat on the edge of a stack of cloth remnants at the back door and watched Vincent stride toward the railroad tracks. "Sure you got a gig," he yelled sarcastically to Vincent's back, but he realized that was probably the only thing Vincent was lying about. *Somebody must know what they're doin'. Somebody must have the story. Miano Tse, he says, and Ghanna and Josh. If I play it cool and watch them, watch what they do, maybe I find out. Gettin' rid of them before I know what they do ain't no good. Soon as I know, ZAP, they're out. William, now all he wants is a few extra bucks. Maybe he has more information. Maybe he'd like to shop the farmers' market once and we could talk.*

Chapter

7

*A*BOUT A WEEK LATER, on a sunny May afternoon, Ghanna was sitting in his park enjoying a bottle of red wine when he saw a Humvee-yellow Corvette pulling over to the curb on Hughler Street, right where William was sweeping the sidewalk. *Hmmm. Looks like The Oxman's car,* Ghanna thought. *What's he want from William this time? Bet that's one of his dealers.*

The guy didn't talk long—just drove up and spoke from the car, then opened the passenger door. But William shook his head and continued to sweep.

As the drug dealer drove away toward the farmers' market, Ghanna got only a glimpse of his slicked-back blond hair and big sunglasses. He took another sip of his wine and stood to watch William walk back toward the maintenance shed, put away his broom and trash barrel, and get into his 2000 Neon. Ghanna shook his head. *William's leavin' early—ain't five o'clock yet. There he goes, down Woodhouse toward the farmers' market. Wonder what's up?*

When William pulled in behind the cloth shop, he saw the Humvee-yellow Corvette. It confirmed he was at the assigned place. But then he saw something else: the looming form of The Oxman sauntering toward him. *Fuck! Of course the Corvette's gotta be The Oxman's. Who else would have a Humvee-yellow Corvette? That other guy must've been one of his dealers.* It looked ominous. For one brief instant William was tempted to hit the gas and zoom out of there before he could be recognized. But the opportunity was lost: The Oxman himself opened William's car door. "Saw you comin'. Don't be scared. Ain't gonna hurt ya. And nobody else will neither, not with me here."

William got out of his car and started to lock it. "Don't worry, William, even if they wanted that rusty piece of junk, no one would steal it from my guest."

William gulped. "Okay." He heard a strange sound that must have been his voice. Now he was in The Oxman's territory, and there was no escape.

"C'mon in my shop," The Oxman said. "We got a lot to talk about, you and me. Got an opportunity for ya. But first let's take a quick look at the farmers' market. Wanna show ya off."

William took a deep breath, turned, and followed behind The Oxman through the alley to the sidewalk at the front of the cloth shop. His eyes were riveted on The Oxman's back. William did not check his surroundings. He just dragged his lame leg the best he could, mesmerized by The Oxman walking in front of him, waving to several of his dealers in his enormous leather jacket. *Must've taken a herd of oxen to make a jacket that big.*

As they passed by a few stalls of the farmers' market, William didn't notice the New Jersey asparagus, the crop of bright red strawberries, or the many customers buying homemade strawberry shortcakes. For William, the sunny, warm May day was clouded over with fear.

When they entered the front of the cloth shop, a burly man yelled, "STOP!" and leaped toward William. "Gotta search ya." Startled and trembling, William was about to submit to a pat-down, but The Oxman intervened.

"Thanks, Joe," he said. "This guy's cool." The Oxman put an enormous arm around William's shoulders. "Sorry about that, William. He's just tryin' to do his job. Good you don't have a backpack. This here farmers' market ain't as safe as it looks. Figured you could get to see some of it, though, if we came around to the front. C'mon up to my apartment."

Haltingly William followed The Oxman to the back of the

shop. The Oxman unlocked a door and led William up a steep flight of stairs, which he climbed one step at a time like a toddler.

"This is where I live. Don't get much company. I ain't sociable. Have a seat, William. Relax—we gotta do some business." The Oxman pointed to a leather sofa torn in a couple of places so that the white stuffing puffed out.

William dropped down warily into the sofa. He glanced around the wallpapered room and noticed that one dingy pattern covered the walls while another covered the ceiling. Both had angular black cracks where the old building had settled; orange and gray stains suggested water damage. *William, get a hold of yourself! How come you're focused on stuff like this? 'Cause you're too nervous to look at The Oxman, that's why.*

Reluctantly he watched The Oxman pull some newspapers off an easy chair, then wriggle back into it, searching for a comfortable position. "It's miserable bein' this big. Nothin', absolutely nothin', ever fits," he complained. "I like leather. It's big. You think it's big? I mean, I'm gonna fix up that sofa you're sittin' on soon as more leather comes in the shop. And this here chair, that too. Soft and big, it's what I like about leather. You like leather, William?"

"Yeah," William patted the sofa. "It's soft and it's b-big. I see what ya mean."

"Glad ya agree. Now, William, remember about them doctors? The two we talked about? I been doin' a little lookin', and I think we got us a chance to make some money. But you gotta help. You got a lot of work to do. You know what I mean?"

"You mean you w-want to know more about the ER doc, Pannell, who's gettin' money from the c-cancer doc, Truesort?" William asked in a monotone.

"Don't be so stupid, man. Course that's what I mean."

William mumbled, "One thing I know f-for certain . . ."

"Speak up. Can't hear ya," The Oxman commanded.

William looked up and started again. "I, ah, know to help patients, they've been bringin' them in without registering 'em in the system. One of the security guys I know well, h-he told me. But he said it ain't harmful. I asked him, 'What kinda patients?' He told me AIDS patients."

"Now why would he tell ya that? A punk like you."

"'Cause, 'cause he don't want me interf-ferin'," William stuttered. "I, ah . . . I'm supposed to keep an eye on who goes in and who comes out. S-see a stranger, I tell Security. People leave late, leave early, I ch-check on that too. I know m-most of the docs and workers that have my shift. This hospital has a good reputation. Lots of employees stay until retirement. It's a good deal. Ya get m-medical and dental as long as ya use hospital staff. I ain't the only one checkin'."

"Yeah, yeah. But AIDS patients. You mean like Vincent?" The Oxman felt he was getting somewhere. "He says the doctor calls him his successful experiment."

"Uh-huh. In fact, the security guy m-mentioned Vincent. Said Miano Tse brought him in. Ghanna and J-josh mighta been involved too, for all I know." William watched The Oxman smile.

"They're gettin' money to help with the experiment. Right?" The Oxman asked.

"Looks that way."

"William, you're in security—you're s'posed to know about the law. Is what them doctors doin' legal?"

"It's helpin' patients, so nobody's stoppin' them," William answered, avoiding the question. "No way is the security guy gonna argue with them doctors. But I'm not security 'xactly."

The Oxman laughed. "Whaddya mean, 'not security 'xactly'?"

"Because I'm disabled," William said, swallowing hard to control his frustration. "I just keep an eye on things is all. The hospital asked me to. I don't work for the security company like the others do. I'm m-mainly outside."

The Oxman laughed again. "You're too smart to just be cleanin' up all the time. Is that it?"

"Somethin' like that."

"Why them docs so sneaky? Why they gotta pay anyone?" The Oxman leaned toward William and scowled.

"I know it ain't r-right to experiment on hu-human beings without permission. I had to sign a paper when other docs operated on me. Maybe these docs hadda get people who d-don't care, no family to sue if s-somethin' goes wrong. I guess . . . I guess the docs just paid the suppliers," William said, holding his head between his hands to stop the shaking.

"Relax, William," said The Oxman. "You're doin' good. Just take it easy and keep talkin'. Anyhow, we don't know for sure the people didn't give no permission. Docs probably didn't wanna find patients themselves. They don't exactly hang out with street people, ya know? So they prob'ly paid someone else to find 'em."

"That's how it looks to me," said William. "B-besides, some sorry-lookin' guys outside of Lefty's were askin' to see the docs 'n' arguin' who would go first."

"Guess you're right. So that's how Josh, Ghanna, and Miano Tse got their money. Josh didn't even wanna help me no more."

"You plan . . . plannin' to supply some patients too?" William asked, relaxing more now that The Oxman slid back in his chair. "You believe we can make some money?"

"Maybe. Maybe. But I'm gonna check a few things out before I decide what to do. I'll let you know." The Oxman stood up, moving out of the easy chair with agility despite his massive body.

"Good," said William in a businesslike tone as he pushed himself up with the palm of his hand on the sofa arm. "I want a cut. Ya know, I did say I'd charge for today."

The Oxman laughed. "I don't remember hearing that, William. You been workin' with them doctors too much. But here's a few bills anyway. One more very important question: any other patients get well—besides Vincent, I mean?"

"Possibly," William called back as he clunked down the stairs past the bodyguard. He locked the doors of his car as soon as he got in, watching his own fingers tremble. That tremble swept through his whole body. William gripped the steering wheel and waited for his quaking to stop. *I should never have asked for money.*

$$\sim\!\!\bigwedge\!\!\sim\!\circ$$

"Happy to give you this, Miano Tse. Business been slow."

Miano Tse had pedaled over to get her payment for another patient she had sent Ghanna's way. They were both sitting on the grass in Ghanna's mini park when the 2000 Neon pulled into the maintenance parking area.

"That took almost an hour. Thought maybe I'd never see him again," Ghanna told her.

"What do you mean?"

"I mean The Oxman askin' too many questions. Afraid he knows what we're doin'. He don't wanna ask us directly, but he will if he has to. Probably leavin' us alone so he won't poison the money well till he's ready to dip in. Instead he just keep talkin' to William," Ghanna said.

Miano Tse sighed. "The Oxman scares me, always watching me with those green eyes, always planning wickedness. I used to buy Egyptian cotton from him to send to my mom. No more. I wish we could get him locked up forever!"

"Vincent told me he had to talk to him. How you think The Oxman found out about Vincent doin' so good?" Ghanna looked right at Miano Tse and saw the answer to his question. She flinched as though stung by a wasp when he alluded to Vincent's local fame.

"Guess he was talkin' about himself," Ghanna continued, ignoring Miano Tse's silence.

All she said was "See you tomorrow" as she rode off toward her apartment.

—◠╲╿╲◡◦—

The Oxman was pleased: William had filled in the missing pieces of the puzzle. Getting patients to the doctors was a simple matter of supply and demand, fine for wimps like Ghanna and his friends, but the supply could be hard to find and the demand might dry up.

No, The Oxman had decided on a more certain way to continue the flow of cash into his pockets—and he wouldn't have to share the money with anyone. He just had to check one more fact: Was Vincent Monique the only successful patient?

Maybe Assam knows somethin'. He sometimes sells his rugs down by Ghanna—hangs 'em over the fence so people can see 'em. Maybe he could ask Ghanna or the street people for me. I can always pay him off in bolts of cloth. He says his wife likes to sew.

The day after his meeting with William, The Oxman drove up Woodhouse Street to Assam Sadur's shop. Assam had reclaimed an old warehouse building, one of the few usable ones left in that part of the city. He sold not only rugs, but also job-lot items he gathered and displayed on the sidewalk and on neatly stacked crates inside. Beribboned children's Big Wheel tricycles in gaudy pink and blue plastic, and racks of sequined clothes, lured customers in from the sidewalk to browse. The colors of the merchandise provided ample decoration. Plastic flowers, dusty Christmas-tree ornaments, bookshelves, and coloring books were for sale, as well as any size rug with a hand vacuum cleaner to keep it neat. Assam always hoped to sell both together, but somehow this marketing ploy never quite succeeded.

A perpetually cheerful man, he never despaired even when business was going badly. And when The Oxman arrived, Assam gave him a lecture on how to sell: "You should have needles, thread, and scissors in your cloth shop. Here, take these," he said, shoving leftover sewing kits into the big man's hands.

The Oxman laughed. "Okay, Assam. But the cloth shop ain't my only business."

"I know. You busy man. You come here because you need Assam to run cloth shop for you. Yes?" Assam smiled, his jet-black mustache emphasizing the upward curve of his lips.

"No. Not this time, Assam. This time I need ya to help me with somethin' else," The Oxman said.

A shadow of disappointment flickered over Assam's face, but he soon was smiling again. "What is it I can do for you?" he asked with both hands opened out toward The Oxman in a friendly gesture.

"Ya know Ghanna?" The Oxman was sure of the answer—everyone knew Ghanna—so he continued. "I need to find out somethin', but it's better I don't ask him myself. Maybe ya could help me out?"

"Sure, sure. What ya want to know? He has no daughters." Assam pressed his fingers together, steeple-like.

"Nah, you got the wrong idea, Assam. This is business."

"Oh. Of course. Happy to help you, my friend." Lowering his voice, he added, "I know some matters are delicate."

"Could you just ask him if he's heard of any other AIDS patients who went into the hospital real sick and came out as healthy as Vincent Monique? And of course don't mention me," The Oxman said.

"AIDS!" Assam paused for moment, startled. "Ah, *very* delicate matter. Yes, I will help you with this. People who had AIDS but now they're healthy like Vincent Monique, and don't mention you." Assam repeated the request. "I ask next time I go take rugs down by Ghanna's."

"Good. But make that next time tomorrow. I need to know the answer right away. I'll stop by tomorrow afternoon."

"All right, all right. It is to be nice tomorrow. My rugs shouldn't get wet, you know."

"Don't worry, I'll buy any wet rugs. Oh, and bring your wife, Sakina, to my shop anytime. I'd like to give her some cloth. Got some nice cotton prints in, perfect for summer dresses."

"Sure, sure," Assam said, continuing to bow to The Oxman's back as he left the store. *Maybe he has AIDS?* Assam wondered.

Assam Sadur was pretty certain of Ghanna's answer. Other patients might be receiving the same medical treatment as Vincent, but none had regained their health.

Vincent Monique was in a class by himself.

The whole neighborhood knew his story. It was the talk of the marketplace, the ballad of the street. Sakina heard a lot of discussions about Vincent as well as the hopes of other potential patients from her customers. She kept Assam well informed.

Sometimes Vincent sang about himself as he strummed his guitar. Lefty's Bar and Tops Tavern near the railroad tracks, which he added to his venues, paid him in beer and sandwiches, and his listeners left tips in the mug at his side. Even some who had known him before he was sick said he'd never looked so healthy or played so well.

Vincent had become an inspiration to many who had decided long ago that they could aspire to nothing more than a life on the street, soothed by the soft, billowy forgetfulness drugs could bring. Now they heard Vincent laugh—not just once in a while at someone else's mishap or the usual obscene joke, but all the time. He cheerfully enjoyed his own songs, the sandwiches, and the beer, telling everyone their applause was better than any drug he'd ever had.

But just to be certain that Vincent was unique, Assam lugged a dozen rugs near to Ghanna's triangular bit of land the next morning. As he had done other days, he ran a strong rope between the broken utility pole and one of the metal posts holding up the chain-link fence, then hung the rugs across it. He didn't expect to make a sale so early in the day, but fortunately The Oxman would make up for that loss. Sakina was tending the warehouse store until he returned.

Ghanna came across the street from his apartment and watched Assam without comment at first. Finally he told Assam, "The ice-cone business been shut down. Nobody gonna buy your rugs without it . . . brought in trade."

"Oh? I did not hear. When did it close? The ice-cone business, I mean."

"Ah, some time ago."

"They don't pay off the right people," stated Assam.

"You know the right people?" Ghanna asked.

"No. It's why I have to watch. Somebody might not like me selling my rugs here." Assam went over to sit next to Ghanna, thinking, *This is going to be harder than I thought.*

"It was the board of health, I think. Nothing unhealthy about rugs. You should be okay," Ghanna predicted.

"Ah, good, good." Assam sat leaning against one of the trailers and idly picked at a few strands of grass. He gazed past his rugs to the walls of the hospital. The two men sat in silence for a while, Assam wondering how to appear casual when he asked about Vincent, Ghanna wondering why Assam chose to sell here today.

"People ain't goin' down your way much to buy?" he asked Assam.

"Business is pretty good at the store, pretty good. Just thought

I'd try this today, might get lucky. Got a good price last time, better than down the street. These hospital workers know quality—they like my fine rugs. But like you say, the ice-cone business maybe helped. We'll see," Assam said. Then he asked, "You ever work in that hospital, Ghanna?"

"No. They work hard. Them people never stop. Work, work, work is all. They walk by here frownin' and mutterin'. They is miserable, just miserable."

"I hear they did a good job with that guitar player . . . what's his name? You know . . . Vincent Monique."

Ghanna's body stiffened. He looked directly at Assam. "What ya know about Vincent?"

"Uh . . . not much. Uh, uh, they made him better, said he was going to die before, yes?"

"He tell you that or someone else?" Ghanna snapped.

"Sakina told me. She said everyone was talking about it in the farmers' market."

Ghanna relaxed. "Yeah. Vincent's some sorta hero."

"Will we have any more heroes," Assam asked, "or is he the only one?"

"He's the only one I heard of. Them docs prob'ly workin' on helpin' others."

"One's enough. For now anyway."

Assam continued to visit with Ghanna, hoping for at least one customer. A few people looked. One nurse admired a red rug but said she would be back later. Finally, toward lunchtime, Assam said, "Maybe you're right, Ghanna. Business is not so good here today. I'm going back. You need a lift anywhere?"

Assam dropped Ghanna off at the liquor store so he could buy his wine and cigarettes. When Assam said good-bye, he told Ghanna, "Stop in to see me sometime. Sakina is a good cook, a very good cook."

"Thanks, Assam. Maybe I will."

—⎍ᶺ⎍ₒ

That afternoon Assam reported to The Oxman that Vincent was the healthiest patient in the experiment so far. The Oxman decided to go right to the source of the money—Dr. Truesort himself, the tall doctor with the white hair—and the best way to do that was to threaten Vincent, the doc's living proof.

The Oxman left Assam's shop and drove his pickup truck several miles, turning onto a dirt road into a deserted area of woods near the river. He parked near the riverbank and relaxed with a cigarette. Then he walked along the road for a while and thought: *Scare Vincent, you scare the doctor. The scared doctor pays for protection, and I can always play the ace and hold Vincent hostage. This thing could be worth many big bills, many big bills.* He chuckled at the possibility of being wealthy as he watched a cat tormenting a baby robin. The Oxman grabbed the cat by the tail and threw it into the river.

Vincent Monique played at Lefty's Bar on Wednesdays, Thursdays, and Saturdays starting around eight. Fridays he played at Tops Tavern. He was starting to make some new friends as well as contacts that might lead to more prestigious gigs. Lefty said Vincent had brought in a high-paying customer for the last few weeks, but Vincent wasn't so sure.

He was a new fellow who always sat in the back. *Thin with blond hair, slicked back. Seen that dude before, but where? Can't remember. He's been coming by, sittin' at the rear table, playin' solitaire. Uses his cell phone now and then.*

"He's a good guitarist, isn't he?" Vincent heard him say to Sally.

"Where did ya learn to shuffle cards like that?" Sally wanted to know. "And how come you always alone?"

"Just a loner, I guess. Just me and my cards."

"But ya like Vincent's music. He sings nice."

"Yeah. Very nice. Bartender, bring my friend here another glass of wine."

"Thanks. I'm Sally."

"I'm Eade, Eade Raschieu, Sally."

They listened to Vincent's songs. Eade played solitaire and joked with Sally but didn't talk with anyone else. Not really. And he and Sally continued to sit alone.

Even when he heard the dude's name, Vincent's mind itched to recall how he knew this man. During a break between sets, he went over to Eade's table. "Okay if I join ya? Name's Vincent, Vincent Monique." Eade stood up and shook Vincent's hand.

"I'm Eade Raschieu. Sure. Sit down. I know you're the one who always sings so good." Eade shuffled his cards, the flash of a ruby ring and gold watch emphasizing his dexterity. "You met Sally?"

"Yeah."

"He likes your music, Vincent," Sally said as she joined them at their table. "You brought in a crowd tonight."

"It's Saturday night."

"I know," Sally said. "It's still busier than it was before you started playing."

"You play cards a lot?" Vincent asked Eade.

"Used to be a dealer at Trump Plaza."

"I used to be a pretty good singer-comedian, ya know? Played the clubs in a few cities," Vincent Monique told him. "I think I might've seen you in Atlantic City. That was many years ago."

"Maybe. What happened?" Eade asked.

"Got sick. I'm okay now, though. Just go back for checkups. That's all," Vincent said.

"You don't have to go back too much, do ya?"

"This coming Thursday and then not for another month. Before it was every week. I even got a card saying two p.m. Thursday. They take good care of me. I'm borin' you. Anyway, I gotta sing for my supper. See ya." Vincent took one more hard look at the man but still couldn't be sure why he looked familiar.

After Vincent started singing again, Eade got up to leave. The hunch of his shoulders and the way he jammed an old cowboy hat onto his head so it came down to his eyebrows finally told Vincent Monique who he was. *The dealer*—and not just with cards. *He supplied some of the musicians in the casinos. A sax player recommended him to me. At first I could still say no, but then . . .*

Vincent strummed a couple of chords on his guitar and started to rhyme a ballad:

> *Dealers, dealers of drugs*
> *End up poorer than users, users of drugs*
> *'Cause they're never free, like you and like me.*
> *Bodyguard selection*
> *Always there for protection.*

The face under the cowboy hat smiled. Then the man turned and strode out the back door with a hard, guttural laugh.

"He one of The Oxman's boys, Vincent?" Lefty asked.

"Yeah, 'fraid so."

"What's he want around here?"

"Dunno. I dunno. His name's Eade Raschieu."

Eade sat down on the leather sofa. "He goes in Thursday for a checkup and doesn't return for another month," he told The Oxman. "I talked to him last night at Lefty's."

"Drive my Corvette. Don't take my old pickup truck. You wanna look successful. Go with him Thursday. For his own protection, of course. Explain to the good doctor you are making sure his patient stays well. You expect payment for the care we're giving Vincent," The Oxman explained with a laugh.

"What if Vincent doesn't want an escort? I can't walk into a hospital with a gun in his back."

"He knows we'll kidnap him otherwise. Keep him here." The Oxman pointed around the room. "He won't refuse. And the doctor knows, no Vincent, no living proof of his experiment."

"I'll dress nice. You know, like I did when I dealt at the casino. No cowboy hat and jeans. Tie, jacket, trousers pressed, shoes shined. I'll carry the small handgun," Eade said.

"No. No gun. This is a friendly visit," The Oxman said. "You dress nice. Nobody'll bother you. Besides, I'll break their heads soon as they're out on the street if they try anythin' at all."

Thursday morning was quite warm. Eade examined his face in the mirror and decided yesterday's shave was still good enough. He put some gel in his blond hair, brushed it back behind his ears, and straightened his tie.

He folded his jacket carefully and put it on the passenger seat before he got behind the wheel. Eade drove The Oxman's Humvee-yellow Corvette, cruising around the hospital, around the junkyard and the farmers' market, looking for Vincent. He found him helping the Chinese woman lash metal strips to her bike, laughing and singing like the world was his. When the woman pedaled off, Eade parked the Corvette and called to Vincent. "I didn't know you sing for free. Get in. I'll buy you a beer. I want to talk to you."

"No. No thanks, I never ride with strangers," Vincent joked, but he moved back into the junkyard, where others were going through the debris.

Eade hesitated. He feared leaving the car. He felt protected having its steel wrapped around him. Besides, he had worked hard pressing his trousers and shining his shoes; he didn't want to get dirty. He drove into the junkyard and called to Vincent, "I thought you'd like a ride over to the hospital. Remember, you told me you've got an appointment today."

"It ain't far. I just walk in the front door like everybody else." Vincent picked up a hunk of steel. He held it in both his hands, ready to hurl it through the windshield of the shiny Corvette. "If you don't get outta here, your car is gonna be ripped apart and thrown piece by piece onto the top of this Mount Trashmore," he yelled at Eade. The other men climbed over the mounds of debris and stood behind Vincent. One began to roll a tire into the car's path. Vincent hurled some rotten boards with nails poking out of them.

Hearing the commotion, Miano Tse pedaled back. "What's goin' on?" she shouted.

The Corvette lurched as Eade shifted into reverse and skidded around the obstacle course they had created, yelling, "You'll be sorry, every one of you filthy junkyard rats! Sorry you refused The

Oxman's protection." They watched the Corvette take off down the street toward the hospital's front door.

Miano Tse had now ridden right up to Vincent. She got off her bike and looked at the frightened and angry faces around her. "What was that about?" she asked.

"I dunno," Vincent told her, dropping the piece of steel.

"You no talk to The Oxman?" Miano Tse asked, her lapse into pidgin English revealing her fear.

"I ain't messin' with him. He's messin' with me. But don't worry. I ain't goin' in no front door of the hospital," Vincent said.

Eade figured he would be too obvious in The Oxman's car now. He drove it back to the farmers' market and borrowed The Oxman's pickup truck. Although he drove around the hospital area several times, he couldn't find Vincent.

Ghanna watched the Corvette from his window. He saw it cruise by and then saw the same driver circle the area in The Oxman's pickup truck. He hadn't gone to his park today. His bones ached, and his head hurt. *Guess ole Ghanna had too much wine.* He sat on his step stool to watch the passersby. He did see Josh come outside for a smoke.

Though he had not seen anyone come up the front steps, Ghanna heard pounding at his apartment door. "Who's there?" he yelled, hoping he wouldn't have to move.

"It's Vincent, Ghanna. Let me in!" Vincent hollered, still banging on the door. "I let myself in the back of the building with my old key."

"Hold on! Let an old man get up." Ghanna tottered over to the door, checked through the peephole, and unbolted the latch. Vincent pushed into the room, nearly knocking the old man down. "Take it easy! Easy, man. You musta come up quick. Didn't see ya."

"Yeah. I gotta see the doctor without The Oxman knowin'. They're after me, Ghanna. They're after me. I don't know why."

"Yeah? I done see The Oxman's pickup circlin' the place. *You* they after? Watch from here. If ya time it right, ya can just get over to the emergency room once The Oxman's pickup goes by. Tell Josh ya need to see the doc right away," Ghanna advised as he held one hand against his forehead to ease its throbbing. "Josh be there now. He always tell me what shift he's workin', only I can't be sure of his overtime."

Vincent watched out the window. The pickup truck was passing by. It didn't look any different from any other: standard black Ford. He saw it pass three times in five minutes. "Ya see a lot from here. He's at the corner. I'm goin'. Thanks, Ghanna, thanks." Vincent raced down the alley.

Ghanna bolted his door and shrugged his shoulders. "For what?" he mumbled as he went back to his window to watch Vincent. First the man disappeared from view behind an ambulance parked at one of the emergency-room bays. Then he reappeared as he entered the doorway. *Guess I better get movin'. Always somethin' happenin' here needs Ghanna's help.* Ghanna gathered up his hat and his boom box and went to his mini park to continue his spying.

Eade parked on a side street and went into the emergency-room waiting area. No Vincent. He walked around the grounds, looking in the parking lots, but Vincent had eluded him. He went into the main lobby. No Vincent. Eade was walking down the drive back to his truck when he finally spotted Vincent, who was hurrying into the emergency room.

Vincent didn't see Josh anywhere, so he went on to the main lobby. "Got an appointment with Dr. Truesort," he told the receptionist, and showed her his appointment card. She looked at him, at the card, and then back at him. She asked his name and called Dr. Truesort's office. Vincent heard Martha say, "Yes, Vincent Monique has an appointment."

"Look, lady. I'm sorta in a hurry, see. I don't wanna be late. I don't wanna be late for my appointment," Vincent told her while watching the entrance.

"Do you have any ID?" she asked in an administrator drone.

"No. But last time I came, the other lady said it was okay."

"I don't care what she said. You have to have an ID to go upstairs. That's the rule."

"Ain't got an ID, but who else would wanna be me? Please, ma'am, I gotta see Dr. Truesort," he pleaded. "And Josh, you know him? He knows who I am."

"No, I don't know any Josh. But all right. All right. You know the way to the second floor?"

Vincent saw Eade Raschieu walk in. "No. Uh . . . no, ma'am. Maybe you could get a security guard to show me how to get to the doctor's office."

Vincent was standing sideways now, speaking to the receptionist, tapping the appointment card on the counter, watching Eade cautiously step closer and closer like a wolf stalking his prey.

"Okay. Okay. Calm down," the receptionist told Vincent, and picked up the phone.

Eade was now standing right next to him. They both heard her say, "I've got somebody here who wants to go to Dr. Truesort's office. Says he's Vincent Monique. Yeah. They say somebody with that name has an appointment. He doesn't have any ID, though. Can you take him up?"

"I'll show him the way," Eade told the receptionist.

"No. The guard's coming right now. And who are you?" She smiled at this gentleman, so neatly dressed in contrast to Vincent's faded blue jeans and torn T-shirt.

Vincent moved toward the inner doorway where patients were admitted, praying the guard would come soon.

"I'm his brother," he heard Eade say.

"Do you have any ID?"

"No, but—"

"Look, I can't deal with this right now," she told him as the guard finally appeared.

Eade swiftly moved next to Vincent.

"Which one of youse guys is Vincent Monique?" the guard asked.

The receptionist answered for them. "The one in the blue jeans. The other one says he's his brother, but he doesn't have any ID either."

"You sit down and wait for your brother over in them chairs," the guard ordered Eade, pointing to the grimy orange plastic chairs in the waiting room.

Eade looked at his clean suit and then back at the chairs. "I'll stand if you don't mind."

The guard ordered Eade, "No. You'll sit until I come back for ya." The guard let Vincent through the doorway and watched Eade sit down before he escorted Vincent to Dr. Truesort's office.

—⋏⎪⌐∘

"How are you feeling, Vincent?" Dr. Truesort listened to Vincent's heart and lungs and drew a blood sample.

"Scared, Doctor. Scared," Vincent said.

"That explains the rapid heart rate. You look good. I don't think the AIDS has come back. You seem to be tolerating the transplant. What are you afraid of?"

"You gotta protect me, Doc. I nearly bought it tryin' to get in here."

"Why? What did you do? Somebody after you?" Dr. Truesort peppered Vincent with his questions.

"Nothin'. Why d'you think I did somethin'? Why does everyone always think I did somethin'? Nothin', man. Nothin'. I've been so straight, I could live in your neighborhood."

"Why is somebody after you, then?"

"Because people around here are fightin', I guess. Everybody wants to supply you and get some money."

"But why do they want you? They can't make any money from you. Or can they? How much do they know about you, Vincent? How much do they *really* know?" Dr. Truesort asked this with his head thrust forward, his posture defying the calm he was trying to maintain.

"They know I was sick. They know you made me better. They also know others are tryin' to get better."

"Do they know you're the only one well so far?" Dr. Truesort sat down across from the examining table. He watched Vincent, afraid of the answer.

"I'm a hero, Doc. Course they know." Vincent quickly added when he saw Dr. Truesort frown, "I never told much. Word just gets around, is all. They even wanna touch my shoulder. Some think I'm some kinda miracle God did." He looked at Dr. Truesort. "Ya know, Doc, sometimes I think they may be right. How else you, even you, gonna explain the Chinese lady makin' me come to the hospital in time? You gotta help get me outta here, Doc. One of The Oxman's boys is sittin' in the waitin' room right now. He even told the receptionist he's my brother. He ain't."

Dr. Truesort said nothing. He looked at Vincent. He looked out the window. At last he got up and went to the phone. Vincent heard him say, "Ingrid, we're going to have a houseguest for a while. He will be coming home with me tonight. Thought I'd better warn you."

"Ya mean me? Ya gonna help me?" Vincent started to shake the doctor's hand.

"Don't thank me yet, Vincent. You have to play a part. From now on you are Dr. Vincent Monique, visiting from Morocco. Your grammar and your manners have to be perfect. Stay here. I'm going to get you some appropriate clothes. Remember, don't leave this room unless I tell you to."

Fred asked Martha to go to the hospital lost and found. She returned with a sports jacket, slacks, a short-sleeved shirt, and brown loafers. "I hope these fit," she said. "I couldn't find a tie."

"Thanks, Martha," said Fred. After she left, Fred added, "Vincent, wear this for now. We'll leave together shortly. Once you're dressed, just go into my office and wait. Here's one of my ties and an old briefcase I've never gotten rid of."

Vincent admired himself in the shiny chrome cabinet in the examining room. He hadn't worn a jacket and tie in a long time. The shoes were a little tight, but that was okay.

"Not too bad a fit," Dr. Truesort told him. "You and I are going to walk to my car in the parking garage. Just keep chatting with me and walking, no matter whom you see. I'll do most of the talking. Just nod and smile, and act like you understand all the medical information I'm talking about. Remember, you are Dr. Monique. Act it."

"I'm cool, Doc. Don't worry." Vincent picked up the old brief-case, stuffed his worn clothes and sneakers into it, and followed Dr. Truesort. The pair walked through the hallways without incident. Fred checked out so hospital staff knew he was not in the building. He nodded hello to the guard as they entered the parking garage.

When Dr. Truesort unlocked the Porsche, Vincent got in and asked, "How fast can this vehicle accelerate?"

Fred laughed as he opened the window slightly until the air-conditioning cooled the car. "Don't tempt me. And by the way, your vocabulary is improving already." He waved to the guard as his car went through the open gate, then started for home.

"I appreciate this, Dr. Truesort," Vincent told him.

"You'll be safe as long as you stay in my house. I think your clothes will need some improving. Tomorrow we'll ask Ingrid to see what she can do about your wardrobe. My wife loves to shop. It'll give her something to do," Dr. Truesort said. "She used to teach English. How would it be if we had her tutor you?"

"Okay, if it helps me hide. But why? Why do you think they're after me?"

"I suspect somebody wants to kidnap you or blackmail me. Either way, you are in danger on the street. You are proof my methods work. Valuable proof. In any case, we want you around, right? Just trust me. But stay in my house. Do not leave until we find out who is doing this."

"Probably The Oxman, Doc."

Eade realized Vincent would probably find another way out. He would not be stupid enough to return through the main lobby or emergency room, but just in case, Eade waited a while before slipping out to resume his search. Again he drove The Oxman's pickup truck around the hospital complex and nearby side streets. Finally he admitted defeat and drove back to the cloth shop.

"He's not anywhere. He gave me the slip," he admitted to The Oxman.

"You got all dressed up for nothin'," The Oxman mocked him. "And you ain't got no skill," he shouted. "Fortunately I have another idea, but it don't include you. Get outta here. Get outta here and outta my sight."

He lunged at Eade, pulled him high off the floor, and held him up by the scruff of his neck like a dead animal. "Blackmail, my incompetent friend!" he shouted. "Blackmail!" he yelled, dropping Eade to the floor.

Vincent awoke at Fred's house the next morning. After descending the stairs and finding the kitchen, he found a note from Ingrid on the refrigerator door:

Good morning, Vincent. I had to go out for a couple of hours. Please help yourself to anything you want for breakfast. Fred said to remind you:

1. Take your meds, and
2. Don't go outside.

Back soon,
Ingrid

As he ate toast and drank coffee in the kitchen, Vincent gazed out the window and admired the shimmer of the sun on the river, gleaming through the oaks and blooming dogwoods near the water's edge. He could hardly believe the luxury of his surroundings. *Just six months ago I was dyin' in a freezin' warehouse. Never thought I'd be in a place like this! Life sure can surprise ya sometimes.*

He set his dishes in the sink, found the morning's paper on the counter, and took it back upstairs to his room to read. Half an hour later, he'd finished the sports section and the comics. *I wonder if the doc would mind if I explore a little? Can't do any harm, long as I don't swipe or break anything.*

He peeked into the master suite, which extended across three-quarters of the back of the house. He stared at the polished mahogany furniture, the canopy over the bed, the gold draperies framing tall windows with a lovely view of the backyard and river. *Jeezus. I knew the doc was rich. Didn't know he lived like a king.*

Next he opened the door of a room adjacent to the master suite and discovered a guest room about the size of his but decorated in a more feminine style with pastel florals. He could see through two partly open doors that, like his room, this one had a private bath and walk-in closet.

Vincent went back downstairs, admiring the marble floor in the hall below. He continued moving from room to room, admiring the paintings and the antiques, the Persian rugs and the quilted wall hangings. "I'm livin' in a museum. This place is a private museum," he said to nobody.

He walked through the living room to the library, where he examined books on shelves, pulled a few off, and found some filled with words in some other alphabet. *What crazy language is this? I wonder what it says.* He rubbed the dusty, tooled-leather covers across the palm of his hand. *I wonder if the doc can read it or if he just collects stuff. These books might be antiques. Probably worth a lot.*

Almost every room's got a telephone—guess that's important when you're a doctor. Two video recorders, a huge CD collection, DVD and VHS players, wide-screen HD televisions . . . this place has more than an electronics store. Whew, put that thought out of your head, Vincent. This guy is keepin' you alive. Don't swipe nothin'. Don't make him mad.

Turning his back on this tempting array, Vincent opened another door. To his delight it led to a music room, with a baby grand piano and stacks of sheet music on the bench.

Vincent could not resist. He sat down at the piano and began to play some scales, then leafed through the music scores and tried some songs from Bernstein's *West Side Story*.

"What a pleasant greeting," Vincent heard Ingrid call as she arrived home.

Ooops. "I hope you don't mind my playing, Mrs. Truesort. The piano was just sitting here. . . ."

"That's perfectly fine. I didn't know you were so talented," she told him as she entered the music room.

"I don't play the piano very often. In fact, this is the first time in years. Guitar is really my favorite. Doc Truesort brought me here so quickly, I didn't have a chance to get my guitar."

"I think I can fix that." Ingrid opened a closet and began rummaging through out-of-season clothing, boxes of Christmas decorations, and a pile of medical journals. "Here's what I'm looking for," she announced, pulling out a guitar case. "Fred played this in college. He never would let me get rid of it. Now I'm glad I didn't. Go ahead: open it."

Vincent felt overwhelmed. "You sure it's okay?"

"Why should this sit in the closet? Go ahead."

Vincent lifted out the guitar, tuned it, and tried some chords.

"Do you like it?"

"It's a beautiful instrument. I'm glad he made you keep it."

"I can lend it to you until you get back your own. Just take good care of it, that's all. I'd give it to you, but it isn't mine to give."

"Thank you. Thank you, Mrs. Truesort! I'm so much happier when I can play guitar." He strummed a jazz riff. "The strings sound kinda dead because they're so old. I didn't dare tune them quite up to pitch."

"I'm sure they haven't been replaced in years. I'll go to the music shop and get you new ones. I'll be shopping in that area tomorrow morning anyway."

"Perfect. I can't thank you enough."

"You can play 'Maria' for me. That will be my thank-you."

part FOUR

Fred's Summer from Hell

Chapter 8

MARTHA HAD JUST FLIPPED HER DAILY CALENDAR page to Tuesday, June 12, 2007, when the phone rang. A minute later she buzzed Fred on the intercom. "Patsy Willington is on the phone, Dr. Fred. She says she feels tired all the time . . . afraid her symptoms are returning. Could you write a prescription for a blood test and have it analyzed at our hospital lab? Patsy's voice is a whisper. I think she's crying."

"Get her over here now if you can," Dr. Truesort said. "I'll draw her blood; Cory can analyze it. We'll get the results quickly. Can't get better service than that."

"Is she the tall, slim girl with her brown hair in a single French braid?"

"That's the one."

"She's beautiful. I hope she's okay. I'll tell her to come right in." Martha got back on the phone and a moment later reported, "She's on her way.

"Good." He was eager to know Patsy's status. Her bone marrow was vital to the success of his experiments.

"Thanks for taking me so quickly, Dr. Truesort."

"You're welcome. No sense brewing and wondering what's going on. Occasionally patients who have recovered from a cancer are overly cautious and panicky when they feel symptoms similar to those they had before. It may be that's what you're feeling, but we don't want to take any risks. The sooner we find out what is actually happening, the better off we are." He smiled at her encouragingly. "You can follow Martha right to my examining room. Just sit down in there and roll up your sleeve. I'll be along in a minute."

After drawing Patsy's blood, Fred reassured Patsy that he would call her as soon as he had the test results.

"All right. Thanks again, Doctor." Patsy smiled. "I feel better already," she said as she left.

"Martha, get Cory on the phone," Dr. Truesort said. A moment later, he said, "Cory, come on up. I need to talk to you."

"Now what?" Cory walked into Dr. Truesort's office a few minutes later without knocking and sat down in the chair across from Fred's desk. He did, however, say hello to Martha on his way in.

"Martha, would you excuse us for a few minutes?" asked Fred. "We need to caucus."

"Sure. I'll take my lunch hour now—I'll be in the cafeteria if you need me." Martha took her pocketbook out of her desk drawer and left. She looked smart in her white, long-sleeved blouse and slim navy-blue skirt. Her high heels added a few becoming inches to her shapely legs.

"What's going on?" Cory asked.

"Patsy Willington was here. She thinks her cancer is coming around for another try."

"Oh, shit!"

"Now, Cory, calm down. Her symptoms could be caused by any number of factors, but just in case, I told her to come over immediately and I drew her blood right away." Dr. Truesort pushed the vials across his desk. "Here it is. Analyze it for us."

"You're not suggesting that I falsify the results?" Cory did *not* pick up the vials.

"I'm not suggesting any such thing. Whether we like it or not, we need to know what the analysis reveals. Besides, I have to do my rounds now."

"And if the analysis shows her cancer is returning?"

"We will treat her as best as we can."

"Maybe we could do a reverse," Cory suggested.

"What do you mean?" Fred wanted to know.

"Take some of Vincent's marrow and give it back to her."

"That would never work. We would have two dead instead of one."

Cory stood and picked up the vials. "I'll get the analysis started today and give you a full and accurate report in twenty-four hours. What you do with it is up to you and your *conscience*."

The next day at one o'clock sharp, Cory dropped off Patsy's laboratory report. Dr. Truesort groaned when he read it. Her cancer had indeed resurfaced. His usually firm voice quavered when he phoned her: "Patsy, you'll . . . uh . . . have to come in to the hospital again. I . . . a . . . I need to harvest some more bone marrow to study. Your cancer is no longer in remission. Come on in tomorrow morning. I will examine you first thing, and we can go from that point."

Patsy felt he sounded compassionate, but Dr. Truesort knew he had taken a risk and lost. He had given all of her bone marrow to Vincent.

"But why, Doctor? I already have some stored. Don't you remember? In case I would need it. I need it now. Why should I give more to be studied?"

"To be sure you really have a fresh supply, and in case there have been any changes," Dr. Truesort lied. "But we will go over all our possibilities and discuss them tomorrow."

"Doctor, believe me. This is how I felt last time. You weren't so cautious then. What's wrong with getting me started? I want to get better *now*. You know, Doctor, I think I'm going to get another opinion on this."

"That's your privilege, of course, but this approach seems wise to me since your cancer has come back for a second try. It may be slightly different than it was the first time around."

"Maybe. But it's still my body. I don't understand why a small sample wouldn't be enough to study. Why can't my transfusion start at once? I thought that was the whole purpose of having some of my bone marrow on hand. That's what you claimed originally."

Patsy slammed down the receiver with more energy than she had felt in weeks. *Anger certainly gets you moving,* she thought.

Yet she burst into tears. Her mother ran from the kitchen and hugged her. "What happened? What did the doctor say? Why are you crying?" she asked, dreading the answers.

"I hate that doctor. I hate him! He won't give me my bone marrow. Says I have to get more harvested to be studied. God, it's my bone marrow. Why won't Dr. Truesort just give it to me?" she yelled.

"I should have talked to him myself. I'll give him a call." Mrs. Willington gave Patsy another hug.

"No, Mom, no!"

"How about if I ask Dad to call? He's in his office today, not on the road."

"Not Dad either. I told Dr. Truesort I would get a second opinion, and that's what I'm going to do." Patsy strode to the little phone table and yanked open the drawer. She rummaged through it, found the list of oncologists from her local cancer-survivors' support group, and made an appointment for early the following afternoon with Dr. Todd Quintel.

Ever since Vincent's disappearance nearly three weeks before, The Oxman had sent his network of drug pushers out around the city to search for him. They found the junkyard crew conducting business as usual. Ghanna was asleep in his little park, except during several days of heavy rain. Sally shuffled from the garbage pails to the recycling center, then to Lefty's Bar, following her usual pattern.

Lefty complained, "Business is down since Vincent stopped singing." Many people in the neighborhood thought Vincent had died in the hospital.

The Oxman's pushers told him some of their customers had been trying to be like Vincent. When the addicts learned Vincent had disappeared, the flicker of hope he had inspired for their future was snuffed out, and they quickly resumed old drug habits.

But The Oxman was not placated by this small rise in revenue, although he told his drug pushers to sell more now that Vincent was out of the way. The Oxman had not forgotten his "protection plan." *Vincent wouldn't be stupid enough to go to the doc's house,* he decided.

The Oxman drove around the farmers' market and on to Lefty's for a beer. *It's after quittin' time. Probably find Josh there—best person for me to talk to an' begin the search. He works in the hospital an' knows how to work the street. Told Josh I wanted a piece of the action. Gotta be careful not to frighten him away. First he gotta tell me what I need to know. After, he won't be of no use. I'll get rid of him. Good I didn't let Eade take no gun. He coulda killed Vincent. Might not have a chance to capture him.*

$$\sim\!\!\bigwedge\!\!\!\frown\!\!_\circ$$

As word of Vincent's disappearance got around, few junkies came to Lefty's back door asking for medical help. Miano Tse complained to Ghanna that they were losing money, but he just shrugged his shoulders. "You got scrap metal; me, I got scrap people. I'll sell hypos again, I guess."

"Yeah, but I want more than scrap. I'm gonna get a real job, like I had back home."

"You go for it, Miano Tse. You sure got a good head on your shoulders."

Both Ghanna and Josh knew that Vincent was not dead. Ghanna had seen Eade follow Vincent into the emergency room and emerge alone about an hour later, then prowl around the ambulance bays and the parking lot. Josh had learned from Bob Pannell, and then told Ghanna, where Vincent was now. Josh and Ghanna agreed not to tell anyone else except Miano Tse.

Vincent's presence at Lefty's and Tops Tavern had certainly helped them get more business, but Vincent could not possibly return while The Oxman was hunting for him. Ghanna had seen six of The Oxman's pushers stationed at strategic points around the neighborhood, such as driveways and the hospital parking facility. For the time being, Vincent must hide.

It was now June 13. Vincent had become bored and unhappy staying at the Truesort mansion. Despite the loan of Fred's old guitar, he
missed his freedom, missed his friends at Lefty's. At Dr. Truesort's
insistence, he had stayed indoors for two weeks and was going
stir-crazy. It wasn't safe for him to go outside with The Oxman
still on the loose. But Ingrid had gone to some luncheon, and the
housekeeper and cook were sharing complaints about her in the
kitchen. *Nobody will notice if I just go outside for a while. I feel like a
chicken in a coop even if this house is big.* He found an old baseball
cap in the guest-room closet and put it on catcher style, then went
down the front staircase and out the front door. The two in the
kitchen at the rear of the house never noticed.

Vincent walked across the driveway to his left and followed
a hedge-lined garden path around to the back of the house, past
a garden full of fragrant roses. When Chewy bounded over and
rubbed his nose in the palm of Vincent's hand, Vincent patted
the dog's head and followed him. Together they ambled down the
path, past the terraced lawn and pool, toward the river. Near the
riverbank the lawn yielded to forest growth until there was a sudden vertical drop of seven feet where the swift-moving river had
eroded its bank.

Chewy and Vincent sat at the top of the bank, surrounded
by trees and underbrush, watching mini whirlpools swirling by.
Farther downstream Vincent could see the spray misting and bil-
lowing into clouds as the water hurtled over the rocks at the rapids.
Heavy rains earlier in the week had made the river high. It often
reached flood level because drainage was poor upstream and over-
development had filled in the natural flood plain.

Vincent sighed, enjoying the sunshine, the noise of the river,
and the feeling of safety. "Chewy, this is great! You don't know
how lucky you are to be able to run around here whenever you
feel like it." After a while Chewy led him to a narrow stone stairway invisible from the house, and the two of them descended to
the yard-wide path below the eroded bank, right next to the river.

Vincent would have liked to go wading, but he didn't dare, because the white water pounded so hard against the boulders. The current was treacherous this close to the rapids.

The riverside path stretched between the two high stone walls at the sides of the Truesorts' property, hiding the areas beyond from view. Vincent realized money bought safety, money bought beauty, and maybe money even bought peace.

Eventually he got hungry and returned to the kitchen. The housekeeper and the cook were still talking. They hardly looked up when Vincent began making himself a sandwich, piling lettuce and cold cuts on a roll, eating bits as he constructed several layers of meat and cheese. He stood over the sink, eating his sloppy sandwich and drinking his soda.

Vincent spent the rest of the afternoon playing Fred's old guitar. He was starting to write several new songs, hoping someday he'd get to play them for an audience. But he still felt restless.

At dusk he went back outside, this time through the kitchen door. Chewy joined him once again. *Think I'll check out the other side of the yard this time. Looks more private over there, too.* Vincent carried a lounge chair from the pool area across the wide lawn. He found a good spot near the northern stone wall, about twenty feet from the riverbank. After fully opening his chair, he stretched out and gazed upward through the lacy filigree of tree branches. The first few stars were just coming out against the rich blue backdrop of the sky.

But Vincent felt melancholy. *What will become of Vincent Monique now that he's alive again? I can't go on livin' here. It's fancy, but it's a cage—it's beautiful but lonely. I'll never be free until The Oxman is dead or locked up in jail forever, no parole. I can't do anything about that from here . . . or can I?*

Chewy's growl interrupted Vincent's musings. "What's the matter, boy? What's wrong?"

Chewy's answer was to bark at Vincent and run up the hill along the stone wall and then repeatedly back and forth to him. Vincent stood up and began to follow Chewy. Then he heard it: furtive male voices on the other side of the high stone wall.

Vincent froze and listened intently, but the gurgling water below muffled the sound. He couldn't identify the voices. What were the men saying? It scared him.

Some of The Oxman's boys checking out the mansion? Planning a hit? Oh my God, they've tracked me! Ain't safe even here. No wonder Doc Truesort told me to stay inside.

His heart pounding with panic, Vincent sprinted up the hill to the house, Chewy beside him. The moment they were in the kitchen, Vincent locked and bolted the door. Then he sank into a chair, put his hands over his face, and cried. His whole body was trembling. Chewy put his front paws on Vincent's knees and whined.

I can't live a life of fear. Every day scared. Every night sleepless. Help me, God. Jesus, help me.

At two fifteen on Thursday, sensing Patsy's anxiety, Dr. Quintel's nurse led Patsy directly into the exam room to speak to the doctor. Patsy explained her case to him, referring to her diary, which detailed the progression and remission of her cancer. Dr. Quintel leaned back in his chair and listened. "Quite a thorough account. Hop up here on the table, Patsy."

"Dr. Truesort already analyzed my blood."

"Like you, Patsy, I want a second opinion."

Dr. Quintel examined her and took blood samples. "Patsy, I'm sending your blood to the lab by special courier. I'll ask that it be analyzed immediately. As soon as I receive an answer, I'll call you with the results. Make sure my office staff has all your contact information. You say Dr. Truesort is your physician? Have his staff fax your medical records to me right away. They need your consent to do that."

Patsy squeezed back her tears. She could only nod yes.

"I'll call him with my opinion, too. Don't worry." Dr. Quintel, a Humpty Dumpty sort of man with a warm smile and genuine concern, patted her hand. "You did the right thing by coming to both of us as soon as you felt something might be wrong."

When she left, Dr. Quintel called Dr. Truesort's office and asked to speak to him concerning the case. Martha told him that Dr. Truesort was not available but would get back to him as soon as possible.

~\|~。

Late that same afternoon, Ghanna was sitting in his park, listening to some island music. The heat of the day was making him sleepy. William was in the parking lot behind him, picking up trash by the fence.

Suddenly there was a screech of brakes. The Oxman spun his Corvette around to block William's progress, then rolled down the window and yelled, "William, git over here! I wanna ask ya a question."

The noise startled Ghanna awake, but he merely turned his head very slightly to have a better look.

William yelled back, "Aw, j-just wait a minute! You think you're everybody's boss?"

The Oxman got out of his car. "Watch your mouth, punk. You're gettin' too wise for your own good."

"Well, whaddya wanna know?"

"You remember a guy named Vincent? Was a patient in your hospital for a while. Guitar player at Lefty's."

"Yeah, I know who he is."

"Seen him lately?"

"Nah."

"My boys have looked all over and he ain't around here anywhere. Gotta look farther afield. Ya think he left town?"

"Dunno. The word on the street is he's dead."

"Yeah, but what if he ain't? He gotta be somewhere. I got a score to settle with him, an' I don't give up easy."

"If I hear anything, I'll let ya know."

The Oxman flung a handful of loose change onto the macadam and laughed as William limped over to pick it up. Without another word, The Oxman got back in his Corvette and zoomed away.

Ghanna frowned. *This ain't good. Know what I gotta do about it, though.* So he walked over to Lefty's and ordered his usual red wine. The bar was crowded with happy-hour customers.

"Got some news for ya, Lefty," he said. "Your friend Vincent, who played guitar here?"

"Yeah. You know where he is?"

"Florida. Saw him yesterday, just before he left. He was standin' at the bus stop with his suitcase and guitar. Said to tell you sorry he didn't have time to say good-bye. He used to play in a band down there, wants to start it up again."

Lefty sighed. "Well, I wish him luck, but I'll miss him. Gotta try'n find another musician for the weekends."

After finishing his wine, Ghanna went home and phoned Josh's cell, asking him to come over during his break. When Josh joined him that evening, Ghanna hurriedly told him about the disturbing conversation he'd overheard that afternoon and the rumor he'd started at Lefty's. "I was there durin' happy hour," Ghanna explained, "so the story will spread fast. An' tomorrow I'll be sure'n tell Sally, Assam, and Alvarez upstairs." He chuckled. Then his face grew serious. "It ain't no joke that The Oxman's still after Vincent."

"You got that right," said Josh.

"He ain't safe at the doc's house no more. The Oxman's gonna find him. My story might buy Vincent another week, not more."

They agreed that Josh must tell Dr. Pannell immediately and urge him to warn Dr. Truesort. Vincent had to be moved quickly to a safer place. Josh dashed back across the street to the hospital.

─᠕╿╰╴o

Ten minutes later, Josh met Bob in the supply closet and conveyed Ghanna's urgent warning about The Oxman, explaining the rumor that Ghanna had intentionally started. "The Oxman's gonna look all over till he finds Vincent. Big, mean hulk that The Oxman is, he won't give up. He's not stupid, either."

Bob had a sudden flash of intuition. "Big hulk? Is he a *really* big dude?"

"Hell, yeah! How'd ya think he got that name, anyway? He's big as an ox an' crafty as a fox. Big enough to pick up a grown man by the collar and throw him to the floor." Josh rubbed his neck ruefully, remembering that day at Lefty's. "He could cram Doc Truesort in the trunk of his Porsche and pitch it into the river."

"And does he have long, brownish-gray hair? Wear a leather jacket sometimes?"

"That's him."

Dr. Pannell paused a moment, then began humming to himself. *I wonder if he was the prowler I saw around Fred's place a few weeks ago? It's gotta be. Gotta be. Shit, if he's hunting all over for Vincent, it's only a matter of time before he goes back to Fred's place. I wonder if he's been onto Fred all this time? Wonder if he's onto me, too?*

Josh just stared at him, wondering what he was thinking. At last Dr. Pannell looked up at him and explained he had seen a huge man prowling around Dr. Truesort's mansion one night. He patted Josh on the shoulder. "I'd better warn Fred what's up. He doesn't have our street smarts; no experience with drug dealers, no idea what he's up against." Bob went into his office and picked up the phone.

Later that Thursday night, Cory had just bolted his apartment door and turned off the lights when the phone rang. Thinking something might have happened to his daughter, Nora, he hurriedly picked up the phone. It was Fred—his speech clipped, his words tumbling out rapidly. Cory had never heard him so upset.

"Home isn't safe anymore. Not for Vincent or Ingrid or me. Security camera, high stone wall—all useless!"

"Slow down, Fred. What the hell are you talking about?"

"Bob called me earlier tonight. He saw an intruder in my yard last April. Bob phoned me at the time, but I didn't want to involve the police. Tonight Bob realized it was The Oxman—that drug lord I told you about. Recognized him from Josh's description."

Cory frowned. "Yeah? That's not good, but that was last April."

"But Bob also found out The Oxman's still looking for Vincent. Cory, this is disastrous. Bob described how persistent The Oxman is and what he does to his victims. Now this guy is after Vincent because that's how he can get at me. Maybe he's after Ingrid. Maybe you, too. How the hell did I get into this?"

"Fred, never mind that now. Solve one problem at a time. You want to get Vincent out of there?"

"Now! Immediately!" shouted Fred into the phone.

"Calm down. Let's think."

"Cory, don't your ex-wife and daughter live in upstate New York?"

"Yes, in Oneonta."

"Can you arrange to have Vincent stay with them?"

"My ex would never go for that. But actually, my daughter was just telling me she cleans house for a lady who rents rooms. Nora said she has one room vacant. We could—"

"Rent it, Cory. Right now," ordered Fred. "I'll reimburse you. Vincent can stay there. Going forward, I'll set up an online bank account for his expenses. What the devil are we going to do about his blood tests and exams, though?"

Cory answered, "I visit Nora every other weekend, so I can take blood samples when I'm up there and bring them back to analyze. I plan to leave around two tomorrow afternoon. I'll call and confirm all this with you, Fred, just as soon as I can."

"I'll still need to see Vincent in person from time to time," Fred pointed out.

"I can take you up for a visit too if you feel you need to examine him," Cory suggested.

"All right," Fred agreed. "We've got to move quickly. Bob was clear about that. Let me know what Nora says as soon as you can. I won't discuss it with Vincent until I hear back from you."

After closing the library door, Fred ascended the stairs to the master suite. Ingrid was sitting on the chaise lounge, watching a late-night movie. "Oh, are you finally coming to bed?" she asked, turning off the TV. "It's almost one o'clock."

Fred sat down next to her and told her that Vincent would be moving out. He thanked her for being so gracious to their guest, adding, "Sharing your home with a stranger isn't always easy." He also told her he was deeply concerned about several break-ins nearby, so she should leave Chewy outside for extra protection.

"Tomorrow," he reassured her, "I'll order a top-of-the-line upgrade for our security system."

After a flurry of phone calls the next morning, Cory and Nora had worked out Vincent's new lodging arrangements by noon. Fred had stayed home that day and explained the situation to Vincent early in the morning, asking him to pack quickly and be ready to leave by two.

Fred felt that he couldn't possibly focus on anything else until Vincent was safely away from Hughler City and until his own new security system was installed. *Good thing I'd planned to work at my own lab today; don't need to cancel any appointments. Martha will call with any important messages.* He never thought of explaining his absence to Abby and Ian, who wondered why he wasn't at the private lab and why Cory was on the phone all morning with his office door locked.

Anxious to give Vincent one last thorough checkup before his departure, Fred knocked on Vincent's bedroom door. He found Ingrid busy pulling clothes out of the drawers and closets, gathering the complete wardrobe she had bought for Vincent. Clothing was piled all over the bed: dress shirts and casual shirts, slacks and designer jeans, sneakers, ties, sweaters, shoes, and a handsome raincoat. Vincent was valiantly trying to pack the suitcases sprawled across the rug. He was sitting on the lid of one when Fred suggested that they go to the master suite for his checkup.

Fred made sure Vincent's meds were up to date. He reviewed the purpose of each medication with him and told Vincent to let him or Cory know immediately when he needed a refill. Fred took a blood sample to analyze. "We're all doing our best to keep you safe, Vincent. But don't forget, you're in danger from more than just The Oxman," Fred warned him. "If you stop taking your meds and getting regular checkups, you will die. You must maintain a strong immune system capable of warding off diseases. Cory and I must always know where you are. Don't even *think* about leaving Oneonta and taking off on your own. Don't you dare give your HIV a chance to come back."

Vincent sighed, but he knew Fred was right. "Don't worry, Doc. I know I'm going to miss my friends here and my guitar gigs. I was just gettin' started makin' new contacts and all. I'm comin' back as soon as it's safe."

"Good," answered Fred. "Once it's safe for you to return, you will continue to be well cared for. Cory will be our go-between. He will take your blood samples for analysis, and I will give any meds you need to him. Be sure you take them as prescribed. Call me anytime if you have medical concerns or questions."

"Okay, Doc," Vincent answered, taking the card Fred handed to him.

"If you need medical help while you are living in upstate New York, don't go to any other doctor unless it's an absolute emergency. I will fly up to take care of you. My friend has a nice little plane; he uses the Lincoln Park airport."

Vincent smiled. "Thanks, man. I really appreciate all you've done for me."

Although Vincent was relieved to be getting farther from The Oxman, he was sorry to leave behind everyone and everything he knew. *I'm still not free. No matter where I live, I'll never really be free.*

When Cory arrived shortly before two, Ingrid asked him to help with Vincent's suitcases. Cory mentally groaned when he first saw the pile of luggage but managed to cram all the suitcases and garment bags into the back of his Chevy station wagon.

Vincent thanked Fred for the loan of his guitar. Then he said his good-byes, shaking hands cordially with Fred and giving Ingrid a hug. Cory got right into the car, promising to call when they arrived.

During the trip, Cory told Vincent what his new situation would be like. "My daughter, Nora, helped find a room for you. I visit her every other weekend. Nora and I will help you settle in and give you a tour of the area. I told her that you play a cool guitar, Vincent. She's looking forward to hearing you. She plays a little herself. Might get a kick out of jamming with you sometime."

Once Cory's car drove away, Fred sat down in his recliner with a sigh. *I pray no harm comes to Vincent. I really like the guy.* Fred's eyes closed. The constant concerns of the week had overwhelmed him. His hands were across his chest, his head was back, and his breaths were softer than a whisper.

Ingrid hated to wake him. "Fred, FRED, wake up." She pulled his shoulders forward, repeating, *"Fred, wake up!"*

His eyes opened. He rubbed his face with his hands. "I must have fallen asleep. What's the matter?" he added in a grumpy tone.

"Bob Pannell wants to talk to you. Says it's urgent."

Still groggy, Fred stared at the phone as though it were some foreign creature. Finally he picked it up and said, "Dr. Fred Truesort here." Ingrid quietly walked out of the library and closed the door.

"Bob Pannell, Fred. We have a situation. Your patient Midgin took off."

"What?"

"Yeah, his nurse just reported it. I'm calling from his room now, on my cell. Josh is out looking for him—just checked the railroad station where he originally found Midgin. No luck there."

"But Midgin's got no immune system at this point! He can't just go walking out. Where the hell was that nurse, anyhow?"

"Just making a quick phone call across the hall, she said. When she saw his vacant room, she panicked and tried to call you. Martha told her you had left for the day and advised her to call me instead. . . . Fred, are you still there?"

"Yes, damn it. Bob, the fool is committing suicide! He's got no chance without my medical support. He's a walking dead man. How the hell did he get out?"

"Sometime around four thirty this afternoon, he must've simply unplugged the monitor and removed all the wires on his chest. To halt the bleeding from the IV, he used some towels and dropped them on the bathroom floor. He took gauze pads and broad tape from the supplies on his bed stand. Probably a heavy user; he knew how to handle the IV needle. You had leftover clothes in the closet here, right?"

"Yes."

"Well, now there's a pile of clothes on the floor," continued Bob. "Midgin must've found some street clothes and gotten dressed, then slipped out the door when no one was paying attention."

"The stupid bastard! What the *hell* did he think he was doing? Goddamned idiot."

"The nurse wants to speak to you, Fred. I'm putting her on the phone."

"I am so sorry, Dr. Tr—"

"*You're* sorry," Fred interrupted. "How do you think *I* feel? This is catastrophic. Do you realize how weak the patient's immune system is? He's going to *die* out there on his own!"

Fred could hear the nurse's stifled sobs. "When I went across the hall to phone my daughter, Midgin was sound asleep. On my way back to his room, I saw someone go out the hallway door to the back staircase. It was probably Midgin, but I didn't realize it at the time. He'd complained a lot for days—really hated the chemo, as I told you earlier—and seemed impatient with the lack of progress in his condition. I guess he just decided to take matters into his own hands."

"Must have been a damn long phone call. I promise you, I will see that your status as an RN is revoked. Go, and don't expect pay for any of your hours." The sobs on the other end of the line turned to wails, but Fred felt no sympathy.

"Fred, Bob again. I did some discreet questioning on the ground floor near that staircase exit. One of the interns used his ID card to go outside, and some short guy immediately followed him out, avoiding any alarm. From the intern's description, it could have been Midgin. You know—skinny, medium height, baseball cap. Looks like he just took off."

"Don't involve Security or the city police. Leave the room exactly the way you found it. I'll be over tomorrow to see it myself."

"Okay. Josh will keep looking for him and keep me posted, and I'll ask Étoile to watch for him in the lobby, waiting room, and ER. You will know instantly if I hear anything. I'll also check Midgin's room again before I leave, just in case he decides to return."

"If Midgin doesn't show up at the hospital by late evening and Josh doesn't find him, tell Josh to go on home. Of course we'll take Midgin back if we can find him and he's willing—the treatment could still save his life—but if he doesn't want to cooperate, there's not much we can do."

"Okay, Fred. I agree: we can't hold patients here by force."

"But from now on, nobody gets paid up front. No recruiter will be paid until a patient *leaves* with my permission. If anyone else walks out early, the recruiter gets nothing!"

Bob objected, "I'm not so sure that's reasonable, Fred. We can discuss it later."

"Okay, but we need to adjust the payment soon. I can't continue to finance reckless patients who throw their health away without moving my research forward. In any case, Bob, thank you for your thoroughness." Fred hung up the phone.

Christ, he thought, *why all these disasters at once? Should've checked Midgin myself yesterday and today. He must have become despondent.*

Ingrid knocked softly on the library door and came back in. "What happened?" she asked.

"A very ill patient fled from the hospital. Nobody can find him."

"What are you going to do, Fred?" Ingrid asked, filled with concern.

"Me? I'm going to bury myself in a big martini."

--\\/\\~o

Saturday morning Fred looked at Midgin's room, cursed in disgust, and then phoned Bob. "Get Josh up here. Tell him to clean up the wreck Midgin left in room 424."

"But it's Josh's day off," said Bob. "He rarely gets a Saturday—was going to spend it with his girlfriend."

"Having one of our own team take care of this shambles will stop any potential gossip, and we'll all be safer for it. He's got to come."

When Josh's cell phone rang two minutes later, he and Miano Tse were packing a picnic lunch. "I'm sorry to ask you this," said Bob, "but Fred insists that you come in today to clean up Midgin's room."

"Jeezus, does it have to be *now*? I never get a Saturday off!"

"I know, Josh. Sorry, but Fred is in an apoplectic rage. He doesn't want the hospital staff to see the mess in room 424—they'd ask too many questions. And there's still no sign of Midgin. He'll die if we don't find him."

"I feel bad about that too, but it's not like I knew he was gonna quit. Damn it, man! Last night I hunted for Midgin all over town! What more does the doc want from me?"

"Come clean up the mess. He told me he'll pay you."

Josh grunted. "Yeah? Then you owe me, Doc. I want the next three Saturdays off."

"Okay, you've got it, Josh," said Bob. "And thanks."

Half an hour later, Josh *and* Miano Tse were at Hughler Hospital, ascending the back staircase. To blend in with the hospital staff in the hallways, Josh wore his white emergency-room coat and Miano Tse wore a hospital volunteer jacket. After closing the door to room 424 behind them, they reconnected the monitor, cleaned up the soiled laundry, and scrubbed all the surfaces with disinfectant. Soon the room was ready for another patient.

Afterward Josh led Miano Tse to Fred's office and knocked on the door. "Hey, Dr. Truesort. Just wanted to tell ya the room is cleaned and disinfected. And I want ya to meet my girlfriend, Miano Tse Liu. She helped too. Used to be a lab tech in China."

Fred looked at the two and with a deep sigh invited them in. "Glad to meet you, Miano Tse. Thanks to both of you for your help today." He handed each of them a $100 bill.

—◠╲╿╭◠ₒ

Dr. Quintel continued to call Fred several times over the next few days, but Fred never returned his calls. Not until Tuesday, when he received a letter from Dr. Quintel by special messenger, did Fred realize he had no choice but to respond. The letter strongly advised him to administer Ms. Patricia Willington's stored bone marrow to her at once. Fred called and explained, "You're not going to believe this, Todd. Her bone marrow is missing for some unknown reason. I didn't want to alarm Patsy. I was going to quickly harvest more, cleanse it, and give it to her, but she became upset and insisted on seeking another opinion."

"Have you spoken to that new guy, Wimpler, about this foul-up?" Dr. Quintel asked. "I'll write a confidential memo to him if you want me to."

"No, no. I'd better handle it from my end. Thanks anyway. These things can happen."

"Not to me they don't. I'm going to say something to him or drop my privileges at Hughler Hospital. Next time it might be one of my patients."

"I'll take care of it," Dr. Truesort insisted, but Dr. Quintel had already hung up. Dr. Truesort put down the phone. "Fuck you, Quintel," he yelled across his empty office. *How the fucking hell am I going to get through this mess? Spent too much money already. Can't let it fall apart now.*

The office intercom interrupted his tantrum. "Mr. Wimpler is on line one for you, Dr. Fred," Martha cooed in her Muzak voice. "Oh, and Mrs. Culmantski called to confirm her appointment tomorrow. You know, the judge's wife."

Shit, Quintel didn't waste any time. Probably scared that Mr. Goody Two-shoes.

"Thanks. I've got it, Martha. Hi, Harry, how are you?" he asked, pretending cordiality.

"Got a problem. A big problem. Okay if I come up to your office in a few minutes?"

"Sure. I've been meaning to call you." *It will take him at least twenty minutes to weave his way through the labyrinth of tunnels and hallways of this old hospital.*

The instant he hung up from Harry Wimpler, Fred called Cory. "Bring everything you've got on our research so far to my office in five minutes. We may need it. And don't let anyone see you or those papers."

"But I'm in the middle—"

"Now!" Dr. Truesort barked.

When Harry Wimpler entered Fred's office, Cory was standing at the wide window. Harry glanced in Cory's direction. "I wanted to speak to you privately, Fred."

"Cory's my closest friend and a trusted colleague. You will soon understand why I want him to stay," Fred announced, and closed the door. "I think I know what brought you here."

Harry, like a rabbit that trusts to stillness to keep him safe, eyed each man quietly. He remained standing and waited.

"Sit down, Harry," said Fred. "We're not going to hurt you."

Cory pointed to a chair at the conference table for Harry, then sat down across from it. Once Harry was seated, Fred joined them at the head of the table. "What prompted your call, Harry?"

Harry countered, "You mentioned that you wanted to see me." Harry pushed his chair away from the table as though he were already preparing to leave.

"That's true, but you said you needed to see me immediately. Believe you said you have a big problem."

Staring again at Cory, Harry still said nothing. "Maybe I should come back later," Cory said, beginning to stand.

"No. You stay. You're fine, Cory." Fred seized the advantage. "Come on, Harry. I'm busy. I can't wait all afternoon." He looked at his Rolex.

Now staring down, Harry mumbled, "None of what I'm going to say leaves this room. Okay?"

"Stop talking to your shoes, Harry. Cory and I can barely hear you."

With a sigh Harry looked up. "I said, none of what I'm going to say leaves this room."

"Of course. We both understand some issues have to be kept confidential," Fred replied, smiling at Harry's discomfort.

"Cory? You okay with that?" Harry looked at Cory directly.

"Certainly." Cory was slouched in his chair with his legs extended out in front of him. He yawned as Harry began to speak.

"Well . . . well . . . I had a call about a half hour ago from Dr. Todd Quintel. He said we're missing bone marrow . . . one of your patients'. He said I'd better make sure it doesn't happen to any of his. Then he told me about some patient of yours, Patsy . . . Patsy Willington, I think, who came to him for a second opinion. Told me to check with you about it." Harry's shoulders slumped. He looked at Fred and then at Cory.

"Did you check the bone-marrow bank? Is any missing? Did you make sure what he said was so?" Fred countered, leaning across the table as he spoke.

"No, no, uh, I didn't . . . d-didn't think of that," Harry stammered. "I . . . well, I just came up here right away." Harry began squirming in his chair, fearing opposition from this famous oncologist. *Truesort could ruin my career climb—put it in a downward free fall forever.*

Fred, surprised at how easy it was to make this weasel cower, continued in his accusatory tone, "Exactly what did Todd tell you, Harry?"

"Just what I said. One of your patients' bone marrow is missing. He happened to find out about it because the patient went to him for a second opinion."

"That's all?" Dr. Truesort asked with withering sarcasm.

"He also said we, uh, we were very careless around here. Um . . . should hire better help to be in charge of the lab." Harry paused. "Sorry, Cory. I know you're the one who instituted the bone-marrow bank."

Dr. Truesort rocked back in his chair. "Relax, Harry, relax. I've worked at this hospital for decades. I'm respected in the medical community, as you know. After peer review I've published papers on much of my research in prestigious medical journals. Now, Harry, I tell you that when you go downstairs to the freezer you will not find any bone marrow for my patient Patsy Willington. It is not because Cory or any other member of the staff has been careless, mixed it up, or mislabeled it. Cory and I are doing some research. I know I can trust you to understand its importance and the need to move along quietly even when these unusual incidents occur. I must insist on your utmost cooperation. Naturally you will receive credit, too, for facilitating the research when it is finally publicized."

Harry's jaw dropped. His eyes were fixed on Fred. "I never, I don't know. Research, never thought—research."

"Can I trust you to be discreet? Do I have your cooperation? Can I put my trust in you and know you will keep this confidential?" Fred asked again, leaning toward Harry as he spoke.

"I never suspected anything like this. What is the research about? Of course, anything you say is absolutely in confidence. You can always trust me, always," Harry said.

So Fred summarized his experiment for Harry. "Do you follow me so far?" he asked.

"Yes—yes, I think so."

"Good. Cory," Fred ordered, "show Harry our log, photos, and notebooks."

Cory spread their findings across the length of the conference table. Harry got up to look at photos of Lee Ribbentrop and Vincent Monique, along with photos of the cell configurations throughout the research and detailed treatment reports of both cases.

Cory explained, "We have monitored two HIV/AIDS patients. The first one, Lee here, was responding to our treatment when he died of a heart attack. Unfortunately we didn't get a photo when he first came in off the street, but Lee looked even worse than Vincent; his Kaposi's sarcoma was far more advanced. Vincent, our second case, is doing quite well. He returns for checkups periodically and has remained healthy so far. We've recently started working with several other patients."

"Wow, Vincent looks remarkably robust now," Harry said, looking at the before-and-after photographs.

"We hope to progress to a procedure that would allow a recipient to adapt to a noncompatible donor," said Cory. "All this was Fred's idea."

Fred continued, "You see the need for absolute secrecy, Harry, until we have enough cases to make a valid and comprehensive report. No other patients want to be near HIV/AIDS patients. We could lose insured patients who can pay and consequently lose revenue. Experienced nurses might choose to go elsewhere, too. So it's best not to make anyone aware of how many we will be treating to form a statistical study. Plus, we could raise false hopes if we say we have a method of treatment before we are certain. I'm sure you understand our concerns."

"Of course. Of course I'll do all I can. So what you are saying is that you think you have found a way to put AIDS into remission," Harry said.

Surprised that Harry understood at all, Fred replied simply, "That's right."

"But what about your patient Patsy Willington?" Harry asked with a slight frown.

"She'll be all right. I'll harvest more marrow and cleanse it. We will return it to her body as soon as I give her a few chemotherapy treatments. The short delay will really do her no harm this time," Fred assured Harry.

Harry shook Fred's hand and then Cory's. "I will do everything from my office to smooth the way for this valuable work. But be thinking how you will present it to the medical board. They will not like to know you have used human guinea pigs. How did you sign the death certificate of the first patient?"

"Like I said: died of heart failure. That's all. He was a ward of the state. The morgue disposed of the body," Fred explained.

"Draw up an informed-consent form," Harry insisted. "Have the patient and/or next of kin sign it. They must know about and agree to the experimental treatment. Warn all concerned not to publicize the treatment. *No. Not. Never,*" Harry emphasized.

Fred just sat back and smiled at Harry's little outburst. "I don't think we have to draw up a form. Give us a copy of the one you want us to use, and we'll take care of it. But I should warn you, many of these people don't even read. Their signature will be an *X*. Next of kin is no problem. So far our candidates don't even have an address. The hospital bed is their home. And don't tell us to advertise for candidates; we're too small an operation to handle any large-scale program."

"Don't worry. This is overwhelming." Harry shook their hands and left the office, closing the door carefully behind him. He slumped against it for a minute as the full import of what was going on began to sink in: *I'm a part of potentially groundbreaking research!*

He looked around hurriedly to see if anyone had noticed him. Relieved to find an empty hallway, he slunk off to the nearest elevator back to his office. While the meeting was fresh in his mind, he dictated his notes and locked the confidential tape in his secure file cabinet.

$$\text{—}\wedge\!\!\!\!/\!\!\!\!\backslash\!\!\!\text{—}\circ$$

"Do you think it was wise to tell him so much?" Cory asked. "I thought we were going to keep this among ourselves."

"I can control that ambitious creep. He's so eager to succeed, he would hang by his fingernails if necessary."

"Better if he donates some bone marrow." Cory laughed.

"That's not a bad idea. But no way would his donation go unnoticed." Fred laughed too. "He can be very useful. We're going to be getting more and more patients. The bigger my study, the more convincing it will be."

"True. But Fred, you really shouldn't have told him that all our patients are homeless and illiterate. That was a lie."

"Close enough. Come off it, Cory. Harry will never know the difference."

Cory shook his head but dropped the subject. "Any reason you didn't mention that Patsy's marrow was a remarkably good match to Vincent's?"

"I don't think such personal information should be divulged," Fred answered. "Some of Ms. Willington's ancestors are from French Morocco. I suspect Vincent's are also. But that's for your ears only. We ask possible marrow recipients or donors to cite their ancestry if they wish on the registry form, and it goes into their file. It adds to our knowledge."

"Yes, it's valuable information."

"I keep the ancestry and genealogy data locked up. It's not on any computer; didn't think it would be safe. Some people give us the information and others don't bother. Hear anything from Pannell today?"

"Nothing. And we sure could use something. Why don't you give him a call." Cory gathered up the slides, photos, and spreadsheets, then left Fred's office.

Chapter

9

BY LATE JUNE CORY AND FRED DECIDED it had become too risky to continue any of their private research at the hospital lab even though it was conveniently close to the patients. Harry Wimpler might snoop around and notice that they were using their own computers to bypass the hospital network. So they painstakingly expunged all evidence of the HIV/AIDS research work from the hospital oncology lab and transferred everything to Fred's private lab. To camouflage this removal, Fred and Cory placed slides and test tubes of samples in coolers. They carefully packed Fred's personal microscopes, and they neatly filed hard copies of documents into hospital archive storage boxes and slipped portable hard drives into their briefcases. Both of them moved out small items inconspicuously over a period of a week.

But their subterfuge did not go unnoticed.

About four o'clock the last Friday in June, William saw Cory's car parked at the back door of the lab. The brown Chevy station wagon was right at the foot of the loading ramp that ran parallel to the building. Surrounding the ramp was an uneven area of gravel where delivery trucks parked when bringing supplies to the lab.

William watched Cory going back and forth, loading his car with coolers and large boxes. _Well, how 'bout that. Cory's wagon ain't been in the employees' parking garage all week, but I did see Cory around_ *a couple of times, so he wasn't on vacation. Might've parked back here the whole time, and this would explain why. Better check it out.*

William pushed his wheeled trash bin over closer to get a better view. *Wonder what he's stealin'?* Grabbing just his push broom for support, William limped even closer to the station wagon, hiding behind some bushes near the high end of the ramp. *If he'd just go back inside, I could get a good look at what's in the car.* But Cory continued loading more stuff. Finally, when the station wagon was full, Cory locked the lab door, got behind the wheel of his car, and started the engine.

Meanwhile William had limped to the driver's side of the car, holding on to its side for balance. "Where ya think you're goin' with this gear?" he yelled at Cory.

Cory laughed. "Can't you see? I'm going on a picnic. Want to come?"

"You ain't goin' on no picnic," William said. "You're stealin' stuff."

"So what if I am? You would never believe me if I told you a lot of this stuff is going into the offsite archives. Move out of the way! I don't have time to fool around; some of these specimens are on ice." Cory impatiently shifted the car into gear, and it lurched a couple of feet.

William stumbled forward, nearly falling. Cory cursed to himself, slammed on the brakes, and got out of the car. He then led William back to his trash bin and handed him the push broom he'd dropped. "Your curiosity is going to get you in real trouble someday," Cory advised. Then he abruptly turned, got back into his car, and sped away, accidentally shooting gravel onto William's arms and hands.

William returned his trash bin and push broom to their storage shed, struggling to balance the overloaded bin as it bumped across the uneven surface. Only when he leaned against the shed did he see the bloody pockmarks the gravel had left. *That asshole, Cory. I think The Oxman needs to know what I saw.*

William parked behind the cloth shop, as he had about a month earlier. He was debating whether to knock on the back door or walk around to the front when one of The Oxman's boys yelled, "Hey, you!" and spat on the ground.

William turned his head.

"Yeah, *you,* fuckin' idiot. Can't you tell this here's private parkin'? Get your car outta here unless ya want the tires slashed!"

William turned and looked straight at him. "I'm l-lookin' for The Oxman," he called.

"Yeah? He don't like no company. Whatcha wan' him for, anyways?"

"It's okay, Gus," The Oxman said, opening the back door. "He's harmless." Then he got a good look at William. "What the hell happened to ya, William? I told ya, puny guys should never pick a fight. Why don't ya go to the hospital and get taken care of?"

"Oh, *halt's Maul!*" William lapsed into his grandfather's native German. "Cory did this, sprayed me with g-gravel when he drove off in his car. He's s-stealin' stuff from the hospital lab. Thought you'd l-like to know."

"Who's Cory? Another crooked doc pretendin' to be straight?"

"Nah. Cory Maxwell," William answered. "He's some kinda chemist, works in the lab with D-doc Truesort. Maybe he's in on the same scheme. Ya never know."

"What kinda stuff he stealin'?"

"Archive stuff and s-specimens. That's what he *said,* anyways. A lot of coolers an' boxes."

"Yeah? Where was he takin' it?"

"D-dunno. He said something about offsite archives, but I bet he was lying. You could f-find out by following a brown Chevy station wagon, a ninety-five, I think. He always drives old, worn-out, secondhand cars. Somethin' about havin' to pay too much alimony. I'll try to g-get the license number for ya tomorrow."

"Nah, don't bother. Just puttin' away old stuff in an old car? He ain't important. But here's a little cash for your trouble."

—ᴧᴧᴦ∘

When Cory parked close to the back door of Fred's private lab, Fred opened the door for him. "It's just you and me here to unload all this lab stuff, Cory," he said irritably. "Abby and Ian decided to take a week's vacation over the July Fourth holiday. They left early this afternoon."

"Too bad," said Cory. "But you and I can get these things put away. This is the most important stuff, anyhow."

"I've got everything for the freezer—all the tissue samples and the bags of bone marrow we selected for our three current private patients. Also brought your own microscopes and the confidential files, like Patsy's."

"Thanks, Cory."

"One more carload of the usual stuff should do it."

"Good. After the holiday, Abby, Ian, and Martha can unpack the rest."

Fred and Cory worked for an hour in the hot sun hauling in all the equipment. Once the microscopes were set up in the clean room and the samples had been stacked in the freezer, Fred collapsed into the executive chair at his desk. Cory went down the hall to the kitchen and got two tall glasses of ice water. The air-conditioning was struggling to keep up with the heat.

"I've been wanting to give you a more thorough update on Vincent," Cory said as they sipped their water. "We've both been so busy lately, I haven't had much time to brief you, except on the basics."

Fred asked, "How's he settling in?"

"He's living in an old home that's been recycled into a guesthouse. His room has a window air conditioner and a TV. It's on the second floor, overlooking a park. Nora and I drove around the neighborhood with him. In addition to the park there are shops, a cinema, and a library nearb—"

"Thanks for the real estate report, Cory," Fred interrupted. "How is his health? Is he taking his meds?"

"He seemed very relaxed. He runs on the high school track to keep in shape and feels safe at last now that he doesn't have to contend with The Oxman. Yes, he was taking his meds. When

I picked him up to go for a ride, I went up to his room. I actually saw him take his pills. I also reminded him that he must be strict about his meds for the rest of his life. He knows that our treatment hasn't cured the HIV, just held it at bay. If he skips a dose, the virus can mutate into a deadlier strain. I do think he takes that danger seriously."

"He'd *better*," Fred replied. "Originally I was afraid he might flee to Canada. Yet when I spoke with him just before you both left that Friday afternoon, he seemed determined to return to New Jersey once it was safe. He thanked me in a truly sincere manner for all I had done."

"Glad to hear it," Cory responded. "While we drove up there, I told him he would be reasonably safe, but if he ever saw anything unusual, like someone following him, to let you or me know immediately. I also pointed out that you and I—and my daughter, Nora—are all in this together."

"That's true; that's true," said Fred.

"By the way, Vincent was pleased to find out that Nora plays guitar. He's been practicing and hopes to sing at a local pub up there. No great shakes compared to some of his earlier gigs, but better than nothing."

Fred sighed and leaned way back in his chair. His eyes started to close and then fluttered open again. He looked at all the boxes and empty coolers still piled around his office and along the hallway. "You know, Cory, all this mess is a good metaphor for our research: completely chaotic," he said in a bitter tone.

Cory had never seen Fred so drawn and weary. "I've got a suggestion that might help."

Abruptly Fred sat straight up and looked at Cory.

"You need more help, Fred. Abby and Ian deserve this July Fourth break. They are extremely conscientious and have put in plenty of time. They need an assistant lab tech."

"It's not that simple, and you know it. Another expense? All this cash layout will ruin me soon if I don't get some revenue," Fred complained. "Besides, confidentiality is a major problem. We can't just put an ad in the city paper."

"We don't need to. We've got Miano Tse."

"*Who?*"

"Miano Tse. You remember: one of the local people finding patients for us—Josh's friend. I had a drink with Bob Pannell the other night. He was telling me he's quite impressed with her. Apparently she was a lab tech in China. You met her when she and Josh cleaned up Midgin's room, remember?"

Fred snorted. "So we know she can clean up a bloody mess. Does that mean she's a qualified *lab tech*? I thought she was just someone off the street who knew a lot of homeless people."

Cory shook his head in disgust. "Oh, come off it, Fred; you've got to look beyond the obvious. A lot of people have skills you know nothing about. Yes, Miano Tse has years of experience as a lab tech. Bob Pannell said she's been away from that field since she left Shanghai, but I'm sure she must remember the basics. Bob says she's kept meticulous records about all the patients we've treated as part of this project. Speaks English quite well, too. Besides, she already knows about our research and has proved she can keep a secret."

"You sure?"

"Ask Bob Pannell about her. Interview her. Find out for yourself. You could hire her on a trial basis, say, four months."

"All right," Fred reluctantly agreed with a sigh. "But I'll see her at my hospital office, not here. Not taking any chances till I know more about her myself."

⌁

The following Monday afternoon, Miano Tse hurried along despite the broken sidewalk surrounding Ghanna's park. Her high heels clicked smartly as she walked, and she was wearing the business suit and carrying the briefcase of a successful career woman. Miano Tse had an interview with Dr. Fred Truesort, chief of the oncology department.

Miano Tse had been careful to get the proper papers and apply for permanent citizenship. She now had a bona fide green card—not the usual street-artist forgery—and felt confident she would be able to get "real" professional work.

The people at the community center had advised her. One volunteer had even helped write her résumé. When Miano Tse had trouble explaining her background as a medical lab technician, the volunteer went to the Hughler Hospital language bank to have it translated from Mandarin into English. Then she helped Miano Tse practice for an interview by asking questions and helping her refine her answers.

Brimming with the confidence this support had brought, Miano Tse now had a chance to discuss her work as a medical technician.

Fred looked over Miano Tse's résumé and saw that she did indeed have ten years of experience as a lab tech in Shanghai. She explained to Dr. Truesort that she'd had a hiatus in her career when she arrived in the United States because it had taken her a while to acclimate to the culture and learn English. She was proud of the fact that she soon would become an American citizen. She told Dr. Truesort she had been in the United States for four years and had only one more year to wait. He nodded and seemed to understand. "Now tell me what it is like to be a lab technician in Shanghai."

A smile blossomed across Miano Tse's face. She told Fred about her schooling and experience, and they discussed some of the differences between traditional Chinese and Western medicine. Miano Tse had prepared frozen tissue specimens for slides, slicing them with a microtome so they could be studied under the microscope, and she had been the lab tech for a rare Chinese study of immune-system cells.

Fred realized with surprise that he had the perfect fit for his private lab. "Miano Tse, you appear to have the skills I am looking for. But there is something else: confidentiality is extremely important in my research. I must insist you do not discuss anything about my experiments with anyone except your professional colleagues in the lab. Do you understand? Do you agree to this?"

"Yes, of course, Doctor. I have been keeping your secrets for a long time already, you know." Miano Tse calmly opened her briefcase and pulled out a spreadsheet she'd begun when Lee arrived at the hospital, listing all the patients she, Ghanna, and Josh had screened for Fred's research study. The chart tracked each patient's progress, including treatment and outcome. For those who had been rejected during the screening, the chart stated why.

"Impressive, Miano Tse. I can see you're a good organizer. All right, I would like to hire you on a trial basis for four months. You can start next Monday, July ninth." He wrote a figure on a piece of paper and handed it to her. "Would this weekly salary be all right with you?"

"Those terms are acceptable. Thank you, Doctor."

Fred explained that Miano Tse would be employed only at his private lab, although he worked both there and at the hospital. "Remember, don't say anything to anyone. Not even your cat— that is, if you have a cat."

Miano Tse smiled and shook Fred's hand. "I understand. It will be an honor to work with you."

As she was leaving his office, Fred added, "Enjoy the fireworks on Wednesday night."

On her way home that evening, Miano Tse intentionally walked by Ghanna's park, but it was empty. For an instant Miano Tse wondered whether she needed to count Ghanna among her friends anymore, but she brushed the thought aside, ashamed. *I should tell him about my new job, in case he's looking for me at the junkyard.* She walked down the alley and knocked at Ghanna's back door.

"Saw you were looking for me," Ghanna told her as he held the door open. "C'mon in."

Miano Tse smiled, glad she had made the right decision. "I just got a real job, Ghanna! Going to work at Dr. Truesort's private lab. Wanted you to know."

"Ain't that somethin'! Knew you could do it, Miano Tse. You got brains. Where his lab at?"

"I'll have to use my bike or ride the bus. It's about five miles from here."

"Nah, that bus is often late. Bike's no good in bad weather, and you gotta dress nice and all. Won't you be needin' a car?"

"Yeah, but I can't afford one yet. Have to keep wiring money back to my mom in Shanghai."

"You got a driver's license?" persisted Ghanna.

"No, but I can get one soon. I heard about it at the community center."

"You need a car, Miano Tse. Ghanna'll see what he can do."

"Thanks, but I don't want anything stolen anymore."

"Huh. So just 'cause you goin' legit, don't start lookin' down your nose at your ole friends, Miano Tse."

She felt herself starting to blush. "It's not that, Ghanna. It's just—"

"Don't worry. Josh and me, we find somethin'. We get you one of them reconditioned cars. You know. Won't cost ya too much. I talk to Assam. His brother runs the auto-parts shop down near the farmers' market. You prob'ly have to pay cash, but it'd be cheap," Ghanna said.

"You're too good to me, Ghanna."

"Nah, I just look out for all my friends," he answered. "But another thing, Miano Tse: now you workin' for Doc Truesort, you got even more reason to watch out for The Oxman. You hear me? You watch yourself. Look how he tried to kidnap Vincent."

Miano Tse sighed. "I know, Ghanna. I'll be careful. Hopefully The Oxman will never find out about my new job." She shook hands formally with Ghanna and left.

Don't worry, Ghanna. It'll take more than a new job to make me lose my street smarts. She glanced quickly to the right and left, then walked back down the alley.

—ᐱᜒᜒ∘

On Wednesday morning the neighborhood was awakened by drumbeats and trumpets as the participants in the city parade began to march down Main Street. It was the Fourth of July.

Josh and Miano Tse walked up Hughler Street to Main Street. At the corner where they'd arranged to meet, they were soon joined by Ghanna, Alvarez, Asunta, and Ramiero, and then by Sally, winding her way through the crowd. Everyone had a folding lawn chair since Josh had brought extras for Sally and Ghanna.

While these neighbors waited for the parade to go by, Miano Tse announced, "I've got a new job, everybody. No more junkyard boss. Told my crew yesterday. They actually shook my hand and wished me well. They chose Carlos, my assistant, to take over and settle any arguments."

Miano Tse's friends congratulated her, but soon their questions were drowned out.

A band of mummers paraded by in shimmering, satiny costumes, playing lively music on their stringed instruments. Men and boys marched past in Revolutionary War–style uniforms to the beat of the fife and drum. Ramiero was fascinated by their muskets.

Girl Scouts walked out of step, busy chatting with their friends and waving to their families along the sidewalks. The chief of police drove by in a shiny black convertible, chauffeuring the beauty queen and her escort, the mayor. Both waved enthusiastically at the crowds.

Boy Scouts came next, led by a weary Eagle Scout carrying a large American flag. He stepped slowly as he tried to wipe the sweat from his forehead. Fire trucks rolled along, sounding ear-splitting sirens while the firefighters tossed peanuts and candy to the crowd. The city police force, in uniform, stepped smartly with backs straight and arms swinging, keeping their ranks in straight lines, with all eyes looking straight ahead. They received loud applause as they marched.

All the while, clowns pressed their way along the sidewalks, giving out candy. Vendors sold Mickey Mouse balloons. Several politicians worked the crowd, eager to shake everyone's hand.

In the afternoon Alvarez and Josh put the lawn chairs into the two cars and drove the group up the mountain to the park. Asunta and Miano Tse had brought a huge bucket of Kentucky Fried Chicken. One of Sally's friends at the farmers' market had given her some fresh produce for a green salad. Asunta had baked a sheet cake and covered it with white cream cheese icing topped with a square of blueberries and stripes of sliced strawberries to form the American flag. Josh had brought a large insulated cooler filled with fresh-squeezed orange juice.

After their picnic Ramiero played on the swings, the slides, and the jungle gym. Alvarez studied the latest racing form, then took a nap in the shade. Ghanna dozed off too. Josh and Miano Tse took a hike around the park while Asunta and Sally chatted and kept an eye on Ramiero.

As the sun faded in the sky, many gathered on the upland meadow, which was reported to be the best place to view the fireworks. Ramiero's dark eyes shone with excitement when Ghanna gave him some sparklers and showed him how to light them safely.

Miano Tse held Josh's hand as they watched the bright colors explode across the black sky. "I've never seen such beautiful fireworks," Miano Tse whispered in his ear. "Ever."

"Miano Tse, we cleaned out some file cabinets for you," Martha said Monday morning in Fred's private lab. She was dressed in jeans, a gray sweatshirt, and sneakers. "Cory heaped boxes everywhere in my office," she explained. "Oh, Cory did ask me to get you an ID so we don't have to keep buzzing you in. It's locked in my desk. Remind me to give it to you before you leave today, Miano Tse. Sorry everything is so disorderly on your first day."

Miano Tse watched in amazement as Martha shouted orders at her superiors. "Cory, put those archive boxes by the file cabinets. Dr. Fred, do something with those briefcases. Miano Tse, you're not too new to help Ian find a place for these portable hard drives." Martha changed her mind. "No, Miano Tse, better yet, help Abby get the boxes of new file holders and manila folders down from the storage shelves. You can start organizing those hard-copy documents. Wait, Miano Tse, put this lab coat on so you don't get your pink blouse dirty. Great outfit. I didn't think to call you and suggest you wear casual clothes today. Maybe the lab coat will help."

"Thanks." Miano Tse put it on.

Later Fred called Martha into his private office/lab suite. "Martha, I've checked off the reps I want you to contact from various pharmaceutical houses. I used the list you made up for me. We know most of them. Look over my schedule. I'll meet with each one in my hospital office."

"Sure, Dr. Fred."

"Set up appointments with them ASAP, but make sure you stagger the times so they don't run into each other. It could prove embarrassing."

"I see what you mean," answered Martha with a slight smile.

"Actually, before you do that," Dr. Fred continued, "get Dr. Zelban on the phone. He's Abby's dad, by the way. Abby mentioned that he's still at their country home in Connecticut. Use that number."

Fred tipped his chair back and rested his feet on his mahogany desk before picking up the phone to talk with *the* Dr. Charles Zelban, eminent plastic surgeon. "Hey there, Chas. How are things in your neck of the woods?"

"Can't complain. Busy, as usual. I'm about to leave for a big conference in Minnesota, at the Mayo Clinic. Then heading out to San Francisco and on down to Southern California to look at some pharma labs I'm considering investing in."

"Really? Didn't know that. Maybe you can put in a discreet word or two about our research project."

"Wish I could help you there, but of course it's not my field. I'd also need to know more about your progress."

"Chas, it looks like we may have something; we're moving closer to a cure. I'm looking for some smaller pharma firms interested in buying our research. Can you suggest any contacts? How about any of the firms you're visiting?"

"You must be moving pretty fast, Fred."

"Yes, but I've already had some encouraging results. Figure we should send out some feelers now. And of course, I wanted to keep you posted."

"Well, I'll keep my ear to the ground, but I can't promise anything," Chas said. "You never know—some plastic surgeons at the conference might consider investing a few dollars in a project like that. Let me think it over. I'll get back to you."

"As we move into the next phase, Abby will need access to an electron microscope. I told her to write a proposal, which I'll submit to your company."

"I'm just a trustee at Kingencorp. Great work, though. I'm going to be away for three weeks. I'll look into all of this when I get back. Good talking to you."

Fred said, "Thanks, Chas. Your daughter's doing a great job," but Chas had hung up the phone.

Fred was miffed. Even his trusted friend had no time for him. Chas had been helpful in the past, recommending an excellent business lawyer who had guided Fred through the formation of his research company and drawn up the contracts for his staff. *Guess I caught Chas at a bad time. He did say he'll call when he gets back.*

Fred rose from his desk and walked down the hall to the main lab, which he had outfitted several years ago. *Glad I bought this building. Well worth it to have my own lab. Hughler is okay for routine requests, but I need privacy for my real research.* He was pleased to see that the hall was now free of boxes and equipment; Martha and the rest of the staff had found places for all the gear and office supplies. The move from Hughler Hospital's lab was complete.

_/\/\o

Abby and Ian had returned from the Jersey Shore the night before, refreshed and ready to concentrate.

Abby was at her PC, typing notes rapidly, when Fred interrupted her. "Oh, hi, Fred," she said, looking up. "I'm just starting to write a proposal so we can use the electron microscope at Kingencorp."

"Good, glad to hear it. Say, Abby, have you talked with your dad lately?" Fred asked.

"Yes. Unfortunately he's on the planning committee for a big medical conference. Some of the equipment that was supposed to be displayed by several vendors was delivered late. He was trying to find out why. I think he finally told the salesmen that the carriers were expecting a large tip—otherwise known as a bribe—before they would deliver."

"I asked him to suggest possible pharma companies that might be interested in buying our research," Fred told her. "He seemed a bit standoffish."

"Oh, you know him. He's like that . . . always overextending himself, always in a hurry. Maybe he'll learn of some possibilities at the conference. But it's kind of early in the game, isn't it?"

"Not necessarily; some pharma firms might buy a promising idea even in the early stages of research. Cory just brought in the latest blood and tissue samples from Vincent, taken in Oneonta yesterday."

"Great. I'm eager to confirm that the adjusted dosage of the medication is working properly. It's been fascinating to see the recovery of his immune system since he first arrived at the hospital seven months ago."

"Let me know his med levels as soon as you're finished testing them," Fred added. "We've got to keep taking good care of our survivor for his own protection."

Abby said, "And we have to find out *why* he's surviving so well."

An hour later Abby knocked on the door of Fred's office/lab suite. "Good news about Vincent," she announced. "His HIV level is still undetectable, and his cancer is still in remission. Is this guy a fluke or what?"

"We hope not. We've still got to monitor him closely."

"Fred," said Abby, "I keep wondering if the source of the HIV infection and the age at which patients contract it might impact the patients' survival rate."

"That's an interesting point."

"Do we know how Vincent contracted the disease?"

"No," Fred admitted, "but many patients don't know that themselves."

"Did he ever use other people's needles or just his own sterile ones?" Abby wondered aloud. "Has he always been careful about safe sex?"

Fred handed Vincent's phone number to Abby and suggested that she call him herself.

Vincent was happy when Abby told him about his latest lab results. She paused a moment, then continued, "If you don't mind my asking, Vincent, I do have a few personal questions that might help with our research. Your input is important and would remain confidential. Are you okay with that?"

"Sure. What kind of questions?"

"Do you know how and when you got HIV?"

Vincent answered, "I'm not sure. Started feeling real sick about five years ago, after I'd been using heroin awhile. Always used sterile needles, though—well, almost always. Maybe got unlucky once? Always had safe sex. My girlfriends insisted."

"I understand. And how about your mother, Vincent? Is it possible that she had HIV and passed it on to you? Now we know this virus can be quiet for years before striking."

"Well, my mom was a heroin addict. She died real young—coulda been from AIDS, from what I heard. The docs weren't really lookin' for it back then. My grandmother raised me."

"I'm sorry to hear about your mother. You must've had some rough times. Thanks so much for sharing this with me, Vincent. Stay well."

Wish we knew for sure how Vincent contracted AIDS, thought Abby, *but the information he gave me is helpful, anyway. Such a nice guy; hope and pray the treatment continues to work.*

Abby selected one of Vincent's most recent samples, went to the prep area, and started to prepare the sample for analysis.

"Abby," said Fred as he walked by, "could you do a careful analysis of Camilla's immune system today? I'm concerned about her. The highly nutritious diet we put her on when she first arrived did help her gain weight, but now she's not responding well to the chemo. I don't want to increase the potency, though—don't think her system could handle it."

"Sure, Fred, I'll be glad to take a look. But I've got Vincent's slide ready. Okay if I do him first and then Camilla?"

"Of course. I keep wondering if there is something we've overlooked with Camilla. I can't explain it. It's just a feeling in my gut," he told Abby. "She just does not seem well."

Fred left Abby to her research, then locked himself in his private suite to begin writing up his experiments along with their documentation, working from his notebooks and charts of the treatments, including those prepared by Miano Tse.

He stopped long enough to ask Martha to make an appointment with the lawyer Chas had recommended.

I need guidance on how to put my work into the marketplace as quickly as possible. Running out of cash; can't keep spending at this rate. Sale of the initial research will help finance the rest of this project.

Half an hour later, Abby knocked on the door of Fred's suite. "Bad news about Camilla, I'm afraid," she told him. "Her HIV has suddenly mutated to a more virulent strain."

Fred scowled and cursed, then turned back to Abby with his professional face on. "All right, Abby. Thank you for letting me know."

She nodded, then quietly closed Fred's door behind her as she walked out.

Fred called Cory into his office, and after a brief discussion, they agreed that they could do no more for Camilla. "All that preparation was for nothing!" Fred complained. "We will have to send her home."

"She doesn't have a home," Cory reminded him, one eyebrow raised sarcastically. "And she has a husband who will beat her if he finds her. You want to send her back to *that?*"

"I've already wasted my time and money on her. She's no longer a good subject for this research project. I'm not paying for any nursing facility," Fred countered angrily.

"Oh, for God's sake, Fred! She can't stay at Hughler. Bob told me her husband has come into the ER twice to find out where she is. Maybe Bob has some suggestions. Want me to talk to him?" Cory asked.

"Yeah, he may have come across situations like this. He sees everything in the ER."

Within a few days, Cory and Bob arranged—at their own expense—for Camilla to be accepted at a critical clinical care center sequestered outside the city. Two women from the facility's staff drove Camilla to the center in a private car. They refused to say where the center was located, since abusers often tried to seek out their victims.

"TGIF! Great to be home," said Abby as she tossed her backpack onto the sofa the following Friday evening. "That lab is getting to me. We have to promise ourselves to get out of there by five thirty every night."

"I'm going to hold you to that, Abby," Ian told her. He was foraging in the refrigerator for supper.

"I know. I get focused on what I'm doing, and the time zips by. I thought we'd have years to work on this. Now Fred wants results in months," Abby said.

"Maybe Fred hasn't planned his finances carefully. He may have thought he would have a saleable piece of research earlier."

"Hmm, I hadn't thought of it that way," said Abby, frowning.

"Well, at least Miano Tse seems to be working out so far. She is one smart lady," Ian responded.

"Yes, and she's enthusiastic; even Fred likes her," Abby said. "But he acts strange: really sullen and short-tempered. He yells at Cory all the time now. We should be glad Fred stays in his own private suite a lot these days."

"Abby, he's tense. The stress is getting to him. This project is very expensive. And what if the research doesn't pay off?"

"Well, he doesn't have to take it out on us; we're working hard. The other day when you had run out to get lunch for us, Fred and Cory started to argue in Fred's suite. One of them slammed the door. I suspect it was all about Fred's prize patient, that guy Vincent."

"Vincent is our fortune walking around," said Ian. "Without him, none of us get paid. You want some more noodles?"

"No thanks," said Abby. "I'm sick and tired of Chinese takeout."

"Let's go to Nick's Steakhouse for dinner tomorrow. But in any case, the atmosphere over at the lab isn't exactly stable," Ian commented wryly. "The place may not last. So you know what I'm doing? I'm keeping two extra copies of all our research on two separate portable hard drives. I thought we could stow them in the storage unit we're renting. With all the stuff you and I can't part with, it should be well hidden. It's climate controlled and has security guards. Nothing to worry about. We need to be certain we have a backup."

"You're right. Fred goes into my files—the originals, not copies—and I'm always afraid he'll change or delete something. I've asked him not to, but he still does it anyway. That drives me wild!"

"Oh my God, Abby, that's really inexcusable. We *definitely* need to save your work before he interferes with it. Besides, their security is nonexistent. We are doing Fred a favor by ensuring the safety of this research."

"I'll take it out in my laptop also," Abby suggested.

"Okay, good."

"You know what else is odd? I overheard Martha calling a lot of reps to set up appointments. We're nowhere near ready for any drug manufacturer. Yet Fred seems to think we are. Why would he be seeing reps? When I talked to Dad, he mentioned that Fred was interested in suggestions of pharma houses that might want to buy our results. Dad was surprised, but later he congratulated me on my work, something he never does. I thought Fred was hoping to learn something from Dad or from some of the sales reps he works with, but now . . . well, now I wonder," Abby said.

"Maybe your dad or some of those sales reps have some information about our research but need more facts before making a commitment. Either way, from how you talk, we could use help," Ian said. "Ask Cory, if it bothers you so much. He may know something we don't. Anyhow, let's quit talking shop. It's Friday night. We deserve a break. I feel like seeing a movie. What's playing downtown?"

"I don't remember," said Abby. "If it's nothing good, we could watch that Netflix movie that just arrived yesterday."

$$\sim\!\!\!\wedge\!\!\!\wedge\!\!\!\sim_\circ$$

The next morning, July 14, Cory looked in his rearview mirror and noticed that a green Mazda had been behind him for several miles now. He deliberately went into the hospital's parking garage to see if the driver would follow. Cory looped up and back down the spiral of parking levels, finally going along the exit ramp to search, but the Mazda was gone. He did see William, though, sweeping up litter from the first floor of the garage and pushing his wheeled trash bin.

"Hey, William. Don't usually see you here on Saturdays."

"The regular weekend maintenance guy c-called in sick. I had a chance to earn some overtime."

"Oh, I understand. William, you see a green Mazda go by?"

"Yeah. Just sped past. Went t-toward Hughler Street."

"Thanks." Cory drove out of the garage.

William chuckled. *Went toward Main. But I'll teach ya to be nice to William. Your tub of a station wagon'll never catch up to no Mazda anyway.* William wandered on down the walk, pushing his trash bin. A few minutes later he saw Cory just parking the station wagon alongside the wall at the back of the hospital oncology lab. "You still lookin' for that g-green Mazda?" he called to Cory.

"You know who drives that car?" Cory asked.

"How much is it w-worth to ya?"

"You really won't tell me without putting a price tag on it?"

"A guy's gotta live."

"Oh, never mind!" Cory grabbed a large cooler out of the back of the wagon. Today he was returning the last of the empty coolers and file boxes he had used to carry materials to Fred's private lab.

"You planning on another p-picnic? What a lousy way to hide stuff. Everybody knows you're st-stealing."

"Stop spreading rumors, you creep. What are you going to do, sell the name of the Mazda's owner to the highest bidder?" Still balancing the cooler against the brick wall, Cory unlocked the lab door and tossed his keys onto a lab bench as he maneuvered the cooler through the door.

But he could hear William's taunts: "Who's d-driving a shiny green Mazda? Why is Cory being followed? He usually don't get the Saturday shift anymore. Thought he was t-too important."

"Shut the fuck up," Cory yelled out the doorway, "and get the hell off my car!" He waited with a scowl till William slid off the hood. Then Cory spun around, startled, as Fred entered the lab from the inside corridor.

"What's going on, Cory?" Fred demanded.

"That creep William gets to me."

"I can see that, but he's nobody. Put down the cooler and come on up to my office. I want you to meet Royce Barkley, a sales rep from Sirgentec Pharmaceuticals. Bring your notebooks. I knew you'd be here shortly, so I went ahead and made this appointment when Royce called to say he was in the area."

"You think we've got enough to show him? And wouldn't it be better to meet with him in your private lab?"

"We've got enough to get some backing, and I didn't want to risk his seeing anything too confidential. Royce is waiting in the lobby. I had a security guy check him out when he arrived."

"You aren't taking any chances," commented Cory.

"I don't trust anybody."

"I know, but this time I happen to agree with you. It sends the right message. I'll play the brilliant but naive scientist."

"Just tell him enough to entice him," said Fred. "You got our notebooks?"

Cory grabbed a couple of blue notebooks off his lab desk and held them up.

"Come on. Let's go. Don't want to keep him waiting."

"Yeah. Especially if Sirgentec is going to give us big bucks," Cory said as he and Fred rushed out of the lab.

$$\sim\!\!\wedge\!\!\!\wedge\!\!\circ$$

William looked closely at the lab door and saw what Fred and Cory had not: Cory had accidentally tracked a chunk of gravel into the doorway. Instead of automatically swinging shut and latching, the door had remained slightly ajar, allowing William to overhear the entire conversation in the lab.

He couldn't resist going in. The set of keys was lying on the bench. William grinned, grabbed the keys, and limped back to the exterior lab door. Carefully he tried each key till he found the one that fit the lock, then grinned again. *A quick trip to the machine shop, and Cory will find out who's boss. I can duplicate it and be back here easy before they finish their meetin'. Just put it back on the ring. This could come in handy when all the lab stuff is found missing.*

Cory and Fred cleared the welter of paperwork off the conference table in Fred's office. Then Fred phoned the security guard: "We're ready, Al. Just bring him straight to my office." After hanging up, he reminded Cory, "Remember, we don't want to give away any answers, just discuss the questions in general terms."

"Yeah, yeah, I know. You got anything to drink in this little refrigerator? You should offer something to your guest."

Cory was placing some bottled water on the table when Alvarez Delgado escorted the sales rep in: a man in his early forties with curly brown hair. "Call me when he's ready to leave, Dr. Truesort. I'll escort him out. This place has been added to so many times, it's confusin'. We've got halls to nowhere."

"Glad to meet you," said the rep, extending his hand toward Fred as Alvarez left. "Royce Barkley from Sirgentec Pharmaceuticals. I'm impressed with your safeguards. Guess you can't be too careful."

"Dr. Fred Truesort here, chief of oncology. And this is my assistant, Dr. Cory Maxwell, medical research chemist."

Royce firmly shook Fred's hand, then Cory's. All three of them sat at Fred's conference table near the window. Cory couldn't help noticing Royce's Movado wristwatch.

Cory put his closed notebooks on the table and began to explain the research project he and Fred had done with cancer cells and their possible application to HIV/AIDS, occasionally tapping the notebooks for emphasis. Royce stared at the notebooks or glanced around the room, occasionally sipping some water or clicking his pen.

After just a few minutes, Royce interrupted Cory's explanation. "Sounds like you're onto something," he said. "Where's your lab?"

"We have one lab downstairs and another off-site. Why do you ask?" Fred said.

"You'd need some sophisticated equipment to even begin to do what you're talking about," Royce observed.

Fred bristled with outrage. "Are you questioning our ability?"

"No. We just usually meet with researchers in their labs," Royce said, still clicking his pen. "It helps us understand what they are doing and how they do it."

"I'm sure it does," Fred said with contempt.

"I'm not suggesting anything else," Royce added defensively. "Sorry to interrupt, Cory."

"No problem," Cory answered. "I've given you just a brief overview. I covered the concept and theory. I won't bore you with any more."

"Royce, what do you think Sirgentec would want?" Fred asked.

"They would have to meet with both of you."

"The sooner the better," Fred said. "We want to keep pushing forward. We will need to know what kind of backing they normally provide. I certainly would need to have a definitive answer within ninety days. And I'm prepared to give an exclusive on this. I realize you don't have any of these answers now."

"I can't tell you dollars and cents today. With recommendations from me, Sirgentec should be willing to meet with you in about a month. Fortunately, we are not a big pharmaceutical house with a long chain of command. We are small enough to be flexible and move quickly."

All three men got out their smartphones to check their calendars. "August sixteenth sound good to you?" asked Royce. "As for an offer in ninety days, I honestly don't know. Even for us, that's pretty tight. But an absolute exclusive for the complete procedure might be an incentive."

"Sorry, I'll be out of town on the sixteenth," Fred lied. "How about August first or second?"

"Well . . . ," said Royce, raising his eyebrows.

"Find out if the Sirgentec people are available, and meet with us right here," Fred commanded.

"We'll try. Just one thing. Don't meet with anyone else until you hear our offer," Royce said.

"We won't, and I have to insist you keep today's meeting confidential," Fred countered.

All shook hands to seal their mutual trust. Fred called Alvarez, who escorted Royce out. Cory tossed the empty water bottles into the recycling bin and began replacing all the files, binders, and piles of unopened mail back on the table in neat stacks.

"Are you one of those obsessive neat freaks? I never noticed you worried about orderliness in anything but your experiments." Fred grabbed Cory's notebooks. "Don't forget these. I know you never referred to them, but they are part of our signed documentation."

"Open the notebooks," Cory said.

"They're empty!"

"Like you said: I don't trust anybody. Royce is probably like me and reads almost as well upside down as right side up. When you know a subject, you don't need to look at your notes. It just makes a good prop. I did keep my hand on the notebooks, because I was afraid he'd try to leaf through them and find out all the pages were blank. Of course, Royce probably misconstrued the whole thing and thought they were too valuable to show him."

"Ha! Great job," said Fred, breaking into a snicker. "Empty notebooks! You had me fooled. I'm sure he fell for it too. Never knew you were such an actor!"

"Glad to help. I'm going to finish putting away the boxes and coolers downstairs in the lab. We'll have more room there for our hospital work now."

"Thanks also for working on a Saturday, Cory. I'll come down to the lab with you."

Sometimes, thought Cory, *Fred really isn't so bad.*

As they put away the last items in the lab, Cory said, "Can you update me about what a sales rep like Royce does? I used to think they just pushed pills. Apparently they also look for new innovations, but don't pharma houses have their own research and development departments?"

Fred answered, "Reps sell meds but also ask doctors for feedback. From our direct experience with patients, we tell them which meds work best and what diseases need better treatment strategies.

Reps listen to the needs of the medical community so the pharma houses can try to fulfill them."

"Makes sense. Okay, I think we're finished here. See ya on Monday." Cory picked up his keys, which were exactly where he'd left them on the lab bench. Fred left through the interior door and walked back through the hospital corridors.

From behind a maintenance truck, William watched Cory lock the lab and get into his station wagon. Holding up a brand-new key, William shook it while laughing and yelling, "Gotcha, Cory, gotcha," as Cory drove away. *I could sell this little key to The Oxman, or I could sell it to the sales rep I heard them talking about. Or I could keep it and open the door myself. Myself, yeah, myself, that's what it'll be—a little service to someone interested enough to pay good money for it. Maybe even show that person around. The alarm on the outside door has been disconnected for years—since back when this place was renovated. Never did get around to connecting it again.*

William got into his rusty Neon and drove from the maintenance parking area over toward the parking garage, then parked across from the exit. *Gotta see if that sales rep is still here.* William left his car and stood by the exit gate. From there he could see much of the garage's ground floor. Many parking spaces were empty, but a baby-blue Lexus was parked in the doctors' reserved parking area, near the exit. A curly-haired man in a gray suit stood next to the car, talking on a cell phone. *Wonder if that's him? Gotta get a better look.* William limped closer, pretending he was walking toward his own car parked farther up. *Never seen him before. Could be the guy.*

"Yeah. They're working with cancer cells and HIV, and bone-marrow transplants. Apparently saved the life of some guy at death's door. Must be something real interesting in the lab—they didn't want me to see it. Cory, Truesort's assistant, did most of the talking. He had a couple of notebooks. I peeked. They were empty. Sure, I'll try to find out more. I'll call you by Wednesday. You'll have the cash for me? Great. See ya."

William heard it all. *Uh-oh, looks like I got competition. Who could this guy be spyin' for, except The Oxman? Maybe I can get a piece of this if I play it cool.*

The man opened the door of the Lexus.

"Ex-excuse me, sir. S-sir, excuse me," William called.

Royce looked at William shuffling toward him. "What do you want? I know I'm not supposed to park in the reserved area, but—"

"Don't worry. Ain't parkin' I w-wanna talk to you about. Couldn't help hearin' s-some stuff. Think I can help you."

"What did you hear?"

"Cory and Doc Truesort ain't l-levelin' with you."

"How do you know?"

"J-just hear. Wanna set things straight."

"Sure, sure. How much is it going to cost me?"

"A b-big one. Thousand."

"Where are you parked?"

"At the c-curb."

"Hold on." Royce got into his Lexus and popped the hood. "Check it out," he told William. "Figure we'll attract less attention this way."

Royce fiddled with a wire under the hood. "Used to work in an auto shop. Never on anything like this, though. It's pretty cool. Didn't work on any stick shifts either. This isn't mine. It's a company car. Helps impress clients. Who are you, anyhow? How come you think you know so much?"

William glanced around. "Um, it's k-kinda easy to hear things in this garage. Wanna take a walk with me to the street, so we can t-talk?"

"No, I noticed it's hard for you to walk; I don't have all day. Let's just sit in my car." William agreed. Royce lowered the hood of the Lexus carefully. "Don't want to hurt this baby," he told William, smiling.

"So," William began once they had settled in the front seats, "I'm William Meddlebach. You might s-say I'm part of the hospital security."

"Uh-huh. Royce Barkley here. And what have you got?"

"The key to D-doc Truesort's lab."

"Now, how could a guy like you get a lab key?"

"Security. Come to the lab. I'll make sure you get in and out without any t-trouble. That's where the bone marrow is. I heard Cory say so."

"You sound serious. But why?"

"Two reasons. I d-don't like Cory, and I need money. Simple." *Plus, Mr. Fancy Watch, you're musclin' in on my territory, and it ain't right. I told The Oxman 'bout Doc Truesort in the first place.*

"You're on. When?"

"T-tomorrow, Sunday. Sundays are busy, so less ch-chance you'll be noticed."

Royce pulled out his BlackBerry. "No, not tomorrow. I've got tickets to the Yankees game. Next Sunday, the twenty-second, is okay."

"Okay, n-next Sunday, about one. Too risky for me to l-let you in the back door of the lab in case anyone sees us together. Nobody'll care if they only see *me*, 'cause I'm doin' m-maintenance all the time. I'll go in the b-back and unlock the hall door for ya."

"Okay," said Royce. "But how do I get there?"

"J-just get a visitor's pass at the front desk. Ask for room 125. It's almost always occupied—got four beds. G-go around the corner and down the hall. You'll s-see the lab. I'll let you in."

"What if I want to talk to Truesort in person? Call his service? Tell him it's an emergency?"

"You could. Kinda risky. N-number's probably in the Rolodex in the lab."

"I'll tell him it's an emergency. How do I get out?"

"Surveillance c-cameras ain't everywhere. C'mon, I'll show you a side exit. No cameras there."

"Let me grab a pencil and pad. I'll make myself a map. Maybe I should be in disguise somehow? Summers during college, used to help my old man put in security systems and stuff. He was an electrician. Don't have any work uniforms now, though. I'll just wear sneakers and jeans . . . maybe my lightweight Yankees jacket if it's rainy out."

"Might be good if you look like a workman when ya leave. I'll put a uniform for you in the closet next to the lab hall door. The c-closet would be to the right. I'll unlock it next Sunday for you."

"Here's my card. It's a deal. One thousand if I learn something. Five hundred if I don't."

"S-seven hundred even if you don't. In cash," William insisted. They shook hands.

William drew a detailed map for Royce and jotted down his name and phone number. Then they drove together around the hospital, with William pointing out the camera-free side door and the back entrance to the oncology lab. Royce drove William to his car afterward.

"Okay, got it," said Royce. "Thanks for the tour. See you next Sunday."

William watched Royce drive away before he got into his car. *Not gonna be seen with that guy more than I have to.* He patted the key in his pocket. *You're gonna bring me a nice piece of change.*

Miano Tse parked her green Mazda in the alley behind Ghanna's building and walked to the front sidewalk. "Come see what I've got," she called to Ghanna, who was sitting in the trailer, door ajar, reading a story to Ramiero. The boy sat cross-legged on the grass in front of him. He wore blue jeans, a red T-shirt, and shabby red sneakers.

Ghanna took Ramiero's hand. They crossed the street and followed Miano Tse into the back alley, where she proudly pointed to the Mazda. "Look. Thanks to you, Ghanna, it is all mine. You don't want to sit around here on such a beautiful summer Saturday afternoon. Want to go for a ride?"

"Sure." Ghanna doffed his hat, bowed low, and kissed her hand. Ramiero hugged her around the waist. "Go ask your mama, Ramiero. Make sure it's okay with her," Ghanna told the boy.

Ramiero was around the corner before Ghanna finished speaking to him, yelling up to the open second-floor window from the sidewalk below. "Mom, Ghanna and I are going for a ride in Miano Tse's new car. Okay?"

Asunta poked her head out the window. "Yeah. Be sure and tell Miano Tse and Ghanna thank you, Ramiero," she managed to call back before a fit of coughing overwhelmed her.

—ᐯᐱo

As Miano Tse drove, Ghanna told her, "Ya know, I'm glad I helped you with this, Miano Tse."

"Me too, but I'm trying to be independent now, Ghanna, and not cause you any trouble. Like I told you before, from now on I have to do things legally. I could lose my job."

"Yeah, I s'pose you're right."

"How about a drive up to the mountain?" Miano Tse changed the subject. "You could play up there for a while, Ramiero, and even look down on some of the farmland in the same big valley where you live."

"Sure. Can I drive your new car, too?"

"No, absolutely not. You are still too young. You have to have a driver's permit and be at least sixteen. How old are you?"

Ramiero sighed. "Only seven."

Once they arrived at the park at the top of the mountain, they headed along the dirt path toward the overlook. Ramiero romped alongside the trail, then ran up to Miano Tse and Ghanna to show them a pretty rock he had just found that sparkled with mica; he proudly announced that he would give it to his mom.

"She'll like that, Ramiero," said Ghanna, and the boy darted away again. "So how's your new job goin', Miano Tse?"

"I like it," she answered, "but some things are strange. Fred spends most of the day locked in his suite. When I do see him for a minute, he seems tense."

"Yeah? Josh say that doc is a snob. I say maybe his research ain't goin' too good."

"Cory can be weird, too—he's a research chemist who's worked for years with Fred. When I was coming over to see you today, I happened to drive behind Cory. It was just because we were both headed in the same direction. Maybe he thought I was following him—didn't recognize me with my sunglasses and new car. But suddenly he whipped into the hospital parking garage like he was scared."

"Why he comin' to work on a Saturday?"

"Who knows? Unless they had some kind of emergency. He might be on call, but he rarely works Saturdays anymore, Abby told me."

When they arrived at the overlook, Miano Tse took Ramiero's hand, and the three of them stood at the railing to admire the view. They could see the rooftops of their city clustered at the eastern end of the wide valley below, while farmland sprawled across the west. The river meandered across the valley like a shining necklace.

Afterward they walked to the playground, where Ramiero went on the swings and the seesaw with other children. The two adults sat on a park bench and watched him.

"By the way," asked Miano Tse, "has Dr. Pannell asked for any more patients?"

"Yeah, he say he needs a comparison study. What the hell's that?"

"Dr. Truesort gives other patients the same treatment he gave Vincent and sees if it works the same for them," Miano Tse explained.

"We ain't found nobody yet. Everybody scared since Vincent gone," Ghanna said.

"I know. I told Josh last night I think The Oxman has been watching me more closely. One of his boys came around to the junkyard a couple of days ago and asked where I was. I don't like that, Ghanna."

Ghanna spat. "Shit. What they tell 'im?"

"Nothing. They don't know anyway, for their own protection. But if The Oxman is after me, of course he'll notice my new car right away, maybe have me followed to my job. Josh is really worried about it. Says he'll strangle The Oxman with his own hands if anything happens to me."

Ghanna drummed his fist on the arm of the park bench. "The Oxman ruinin' life for *everybody*: Vincent, you, Josh, me, the docs, the patients. We gotta do somethin'. Gotta trap The Oxman, lock him up. That's all I can figure."

"That won't be easy."

"I know, Miano Tse, but what else we gonna do? None of us safe anymore."

"I want him locked up for good," said Miano Tse, "but to trap him? It's like trapping lightning."

"Let me talk to Josh about it," Ghanna said.

Miano Tse looked at her watch. "It's getting late, and I want to take Ramiero down to the merry-go-round in Riverside Park. I know he'll like that."

part FIVE

To Trap Lightning

Chapter 10

*O*N SUNDAY, JULY 22, A PORSCHE screeched up to the curb by the hospital parking garage. "Find a parking place for this," barked the driver. "I have an emergency!"

William was leaning on his broom near the filled VIP parking area. He laughed and yelled back, "Happy to, Dr. Truesort."

Ghanna viewed all of this because he happened to be walking by on his way home from the corner store. *Why William here on a Sunday?* he wondered. *What William think so funny? That William's crazy.* Ghanna quickened his pace. *But Truesort's up to somethin'. Gotta see what's goin' down.*

The white-haired doctor left the car keys in the ignition, then ran to the nearby side door of the hospital, which slowly closed— but not before Ghanna slipped in behind him. Helping himself to a large visitor's pass lying on a cart, Ghanna followed the doctor down the hall.

"Truesort here. Where's my patient?" thundered the doctor into his cell phone. "You just called me. Did you send him up to ICU? What the hell are you bumbling idiots doing?"

With his weak leg, Ghanna could not match the doctor's rapid pace, but he could hear every word.

"*What?* That call wasn't from the ER? But my phone said Hughler Hospital's main number. Well, find out who called me, you fool! Have the call traced, Goddamn it! This is critical!" Dr. Truesort immediately did an about-face and ran down the hall, back toward Ghanna, stopping only to punch a number into his cell phone. "ICU? Truesort here. Do you have an emergency oncology patient for me? No? Then what the fuck is going on?"

Ghanna took a sip of water from the fountain as Dr. Truesort jogged past him so fast that he made a breeze when he went around the corner. Ghanna followed and saw the doctor slide to a halt by a door that stood ajar. "Oh my God. What the HELL?" shouted Dr. Truesort, yanking the door wide open and striding in. Ghanna caught a brief glimpse of the guy Dr. Truesort was cursing out. "Who are you, you son of a bitch, and what are you doing in my lab? Where's the emergency case?" Ghanna heard him shout.

Leaning against the opposite wall, Ghanna heard something about bone marrow before the door slammed and the two voices faded like a train disappearing in the distance. ONCOLOGY LAB, read Ghanna on the door. *What the heck's "oncology"? Reckon I'll go on to the ER. Find Josh. Don't wanna get caught snoopin'.*

Royce walked back toward the exterior lab door. "I'm your emergency, Dr. Truesort. I need some bone marrow."

"You look perfectly healthy. How did you get in here?"

"A friend."

"Who the hell are you? Is somebody critical or not?" Fred stepped closer. This guy looked maddeningly familiar. *Where the devil did I see him before? A former patient?* Royce's disguise was buying him time.

"No one's critically ill yet. But it's why I figured you would be happy to sell some bone marrow from your stockpile. I bet it's in this freezer right here, huh? With the research you were doing, I figured you might be in a position to help some patients on the side. One of the reps you saw last week seemed to think you might."

Rep! That's who the bastard is. Thank God the freezer's got a combination lock. "Get the hell out!" Dr. Truesort lunged toward Royce, who easily swiveled behind a lab bench. "This is Hughler Hospital's bone-marrow bank. If I call in Security, you may need a transfusion yourself, Royce Barkley!"

"Don't get excited, Doc. By the way, I thought we had an exclusive deal just between us. And of course, everyone can always use a few extra dollars on the side. Even you," Royce sneered. "But I hear you've been talking to other pharma houses too and doing all the research at your private lab. That's why I called you, claiming an emergency. Figured you're almost dedicated enough to rush over here. I want to know more about this research you're doing so I can explain it to my boss. You and I could help move this process along more quickly, which means we get paid sooner. By the way, I knew Cory was just bullshitting me. His head was as empty as those notebooks."

"Now who's bullshitting?" Dr. Truesort picked up a beaker and glared at Royce. "Your part of the research *was* exclusive. But you've got no deal now. NONE!"

Royce eyed the beaker. "Don't you even try, old man." While watching Fred, Royce slid along the lab bench and circled back to the interior lab door. "You couldn't even remember me. Yankees cap and jacket, sneakers, jeans . . . I ditched the suit and tie, don't look like a sales rep today. Even left my Movado watch at home."

Dr. Truesort threw the beaker at Royce, catching him on the elbow, but Royce only laughed. Broken glass littered the floor.

"Okay, okay, I'm going." Royce slowly placed two of his business cards on the lab bench with an exaggerated bow, arranging them neatly so the corners were perfectly aligned. "Here are a couple of my cards in case you change your mind." He smiled at Fred and walked slowly to the hall door.

Fred pulled out his cell phone and strode toward Royce, only to have the door slammed in his face.

"Hello, Security?" said Fred, shaking with rage. "An intruder broke into my lab."

Royce slipped into the broom closet next door to the oncology lab. Sure enough, there was the maintenance uniform William had promised. Royce took off his Yankees cap and stuffed it into the pocket of his jacket, then shrugged it off and dropped it on the floor. He stood silently for a moment and heard the click of a key, a sigh, and then the quick cadence of footsteps passing by. Hastily he pulled on the maintenance uniform over his clothing and grabbed a broom. The blue maintenance cap completed his new disguise. After peeking out the closet door to make sure the coast was clear, he began sweeping along the hall toward the side exit William had showed him. Once he was outdoors, a light rain reminded him: *Damn, I left my Yankees jacket and cap in the closet.* But the side door had locked behind him.

From the top level of the parking garage, William saw Royce drop the broom, rip off the maintenance outfit, and toss it into a Dumpster, then jog toward the garage entrance. "Hey, Royce," William yelled. "How'd it go?"

"Not good. And I left my jacket."

"I'll look for it."

"Good. I'll give you a call."

"Wait a minute. You owe me—" William yelled.

"Look in the broom closet," Royce shouted back.

William took the elevator down to the ground level and entered the hospital side door with his ID card.

Ten minutes later William put the broom back in the closet. *Hmm . . . nice jacket and cap, but jacket doesn't fit me. Still looks new. Could get a piece of change for this here, especially from a Yankees fan. But don't see any money yet.*

William searched the jacket pockets. "Fifty bucks! Is that all?" In another pocket he found an IOU for $650. "The s-son of a *bitch!*" William punched the wall in his anger.

$$\sim\!\!\Lambda\!\!\Lambda\!\!\sim\!\!\circ$$

"Ghanna, what are you doin' in here? Where ya get the pass?" Josh asked.

"Ya look good in that there white coat, Joshua," Ghanna said quietly, using his friend's real name. "I need to talk to ya. Come by when you done."

Seeing Étoile approaching, Josh said in a formal tone, "We will let you know as soon as the doctor gives us the information, sir."

Ghanna rolled his eyes, tipped his hat, bowed, and smiled. "I'll look forward to hearing from you," he replied in the same tone.

That night, as had become their habit whenever Josh came over, Ghanna sat on the step stool and Josh on the red chair. "I gotta be able to contact you faster, Josh. Just stoppin' by my little park ain't no good no more. Things happenin' too fast. We gotta be careful. Can't be seen together too much, neither."

"So how come ya don't get a phone like everybody else?"

"Hate to pay all that money, but maybe I need one now."

"Yeah, ya do. I'll get ya one and pay for it, so don't worry, man. How ya get in the hospital? What did ya want?"

"I just slipped in 'cause I needed to ask you to stop by. But on the way I done heard some dude in the oncology lab wantin' to buy bone marrow from Doc Truesort. What the hell's oncology? And what's bone marrow?"

"Oncology is cancer science, Doc Truesort's specialty. Bone marrow is mushy stuff in the center of your bones. It helps make your blood and other things ya need."

"Is it expensive?"

"Yeah, and illegal to just take it and sell it without tellin' anybody."

"No wonder the doc was yellin' and cussin' worse than a swarm of hornets. You shoulda heard him." Ghanna chuckled.

"But who was that other guy, and how'd he break into the lab? And how come he knew the bone marrow was there? We gotta find out."

Ghanna grabbed his broom and began banging the broomstick on his ceiling. "Just our little intercom. Alvarez is right up above me." The two heard three taps in reply. "You hearin' how he checks up on me since I live alone. But if I tap, he come on down to see what I need."

A minute later they heard footsteps descending the stairs. "Al, c'mon in. How are ya, man?"

"Enjoyed my day off. Took Ramiero to the park. Even won a hundred twenty bucks on a pony," said Alvarez with a grin.

"Way to go, Al!" exclaimed Ghanna.

Alvarez exchanged fist bumps with him and Josh before taking a seat on the foot of the bed. "Was having a peaceful evenin' till you started bangin'."

"Sorry 'bout that, Al," continued Ghanna, "but me an' Josh here got a problem. Thought ya might be able to help us out. Some guy broke into Doc Truesort's lab this afternoon."

Alvarez frowned. "*¡Maldito!* How d'ya know?"

"Let's just say it was a reliable source," Ghanna said.

"Anybody hurt?" asked Alvarez.

"Not that I heard of," said Josh. "Nobody showed up at the ER, anyways."

"Any damage? Anything stolen?"

"Dunno. Guess you better call the security company an' find out," said Josh.

"I finally get a day off and look what happens," said Alvarez with a scowl. "What time did your 'reliable source' see this guy?"

"Maybe 'round one fifteen," Ghanna said.

"Good, that helps. Ya got a description? What'd he look like? What was he wearin'?" Alvarez asked.

"He was ordinary," said Ghanna. "White guy, wearin' one of them . . . baseball jackets, ya know . . . Yankees, I think. Dark blue. Baseball cap, too. Little shorter than the doc, who was yellin' at him like an army sergeant."

"That's a good description," Alvarez said. "I'll look at today's videos and let you know if I find him. Josh, did you see this guy too?"

Josh said no, he hadn't seen him, but described the frantic phone call Dr. Truesort had made to the ER about some critical cancer patient who didn't exist.

"I heard him makin' a coupla calls," added Ghanna, "cursin' at everybody. He was shoutin' so loud, his cell phone coulda busted into pieces right in his hand."

Josh laughed. "I guess we all know who's the 'reliable source.'"

Alvarez rolled his eyes. "I figured that all along," he admitted. "Well, thanks for reportin' this, Ghanna. The guy on duty today musta already told my boss about the break-in, but he prob'ly didn't have a description. I could get a bonus for trackin' the guy that broke in."

"Hold on," Ghanna insisted. "You ain't understandin' me right, Al. Josh an' me gotta find out more about that dude: who he is an' how come he done it. Can you tell us what you find out without lettin' anybody know you're tellin' us? Show us pictures, if you got 'em?"

Alvarez hesitated an instant. "Hospital business is supposed to be confidential . . . ," he began. "Why do you guys wanna know?"

"Al," said Josh, "we got our reasons. That guy might be messin' with somethin' that's our business, an' he might be workin' for somebody you don't want comin' after ya. Once we're onto the guy in the lab, maybe we can catch him *and* his boss red-handed. Trust us, we know what we're doin'."

"An' ya better work quick," added Ghanna. "Them videos liable to disappear."

"Out of the hospital CCTV room? No, I don't think so," said Alvarez.

"You'd be surprised at who knows who, an' where they might be sneakin' into," warned Josh. "I've seen it too many times."

"So if you see this guy on them surveillance cameras, could you show us?" Ghanna asked again.

"Okay, I guess I could do that. If this guy shows up on the videos, I'll print out stills for ya. Now I gotta get back upstairs or Asunta will wonder about me."

The three of them said good night, and Alvarez left.

"Al's a great guy an' all," said Ghanna, "but sometimes he's too honest for his own good."

"Uh-huh," answered Josh with a grin. "You an' me, we gotta make him a little more crooked, an' then he'll be perfect."

—ᴧᴧᴑ

As Alvarez read a bedtime story to Ramiero that night, his mind kept straying back to his troubling conversation with Ghanna and Josh. Once Ramiero was asleep, Alvarez quietly told Asunta that he had to return to the hospital for a while because there had been a break-in that day. She was distressed by the news but kissed him and told him to be careful.

As a supervisor, Alvarez was allowed to come to the hospital when it wasn't his shift. After passing through the lobby, he took a brief detour to the vending machines near the cafeteria, where he bought a candy bar and the city newspaper. Then he went to the CCTV room and unlocked the door with his security key card.

After greeting Pedro and Calvin, who were absorbed in monitoring the current videos from the security cameras, he sat down at the extra monitor in the corner and called up the videos from that afternoon: SUNDAY, JULY 22. *Wonder which door he came in? Might as well start with the camera in the main lobby. If this guy came in as a visitor, he'll show up there.* Alvarez fast-forwarded to 12:30 p.m. and watched.

Hey, that's gotta be him! Jeans, sneakers, lightweight Yankees jacket and cap, just like Ghanna said. The man walked straight to the information desk and picked up a visitor's pass. Alvarez zoomed in on the pass, which fortunately had large print: GENERAL SURGERY, FLOOR 1. ROOM 125. *Same floor as the oncology lab. How the heck did he know that?*

The volunteer at the desk pointed to the elevators, apparently telling the visitor where to find the room. Alvarez saw the guy in the Yankees jacket disappear into the elevator. *Once he found the lab, how'd he get in the door? He'd need a key for that.* But there was no security camera anywhere in that hallway. Alvarez could see nothing. *When did that Yankees fan leave? Never came back through the lobby. Must've gone out some other door.* Munching his candy bar, Alvarez checked the input from all the other cameras, hoping to catch a glimpse of the intruder, but somehow this guy had evaded them all. *Maybe he got out the back door of the lab, but then how come the alarm didn't go off? Or maybe the side door, that one with no camera?*

Alvarez instantly understood that this person knew the hospital buildings and the peculiar labyrinth of hallways connecting new sections to old in a hodgepodge of corridors and dead ends. He also recognized something even more significant: this was not the first time he had seen this man. He reversed the video to the clearest view of the man's face, then zoomed in. *Uh-huh, just as I thought.* He printed out several stills, including close-ups and full-body shots, slipping them casually between the pages of his folded newspaper.

Then he switched to an earlier set of videos: SATURDAY, JULY 14, the preceding weekend. *Yup, there he is: Royce Barkley the sales rep, walking right next to me up to Doc Truesort's office. Different clothes but same face. I remember he mentioned on the way out that he wanted to see Doc Truesort's lab. I guess the doc said no, so he found a different way. The bastard!*

Alvarez was dismayed at the inadequacy of the hospital's security system. *No excuse for exits without cameras! No excuse! I've warned my boss before, but he says the hospital is too cheap to pay for more cameras. And of course the security supervisor on duty gets blamed if anything goes wrong.*

Alvarez printed plenty of stills from July 14 as well. After saying good night to Pedro and Calvin, he walked back across the street, his folded newspaper tucked under his arm. *Better show these photos to Ghanna and Josh. Then discuss a better protection system with the boss first thing tomorrow. Maybe after today's break-in, he and Wimpler will wise up.*

—ᴧ|ᴧ‿ₒ

Early the next morning, Ghanna was awakened by taps on the ceiling. A minute later Alvarez was at the door, dressed in his security uniform.

"I looked at yesterday's CCTV data from all the hospital surveillance cameras until late last night," Alvarez told Ghanna. "Made printouts for ya."

"Thanks, Al, thanks! Did ya find that guy?"

"Uh-huh. Here he is in the lobby yesterday afternoon, wearing that Yankees jacket, just like you said."

"Yup, that's him all right. How'd he get out?" asked Ghanna.

"Dunno. Never did see him leave on yesterday's videos. Maybe an exit alarm needs repair. Who knows? I better have Maintenance check all the exit alarms, make sure they work right."

"Yeah, good idea. Maybe double-check 'em yourself after, just to make sure," Ghanna added drily, thinking of one hospital maintenance worker he didn't trust.

"But check this out, Ghanna: here's a sales rep a week ago Saturday. Said his name was Royce Barkley. He's walkin' next to me on the way in an' the way out. Same guy as yesterday!"

Ghanna looked at the photos. "You show these to anybody else?"

"No. Just you so far, Ghanna. Of course I'll show 'em to my boss right away. Gotta get over there in a few minutes. But I think this sales rep knows our hospital layout pretty good," Alvarez said.

"How ya know?"

"Once he got in, he avoided all the interior surveillance cameras we got. He knew the oncology lab was on the first floor. Asked for a patient's room right around the hall from it. I saw him get in the elevator."

"Why he need the elevator? I thought it was on the first floor," said Ghanna.

"It is if you come in from the back, 'cause the land slopes. If you come in the main lobby, you're on the ground floor. You gotta take an elevator to floor one."

"Oh, I gotcha. Last Saturday's face do look like yesterday's face." Ghanna was squinting at the photos. Finally he put them on the bed and stepped back. "Gotta get me some eyeglasses over at the drugstore. Can't see good up close."

"You ever see this guy before?" asked Alvarez.

"Nope, not till yesterday. Maybe Josh knows him."

"Might be someone who used to work at the hospital," said Alvarez.

"Yeah, could be."

"If so, I can track him down even if 'Royce Barkley' is an alias. All the employees' ID photos are kept on the computer network for five years after they leave."

"Cool. I'm glad you in security, Al."

"Thanks again for the tip about this guy, Ghanna. Woulda been much harder to track him down without a good description."

"Glad to help out. You helped Josh an' me too, gettin' us these here photos and the guy's name. You done good, man! We thank ya. Ya work fast, didn't give nobody the time to make them videos disappear."

"No problem, man."

"But you be careful now, Al," Ghanna added with a touch of concern in his voice. "Some of The Oxman's boys could be keepin' tabs on this, ya know? Seems like if anythin' crooked goin' down around here, he's behind it one way or another."

"I'll keep my eyes open, Ghanna," said Alvarez, touching the handle of the gun at his belt. "I got a family to take care of. Now I gotta run. If you need help again, just let me know. See ya, Ghanna."

As Alvarez hurried across the street, Ghanna punched in a number on his brand-new cell phone. "Hey, Josh. Stop by my place on your way to work. Got somethin' to show ya."

"Sally, you seen Alvarez?" Ghanna was spending Tuesday morning on his front steps.

"No, not yet. He's takin' Asunta to the doctor's this mornin'. I just came over to take care of Ramiero."

"Asunta feelin' poorly?"

"'Fraid so," Sally said, while looking at the cracked concrete steps. "You reckon Ramiero could come out here? I don't like climbin' up them steps."

"Just holler up to the window. He'll come out."

Sally pushed her feet up the sidewalk in her flat slip-ons, her ankle-length flowered skirt swaying in the rhythm of her uneven steps. Her *yoo-hoo*s carried above the noise of the rush-hour traffic.

Ramiero joined the pair. He brought along bananas and bagels for his babysitters and himself. "Mom not feelin' good, Ramiero?" Ghanna asked.

"No. She's coughing a lot. Dad's takin' her over to the emergency room. Her doc's gonna meet her there."

Sally patted Ramiero's shoulder sympathetically. "Don't you worry none," she said. "The doc will help your mom feel better. I'll stay with you till your mom and dad come back this afternoon."

"I'm supposed to see if I can clean up Lefty's," Ghanna said. "Both of you wanna help?"

The three went on down to the tavern. Sally and Ramiero collected the aluminum cans around the building and threw them in a garbage bag. Ghanna propped open the front and back doors, then plugged in fans at both of them to let in some sunshine and breezes to dissipate the distinct aroma of beer. Then Ramiero went inside and swept the dust out the open doors with a push broom, occasionally imitating a motor as his imagination changed the broom into a supersonic jet.

Lefty stood in amazement when he came in to wash the glasses. "This place never looked so good. Really got a good airing out. Now I'll have to clean and paint the patterned tin ceiling. It doesn't blend in anymore. My wife has been asking me to paint it for years. She says tin ceilings are rare."

He unlocked the storage room and checked to make sure none of the beer or liquor was stolen. When he saw everything was intact, he ordered pizza for his workers.

"The Oxman ever come in here, Lefty?" Ghanna asked.

"Not since Vincent's gone. He messed Josh up in the back room once. That was before Vincent played guitar here. Between The Oxman's temper and his size, he's deadly. Must've wanted somethin' from Josh or he would've strangled him. . . . No yoking The Oxman." Lefty laughed at his little joke.

"Yeah. I s'pose he's used to havin' his way." Ghanna looked at Sally and Ramiero. "You two stay away from him, hear? He ain't no good."

"I'll make sure Ramiero stays outta of his way," Sally promised.

"Come on, Ramiero. We'll go back to your apartment for a while even though I have to climb those stairs. It's time for a siesta."

"I'm not tired. I don't want any siesta."

"Okay. But come along anyways, 'cause I do," Sally said. She put the garbage bag of aluminum cans in a corner behind the bar. "I'll be by tomorrow. Don't let no one take this," she told Lefty. She took Ramiero's hand and went out the door.

"What's really on your mind, Ghanna?" Lefty asked once Sally and Ramiero were gone.

"'Fraid for that boy an' his mom. The Oxman done make a coupla passes at Asunta awhile ago, back when she was so beautiful. She just ignore him an' keep on walkin'. Now he only whistles at her, calls out nasty comments from his truck when he drives by. When she ain't feelin' well, it really upsets her."

"What a shame," said Lefty. "He's bad news for everyone, all right. No respect for anyone or anything."

"Ramiero even told me it made her cry sometimes," continued Ghanna, "an' he was so mad, he wanted to throw a rock right through The Oxman's windshield. But if the kid ever tries anythin' like that, who knows what The Oxman might do? Maybe hold him or Asunta hostage, even. Lately, though, that truck ain't been cruisin' around here."

"That's good. Asunta's a nice lady," said Lefty.

"Guess The Oxman figures on pickin' up somebody else."

"Yeah. Sounds to me like you got somethin' else goin' on, though. Know anything about all the druggies hanging out behind my building?" Lefty paused, but Ghanna made no reply. "Anyhow, if I see The Oxman around, I'll let you know," Lefty promised.

"How much I owe ya for the pizza and drinks?"

"It's on the house. Thanks for cleanin' up good."

"But you already done give me my bottle of wine."

"Let's say you earned a bonus today. We're even." Lefty continued to rub a scrap of a towel over the bar in a vain attempt to bring back its shine.

The next evening after work, Miano Tse opened all the windows in her sweltering Mazda, which had been sitting in the sunny parking lot at Fred's lab all day. The air conditioner would take a while to cool down the car to a more comfortable temperature than ninety degrees.

On a whim, Miano Tse abandoned her usual route home from work and decided to take a scenic drive along River Road to enjoy some cool breezes. The isolated dirt road passed behind the beautiful gardens of several mansions and then through Riverside Park, with its majestic original forest of oaks and dogwoods and the merry-go-round where she and Ghanna had taken Ramiero a week and a half earlier.

She was enjoying the drive and didn't pay much attention to the car that sped past her from behind. *Maybe I should drive more quickly,* she thought. Then she glanced in her rearview mirror and saw another car tailgating close behind her. Now the car that had passed her before had slowed down and stopped right in front of her. When Miano Tse stepped on the gas pedal in an attempt to swerve around him, the driver behind her veered into the on-coming lane and slammed on his brakes, blocking her.

"We gotcha boxed in," he yelled, just as a third car parked in back of her. "Now it's into the rapids for ya, just where we wanted ya, Chinkie Brat," he sneered. "No trees, no fence—just a nice steep riverbank."

Suddenly ambushed, Miano Tse immediately closed all her windows and locked her doors. The right-hand wheels of her car were at least a foot onto the muddy shoulder of the road, and the abrupt slope to the rapids began only a few feet beyond. She could hear the three men in the other cars laughing and calling out to her through their open windows. "The Oxman's gonna come see you tonight. He thinks you're cute, Chinkie, Chinkie," they taunted.

Miano Tse ignored their scoffing and called 911 on her cell. "The Oxman's men have me surrounded in my car on River Road, by the rapids near the merry-go-round in Riverside Park. Get the police here immediately," she ordered the operator.

Though Miano Tse was terrified and angry, she told herself to remain calm. *You're resourceful enough to figure out how to overcome this trap,* she thought. She turned her steering wheel to the left and began to maneuver her car at a slight angle. Her heart skipped a beat as her rear wheels skidded onto the steep riverbank. She could feel the ground vibrate with the pounding of the rapids. Yet gradually she turned her car so that it pointed between the car on her driver's side and the one in front of her. *Those stupid men can't even figure out what I'm doing.*

Suddenly she stepped on the gas pedal, sent her Mazda lurching forward through the narrow gap between the two cars, swerved through the underbrush on the other side of the road, and took off down the dirt road, ahead of all three cars.

Miano Tse was being chased by the car that had been on her driver's side when the policemen showed up in their patrol cars along with a detective. One patrol car cut off the hit man's car. The hit man attempted to run away on foot but was quickly subdued and cuffed. Another police car continued down River Road at top speed, causing a dust storm, while a third police car approached from the opposite end of River Road to the entrapment site.

Miano Tse parked on the shoulder of the road. The detective tapped on the window and showed her his badge. She opened the window and gave him a full report of what had happened, including the license number of the car in front of her and the fact that all three cars were black.

The detective asked if she would like an escort home. Miano Tse refused, pointing out that a police escort could make her life even more dangerous. "You are The Oxman's enemy. I don't want to be seen with you." Miano Tse sobbed, "I was terrified!"

Then she admonished him, "When are you going to get The Oxman and his violent gang of hit men off the street? It's been years!"

"We're workin' on it, ma'am," said the detective.

Yeah, sure you are, thought Miano Tse.

Miano Tse watched the detective drive toward the crime scene before she called Josh on her cell and told him what had happened to her. "I'm on my way to Ghanna's, Josh. I'll park in the alley by his back door. No, no cop is with me. They went down River Road. Yes, the passenger front door was scraped loose. The lock must be damaged. The door popped open when I hit a pothole, but I was able to latch it. My beautiful new car! Okay, I'll meet you at Ghanna's."

Ghanna was startled when he heard the pounding on the back door of his building. He took another mouthful of macaroni and cheese before he put down his fork, limped to the far end of the hallway, and looked out the tiny peephole in the door. "Okay, Josh, stop bangin'. I gotta get this here lock undone. Can't eat my dinner in peace with you around. You here too, Miano Tse?" continued Ghanna, opening the door. "What happened? You been cryin'?"

"She had a bad scare, Ghanna." Josh looked ready to explode with rage.

"C'mon into my apartment. That's right. Sit down, Miano Tse. Josh, you too," Ghanna insisted, closing the door behind them. "Now tell me what got ya all upset, Miano Tse," he continued in a soothing tone.

Miano Tse explained how The Oxman's men had trapped her by the river and how she had escaped. "They tried to force me to back into the rapids! I could have been captured and tortured by The Oxman, or drowned."

"Jeezus, Miano Tse," said Ghanna, glancing back and forth between her face and Josh's. "No wonder you so scared."

Suddenly Josh stood up. "I can't *stand* the bastard," he yelled. Miano Tse winced at the sudden noise. "I'm gonna *kill* The Oxman!" he yelled again. "I'm gonna mangle him till he begs to die!"

"Hey, Josh, I understand you mad, an' you got a right to be, but you just upsettin' Miano Tse more by your yellin'," said Ghanna calmly.

"Sorry, Ghanna," said Josh, pacing the floor. "Sorry, Miano Tse. But I ain't kidding, Ghanna. I'm gonna kill The Oxman even if I use my bare hands!" Josh grabbed his own neck to demonstrate.

"No, Josh. You ain't gonna kill no one. You hear me?" Ghanna stood and pulled Josh's hands down. "Not with your hands or feet or nothin' else."

Josh stared sharply at Ghanna. "What else can I do? The Oxman's so powerful, nobody will touch him, and he's controlling all our lives! I swear, if anything happens to Miano Tse . . . The cops too corrupt to do anything. If they ain't protectin' us, we gotta protect ourselves!"

"That's true, Josh," said Miano Tse, "but I can't stand hearing you talk about killing people—even someone like The Oxman. Don't let that pig bring you down to wallow in his mud."

But Josh kept pacing back and forth, pounding one fist into the palm of the other hand and kicking the door, repeating, "I'm gonna bring him down. Gonna kill him."

Miano Tse frowned and looked away, ignoring Josh.

Ghanna sat back down on the step stool. "What happened when the cops came, Miano Tse?" he asked.

Miano Tse moved the red chair closer to Ghanna and sat. "The detective jotted down what I told him and went in the right direction to see the ruts on the riverbank. And that will be the end of their investigation. They won't pursue the problem. The police may go after The Oxman's dealers and hit men, but they'll never go after The Oxman himself," Miano Tse said, looking at Josh and then Ghanna.

"Did the detective give you a copy of his notes?" Josh asked.

"No. He gave me his card, though. In case I want to call him directly."

"That's good. Maybe he ain't as corrupt as the others," Ghanna said hopefully.

"Bullshit!" said Josh. "Those motherfucker cops won't do nothin'. I'm gonna kill The Oxman myself!"

Ghanna warned him, "Control that anger before it kills *you.*"

"He's right, Josh," pleaded Miano Tse. "Don't you see? The Oxman *wants* all of us to get angry. Don't fall for it! He could kill you in one blow. Trying to kill him is hopeless. Instead we have to find a way to trap him, get him locked up for the rest of his life."

"I'm tellin' ya," Josh argued, "lockin' him up still ain't good enough. What if some crooked, half-assed judge lets him off? Nobody'll be safe till The Oxman's *dead.*"

"So, you gonna shoot him and try'n explain that to the same crooked, half-assed judge yourself?" countered Ghanna. "We all wish The Oxman would get run over by a train, but you gotta stop talkin' like this or ya gonna be in jail yourself. I agree plannin' a sting ain't easy if ya wanna get away with it. Just ask my buddy. He's doin' life over at the state prison 'cause he didn't listen to ole Ghanna."

"But The Oxman got plenty of enemies," Josh persisted. "What if some of them would *help* us kill him? Or maybe we should use a hit man—a pro, no amateurs. You been in this city a long time, Ghanna. You got any connections?"

"Used to, but not no more," said Ghanna. "They all got wasted, or doin' time, or moved away."

"Count me out," said Miano Tse coldly. "Murder will haunt you the rest of your life, Josh, whether you do it yourself or hire someone else. This is not the America *I emigrated to*. Trap The Oxman, maybe wound him, but don't kill him. Like I told Ghanna before, catching him will be as hard as trapping lightning. We need a really good plan. I know we can figure something out."

Josh paused. He looked at Ghanna. He looked at Miano Tse. Then he murmured, "You're both right."

Ghanna stood once again to give Josh a fist bump. "Now you're talkin' sense."

Miano Tse leaped up and hugged Josh around his waist with gratitude and relief on her face.

That night the three of them pledged to work together to snare The Oxman somehow and get him behind bars. They decided to meet the next evening in the trailer in Ghanna's park to begin working out a viable plan.

Ghanna said he would clean up the trailer a little bit and get the air conditioner going before they came. He added with a sly smile, "Them construction men were smart. They ran a high-capacity A/C line right to the utility pole. It still works."

Thursday evening Josh and Miano Tse stopped at a Chinese takeout and brought supper along to Ghanna, who was waiting for them in the trailer. As Miano Tse placed the containers of food on the desk, Ghanna could see that her hands were trembling. Miano Tse was still upset. "Would you wanna wait till another time to talk about The Oxman, Miano Tse?"

"No," she answered, "let's talk about it now. That bastard. The sooner he's stopped, the better it is for all of us."

"You got that right. Especially now you're workin' for Doc Truesort," Josh agreed.

"I need a different apartment. Now that I have a better job, I can afford a bigger place." Miano Tse's face grew troubled. "The worst thing is that I don't feel safe at home anymore. I used to love being near the farmers' market for all the fresh foods. Now I just want to get away from The Oxman. I *hate* living so near to him! I swear he watches me every time I walk to my car, and then I think he's watching even when he's not."

"The Oxman's boys did ambush you. It's only natural you gettin' paranoid, Miano Tse. I don't like you livin' there either, especially alone," Ghanna added. "Get Josh to stay with you. Together you can find a better place, an' Josh'll help ya move."

"But living a little farther away won't really solve anything," said Miano Tse sadly. "No, like we said last night, we have to lock up The Oxman for good."

"Sure, but how we gonna do that?" said Ghanna. "He's tough—tough to trick and tougher to catch. Whole city police force been tryin' to nab him for years."

"I ain't so sure 'bout that," said Josh. "You know most of them cops crooked—he pays 'em off easy."

"Okay, okay, ya got a point there," Ghanna admitted. "But maybe us three, an' maybe the docs too, all workin' together—maybe we can trap The Oxman in some way he wouldn't see comin'. Somethin' the cops ain't thought of. Like, we could bring Vincent back an' use him for bait."

"Like baiting the hook?" Miano Tse said. "Not a bad idea."

"Too risky, man. Too risky. You gotta be crazy," said Josh.

"Maybe the cops got somebody for a phony Vincent, plain-clothesmen they call 'em," Ghanna said. "You know anybody good with a gun? Just in case somethin' goes wrong?"

"Alvarez, he's in security," said Josh. "Maybe he'd help us out. But you'd practically have to be a sharpshooter, man."

"We all gotta think about this some more," said Ghanna.

Ghanna spent Friday afternoon at his little park. He settled himself comfortably on the trailer steps, finishing a bottle of red wine. While sipping a little wine from the bottle, which he had swathed in a brown paper bag, he tipped his straw hat down over his eyes. The soft rhythms of the island music from his boom box gradually lulled him asleep.

"Hey, old man," Josh said as he turned off the music.

The sudden silence woke Ghanna up. "What ya doin' here?"

"I'm on my way to church," Josh joked. "Nah, it's my day off."

"Thought so. You ain't ever been to no church. Ain't Sunday anyways."

"I was only jokin', Ghanna. You and I know them church ladies don't want no sinners like us joinin' their hymn singin' and prayin'."

"You got somethin' important to say, or can I go back to sleep?" Ghanna closed his eyes.

"Important," Josh pushed hard on the trailer door as he poked his pocket knife into the lock. The door swung open. "C'mon, Ghanna. We'll talk in here." But before entering the trailer and closing the door tightly behind him, Josh took a careful look around to make sure no one—particularly William—was nearby. They settled themselves on some dirty orange plastic chairs left over from the hospital waiting room.

"This is private, man. I got an idea. You know Dr. Pannell, the one who gives us the money for patients?"

"Josh," said Ghanna with disdain, "I *never* forget a business associate."

"He was a Green Beret."

"A what?" Ghanna's eyelids were only slightly open now.

"A Green Beret. He's got medals. You hear what I'm talkin'?"

"Yeah, I hear ya, but it ain't makin' no sense."

"How much wine you been drinkin'?"

"Not enough to put up with you." Ghanna started to take another swallow.

Josh held Ghanna's hand back. "Not now, Ghanna. I need ya to listen up. Like I say, it's important."

Ghanna replaced the cork in the wine bottle with a heavy sigh. "Sometimes you ask too much of ole Ghanna. . . . I'm listenin'."

"Green Berets are real strong superathletes, man. They're great at close combat and sharpshooting. We'd all be safer with the doc on our side. If we can draw out The Oxman, get him alone somewhere, Doc Pannell could nab him easy. The doc would know what to do if somethin' goes wrong. Believe me, he ain't the type to panic in emergencies."

"Yeah, but how we get Doc Pannell interested? How we know he won't squeal on us instead of helpin'?"

"He's hated The Oxman for years. He's sick of fixin' all the bones The Oxman breaks."

"Any way you could see how he feel about helpin' us bring The Oxman down?"

"I could ask him. Back when I was first working nights with him, we talked, had some cheeseburgers. You know . . . when the ER was kinda quiet."

"What he say?"

"He fought in Desert Storm with the Green Berets. Said he had medals, but he don't like to talk about it much. I know he's always workin' out at the gym."

"Yeah, Josh, but somethin' made him give up bein' a Green Beret if he was so good at it."

"As I recall, he said his war experience made him wanna go to school an' become a doc."

"He don't sound like our man to me, Josh. Maybe he's in great shape an' knows what he's doin', and he's a good shot an' all, but sounds like he too damn honest."

"Yeah, but he ain't no Boy Scout. Him and me almost even—we got enough on each other 'cause he's paid us for getting patients. Ain't ethical."

Ghanna chuckled. "Nope, it ain't. Think he would do it?"

"Maybe. I'll try to catch up to him tomorrow."

"Okay. Eat some more cheeseburgers with him. See what you can learn."

"I'll try to persuade him to have a meeting with you and me and Miano Tse."

"Okay, cool," Ghanna said.

Chapter 11

"**W**HAT CAN YOU TELL ME about this patient?" Dr. Pannell asked as he began examining a new patient on the last Saturday night of July.

"Found him over against a fence near the interstate," answered Patrolman Cairnly. "No trace of tire tracks or anything. We brought him to you as fast as we could. Whew," he added, taking off his cap. "The A/C in here feels good. Hotter'n hell out there."

"Any ID?" Dr. Pannell asked. "You ever see him before?"

"No, I'm new to the force. Like I say, there's nothing, nothing but grass stains and blood. The detectives want to talk to him once he comes around."

"Leave a phone number at the front desk. I'll call you once I examine him and feel it's okay for him to talk."

"Okay. Thanks, Doctor," the policeman said on his way out.

"Feels like a cracked rib on the left. Breathing okay. No punctured lung. Broken nose. Probably a concussion. This little guy is lucky," Dr. Pannell noted to Étoile as he cleaned up the patient.

The injured man groaned and began to stir. "Get the fuck off me," he muttered.

"It's okay, pal. Nurse Étoile and I are just trying to bandage your side here. Who did this to you?"

"The Oxman. Who else?"

"We haven't seen any of The Oxman's victims in a few weeks. Why's he mad at you?"

"He's pissed off because business is way down. I didn't bring in the cash he was lookin' for. He had a fit, took it out on me."

"The Oxman's got fewer customers now because his dealers were selling bad stuff. It killed at least six people—and probably more who never got to our ER."

"Yeah, but he don't care. 'Lucien,' he say, 'you got a territory to work. Get busy.' My old customers weren't around. Couldn't find no new ones. Almost got arrested over by the schoolyard. The cash I brought in this week was pitiful, but The Oxman thought I'd stolen most of it."

"Lucien, you got anyone we should call?" Dr. Pannell asked.

"Nah. My old lady split a long time ago."

"You're lucky he didn't kill you."

"I might as well be dead. Get the whole thing over with. If I don't do what he say, he'll kill me anyway."

"Would you be willing to tell all this to the police?"

"What've I got to lose? I'm already a dead man."

"Think it over before you make any decision," Dr. Pannell advised him. "We can help you heal and maybe even make it possible for you to have a better life."

Dr. Pannell asked Josh to take Lucien to a private room and wait there until a hospital security guard arrived. "I'll send Alvarez if he's still on duty."

A few minutes later, Alvarez arrived at Lucien's room. "Glad you could come, Al," said Josh. "You see what The Oxman did to his own dealer?"

"Yeah. The Oxman is a total psycho. Oughtta be locked up in a padded cell forever," Alvarez declared.

Josh stepped into the hall and signaled to Alvarez to join him. "That might just happen," he said softly. "We gotta get him off our streets. I'm gonna ask Doc Pannell to help us."

Alvarez shook Josh's hand. "Let me know if I can help."

When Josh returned to the ER, he beckoned to Dr. Pannell. "Hey, Josh. What's up?"

Josh murmured his suggestion that they meet in the supply closet in a few minutes. As usual, they arrived individually after checking to make sure the coast was clear and walked out carrying a few supplies, which they either used in their work or returned.

Once the door was shut, Josh said, "Lucien ain't the only one on The Oxman's list. Miano Tse, too—and what she ever done to him?" Pacing with agitation, he told Dr. Pannell about Miano Tse's close call on River Road earlier that week. "They tried to force her to back up her car into the rapids!"

Dr. Pannell's eyes narrowed. "She get hurt?" he asked.

"No. She didn't panic, got away."

"Thank God. She call 911?"

"Of course," said Josh. "The cops came. Also a detective—he gave her his card and wrote some notes."

"Good. Now it's a matter on record."

"What good is that?" demanded Josh, clenching his fists. "The cops will just put the case report in a shredder. Doc, we can't take The Oxman no more. Cops ain't doin' nothin'! We gotta bring him down ourselves. *Now!*"

Dr. Pannell heard the desperation and pent-up fury in Josh's voice. "I agree, Josh. This whole city's had enough of The Oxman. I will help you lock him up. That's a promise. But I'm warning you: we'll have to work with the police."

Josh stiffened slightly and took a step backward.

"I know you'd rather not," continued Dr. Pannell calmly, "but you know how The Oxman operates. He plans everything and gives the orders, enforces them with an iron hand. But he makes his boys do the dirty work, so even if the cops catch anyone, he still gets away with it."

"Yeah, that's him, all right," said Josh.

"There's never enough evidence to implicate The Oxman directly, especially since his victims are too terrified to testify against him. But now Lucien Walters says he'll testify."

"Really? Man, he's one brave dude."

"Yes. But unless we catch The Oxman red-handed, doing something big, he won't end up in jail. The cops have to be there to see it for themselves so it won't be just our word against The

Oxman's. Only by working together with our friends, our neighbors, *and* the cops will we be able to make a difference. Remember, he's got plenty of cash to bribe witnesses—and cops, too. Maybe I can point out to Detective Mouski that he and his men will be heroes. The city will applaud them if he succeeds in capturing The Oxman. Appealing to Mouski's ego might work for us."

"Yeah. An' let The Oxman bribe a few cops, or else he's gonna think something's going down."

"Good point, Josh."

"I'll do anything you say, Doc. I got a few friends who wanna see him gone. Maybe they'll join us."

"Okay. Actually, there is something important you can do for me. I saw The Oxman once last April, but it was just for a second, after dark, and I didn't get a really good look at his face. You've seen him a number of times, haven't you?"

"Yeah. Wish I never had."

"Could you draw him for me? Like mug shots, face from the front and in profile?"

"Sure! That is totally cool, Doc. I can do it from memory," answered Josh. "Once you see his face up close, you ain't gonna forget it."

During that same hot Saturday night, Royce Barkley lost his cool. He attempted to break into Dr. Truesort's private lab but was thwarted when he saw Ian's car in the parking lot. *Somebody working even on a Saturday?* So Royce parked nearby and waited, then followed Ian and Abby when they drove away—but Ian led him on a crazy chase, and finally Royce lost track of their car in the city's worst neighborhood. Gangs of young men sauntered down the sidewalks, past the boarded-up windows and empty lots filled with litter and weeds. *Ian must have figured out I was following him. Better call the boss and admit my failure. Damn! He won't want to hear about this.*

But Royce was afraid it wasn't safe to pull over and make the call. He did manage to leave a voice mail message while waiting at a red light. Even then, a drunk wove his way toward the car, demanding money, before Royce could speed off.

Christ, thought Royce. *Why'd I ever agree to do this? But the money's spent. Too late to get out of it now.*

—√√—∘

"Officers, we put him in a private room. Thought it was safest. Got our own security guard there until you get one of your people over here. You're kind of slow, aren't you? He came in last night around ten. It's already Sunday afternoon," Dr. Pannell pointed out.

Chief Detective Mouski, a balding, muscular barrel of a man, raised his eyebrows. "Youse guys at the ER ain't the only ones with busy Saturday nights, Doc," he claimed.

Dr. Pannell shrugged in reply and turned toward his patient.

"Lucien Walters, meet Patrolman Cairnly and Chief Detective Mouski." Lucien mincingly shook the two men's hands from his hospital bed.

"Patrolman Cairnly was the one who found you, Lucien." The policeman nodded politely.

"Thanks, man," said Lucien.

"I told these two gentlemen you wanted to talk, Lucien," continued Dr. Pannell, "but I'm not releasing you until they can assure me of your welfare. There's a hospital security guard outside your door as we speak."

"That guard isn't necessary, Doctor," said Chief Detective Mouski.

"This is my patient. It is my duty and the hospital's duty to protect him while he is receiving our care. Nothing you decide will interfere with that." Dr. Pannell stepped to the back of the room and slumped into the chair usually used by visitors.

"Don't you have some other emergencies?" Chief Detective Mouski asked him.

"Not at the moment. The ER staff knows where to find me," Dr. Pannell said as his eyes closed. He hummed softly to himself.

Giving up any hope of ridding themselves of Dr. Pannell, Chief Detective Mouski and Patrolman Cairnly listened to Lucien's history: years of drug use starting with marijuana at ten and escalating to smoking crack cocaine and swallowing ecstasy tablets, along with alcohol abuse and dealing in drugs. Patrolman Cairnly stood at the foot of the bed and took notes, his long, thin frame towering over everyone else in the room.

"You ever try to come clean? Go to a clinic?" Chief Detective Mouski asked.

"Yeah. I told myself many times I'm goin' clean. Lucien Walters won't deal or use anymore. But I always gave in to my habit. Couldn't resist usin' when I was dealin'. And The Oxman's kept beatin' the shit outta me if I didn't keep bringin' in enough cash. He and his boys were cruel, broke my nose more than once, burned me with cigarette butts. Told me they would kill me if I tried to run."

"So how come you're talking now?" Chief Detective Mouski asked.

"Just look at me!" wailed Lucien, fighting back tears. "This beating was the worst yet. My life is a living hell—I might as well jump off the bridge. I *hate* The Oxman! I can help you track him down and catch him, but I need protection, rehab, and a plane ticket outta here."

Dr. Pannell's eyes opened a slit. "Can you help him? He needs to get out of this quagmire you call a city."

"Thought you were asleep, man," Patrolman Cairnly said.

"My eyes were closed, but my ears were open," Dr. Pannell answered him.

"You seem really interested in Lucien. Why?" Chief Detective Mouski asked.

"I'm tired of seeing people victimized in my own country, sick of trying to patch them up. Lucien was one of the few dealers The Oxman had left. He got beaten because your force swept through and caught a lot of dealers and their customers. It was right after the druggies got bad stuff. Remember at the time you said you got everyone. You didn't. Now it's time to finish the job. Bring down The Oxman himself."

"And I suppose you know how," Chief Detective Mouski said.

"I've given it some thought. How about I meet with you and your chief of police tomorrow or the next day?" Dr. Pannell said. "I hear my page. Let me know when your chief's available." Dr. Pannell left as the city policeman took the hospital guard's place. "Thanks, Alvarez. Guess we got their attention." They walked back to the emergency room together.

"How was your weekend, Fred?" Cory asked on Monday morning.

"Okay. Spent most of the time in the pool. Did you go upstate to see how Vincent's doing?"

"Yeah. His health looks good. But he's itching to get back to Jersey even though he's been playing most weekends at local pubs upstate. To sum it up, he is just plain homesick."

"I can't bring him back, Cory. It's not safe." Fred stood up to leave.

"That's right, and it's getting worse all the time." Fred turned around. "Sit down, Fred. Let me explain."

Fred sat down slowly, watching the solemn look on Cory's face.

"Abby and Ian came to the lab late Saturday afternoon," said Cory. "Abby had some experiments that needed to be checked. They stayed until about nine fifteen. Someone must have been stalking them, because when they left, they were followed."

"Oh my God. What happened?"

"Fortunately Ian knows the city and was able to shake off the driver. It was dark. Abby couldn't read the license plate, but she thought the car was a light-colored sedan, possibly a Lexus, and the driver was a man."

Fred shook his head. "Last week it was Miano Tse by the river; now this. What else can happen, Cory?"

"Whatever it is, it won't be good. You know The Oxman's behind it all."

"I'm afraid you're right. Look—I have to get to the OR now. I should be back around three. I'd like all of us to discuss these events then. We have to warn our staff to be extremely careful—tell them about The Oxman and insist that they must be alert to anything unusual. Get Pannell to join us if he's available."

"I'll get Martha to inform them in person. Be careful," Cory cautioned.

"I'll be alert. Don't worry."

—∿|∿o

Martha phoned every one of Fred's staff to come to his private lab at three thirty for an important meeting. The only message she left was a request for the recipient to call her back ASAP.

By three forty-five Fred and his staff were gathered in the main lab. Bob arrived at four, apologizing for his tardiness. Fred asked Miano Tse to discuss her entrapment on the way home from work. Next Abby and Ian described the car chase through the city they'd been subjected to on Saturday night.

Bob said that Miano Tse's encounter was certainly The Oxman's doing. He wasn't certain Abby and Ian's was, but it definitely seemed like it. He told the group, "I will be working with the local police to help apprehend this individual. We will need all your help. If you see anything suspicious, call 911 like Miano Tse did. I will ask the police chief to assign extra patrols here while we plan how to capture this criminal."

"Will you alert Security at the hospital too, Bob?" Martha asked. Her subdued tone of voice did not reveal the full extent of her fear.

"Yes, Martha, definitely," answered Bob. "I've discussed the problem with Alvarez Delgado. He is working with us and has assured me he will be discreet. This is a delicate matter. If at any time you feel uneasy and would like an escort, let me or Alvarez know. You know Alvarez, don't you?"

"Yes, I've seen him around the hospital."

Ian said, "Bob, I can't get over this. I feel kind of like the time I was driving across the San Francisco–Oakland Bridge during an earthquake. If we weren't so far along with our research, Abby and I would quit," he claimed.

"How can we protect ourselves?" Abby asked. "Our condo has minimal security—just an electronic system, but no doorman or anything."

"I suggest that you discuss your personal safety with Alvarez. He may have a colleague who could help."

"Good idea. Thanks," said Ian.

"Martha," said Fred, "would you please ask our security company to reassess the protection to my private lab? Also ask Alvarez to do a walk-through to check our safety. I will pay him, of course," Fred said.

"Certainly," Martha said.

"In addition to being alert to unusual circumstances," said Bob, "we can change our habits. For example, vary your schedules and routines so you have no set pattern. Although that didn't help Miano Tse, in general it can be a good strategy."

"I realize," Fred added, "that some of you might not know why we have been protecting Vincent, our patient. It's because this criminal, commonly called The Oxman, has been a threat to him."

Bob continued, "Josh, who's one of my assistants in the ER, has had some recent encounters with The Oxman. Josh will be drawing up-to-date portraits of him from memory for the use of the police. Miano Tse, could you bring copies here when Josh has them ready?"

"Certainly," Miano Tse agreed.

"All of you should take a good look at the drawings for your own safety so that you can recognize The Oxman if you need to—but please keep the drawings hidden. As odd as it sounds, anyone who sees the drawings—a deliveryman, whoever—might pass that information on to The Oxman, and our mission would be compromised," said Bob.

"Thanks for your time," said Fred. "Give me a call if you have any questions. Meeting adjourned."

After the others had left, Bob closed the door again and asked, "Fred, Cory, may I have a word?"

"Sure," answered Fred. Cory nodded.

"We're planning a sting to capture and incriminate The Oxman," Bob began. "The police are involved. So are some people from the neighborhood, including Josh and Miano Tse. We need an out-of-the-way place to stage it. It would be great if we could use your outdoor property, Fred. Since The Oxman tried to kidnap Vincent before, we think he'd try it again if—"

"*What?*" roared Fred. "Are you crazy? *No way* will I let Vincent be used as bait for The Oxman. It's too dangerous!"

"Hold on, Fred—hear me out," said Bob. "We're planning to get someone to *impersonate* Vincent. Probably some cop."

"Oh. That's different," Fred conceded, "but I don't want anyone to get hurt. . . ."

"I understand your concern, Fred," Bob responded, "but we sure as hell need to do *something* about The Oxman, and this is the best plan anyone's come up with yet. He's notorious for evading the cops."

"At this point," added Cory, "The Oxman's doing more than cramping our style. He's threatening the safety of every single one of us, not to mention the success of your research. You realize that, don't you, Fred?"

Fred grunted.

Bob continued, "There will be plainclothes police and detectives, both men and women, to help make sure that everything goes as smoothly as possible. We haven't worked out the details, but you will be consulted every step of the way."

Fred sighed. "Well, if The Oxman were behind bars, all of our lives would be a lot safer and easier."

"Amen to that," said Cory.

"All right," said Fred. "As long as every safety precaution is taken, I will allow you to use the grounds."

Bob shook Fred's hand. "Thanks, Fred," said Bob.

"Great," said Cory. "Bob, let me know if I can help in any way."

Dr. Pannell drove over to police headquarters Tuesday morning on his day off. Patrolman Cairnly had called. Chief Detective Mouski was giving a briefing, and Patrolman Cairnly thought Dr. Pannell would like to be there.

As he drove, Dr. Pannell kept thinking about the preceding Sunday afternoon, two days ago, when he had invited Josh, Miano Tse, and Ghanna to his apartment. Seated comfortably around his dining-room table, munching on fresh strawberries, grapes, sliced nectarines, and mixed nuts, the four of them had discussed how best to trap The Oxman. They'd also talked about which volunteers from the neighborhood would be best at which jobs. Dr. Pannell smiled as he remembered Ghanna's remark that they were lucky *nobody* liked The Oxman and Miano Tse's crisp response: "That's because he gives everyone a tsunami headache."

When Dr. Pannell drove into the municipal complex, he was given a convenient parking space and immediately escorted by Patrolman Cairnly to the conference room.

There Chief Detective Mouski gave a PowerPoint presentation. First were Josh's sketches of The Oxman, which the police found invaluable. "We've heard about this guy for years," said Mouski, "and we had some old pictures of him, but we knew they were out of date. These sketches are great. Where'd ya get 'em, Dr. Pannell? You sure they're accurate?"

"I got them from a local guy who's been roughed up by The Oxman—and who happens to be great at drawing likenesses. Too bad The Oxman didn't realize that," Bob added with a chuckle. "And yeah, I'm sure they're accurate, because I've seen his drawings of people I know."

"Good, good," said Mouski. "We're also fortunate to have a new informant, one of The Oxman's former dealers, who's given us plenty of useful info. Like, The Oxman has an apartment over a fabric store by the farmers' market. Drives a pickup truck and a yellow Corvette. Usually works alone and uses a silencer on his gun."

"If we know where The Oxman lives, how come we don't just go there and arrest him?" asked Patrolman Cairnly.

"Ain't that simple," answered Mouski. "He's got lookouts and bodyguards posted all around his place. The Oxman would stay away for months if they warn him his place is being watched. He steals trucks at random and sleeps somewhere different every night, never at home. His apartment only gets used during the day.

Plus, he's slippery, good at covering his tracks so crimes don't get traced back to him. Naaaah, we gotta catch him in the act so we have clear evidence against him. This time we have a good strategy for enticing and trapping him."

Next Mouski showed satellite photos of the Truesorts' property and maps of the surrounding area, downloaded from the Internet. "Nice place they got over there. Real nice," he said.

Bob stepped in to point out the positions of the stone wall, gardens, potting shed, veranda, pool and patio around it, and the stand of trees at the riverbank. "To the south of the Truesorts' property, just beyond the side wall here, is a dirt road. Beyond that are these woods. North of the property is a rocky field with this path winding through it. Both the dirt road and the path go all the way from Sherwood Boulevard down to the river. There's a perpendicular path down here, along the riverbank. You can't see the paths very well on the aerial photos because of tree cover. The rapids are just a little ways downstream."

Then Mouski continued, "Occasionally the Truesorts give parties that include live music. Here is what I propose, youse guys. We'll lure The Oxman to the Truesorts' backyard by letting him know, through a known snitch, that Vincent Monique will be playing guitar by the river during one of these parties. The guitar player will actually be one of youse, though."

"Who the hell is Vincent Monique?" asked one cop.

"Yeah, what's so special about this guitar player, anyway?" asked another.

"He's a patient who's very important to Dr. Truesort's life-saving research," Chief Detective Mouski answered. "The Oxman has tried to kidnap him before, probably for blackmail purposes, and the doctors want to make sure he stays safe." There were several nods of comprehension.

"So we stage this fake party for him," Mouski explained. "Detectives and plainclothes police, both men and women, will pose as party guests. Youse get to dress up nice. We'll have to rent some upmarket cars, so you'll look like the kinda guests the Truesorts would invite. Our informant says The Oxman is cruel to animals, so the Truesorts' Doberman is being put in the kennel for his own safety. All alarms will be off around the house. Then we put a plainclothesman in position, down here near the river, with a guitar. Any of youse play guitar or wanna just sit with one?"

Apparently there were no budding musicians on the force.

Chief Detective Mouski frowned, then continued to point at the diagrams. "The river is dangerous here—strong current just upstream from the rapids—but Cairnly and I will be hidden near the river just in case The Oxman decides to invade from there. He's far more likely to come over the high stone wall. Youse can see that the wall is hundreds of yards long, surrounding the property on three sides. We got no idea where he might breach the wall, so we gotta all be alert. But once he's in the backyard, it's a safe bet that The Oxman will try to kidnap the plainclothesman. It's no secret that he may *threaten* to kill the hostage, but he won't actually *do* it. Extortion is the name of the game."

"You really think The Oxman is going to grab some guitar player during a party, right in front of everyone?" asked a cop.

"I hear this egotist would go up against the Eighty-second Airborne single-handed if he had a chance," Dr. Pannell said. "He craves recognition; he's an attention-starved show-off."

Mouski grinned. "Uh-huh. We're taking special precautions. We'll have a psychiatrist, Dr. Lexi Bakov here, an expert in negotiating with psychopathic personalities. Also, sharpshooters will be across the lawn behind the potting shed, hidden by these here bushes, as a last resort in case things get out of hand. So when The Oxman tries to grab the guitar player, we nab The Oxman instead, red-handed. Give this creep a big surprise and throw him behind bars at last." Mouski grinned at the prospect. "Now youse got the whole picture. One more time: we need a volunteer guitar player . . . anyone?"

No one spoke. No one moved.

The chief detective scowled. "Aw, c'mon, youse guys. What are ya, a bunch of chicken-hearted wimps?"

More silence.

Finally one cop said what they were all thinking: "Chief, you're talkin' about a suicide mission. We all got girlfriends or wives—some of us got kids. Ain't there some other way to catch this guy?"

"Nobody's thought of one yet," growled Mouski. "Don't worry, I'll speak to one of youse later, so ya better watch your step."

"Excuse me, Chief. One comment if I may," said Dr. Bakov. "From the few behaviors of The Oxman you've described, it appears that he is a very troubled individual whose childhood was a nightmare. People who have been abused as children frequently abuse animals and continue that behavior into adulthood. If he can be captured alive, perhaps there may be some hope of rehabilitation with lengthy treatment, but—as you are clearly already aware—he is extremely dangerous."

"Thanks for that insight, Doctor," Chief Detective Mouski said, and added a few final comments. "If for some reason something goes wrong and I say stop, I mean *everyone stop,* cease and desist from whatever you're doing, and return to your assigned places immediately. That means your team too, Dr. Pannell. And by the way, Doc, don't wear your green beret. Any questions?"

"No questions," Dr. Pannell responded. "Just want to explain to your force that I have some local folks who are going to be a part of this also, serving as lookouts over the mansion and its grounds as well as the approaches to them. They live in The Oxman's neighborhood, know him by sight, and have suffered from his atrocities, so they're anxious to help you get him off the street. Principal among them are a former drug user and dealer, the girlfriend of a former user, an elderly ex-convict, a homeless woman, and a security guard. We are using the practical approach to this sting. 'It takes a thief to know a thief.'"

Annoyed by the interruption, Chief Detective Mouski said, "Civilians involved? Dunno about that, Doc. You and me will discuss that later." Then he repeated, "Any questions?"

"Yeah. What if it rains?" a plainclothesman asked.

"We postpone it. So I'll keep checking the weather forecasts and choose a nice clear evening. I'll stay in contact with all of youse. You'll get only a couple hours' notice."

―⌁⌁―

Monday evening after their supper, Asunta and Ramiero left Alvarez with the dishes to go shopping. Ramiero's red sneakers were worn out, and his red shirt was too small. He took the printed bus schedule from the kitchen counter to check the time the city bus would stop at the corner. Alvarez gave him a hug. "Didn't know you could read the bus schedule, Ramiero. You are a smart boy."

Ramiero found that their bus would arrive in ten minutes, so he called to his mother to hurry. She was changing her dress and putting on her high-heeled shoes.

Asunta picked up her handbag, kissed Alvarez good-bye, and took Ramiero's hand. The two of them left the apartment. Asunta and Ramiero were walking along the sidewalk toward the bus shelter when—

A muddy black pickup truck veered onto the sidewalk and blocked their way. Several pedestrians screamed and bolted out of the truck's path.

Asunta recognized the driver immediately. The Oxman laughed at her as he saw fear spread over her face.

She grabbed Ramiero's shoulders and turned him around. "Run, Ramiero! Run home, *fast,* and stay there!" she yelled as she bent down to take off her shoes. "Send your papa. I'll be right behind you." *Now I can run faster. If that evil man gets too close, I'll shove these heels into his eyes.*

"Yeah, send your little bastard home," The Oxman called. "Hey, harlot, how about you an' me havin' some fun tonight?"

The group of about twenty bus riders and other pedestrians were incensed by The Oxman's lewd comments. Several Good Samaritans, mostly men on the way home from their shift at Hughler Hospital, ran behind Asunta to protect her and Ramiero.

The Oxman shifted gears and began driving up the sidewalk. "You'll have to wait, ladies," he hollered. "It's Asunta I want tonight."

The bus riders shouted and shook their fists at The Oxman as they fled. A couple of teenage boys barred his way to Asunta and themselves by throwing garbage pails and a discarded tricycle in his path. When his muddy black truck stalled with two wheels in the gutter, The Oxman let out a string of curses. But, by rocking the truck back and forth, he regained the street and sped away.

Meanwhile, Ramiero had run back toward the apartment,

wailing, "Papa, Papa! The bad man drove his truck on the sidewalk by the bus stop! Mama—"

Alvarez heard the noise through the open window. Alarmed, he ran down the steps two at a time and sprinted past Ramiero toward the corner. "Get into the apartment, Ramiero," Alvarez called back to his son. "I'll bring your mama home."

By the time Alvarez arrived at the bus stop, The Oxman had driven off. The crowd of bus riders had returned to the corner. Asunta sat in the bus shelter to put on her shoes. She was brushing tears from her cheek when she said, "Thanks for your bravery, all of you. You saved me and my son from a hateful man."

Alvarez asked if any of the bus riders had seen the driver of the truck. No one answered him. He put his arm around Asunta, and they returned to their apartment.

Within ten minutes, people at the bus stop weren't talking about The Oxman anymore. They only complained that the bus was late, as usual.

That night Ramiero sat next to his mother on the sofa with his head on her shoulder. He stayed there until his bedtime.

Once Ramiero was asleep, Asunta and Alvarez sat at the kitchen table sipping glasses of wine. "You know, Al, it definitely was The Oxman again. What can we do? I know this apartment is close to your work, which means you don't have to spend time and money on commuting. . . ."

"You want to move, Asunta?"

"Yes, yes, I do. This neighborhood is not good for Ramiero or me. It's not safe here."

"You're right, *amor mio.*" Alvarez kissed her. "I need to talk to Ghanna about this, Asunta. I won't be long."

"Ghanna, it's Al. Got a minute?"

"Course. C'mon in."

Ghanna watched Alvarez pull his gun out of its holster and repeatedly twirl and aim it at the bed, the chair, and the door. "You okay, man?" Ghanna asked cautiously.

"Yeah." Alvarez paused, stared at the gun, then put it back into the holster.

Ghanna sighed with relief.

"Sorry I scared ya, Ghanna. I was shaken."

"You ain't actin' like yourself tonight, Al. What's wrong, man?"

"I wanna help you take down The Oxman. He tried to attack Asunta this evening. Really upset Ramiero, too."

"*What?* I didn't hear nothin'. Musta been when I was at Lefty's, watchin' the ball game. Some guys had a little too much beer and started to sing."

"It was over by the bus stop. He drove after her on the sidewalk."

"She all right?"

"Yeah, fortunately the bus riders and some fellas from the hospital threw garbage pails and stuff in his way. . . . I don't even wanna think about what could've happened."

"You call the cops?" asked Ghanna.

"No. The Oxman had driven away. By the time the police could've gotten there, all the witnesses on the sidewalk would have hopped onto the bus or walked away. You know, I've never been so angry. I actually wanted to beat the guy up, even though I know he must have some mental issues to be how he is."

"I know what ya mean," said Ghanna. "Just about everyone wanna smash his head in, but good thing you didn't try it. So you wanna help us with the sting?"

"Yeah. Josh mentioned some of you were gonna trap The Oxman, hand him over to the cops. What can I do to help the most?"

"We sure could use your help for this, but it's mighty danger-ous. We need someone to play the guitar like Vincent. Josh heard from Doc Pannell that no cop wants the job. Them cops all too scared of The Oxman."

"I'm not," declared Alvarez. "He depends on people being scared when they see him, but he's just a big bully is all. After what he did to Asunta and Ramiero tonight, I'm The Oxman's sworn enemy, Ghanna. He's met his match."

"What if the sting fail an' he recognize you afterward?"

"Stop, Ghanna. I know what I'm doing."

But Ghanna continued, "You be riskin' your life, man! You sure you wanna do that? Doc Pannell and others be there lookin' out for ya, cops too, but still . . . you got a fine wife an' son an' all."

"I'll risk it. Disguise myself. I'll ask Vincent if I can wear the hat and other clothes he wears for a performance; I think we're about the same size. Ghanna, we gotta get rid of The Oxman, or nobody's safe anyway. He belongs in an asylum, not on our city streets. I know it's the right thing to do. I'm more afraid of losing control, attacking him in a rage the next time I see him, if he does stay here. Ya know what I mean?"

Ghanna shook Alvarez's hand. "Thanks, Al my man. Everyone doin' this here sting will be meetin' at Dr. Truesort's place Saturday evening, workin' out what they'll do."

"Good. I'll go with you, Ghanna. See ya Saturday," Alvarez said, and he went upstairs to his family.

Saturday evening around five o'clock, Josh drove his Ford up Fred's circular driveway, parked, and burst out laughing. "Man, check *out* this place! Don't it just figure Doc Truesort would have this kind of house?"

"Prob'ly the first time an old car was ever parked here," said Ghanna. "You be lucky if they don't tow it away," he added. Josh's two other passengers, Sally and Alvarez, laughed too before getting out of the car.

Cory arrived next, bringing Miano Tse, Abby, and Ian in his station wagon. Ian had offered to be a lookout, as well as Miano Tse, whose car was still being repaired.

Dr. Pannell brought Lucien. He was doing well in rehab and was eager to play a part in the sting operation since he had suffered severely from the beating The Oxman had given him.

Everyone involved in the sting from the neighborhood or from the research project had arrived. Alvarez told the group, "Asunta still shudders when she's reminded of her encounters with The Oxman."

Dr. Truesort shook their hands as they came in. Ingrid was on tour with her church choir—which Fred thought was just as well.

His cook played hostess and led them to the buffet in the dining room. To the surprise of nearly everyone, Vincent greeted them there with hugs and thank-yous for their brave decision to go after The Oxman. "It'll let me move back here a free man," he said. Josh, Miano Tse, and Ghanna were delighted to see him again. Vincent introduced himself to Abby, Ian, and Lucien, who had never met him in person.

Vincent thanked Alvarez for coming. "I think I saw you once or twice when I was in Ghanna's basement."

"Yeah. You looked a lot different then," Alvarez responded, smiling and shaking Vincent's hand. "Good to see you so healthy."

Fred explained, "Cory has seen Vincent regularly this summer. Vincent was eager to help with the sting, and Cory thought he should be given the chance. I finally agreed as long as Vincent promised to stay in the house out of sight while he is here, especially during the sting. We can't be too cautious."

So Vincent and Lucien stayed indoors, but Fred escorted everyone else around the grounds and the areas just beyond them, noting the topographical features important to their plans. While most people were admiring the beautiful flowers, exploring the dirt road and path down to the river, or watching the water rush by, Josh was drawing schematics on graph paper, focusing on features invisible on Google Maps' aerial view, such as the pathways obscured by treetops above.

Like Josh, Bob continued his preparation for the sting. He looked carefully at the sturdiness of the stone wall, then checked the height of the riverbank and the stand of trees in front of it. He looked over the potting shed to see what protection it would provide as he imagined how the sting would progress.

After the group had taken a thorough look at the grounds, Fred asked them to gather in the living room. The room was graciously appointed with sectional sofas, two comfortable Eames chairs, and soft indirect lighting. An illuminated glass case displayed a collection of Hummel figurines. The cook had set out a tempting selection of after-dinner mints, chocolates, and homemade butter cookies, along with decanters of coffee and hot water, plus a variety of teas.

There they planned the sting in detail and exactly who would be responsible for what. Dr. Pannell, Lucien, and Vincent took charge of planning where all the lookouts would be stationed, writing their names on a large map. Bob suggested that Vincent should be stationed on the third floor of the mansion and Lucien on the first floor, warning both of them to stay out of sight.

"But the first floor has no windows higher than the stone wall," Lucien complained.

"You're right," Dr. Pannell admitted. "Visibility would be limited."

"I wanna go upstairs, where I can see *everything*, and help Vincent," Lucien insisted.

Dr. Pannell chuckled at Lucien's determination. "Can you go up all those stairs?" Dr. Pannell asked.

"Sure," Lucien said.

"There are landings as you go up. Use them. And you won't try to throw something at The Oxman in revenge?" Dr. Pannell added.

"I promise, Doc. I won't try nothin'."

Bob told everyone, "The police will be helping us. They have their assigned positions. You each have your assignment with alternative options, in case the situation varies from what we anticipate. So far no policeman has agreed to impersonate Vincent, but Chief Detective Mouski will assign someone shortly."

Ghanna stood up with his hand on Alvarez's shoulder. "I got good news for ya, Doc. Al, my friend here, says he gonna volunteer."

Alvarez stood up to hoorays, whistles, handshakes, and high fives. Once his friends were calmer, Alvarez told them what had happened at the bus stop Monday evening.

Bob shook Alvarez's hand firmly. "Sometimes anger can fuel courage," he said. "I'll be watching your back." Then he turned to the others and continued, "Josh has drawn some portraits of The Oxman from memory, in case any of you need to know what he looks like." Josh opened his portfolio, and a portrait of Miano Tse fell out, to the group's amusement.

"No, that's not The Oxman," Josh protested. "That's my girl-friend, Miano Tse here." Everyone clapped.

Josh asked Miano Tse to hold up the portrait. Everyone admired the likeness, and Ian commented, "It looks just like her."

Bob pointed out to the group, "Miano Tse immigrated from China to your neighborhood, and now she works in Dr. Truesort's lab!" There was another round of applause.

"Okay, let me show you The Oxman. The police already have copies of these." Josh passed around the various views of The Oxman. Some of the people stared intently, trying to memorize his features. Others, like Sally, shook their heads. "What makes him so mean?" she murmured to herself.

Abby and Ian heard her. Ian tapped Sally on the shoulder. "We were wondering the same thing."

Sally smiled at them both, shrugging. "Who knows?" she asked sadly. "But I've run into The Oxman many times—wish I never had! And I can tell ya this: these here portraits are just as true to life as the one of Miano Tse. Josh draws really good."

Cory spoke to the group: "Dr. Truesort is helping us in a true community effort—not only with his medical research, but also by sharing his home to help rid our city of a menacing criminal." The group stood up to applaud Fred. Cory shook his hand. Fred smiled, pleased.

─────ᐱᑊᐱ─°─────

It was Monday, August 13, and the steamy, humid heat common to New Jersey had persisted for the two weeks since Lucien Walters had arrived at the emergency room. In Chief Detective Mouski's office, the air conditioner wheezed and snorted out cool air, dripping condensation over the windowsill onto a soggy towel beneath. Some of the drips had actually washed dirt off the gray-green walls. Chief Detective Mouski puffed on his cigar in blatant defiance under the NO SMOKING sign. Occasionally he banged his fist on the air conditioner lodged in the window behind him in a vain attempt to lower the room temperature. "Glad you could come down, Doc," he said. "Sorry this damn thing don't work too good. What we really need is a cold beer. Jack, our chief of police, couldn't make it."

Dr. Pannell wiped the sweat off his forehead with his handkerchief. He had left the air-conditioned hospital that afternoon after his shift to confer with the chief detective.

"Cold water would do right about now," said Bob. He walked over to the cooler without saying a word, poured two cups of cold water, and handed one to Chief Detective Mouski. "Drink this—doctor's orders—and put out the cigar."

Startled, the detective stared at him for a moment and then did as he was told. "I'm used to giving the orders around here," he grumbled.

Dr. Pannell did not acknowledge the comment. "We have everything in place. My team is ready to go—they even rehearsed. Don't worry about using any of your people for the guitar player; we have a volunteer."

The detective looked up, amazed. "You gotta be kidding. Which is he, a cartoon superhero or an idiot?"

"He's a brave man with good reasons to do what he's doing," answered Bob sternly.

Mouski shrugged. "Well, I, uh . . . wish him the best," he said.

"Me too," said Bob. "We should be ready to move this week. Weather report looks pretty good. Is one of your detectives tailing The Oxman?"

"Yeah. Two, in fact—I put a man and a woman on it. She is excellent. Figured The Oxman wouldn't suspect her. Your patient was right. He sleeps in different trucks, mostly near the river. But I've been thinking: I don't know how the chief is gonna take to this."

"What do you mean?" said Dr. Pannell. "Thought it was all settled. You scared or something?"

The detective glared at him. "Course not! Just, it ain't customary to work with civilians like this," said Chief Detective Mouski.

"You use snitches all the time. You're probably making the

best possible use of concerned citizens this time. These snitches know what they're doing. We want this guy off the streets as much as you do."

"Yeah, well, just don't let anyone get hurt," said the detective, frowning. "Not one. Civilians get hurt, it'll be my ass in the sling, not yours."

"Like I say," Dr. Pannell assured him, "they know what they're doing. On that day they will be preparing from four o'clock on. You've already explained everything to your plainclothes people?"

Chief Detective Mouski paused and looked at Bob for a moment before answering, "Yeah. The timing is gonna be critical. My officers will hang out in the blocks nearby so they can get to their posts at the Truesorts' quickly once they get the word. They'll be inconspicuous, not gathered all in one place."

"Good," said Bob. "When The Oxman makes his move, I'll call you as he progresses. We have some lookouts on likely routes to the mansion."

"Okay. And if The Oxman is just taking a truck to the park or up to the mountain or down by the river for the night, we'll know that from the two detectives I've got tailing him. But if I call it off, you gotta stop. Like I told my team, you must cease and desist, go back to your assigned positions. *I'm* the chief detective. In this sting operation you obey *my* orders."

"Fair enough," Dr. Pannell agreed. "I have a good team with excellent leaders, including Lars, Miano Tse, Ghanna, and Alvarez. The whole team met Saturday at Dr. Truesort's and went over our sting plan in detail." (Lars was actually Josh, who didn't want to use his own name.)

"You didn't have to do that, Pannell. My boys know what they're doing," Chief Detective Mouski said.

"Team members have cell phones, hardwired phones, and/ or pagers," Dr. Pannell continued imperturbably. "I gave some of them more than one type of communication device. Here's the phone list. It is confidential."

"Okay. Thanks." The detective folded the list and put it into his pocket. Then he ripped some pages from a department telephone booklet and starred the names and numbers Dr. Pannell's sting participants would need. "Here you go, Doc. There's twenty of us."

"Great! Thanks," said Bob. "And here are some new schematics to supplement the maps and aerial photos you already have. These pathways here, through the woods and along the river, don't show on regular maps at all."

"Okay, good to know."

"I suggest that your plainclothes officers—both men and women—dress formally for this concert or use any disguise that would be appropriate. Do you have enough women so it'll look like a normal party?"

"Yeah, we got that covered okay."

"And did everyone study the sketches of The Oxman?"

"Yeah. My deputy can work all that out. How about a little snort before you go? I got the bottle right here."

"No thanks. See you later this week."

⎯◠⋀⎮⌒◦

The following evening, Bob drove to Fred's house to finalize their plans. Ingrid had returned from her choir tour but was out again, playing bridge. The two doctors sat on the veranda at the back of the house, sipping cocktails and admiring the sunset.

"We have complete cooperation from the police force, Fred. They liked your idea of a concert," Bob said.

"That was Ingrid's suggestion. She's the musician in the family," Fred answered. "I haven't told her the real purpose, of course—just said I've agreed to help the police capture a thief, and she probably hasn't met any of the guests."

"That's all she needs to know," said Bob, taking another sip of his martini.

"The hardest part was explaining to her why we needed a kennel for Chewy. Finally convinced her he might frighten people."

"She should stay inside that night until you feel it's safe," Bob advised.

"At any rate, the food will be served out here on the veranda. It's easy for the caterer to set up since it's near the kitchen, and of course it has a permanent roof."

The doctors stepped down off the veranda, which was surrounded by rosebushes. "My hobby used to be growing roses," Fred explained. "Come on, let's get some exercise. I'll show you some rare species here in my rose garden. The original owner of this house started the collection. This yellow rosebush here is eighty years old."

"It's beautiful. Such fragrant blooms."

"I once did most of the pruning and mulching myself. But lately I've had a landscaper take care of the place." He gave a wry laugh. "Medical research is my passion now."

They walked down to the river. Bob took one more look at all the terrain, including the distance between the potting shed and the river, as well the gardens, the pool, and the shrubs. Fred said, "Mouski dropped by with Josh's diagrams to check everything out. He was impressed; Josh was quite accurate."

"Yes. Josh really has a gift," replied Bob. "Fred, look toward the river. See how the bugs are swarming? That means it's going to rain. The swallows are swooping down low to catch them."

"You sure?" Fred asked.

A crack of lightning snapped down in the woods several miles away. "Don't take my word for it. Swallows never lie." Bob laughed as they ran up the hill to the house, the first heavy drops splotching their shirts.

Chapter 12

BY WEDNESDAY, AUGUST 15, the weather was cooler and ideal for an outdoor concert. There was no threat of rain.

Wednesday, 12:14 p.m.
Dr. Pannell called Josh into the storage room. "Before you go to lunch, Josh, put that telephone chain to work. Mouski just called, and it's a go! You are now Lars. I gave you another name, since you didn't want to use your real one."

Josh took a long, slow breath, jumped up, and touched the ceiling. "I'm on my way, man. We are gonna net us a big one."

3:35 p.m.
Ramiero was bouncing a soccer ball as he walked along the sidewalk to meet Sally. "Ramiero, hold on to your ball when we cross the street," Sally cautioned. She met Ramiero at the corner and kept her hand on his shoulder as they walked across Hughler Street and turned up onto the sidewalk behind the hospital.

"Hold on, Ramiero. I see William ahead. Need to speak to him today. Got any recycling for me?" she called to William.

"A whole bag. People sure are sloppy." William pushed a wheeled trash bin toward Sally. The recyclables were in a black bag balanced on the top.

"I'll be right back, Ramiero."

Ramiero tossed his ball against the hospital wall and waited while Sally shuffled toward William.

"Thanks," Sally said when she caught up to William. "I'm gonna get quite a bit for this here. Pretty soon I'll be doin' as good as Miano Tse. You know she's workin' a party tonight. Earnin' a few dollars to send back home. Doc Truesort, you heard of him, right?"

William managed to fit in an affirmative nod before Sally chattered on.

"He's givin' a concert tonight. Well, not him actually. Vincent is. He's gonna perform. Right down by the river in Doc Truesort's backyard, Miano Tse said. She's lucky. She's gonna hear him. That Vincent sure plays a sweet guitar. You remember, he used to play at Lefty's an' all."

Sally smiled at William, then held up the black drawstring trash bag lumpy with aluminum cans. "Thanks, William. Gotta get Ramiero home."

William smiled in answer. And Sally watched him take out his cell phone before she turned back to get Ramiero. "Hold this a minute, Ramiero. It's just aluminum. Need to call your mama."

"You carry my ball, Sally. I can carry the aluminum," Ramiero said.

"Thanks. This one leg of mine don't work too good. That's a big help, Ramiero. You are a gentleman." Ramiero walked on.

Sally waited until he was out of earshot, then called Asunta on her cell phone. "Asunta, the seed is planted. You'll need to take that little detour on the way home. . . . Uh-huh. Just gimme a call when your friend goes out. . . . Yes. I'll stay with Ramiero. Gotta go. He's gettin' ahead of me." Then, closing her phone, she called out, "Wait up, Ramiero. Don't cross the street without me."

"I'm just gonna sit with Ghanna, Sally. He's right here in his park."

Sally scuttled along and went to visit with Ghanna, too. "You speak to William?" he asked.

Sally said, "Uh-huh. I'll be keepin' Ramiero. Asunta gotta work late tonight."

Ghanna got up. "See ya. Got some work to do myself."

"Who's gonna play ball with me?"

"I'll come with you, Ramiero. C'mon, we'll go into the alley. You can pitch the soccer ball against the wall an' kick it along the pavement back there. Later we'll have supper together, just you an' me."

6:42 p.m.

Glancing furtively around her to make sure she was not observed, a woman wearing sunglasses and a narrow-brimmed straw hat hurried across the alley behind Miano Tse's apartment building. Using a copied key, she quickly opened the back door and closed it behind her; it locked automatically. She was now in the basement, near the laundry room. She had left work as early as she could, but the rush-hour traffic had still slowed down the bus to Miano Tse's neighborhood.

Then Asunta rode the elevator to the second floor and let herself into Miano Tse's apartment. She rushed to the front window and moved the curtain slightly to peek out. The cars were moving along easily, but she did not see what she was looking for. Asunta peered out the side window too, but that street was nearly deserted. She glanced at her watch. *Took me thirty minutes to get here. Hope I didn't miss him.* After a moment she returned to the front window—just in time to see The Oxman drive down the block in his truck. Asunta dropped the curtain, lifted her right knee, and pumped her bent arm and fist back and forth, cheering herself. "Yes! Yes!" she said with enthusiasm while she watched the truck speed away.

Next Asunta grabbed her cell phone from her purse with trembling hands and called Dr. Pannell. "The Oxman left his apartment a few seconds ago. He's going up toward Hughler Hospital. Oops, he just turned left, maybe toward the mountain."

"Thanks, Asunta. I'll send out the alert. You get along home. Be careful, now. So far everything is quiet here at Dr. Truesort's," Dr. Pannell told her.

Asunta made another call. "Hi, Sally. The detour was worth it. Uh-huh, just saw him leave. I'm about to catch the bus home. Should be there in time to give Ramiero his bath and tuck him into bed. Thanks again for everything, Sally."

7:13 p.m.

Peeking carefully from one of the front second-floor bedrooms, Vincent watched the cars arrive. Ghanna was steering a Porsche into a narrow slot at the corner of the stone wall. He wriggled through the door, helped a plainclothesman out of a stalled Maserati, and parked it six inches away from the Porsche. Then he turned toward the next car coming up the driveway and began to direct traffic. *He gotta have all these fancy cars parked before sundown. Hope he remembers to give the keys back to the owners!* Vincent laughed.

"Hey, Vincent. What's goin' on?" asked Alvarez as he walked into the room.

"Look at Ghanna, Al. He's havin' a ball. That ex-con loves tellin' those cops what to do."

Alvarez joined him at the window, where both were careful not to be seen. "Never knew he liked cars. He's like a kid in a toy store," Alvarez said with a smile. "He's so hyper, he doesn't even limp. Anyhow, I came to borrow your guitar."

"Know anythin' about guitars?"

"Just a little. Used to play when I was a teenager." Alvarez strummed some chords and tried a little melody. "In fact, when I helped my mom move into my sister's home last month, I found my old guitar in the attic behind an even older steamer trunk." He chuckled. "Brought the guitar home. Cleaned it up and began playing again. I've been teaching Ramiero how to play. Didn't know it would come in handy, though. Maybe I shoulda brought my own guitar?"

"No, it's okay. You can fool around some. I doubt The Oxman is a musician. I had a conversation with him once in his store. He won't hear any difference."

"That's good."

"Looks like you have on the pants from your security uniform."

"Oh yeah. Usually just change my shirt when I get home. You think he can see the pants in the dark?"

"You don't wanna take any chances. Those gold stripes down the side may scare him off."

"You got somethin' I can use?" Alvarez asked as they walked down the hall to the stairs.

"C'mon, I got a costume for ya. It's good you asked about it. I've worn it for some gigs in upstate New York. Brought it back with me and put it in the guest-room closet."

"Cool."

"The room where I'm stayin' now is at the back of the house, overlookin' the river on the third floor. Reckon it was some servant's room once. I used to have a guest room on the second floor, but this time Dr. Fred put me up here so I'd be less likely to be seen."

The two men ascended a flight of stairs and walked down a narrow hallway to Vincent's room. "Here's my fancy shirt and jeans. You should look like you're givin' a concert. Think they'll fit okay? I got them out special for ya. This hat goes with it."

Sure enough, the clothing fit Alvarez fine.

"Great. It'll help my disguise," Alvarez said.

"You look good in bright green, Al. Too bad Asunta ain't here." Vincent laughed, then grew somber as he looked at Alvarez's reaction. "Sorry, man. I hear you're doin' it for her. Sorry."

Alvarez just nodded and tossed his shirt and blue security trousers with gold stripes down on the bed. He handed the guitar to Vincent. "Tune it, will ya? And maybe play a little."

Vincent gave Alvarez a lesson. He showed Alvarez the way he slapped the guitar itself to get some rhythm and how to stop the sound suddenly by placing his hands across the strings. Then he handed the guitar to Alvarez and worked on fingering. Alvarez imitated the sounds, strumming and chording accurately.

"You sound good," said Vincent. "Hey, maybe you an' me should have a jam session one of these days, huh? Once The Oxman's behind bars, I'm movin' back to town!"

8:10 p.m.

"It'll be gettin' dark soon," said Vincent. "You better go on down. I'll be a lookout from up here, along with Lucien. He's comin' up in a few minutes. He was gonna stay downstairs on the first floor, but he can't see anything from there. Doc Pannell says Lucien's healed enough so the stairs won't bother him much. See, Al? Take a look. Me and Lucien can look out any window on this floor. We gonna have a great view with these night-scope goggles, an' we can call this special conference number and reach everyone on their cell phones. Everybody's double-checked that their phones are on vibrate."

"Good, said Alvarez, "Can't hardly have The Oxman hearin' phones ringing all over the backyard," Alvarez said facetiously.

"If anything don't seem right, stop the music, Al. Stop it the way I showed ya. That's our signal. All your friends will be listenin' for that. Remember, you're covered on all four sides."

"Yeah. Good thing, too."

"Also, all the guests' IDs are bein' checked carefully. Josh did a lot of that. Ian too, before he went to his lookout post."

8:28 p.m.

Miano Tse pushed Alvarez out the side door. She whispered, "Mrs. Truesort doesn't know you're not Vincent." Miano Tse led Alvarez through the dusk, using her flashlight. She continued to whisper, "Okay, just like we practiced the other day: sit over there by the stone wall. Move your barstool a little if you want, but not too close to the water."

"Okay. This looks like a good spot." Alvarez reckoned he was approximately fifty feet from the river.

"You might as well start playing guitar. Attach this mike to your shirt and check to make sure it's working right. That's it. The guests will stay up on the veranda, not too close to you, unless The Oxman's a no-show. They'll be able to hear you fine without getting in the way. But they can reach you quick if there's trouble. The psychiatrist is with them too, if you need him to negotiate."

"Yeah, I understand," said Alvarez.

Miano Tse glanced at the potting shed, then the veranda. "The guests are gobbling up the food—lots of little sandwiches and hors d'oeuvres. I helped Mrs. Truesort set them out. Gotta get Mrs. Truesort to stop pacing up and down the veranda. She keeps telling the caterer she never uses paper plates and plastic cutlery, but she does know it's a police ploy," Miano Tse added with a grin.

Alvarez managed a slight smile. "The guests got more appetite than me right now."

"Yeah, they probably do. I'll be back soon." Miano Tse slipped quietly up the path to help Ingrid in the kitchen.

8:44 p.m.
Josh was perched on top of the stone wall at the front corner of the property, having climbed up using a chain ladder. Though partially hidden by a tree outside the wall, he still had a good view of Sherwood Boulevard and the dirt road below him, with the dark woods beyond. Cory was stationed at the other corner, behind a large boulder in the field.

Josh felt his cell phone vibrate. "Lars? Detective Zanden here. The Oxman's on his way, in his own black Ford pickup. Should be there in about twenty minutes unless he takes a detour. He was up on the mountain, settling in for the night, when he got a phone call from one of his boys. We were close enough to hear his side of the conversation. He revved up his engine and headed back down the mountain, aiming toward the river and the area of Sherwood Boulevard. We're still tailing him, but real discreet-like so he won't get suspicious."

"Great! Thanks," said Josh. "Keep me posted." He clicked off, then called the rest of the team on the conference number.

At the other end of the dirt road, in the woods near the river, Cairnly and Mouski got Josh's message. They stopped chatting and took cover. "Remember, Cairnly, I want this motherfucker alive," Chief Detective Mouski said in a hoarse whisper. Mouski remained by the riverbank. Cairnly moved into position about sixty feet from Alvarez and hid in forest growth adjacent to the river, resting his palm on the handle of his .45-caliber Glock automatic.

One block north of the Truesort mansion, Ian crouched behind a hedge and adjusted his binoculars, hoping to be the first to spot The Oxman's truck.

Several unmarked police cars within a mile moved closer.

Behind the potting shed, on the upstream side of the backyard, Dr. Pannell and a couple of police sharpshooters adjusted the night-vision scopes on their rifles.

Miano Tse left the kitchen and quickly walked the length of the backyard, within the shadow of the stone wall. "Your music sounds nice, Al," she murmured as she reached him. "Good luck! I'll be stationed right over there in the tall grass at the riverbank."

Alvarez looked at his watch. "Take cover, Miano Tse," he told her quietly.

Miano Tse disappeared into the darkness. Alvarez saw the beam from her flashlight, heard her swish through the grass. Then the light beam was gone.

9:02 p.m.

Lucien phoned the group on a conference call. "I got the truck in sight! The Ox is about to be yoked."

Then Alvarez heard *ahoo-hooo-hoouh*. The owl call was the prearranged backup signal to mean The Oxman had actually been seen. Ian had recommended it, having learned it as a boy when hiking with his grandfather in the Navajo reservation along the San Juan River.

Josh used the chain ladder to climb partway down the inside of the stone wall, out of view. He eased the ladder off the top of the wall, then jumped to the ground as the ladder gave way. Instantly Josh dropped the ladder neatly between a Lexus and a Mercedes and knelt behind the hedge, occasionally hooting like an owl as he waited, hoping for a glimpse of The Oxman.

When he heard the owl call, Alvarez checked what he could see of the front grounds, then turned his head to scan the river area. So far there was no sign of The Oxman. Alvarez settled on his sturdy, three-legged barstool, with his back a few feet from the stone wall on the downstream side of the yard.

He had been practicing before, but now he clutched the guitar so tightly that his fingers began to quiver uncontrolled. He whispered to them as though they were not part of his body, "Calm down, fellas. You have to play this here guitar."

He was so frightened that his own soft voice startled him. Rubbing his shaking fingers on a shrub, he closed his eyes and prayed, "God, be with me." He turned on the mike attached to his shirt, then resumed singing and strumming.

The mike picked up the sound and spilled an anguish-driven tenor voice out across the gardens as he sang "Stand by Me." The hungry guests hushed, listening. The river lapped against the bank, providing a soft background brush rhythm to his music.

9:10 p.m.

Alvarez heard a new sound near the stone wall: the grinding of gears, the sound of a motor, and the valve tap of a poorly tuned engine. He leaned closer to the wall, unconsciously attempting to blend in. Then, about twenty feet away, between him and the house, he saw a dark silhouette come over the top of the wall: a foot, followed by the head and huge shoulders of The Oxman.

Alvarez held his breath in terror and strummed his guitar as fast and hard as he could, propelled by sheer gut-wrenching fear.

The Oxman was amazingly graceful as he eased himself down the wall, clinging to it like a warm blanket on a cold night. When his feet reached the ground, he crouched behind the shrubs to keep out of sight and crawled silently downhill toward Alvarez.

Miano Tse hooted out *ahoo-hooo-hoouh*. Alvarez froze, and the music stopped. The Oxman paused. A silence fell over the gardens.

9:18 p.m.

The stunned silence broken by the guttural laugh of The Oxman shocked the team into action. Miano Tse aimed the bright beam of her LED flashlight at him. The Oxman had pulled Alvarez up to a standing position facing the sharpshooters. His arm was around Alvarez's neck, his gun at Alvarez's temple. "Sorry to interrupt the party. Entertainment was pretty good. You thought it was free. Well, now ya gotta pay for it," The Oxman growled, then kicked the stool and guitar down the trail.

"Nobody shoot," Dr. Pannell whispered to the sharpshooters, laying down his rifle. "Keep him talking. Think I can sneak around behind, going along the riverbank."

"But you won't have a weapon," a sharpshooter whispered back.

Dr. Pannell put on his green beret. "Don't need one." He crept silently to the river, slipped into the water, and let the current carry him swiftly to the downstream side of the yard, just inside the stone wall. Then he noiselessly pulled himself ashore and slid on his stomach toward Alvarez, using the underbrush for cover. Any sound he made was muffled by the rapids.

9:26 p.m.
Alvarez's body was numb with hatred and dread. Only the brightening of his eyes told Dr. Pannell that Alvarez knew he was there.

"You got the wrong man," a sharpshooter yelled at The Oxman. "He's not the one you want."

The Oxman laughed and turned Alvarez and himself slightly toward the guests. "Any hostage will do," he yelled.

Dr. Lexi Bakov, the psychiatrist, moved forward toward The Oxman. "Relax. Just drop your gun. Nobody wants to get hurt. Rest a minute. That climb over the wall was hard work."

Still holding Alvarez, The Oxman yelled, "I'm *The* Oxman. For me, scalin' that wall was easy!"

Dr. Pannell slowly maneuvered into a crouching position and duckwalked closer to The Oxman's back.

Miano Tse realized the doctor's strategy. She clicked off her flashlight. The Oxman blinked in the sudden darkness. That's all Dr. Pannell needed. He sprang as though rocket propelled and caught The Oxman's elbow with both hands, thrusting the huge man's gun to the ground. Pushing Alvarez away from harm, Dr. Pannell slammed the side of The Oxman's head against the stone wall. Blood spilled down The Oxman's face from his temple.

Alvarez slid to the ground, grabbed The Oxman's gun, and scrambled away. He rubbed his sore neck and put his hands over his face. Nobody could see his tears.

The Oxman socked Dr. Pannell in the mouth. In response, Dr. Pannell yanked The Oxman into a full standing position, pinned his back against the wall, and shoved his knee into The Oxman's stomach. The Oxman kicked Dr. Pannell's legs. Moving away from the wall, The Oxman turned to mount it and escape into his truck. Despite his pain, Dr. Pannell dove for The Oxman and yanked him off the wall by his ankles. The two men rolled on the ground, pummeling each other mercilessly about the face and head.

What the hell's going on? thought Cairnly. *Can't see a damn thing from way down here.* Defying orders, he started to creep through the bushes toward the two men struggling on the grass.

Dr. Pannell, lying under The Oxman, finally pushed him off his own body almost in a reverse push-up. The Oxman could not stand. Dr. Pannell dragged The Oxman's bulk up to a standing position facing the veranda with his back toward the river, then gripped his opponent's throat with the strength of a vise. Still facing his enemy, Dr. Pannell took a few steps away from The Oxman to catch his breath.

Suddenly a shot rang out. The Oxman twisted in a dizzying, deadly reel from the impact. Cairnly stared in shock as The Oxman crumpled to the ground.

9:42 p.m.

Down on the riverbank, Chief Detective Mouski had stayed away from harm during the sting operation. At last he climbed up the muddy bank at the end of the stone wall, about fifty feet away from his victim. "God damn you, Cairnly, I told you I wanted him alive! You *bastard!*"

"Maybe he's just wounded, Chief," Patrolman Cairnly said timidly.

"Everybody, stay back," Chief Detective Mouski yelled at his sharpshooters, the guests, and the entire entrapment team. All were somber, staring at the scene.

But Dr. Truesort ignored the chief detective's command. Miano Tse handed him her flashlight. He examined the body and pronounced The Oxman dead. "The bullet entered his spine. He would've been completely paralyzed anyway," he said. "Sorry you had to see this, Ingrid."

Ingrid leaned on her husband's shoulder. *It can't be real,* she thought. *A life gone. All action halted. Why didn't this picture fade to black?*

The two walked back to the veranda. Dr. Truesort got out his silver pocketknife and cut a prize, sweet-smelling Chrysler Imperial rose, which he handed to her as they went inside. "Now we're safe, my dear," Fred said as he hugged her and wiped away her tears.

9:51 p.m.
Chief Detective Mouski snapped out orders. Like a puppeteer's strings, his staccato got the men to perform. "People, care for the body. Get reports from onlookers. Go over the truck."

Patrolman Cairnly collapsed by the river, vomiting and crying out, "I never killed nobody before."

"Make sure Cairnly doesn't drown down there in three feet of water. One death is enough tonight," Chief Mouski shouted.

10:04 p.m.
Vincent, who had been waiting for the all clear, hollered from the upstairs window, "Al, Alvarez, you okay?" The only answer he heard was the chief detective's orders to his men. *Man, them stupid cops forgot about Al.*

Vincent rushed down the stairs, across the veranda, and over the lawn to where he saw Ghanna trying to help Alvarez up. "They forgot about him, Ghanna. He all right? Oh, God, please let him be all right."

"Just shaken. He done fainted. Give me a hand with him. Take 'im to the house. Let the docs check him," Ghanna said.

"Al, it's me, Vincent. You okay. Ghanna and me gonna help you stand. Nothin' feel broken?"

Alvarez shook his head.

"C'mon. C'mon now," Vincent coaxed.

Ghanna wiped off Alvarez's hands and forehead with a towel Miano Tse handed him. "He got muddy. It's damp next to that stone wall."

Miano Tse picked up the guitar. "Just a little mud. Vincent, your guitar looks okay."

Vincent answered Miano Tse with a nod and a smile. Gently he put his arms around Alvarez's waist and lifted him to his feet. He gave him a hug. "You did fine, Al. Moved me to tears. Wished Asunta could've heard you sing."

Alvarez smiled. "It was for her."

Vincent let Alvarez lean on him. With Ghanna leading the way to the veranda, they carefully maneuvered Alvarez onto the chaise lounge. Miano Tse tucked a pillow under his head.

"You rest here as long as you want," she said, and kissed his cheek. "We are all proud of your courage."

10:07 p.m.
Ian called Abby on his cell. "Hi, sweetheart. We got him! The Oxman is dead, accidentally shot by a cop. Everyone else is fine."

"Oh, Ian, I'm so glad you're safe," she answered. "Tell me everything that happened!"

So Ian described the whole sting to her—how he'd hoped to be the first one to spot The Oxman, but Lucien had spotted him first instead. "Most of the action took place on the other side of the gardens. I heard the gunshot but didn't see the struggle up close."

Abby smiled. "I'm glad I didn't go. I probably would've screamed and given the sting away."

"Nope."

"Well, I'm just glad it's over. No more worries about being followed anymore. We can relax now, Ian." She heaved a big sigh of relief. "Come on home. I bought a pint of your favorite ice cream—strawberry!—and there's a good movie on TV."

10:25 p.m.
"Thanks for your bravery, Alvarez," Dr. Truesort said. "You look fine. No broken bones—just a few scratches and bruises. If anything bothers you, give me a call. Bring Asunta to my office for an initial exam, and I'd like to meet your son as well. I have a pediatrician who will be happy to look after him." He shook Alvarez's hand. "Take this. It will safely ease the pain for a while. Here are a few more of these pills in case you need them. Put them in your pocket."

Miano Tse tucked a blanket over Alvarez and washed his hands and face thoroughly this time. She sat beside him for a while to be there in case he needed anything. Then she phoned Asunta to tell her that Josh and Lucien would take Alvarez home soon.

After receiving Miano Tse's call, Asunta went to bed to rest and wait for him, but soon she dozed off. No one had told her the details of the risk her husband was taking. During the planning meeting, when the other volunteers had heard Alvarez comment on her fear of The Oxman, they had understood intuitively not to frighten her any further.

10:47 p.m.

"Well done, Doc," said Josh. He gave Dr. Pannell a fist bump and clapped him on the back.

"Thanks, Josh."

"Mouski didn't do nothin'," Josh complained. "Doc, I told ya to get the county sheriff in here. The cops let you do all the work."

"That's exactly why I didn't get him," said Dr. Pannell. "Figured we would keep it 'in the family.' Then we'd be sure it would get done. Hadn't figured on Cairnly."

"Me neither," said Josh. "That was a surprise."

"Mouski will make sure all legal angles are safely covered. He has to. How else will he look like a hero? Just as well Cairnly shot The Oxman. Fred declared he was dead right after he fell to the ground with a bullet in the spine. Actually he was dead before the bullet hit him, but only you and I know that," Dr. Pannell said. "If it comes to a trial, which I seriously doubt with Mouski in charge, I'll plead self-defense. Mouski and Cairnly will corroborate my plea, and Fred will too."

11:20 p.m.

Dr. Pannell looked at Miano Tse with new admiration. "How did you know to do that?" he asked her. "Turn the flashlight off, I mean."

Miano Tse shrugged. "It just seemed logical. You were ready. Al knew you were there."

"Come on. I'll take you home," Dr. Pannell said. "You too, Ghanna. Josh and Lucien will see to Al."

Midnight

Josh and Lucien rushed to the passenger's side of the car. Alvarez grabbed Josh's hands, then eased himself off the seat and onto the sidewalk. "Never seen anyone so brave, Al," Josh said. "You should be real proud, man. I'll buy you a drink at Lefty's anytime."

"Maybe in a few days. For now just help me in, Josh. Hurt all over. It even hurts when I smile. Just help me upstairs to my apartment. I don't need a drink." Alvarez dropped his keys.

"Here, let me help ya," Josh said, and he picked up the keys. At the top of the stairs, Josh unlocked the apartment door and quietly put the keys on the kitchen table. He and Lucien shook Alvarez's hand one more time.

"Everyone asleep in here," Alvarez whispered.

Josh and Lucien left, closing the door very quietly.

Thursday, 12:15 a.m.
"Josh here, Miano Tse. Did I wake you?"

"No. Dr. Pannell drove Ghanna and me home a little while ago. But I can't sleep. Too excited, I guess."

"Just brought Al home. You were awesome tonight."

"So were you."

"Okay if I come over?"

"Sure."

Fifteen minutes later, Miano Tse hugged Josh as she cried. "I was sooo scared, Josh. Really scared."

"Me, too, Miano Tse. Me too." He hugged her, then realized there was nothing under her silk dragon kimono. "You're beautiful even when you're crying. You know that?"

Miano Tse tried to wipe away her tears with her hands. Josh led her to the couch. "Sit down, Miano Tse. You're trembling." She reached up and hugged him again.

He kissed her neck. She put her arms around him in a yearning embrace, then turned and kissed his mouth.

Josh carried her to the bedroom and gently placed her on the bed. Miano Tse slipped off her kimono as she lay down, pulling Josh onto her. He shoved his jeans and underpants down his legs. Josh groaned when he entered her. Miano Tse let out a little cry. "I love you, Josh."

"That's good. I love you, too."

Their bodies intertwined in bliss.

12:25 a.m.

After making himself a cup of coffee, Alvarez sank down slowly into his easy chair, then sighed and bent over to untie his shoes. He slipped them off one at a time, wiggled his toes and pulled off one sock, rested, and pulled off the other. Then he pushed himself out of the chair and walked into the bedroom. He woke Asunta with a kiss. Asunta gave him a hug and whispered, "I'm glad you're back. I'm sorry. I was so weary. I must've fallen asleep." Alvarez kissed her again and watched her eyes close.

Tiptoeing silently, he went into Ramiero's bedroom, placed his son's teddy bear next to him on the pillow, and patted his head. Then he stood in the hall where he could see both of them and said softly, "Sleep well, *amor de mi vida*. Sleep well, *hijito querido*. You are both safe now. Any other drug lords will think twice before they try dealing here."

Afraid of waking Asunta if he climbed into bed next to her, Alvarez returned to the easy chair and fell asleep. When he awakened, the sky was already brightening. He went to the window and watched a slice of sunlight stretch out across the horizon as though it were pushing the charcoal-gray skies away above it, making room for the dawn.

It's a new day and a new community, he thought. "Thanks, God. Thanks for protecting me and my family."

Friday, 10:00 a.m.

"Hello? Yeah, Royce here. Listen, I heard some news I thought might interest you. That big drug lord is dead. Yeah. Shot by a cop. That little punk William told me about it, saw it in the paper. He actually complained that he'll be losing revenue as a result!" Royce laughed. "Anyway, the people you're interested in will become less careful. Gives us a better chance. The increase in surveillance that I saw will probably be reduced. So figure out what you want done. Yeah, okay. You know where to reach me. Bye."

part SIX

Crashing Glass, Flashing Lights

"**W**ELCOME BACK TO HUGHLER CITY, Vincent!" Abby said. "No worries about The Oxman anymore!"

Vincent had stopped by Fred's private lab first thing Thursday morning, August 30, soon after Abby, Ian, and Miano Tse had arrived. None of them were even working in the clean room yet, and they all greeted Vincent warmly.

"It is awesome. I still keep lookin' over my shoulder, though. It's only two weeks since that night. . . . I just can't shake that scary feelin'. Been referrin' some new patients to Doc Truesort. They ask me a lot of questions."

"Didn't realize you helped people get treatment from Dr. Truesort," Abby said.

Miano Tse said nothing. Realizing that the conversation might put her in an awkward situation, she sat down at her desk and started reading the email Abby had sent her the night before.

"Yeah. I'm his success story." Vincent laughed. "But I'm eager to move ahead with my career now. Great to see my old friends in the city, too. Missed them while I was away."

"I bet," said Ian. "I'm sure they hoped you would return soon."

"Well, just wanted to stop by and say hi, and thanks to all of you for helpin' me get my freedom back!" Vincent looked at his watch. "Josh drove me over here—he's waitin' for me in the parking lot. He's gotta get to work at the ER. And I have to practice today for my next gig."

"Where are you playing?" Cory asked from the hall doorway.

"Over at Lefty's. I don't have to travel far. I'm livin' in the room upstairs above his bar," Vincent said. "Lefty told me I could have it free until I get on my feet."

"That's terrific. What time do you start?" Cory asked.

"Tomorrow evening around four thirty. Usually I start later, but Friday night is happy hour. All of you should come over. You're the ones who made this possible. I can't thank you enough," Vincent said, his voice shaking with emotion.

"Our pleasure, Vincent," Abby said. "And thanks for your invitation, but I don't think I'll be able to make it tomorrow. My experiments are still in process; I'm sure I'll have to work late even though it's a Friday. Take care, Vincent."

Ian said, "I'm told you play a mean guitar, Vincent."

Miano Tse nodded emphatically. "He's very good. Always draws a crowd at Lefty's," she said. "Josh and I will be there."

"I'll drop by tomorrow," said Ian. "Okay if I go with you, Cory?"

"Sure," Cory said. "Vincent is talented. You'll enjoy his performance, I know. I've already heard him play duets with my daughter in upstate New York. Anyway, I can drop you off at your condo afterward. That way Abby will have the car."

"Good. Abby can drive home when she's finished here. You don't mind going home alone, do you, Ab?"

"Of course not," Abby said, a little too boldly. She was not going to show that she felt apprehensive.

As Ian and Miano Tse prepped for the clean room, Abby waved good-bye to Vincent. "You know, Cory," she said, "there's a theory that AIDS patients with a positive outlook on life continue their vocations, and this helps them maintain a healthy life."

"Well, that could be Vincent," Cory agreed. "Or maybe the strain of HIV he had was less virulent than most."

After prepping for the clean room themselves, Cory and Abby joined their colleagues.

"By the way, Abby," continued Cory, "how was your meeting with Fred yesterday? I know he's concerned about obtaining some marketable results soon; he's eager to see what you've found now."

"Yeah, I know," said Abby. "He's always asking me that lately—he seems stressed out all the time."

"Yeah, tell me about it," interjected Ian, rolling his eyes.

"But I think yesterday's meeting was constructive," Abby continued. "We compared notes and discussed how to proceed from here. He's concentrating on his theory and I'm concentrating on mine, though we agree that our two approaches build upon each other. Now we each have a list of experiments we are going to try."

"Thanks for your email about that," said Miano Tse. "I've started preparing specimens for the first experiment on the list."

"Thanks, Miano Tse," said Abby. "Both Fred and I are using sluggish cancer cells to slow down the HIV's rapid changes so we can study it and find out what's going on. So far, our detective work has given us several clues toward an eventual cure."

"Sounds promising," said Cory. "Keep it up."

"Bob was there for part of yesterday's meeting too," continued Abby. "He joined Fred and me for a conversation about poor Camilla. After she died on Sunday, we wanted to review her treatment, see whether we could have done anything differently. Fred had asked me to look once more at the course of her HIV infection."

"I wish I could have been here Sunday. I was visiting Nora. Did you find anything?" asked Cory.

"All I could conclude was that her HIV was too far advanced when she came to us," said Abby. "Really sad. Apparently she hadn't taken her meds consistently. The HIV lay dormant in her liver and intestines, and probably elsewhere beyond the immune system's notice, so the virus was able to attack again whenever she was sick or stressed, like after her husband abused her. I wasn't able to come up with anything to ward off her infection beyond what we had already tried."

"Yes, it's very sad about Camilla," said Cory. "At least we did what we could to help her die in comfort."

Abby added, "Over the past few months, Fred and I have succeeded more consistently in using cancer cells to slow down the fast mutation rate of HIV. This gives the host cells a chance to fight back. Perhaps eventually Fred's approach could help a patient like Camilla, but it was too late for her."

"Heard my name mentioned," Fred said, entering the lab. "Hello, all. Anybody making any progress so far today?"

"Definitely, Fred," called Ian from inside the clean room. "Right now I'm recording some interactions of CD4+ T cells. Come take a look."

"Hold on a minute," said Fred, preparing to enter the clean room. While he went through the air shower and put on his sterile lab coat, Ian moved out of the way so that Abby, Miano Tse, and Cory could view the cells on the workstation monitor. Fred quickly joined them.

"Fred," Ian said, "I think your theory has opened the door. First the cancer cells attacked the HIV, slowing its mutation rate, weakening its assault. See, the CD4+ T cells have taken advantage of the extra time. More of them are surviving to reproduce without being attacked by the virus's RNA."

Fred was elated. "We finally have a base to work from! Abby and I decided to work on this cancer theory of mine first, since it would be helpful in many approaches we might use."

"HIV mutates so fast! This approach *has* to help," Miano Tse observed. "It's strange, Fred: in most cancer patients, cancer cells and CD4+ T cells are enemies. Now it appears they are working together against the HIV!"

"That's right, Miano Tse," said Fred. "We can work with Louella's and Vincent's DNA in some new ways now that the cancer-cell approach is more promising. In fact, it may become a vital part in other experiments we're trying as well. The next step will be to prove its consistency."

"I'd like to help with that, Fred," offered Cory, "by analyzing interactions and the rate of mutations. As you know, I did something similar with cancer cells to check on the accuracy of a drug dosage. I watched the interaction of the drug as it attacked a cancer cell so you could adjust the drug potency if needed. In this case, we can develop an optimum 'dose' of cancer cells and tweak it, depending on the resistance of the patients' HIV."

"Great. When can you get started, Cory?" Fred asked. "I think your approach to this problem would be very helpful."

After Fred had left the clean room, Abby announced, "I told Fred last night that we've been approved for time on an electron microscope by one of Dad's companies. That is, he sits on their board. When the secretary called this morning, I explained that we would wait until we are closer to the final stage of validating our theories. But I'll start writing the official proposal right now, since this application of Fred's theory appears to be successful."

"Cool!" said Cory.

"I'm eager to move ahead with analyzing Louella's immune system. I want to see exactly how she's fighting off the HIV."

"Sure, Abby. Give it a try," Cory answered.

"I can take some still photos and videos of her CD4+ T cells if you want," said Ian.

"Okay," said Abby. "Let me prepare some specimens for you."

An hour later, Miano Tse heard Fred striding down the hall. "Fred, you want to see some still photos of Louella's CD4+ T cells?" she called to him.

"That's nice, boys and girls," he snapped, "but don't bother me now. Can't you see I'm in a hurry? Just let me know what you find once you are finished with these high-priced toys. Damn it, get the job *done*! I've got to get to my lawyer." He stormed out of the building.

Maybe we're getting something after all, Fred thought as he slammed his car door and sped away. *Heaven knows I'm paying the price for it.*

After Fred left, all the others exchanged glances. "What the hell got into him?" asked Abby. "He was on top of the world just an hour ago."

"Beats me," said Ian. "Cory, you've known him a lot longer than the rest of us."

"Yeah. He's just like that," said Cory. "I don't know what set him off this time." (Cory actually had a pretty good guess, but he wisely kept it to himself.)

Miano Tse looked at her colleagues. "Maybe he can't yell at the people who are upsetting him, but it's safe to scream at us."

Abby nodded. "You're probably right." She sighed and turned back to her work.

Ian took some videos of Louella's CD4+ T cells. Abby and Cory realized that they might need the electron microscope sooner than they'd thought. They found some odd configurations on the CD4+ T cells that would require a better-quality image for further studies and experimentation.

In the early evening, after Cory and Miano Tse had left, Abby and Ian were discussing Fred's inexplicable change of mood and sudden exit. "I'm getting sick of working here, Ian," Abby admitted. "The research itself is exciting, but I'm so sorry I dragged you into this place. There's too little communication. Each of us is on our own solitary planet. I'm not sure my research complements Fred's and Cory's like it should, but I know it complements yours."

Ian threw his lab coat and other clean-room clothing into the laundry bin and walked over to sit by Abby at her desk. "Sometimes Fred is so distant and bad-tempered! Maybe he's scared he's in over his head," Ian suggested.

"That makes sense. Lately we've really taken a leap forward with his theory, and I'm trying to use it in all my experiments right along with him," Abby said, "but it's never good enough, never fast enough to please him. He was *really* in a foul mood when he suddenly left today. Did you see? I wonder what's eating him."

"He's been doing that kind of thing a lot lately," said Ian. "He seems desperate about something. Failure? Financial ruin?"

Abby stood up and looked around her at all the lab equipment, then scowled. Suddenly she grabbed a handful of empty test tubes and hurled them across the lab. "I have to blow off steam too," Abby yelled.

Ian walked over to the janitor's closet, got the dustpan and broom, and began to sweep up the glass as he continued the discussion, hiding his anger in a calm, stoic tone. "Let's go home."

Abby put her notes and personal log into her backpack, looked outside, and saw an empty parking lot. "Everyone is gone, Ian. Maybe they're the smart ones."

She took another look at her experiments and said, "Nope, I can't go to happy hour tomorrow. I was hoping to get these specimens done today."

The couple stopped at the local Chinese buffet and enjoyed choosing their dinners from the abundance of enticing dishes, such as green beans in black bean sauce, mussels with ginger, and Alaskan king crab in butter sauce. After they read their fortunes, they drove home in an atmosphere of tense quiet after a hard day that had ended in anger.

At their condo Ian poured them both a glass of Orvieto Classico, and they continued their discussion in a more relaxed manner.

Abby sighed. "When I accepted this job, I didn't realize Fred hasn't kept up with the latest research techniques. But how can he, while treating patients as well?" she continued, trying to be understanding. "I wonder if my dad knows this. Maybe we should discuss the research with him."

Ian seized the opportunity. "Labor Day is coming up—a three-day weekend. I nearly forgot! Let's go to Connecticut. We sure don't want to hang here. You're burned out, Abby. God knows, *I* need a break."

"Yes, we could both use a breather," she answered.

"When we were in California," remarked Ian, "you promised we would spend some time at your dad's country house. That was five years ago, when we were first married. We've lived on the East Coast for more than a year and still haven't gotten up there. Besides, this research isn't something you want to discuss over the phone or via email."

"You're right, Ian. Okay—I'll call him in the morning and see if he's free. Yeah, I agree: talking in person is better, and a weekend away would be the right medicine for both of us."

"It's good that you understand Fred is very busy, Abby. You can understand the 'why' of a situation, but you don't have to like it," Ian said. "You know who first gave me that bit of advice?"

"No."

"Your dad."

Abby smiled. "Maybe I'd better take it, then."

"Fred doesn't really understand what you're doing. He's still working the way he did twenty years ago. Cory is much better."

"Really? How do you know?" Abby asked skeptically.

"This isn't the first place I've worked," Ian answered. "But don't take my word for it. Miano Tse has worked here and in hospital labs in China. She'll confirm what I say."

"She is very careful to make copies of her work and store them in her locked file," said Abby. "Miano Tse told me I should change the passwords on my files more frequently also."

"Right," Ian answered. "And quit breaking stuff when you get mad."

"Okay. I know one day we'll have our own lab."

"That's right, Ab. That's our long-range plan. The reputation and the money we earn here will be our base."

The Victorian home overlooking Long Island Sound was a sanctuary, a walk back into the nineteenth century, a place where you expected to see a wooden icebox near the kitchen door and stables in the rear.

Impatient to get into the pool for a swim and relax in the sun, Abby and Ian made a quick change and asked Dr. Zelban to join them as soon as he could.

Abby dabbled her feet in the water and leaned back on her elbows to look up the hill. "It's almost a California day in Connecticut, and look at that house. With all its carpenter Gothic and gingerbread, it almost bristles with importance. I expect Queen Victoria to come out on the porch at any minute, with her whole retinue following."

"Pray she doesn't. In that bikini, you'd be sent to the Tower for shocking Her Majesty," Ian retorted playfully. "It's so different from the regular California ranch. But it is a beautiful home. I can see why you love it."

"When Dad and Mom bought this house as a weekend get-away, everyone thought they were crazy. My dad was working at Massachusetts General and Tufts Medical Center and didn't have much time to get away. My brother, Steven, warned that the house would be costly to restore and would isolate my parents from civilization. But Dad said he could afford the restoration; Mom said their aim *was* to get away from civilization. They had an architect look at it before they bought it. He recommended that the kitchen and bathrooms be upgraded but said most of the house was structurally sound already."

"That's amazing for a house this old," Ian commented.

"As the youngest, I really have enjoyed it more than anyone. I tell people I was born in Boston, but I had the most fun in Connecticut. I learned to ski right over there." Abby pointed to a slope of tall grass with a stand of maple trees at the top, their yellowing leaves the harbinger of fall's colorful foliage. A brook sliced through at the foot of the hill, where a one-lane dirt road angled over the bridge just before the brook fed into the pond.

"Bridge ever wash out?" Ian asked.

"Mm-hmm. Sometimes. We had to use the other drive down to the main highway. It's the long way around."

"What's a long way around?" Chas asked. He kicked off his flip-flops and dove into the pool before he could hear the answer.

"Why didn't we see him coming?" Ian said.

"He used the path on the left side of the house. You know, by the cliff." She pointed to a trail that followed along a gulley, where the land dropped off steeply. "I'll have to take you on tour later. Here comes Schmutz. He guards the place. Goes on his rounds every morning and naps every afternoon."

Ian looked up to see a 120-pound, dusty-black German shepherd racing his way. "He won't hurt you, Ian."

"Then tell him to stop snarling at me. His sharp teeth are all I can see."

"Here, Schmutz. Attaboy." Abby buried her face in Schmutz's ruff of neck fur. "Meet Ian. Shake hands with Ian, Schmutz."

Schmutz whimpered, sat, and offered Ian his paw. Ian shook it. "You're a good dog," said Ian. Schmutz nuzzled his hand in acknowledgment.

Chas pulled a lounge chair next to Abby and sat down. "She was always good with animals. Constantly bringing home stray cats, birds wounded by them, a baby rabbit, and even a three-legged fawn. Fawn's leg got caught in a thresher. He was hiding in some deep grass. I had to do the surgery. We expected Abby to become a veterinarian or maybe an ob/gyn nurse like her mother, but not a geneticist. How's the research progressing, Abby?"

"Not bad. It's slow, though I think the time will be worth it. I'm zeroing in on a critical component by examining various theoretical possibilities and systematically eliminating those that don't work. Once I have a narrow focus, the research should go more quickly. The electron-microscope time you got us will be a huge help."

"Are you glad you went to Tufts, Abby, now that you are doing some groundbreaking research?" Chas asked.

"Certainly, Dad. It was grueling at the time, but it is finally paying off. I just wish—well, my work would be a lot easier if Fred had kept up with technology as we know it today."

"All the better for you and Ian. You can lead the way," Chas answered.

"That's difficult, Dad. Fred doesn't relinquish power easily. He told us we didn't have to solve the whole problem; just a piece of the puzzle would do. And that's what I think I've got, plus the possibility of much more."

"Abby, just mention to Fred what you have in mind in a casual way," suggested Chas. "I assure you that within a few days he'll unconsciously adopt your idea as his own. And if he has fallen behind on research techniques, as you say, he'll let you take over that aspect of the problem."

"Will he really?" Abby asked in disbelief.

"Positive. I've known him for a long time. Many overbearing people behave that way, and Fred is no exception."

"Hmmm," said Abby. "I suppose it's worth a try."

Chas said, "If I remember correctly from what Fred described over the phone, his little lab will never be able to provide you with all the resources you need. You should be at a lab in a full-scale pharma house. Fred is the one you really need to talk to about that, not me."

"I don't know of any sale in sight," said Ian. "Do you, Chas?"

"No."

"Fred hasn't even dropped any hints your way, Dad?"

"No, nothing."

"Perhaps some pharma house might be interested in my work," said Abby. "I've studied HIV carefully and now feel I'm getting close to making a significant contribution toward a better treatment. I'll work on the most plausible approach first. I may find that some of my work will reveal another approach or could be integrated into a recent experiment."

"And of course Fred is the one to contact any sales rep," Chas said with disdain.

"Fred tends to keep to himself," Ian pointed out, "though recently he and Abby have begun collaborating more closely. His theory about cancer cells can be applied to Abby's approaches. So maybe he'll become friendlier as they go forward. Whenever he's around, I've tried to promote this attitude by showing him the displays of cell interactions we get on my monitor."

Chas paused, then looked from Ian to Abby as he advised, "Abby, for this once, maybe you shouldn't be so thorough. I know you want to solve the total problem and get every piece of this thousand-piece puzzle to fit, even though you claim you're zeroing in on one critical component. That's how you are. But Fred's right: this time, if you get one corner of the puzzle, you'll be doing well."

Abby saw Ian nodding in agreement. "At least," Ian said, "we've got something in our favor: a real, live AIDS survivor whose treatment has been successful. He regularly donates blood and tissue samples to work with during his checkups."

"And we have another subject with a natural immunity to HIV. I'm studying her DNA," Abby added.

"I guess you could say you have both sides of the coin. But

at the same time, Fred probably needs money," Chas suggested. "He's put a lot of his own cash into this. You did say the man that threatened to hold his patient hostage was caught and killed by the police? That should relieve some of the pressure."

"True," said Abby. "Guess at this point it's simply a money issue."

"No money issue is simple, Abby," Chas said.

Ian quickly agreed.

"Dad, Fred is an odd guy, not easy to work for," Abby claimed. "As Ian said, lately he's been conferring with me more often—now we're finding that our two theories supplement each other—but for months the only real discussion we had was when he hired us."

"That's because he knows you're competent," Chas said. "This is a very small operation. The bulk of the research is up to both of you."

Abby said, "I love doing the research, but I'd like to be assured I'm on the right track. A little guidance from Fred would help."

Chas told her, "When my colleagues in the plastic-surgery field have a theory they want to develop, they sometimes discuss possible techniques and treatments with me. I know they want my opinion and that our discussion is confidential. You might say security is an unwritten law."

"That makes sense. Kinda like a brainstorming session. Any of them successful?" Ian asked.

"I don't recall," Chas responded.

"Well, in any case, Fred doesn't trust us," Abby insisted.

"Yes he does, Abby! Sure, he trusts you," Chas protested. "It's just that one comment to another researcher might be all that is needed to give away the key to a valuable discovery."

Abby said, "But he keeps his lab and office locked even when we're working in the main lab in the same building! It's as if he thinks we'll steal his ideas or something. Honest, Dad, I wouldn't take any of his work!"

Her father answered, "Fear of research falling into the wrong hands is well founded. I think you and Ian may be a little naive. This isn't graduate study; this is research for sale. The glory is in the dollars. Everyone wants those—and, if they're lucky, a little fame thrown in."

"Fine," said Abby. "But I still think we should have a discussion about the computerized techniques and processes we're using, at least once."

"That's my side of the research," Ian said. "If Fred knew how to do it himself, he wouldn't need me."

"I suppose," said Abby doubtfully. "But what about us insiders? He should at least be frank with us. After all, we work for him! Did he ever consult you about his research, Dad?"

"Enough, Abby. No more shop talk."

"Think I need to cool off," Ian said. He did a swan dive into the pool and started to swim laps, mulling over what he had heard. *That was weird, how Chas just cut Abby off. I bet he didn't like the way our discussion was headed. Sometimes Abby seems hurt that he doesn't care, isn't more proud of her. Is her work that common? Couldn't be. Smart guy like that: of course he remembers which researchers were successful. But why would he lie about it?*

And Fred's been his friend from way back. Is Chas just aloof, like Fred? Or maybe he's protecting Abby from something. If he knows this project is doomed, wouldn't he advise her to get out? Maybe Fred is doing something crooked, some kind of ethics scandal? That might explain why he's so secretive. Nah, Chas is lying. Better tell Abby she can't believe him.

But Ian, you can't do that. She's so devoted to her father; she'd end up doubting you. He's more involved than he's saying. Maybe so, but how the hell are you going to prove that?

Abby called to him, "You must take lap swimming seriously. Why are you frowning?"

"'Cause I'm swimming alone."

"That's easy to fix."

Abby dove in and raced past Ian with a perfect butterfly stroke. Ian dove high off the board to show off a somersault. Chas watched their can-you-top-this for a while and then disappeared up the path to the house.

Half an hour later, as they toweled off, Abby asked Ian, "You get along with Dad okay? I know you met him only briefly when he came to California for the wedding. I'm hoping you'll really get to know him better this weekend."

"Sure, Ab. We just need a little time to get acquainted."

The Labor Day weekend in Connecticut was over. It was now late Monday afternoon, a week later. Abby had had a good rest and returned with a renewed sense of dedication to her research, but Ian still felt unsettled. He kept remembering his conversation with Chas, whom he still couldn't bring himself to call Dad.

"Abby, seen Fred or Cory around?" Ian asked, walking into the main lab from the hallway.

"No. Why?" asked Abby from her desk.

"Just wondered if I needed to batten down the hatches." He locked the door to the main lab and sat down at his desk. "I think Miano Tse has left for the day. She usually says good-bye, but her car isn't in the parking lot."

"It's late, Ian. Almost seven thirty," Abby said, glancing at the clock above her desk.

"Martha's gone home. She came over from Hughler Hospital around three this afternoon to do the data entry for some recent financial transactions at this lab. I happened to walk by when she was setting up a new account. The beginning balance was five hundred thousand dollars."

"That's pretty substantial, Ian. Didn't know Fred was putting in that much from his own pocket."

"He isn't, according to Martha. Fred told her it was coming from a pharma sales rep, who hand-delivered it to Fred's hospital office this morning."

"A pharma rep, huh? Interesting."

"But how come we weren't told about this, Abby? What kind of an outfit are we working for? The goddamn office administrator knows more than we do. Martha wouldn't let me see the check, either. Just sealed it in a big envelope with some other checks, probably from Fred's patients, and took it with her when she left."

"Stop acting like a control freak," Abby answered. "Who cares where the five hundred thousand came from? It's here. It shows that some pharma house has faith in what we're doing, which is good news. And, Ian here's even better news: I'm making progress at last."

"Louella's DNA finally paying off all right?" Ian asked.

"I hope so," Abby said. "I isolated a sample of her CD4+ T cells, then added an extra virulent strain of HIV. The T cells are still thriving and multiplying. Louella's resistance to HIV is truly remarkable! The more I look at this, the more I think it could indicate a mutation in her DNA."

"Interesting! Let me take a look, Ab."

"I've been anxious to try this for months, but Fred wanted me to work on his cancer-cell theory first and help Camilla if I could."

Both of them prepped for the clean room and went inside, where Ian bent over the microscope. "These cells look completely unaffected by the HIV. Why don't we take some still images and motion shots of interactions," he suggested. "I can slow down the video so we can see what's happening, and you can compare images using the stills."

"Okay, good. Who knows: this may be the break we've been hunting for," Abby said with her fingers crossed.

Both of them knew that the chance of Louella having a bona fide mutation was about one in a million.

"Ian, please document this and make a backup. This is the third replication of these results," said Abby. "Here's another slightly different configuration. Over on that bench is the still, the first image I showed you. I like plenty of backup material. I just hope I'm not being overly optimistic."

"Maybe some mutation is doing Louella a big favor," said Ian. "If so, we will need to figure out which one or more chromosomes were changed, and exactly how. It may hold the secret to how the HIV is defeated! Wouldn't that be fabulous?"

"Yes!" said Abby. "Then the next step would be reproducing the same effect artificially."

Because her dad had warned them about keeping experiments safe from prying eyes, Abby instinctively glanced toward the main lab door to make sure no one was coming as they left the clean room.

"Ian, your skill with that computer has made a huge difference. Now we need the electron microscope to see and document all the minute detail well enough to really confirm what's going on. Can't wait to examine these samples thousands of times larger, with fine resolution and lighting!" Abby said.

"Me neither," Ian agreed. "We really may be onto something!"

"You know, it's strange: I always thought I'd be more excited than this, but now that I see real progress, I'm mostly just weary."

"It's been a long haul," said Ian.

"For both of us. Well, for now, just make the copies of our visual documentation, and we can go home. Then, my love, we will have all the time in the world."

"Okay, Ab. Let me start with the first one you showed me." He started making the copies.

"Thanks, Ian."

Ian finished the copying fifteen minutes later. "Great!" said Abby. "Let's go home. I'm all finished and set up for tomorrow. First thing in the morning, I'm going to run this set of experiments again to make sure this result isn't a fluke."

"Okay, just a minute." Ian finished shutting down his computer for the night.

"Let's stop by our storage unit on the way home. We can leave the backup copies of the photos there," Abby suggested. "The original DNA is safe locked away here, I'm certain."

"Okay with me, Ab."

"Good. With the visual record of the cellular action, we'll have our own video showing the DNA at work. Fred will love us. Maybe I'll even tell Dad," Abby said as she began putting her laptop and a portable hard drive into her backpack.

Then they heard the outer door open and close. Footsteps resounded in the quiet hallway. "Hey, what's going on in there? Abby, Ian, is that you?" Fred yelled as he rattled the door handle.

Abby rolled her eyes at Ian. "Sorry, Fred," she called. "We're working late. Just thought it would be safer if we kept the door locked."

Fred pushed past Abby as she opened the door. "What the hell are you two doing working behind locked doors? You know there's an open-door policy in this building."

"Sorry, Fred," said Ian. "We've been a little paranoid about security lately. I just finished copying photos of an experiment Abby finished today. We think Louella's CD4+ T cells may be protected by a mutation. Want to see what we've got?"

"No, thanks. I've got a splitting headache. I'll take a look at it tomorrow," Fred said. He went down the hallway to his office and closed the door.

As Abby and Ian drove to their storage unit twenty minutes later, Abby said, "I wonder how often he drops into the main lab after we leave. Occasionally I've found some of the microscopes moved. Everything else I either take home or lock in the safe."

"Fred knows the combination," Ian answered. "He probably takes out samples from the locked freezer and looks at them under the microscope. Maybe it was enough to get the five hundred thou."

"Yeah, could be," said Abby. "Hey, how about stopping for pizza tonight?"

"Sure. There's that Italian place near the storage unit. I know you love their pepperoni."

"Mm-hmm. I—"

Suddenly Ian tromped on the gas pedal of the BMW.

"Where are you going, Ian? You were supposed to turn right here. You're heading straight for the toughest part of town." Abby grabbed the armrest. "Ian, what the hell are you doing?" she yelled.

"That guy's following us!"

Abby looked back.

"He got behind us after the first light out of the parking lot. A couple of cars came between us on Main Street. One of them was flashing its lights at me, and I couldn't figure out why. Now that first car is right behind us again, tailgating like he wants to rear-end us. Who *is* that bastard?"

Abby released her seat belt, turned around, and knelt on the passenger seat, gripping the back. "It looks like a Lexus, maybe. Oh my God, Ian—what if it's the same car that chased us before? Driver is a man, no passengers. Can't see him clearly or read the license plate either. It's too dark."

"Fuck!" yelled Ian. As the brakes screeched, Abby got tossed backward toward the windshield.

"Watch it, Ian!" she shouted. "Drive safely, can't you?"

"Not now, Ab." Ian yanked on the wheel. The car swerved violently to the right and screeched down a cobblestoned alley, scaring rats and cats, crashing into garbage pails, and awakening the junkies huddled in the doorways.

Abby fell against the door and grabbed the precious backpack at her feet. "Let me out!" she screamed. *"IAN, LET ME OUT!"*

"No, Ab! Too dangerous. You—" In his moment of hesitation the driver of the Lexus drove onto the sidewalk, then swerved in front of them and stopped, forcing Ian to a halt.

Frightened, Abby lunged into the backseat, still clutching her backpack.

In seconds a Mazda arrived behind the BMW with another screech of brakes. The Lexus bounced over the curb and sped away down the dark alley. Ian was tempted to take off after it and find out who the driver was, but a passenger instantly leaped out of the Mazda behind them, waving arms and yelling, and dashed in front of the BMW, blocking its way.

"Wait, Ian! STOP! It's Miano Tse! I don't believe it," Abby shouted. "She's standing right in front of us . . . just staring. Why? Why? And why is that black guy driving her car?"

Neither Ian nor Abby recognized Josh when he got out of Miano Tse's car and reached their car with two easy strides. He tapped on the windshield. "Need to talk to ya, man. You remember me: Josh King, Miano Tse's boyfriend. We met over at Doc Truesort's place."

Oh, of course, thought Abby, *the one who draws so well. How embarrassing that I didn't recognize him in the darkness.*

"We aren't here to hurt you. We're here to help," Miano Tse added, linking her arm through Josh's. "You can open the window."

Josh held up his hands. "I ain't got no gun or nothin'. Just got somethin' to tell ya."

Ian felt his racing heartbeats begin to slow down to normal. "Kind of a rough way to start a conversation," he growled, rolling down the windows. "But I'm listening."

"What we have to say is highly confidential. Actually, Ian, you picked a good spot. No cops never come down here." Josh leaned over and unlocked the back door through the open window. With a small bow and a wave of his hand, he held the back door open for Miano Tse, who sat next to Abby. Ian unlocked the front passenger door for Josh.

"Cool car, man," said Josh. "Real cool car. Didn't think no Mazda could stop a BMW."

"Cut the bullshit," said Ian sharply. "Tell us what's going on." He took the keys out of the ignition and put them into his left pocket.

Ian looked over his shoulder at Miano Tse. "I thought you had gone home for the day. Were you still in the building? How come I didn't see your car?"

Josh explained, "I came to get Miano Tse after work. My car is in the shop, so she let me borrow hers. I pulled up to the main door, where I figured she'd be waitin' for me."

"Yes. I was in the lobby waiting for Josh," Miano Tse said. "Did you look there?"

"No, didn't think of that," Ian said, and turned to face Josh.

"After I picked her up," continued Josh, "I drove around to the parkin' lot to exit and saw another guy pull up in a blue Lexus. I recognized him. He's a thief. When Miano Tse and I saw him drive behind you out of the parking lot, we figured he was up to no good. So we followed to make sure you were okay."

"Sorry we scared you so much, Abby," said Miano Tse. "When we blinked our lights, we thought maybe Ian would pull over, but he sped up instead."

"Well, I won't deny you scared us half to death," admitted Abby, "but you also scared that other driver away. So thanks for looking out for us."

"Yeah, thanks," said Ian. "But who the hell is this thief you're talking about, and what does he want from us?"

"His name is Royce Barkley," Miano Tse said. "He broke into Fred's hospital lab a few weeks ago—wanted to steal some bone marrow to sell on the black market."

"*What?*" exclaimed Abby. "How do you know that?"

"Our friend Alvarez—you remember him from the night we brought down The Oxman," Josh said.

Ian nodded. "Hard to forget."

"You got that right," said Josh. "Anyway, he's a security guard at the hospital. So on a Saturday in July, he escorts this Royce Barkley dude to a meetin' in Doc Truesort's office with the doc and Cory. Barkley's supposedly a sales rep for some pharma company."

"July," said Abby. "That was about the time that Fred asked my dad to suggest sales reps who might be interested in our research, wasn't it, Ian? But my dad and I both thought it was premature."

"Then," continued Josh, "the very next weekend, somebody breaks into the doc's hospital lab. Alvarez looked it up on the surveillance tapes. Definitely the same guy. Me and Miano Tse and our friend Ghanna all seen the printouts."

"I don't think he really worked for any pharma company," Miano Tse said. "Did Alvarez ask the company if he was one of their employees, Josh?"

"I don't know," Josh said. "If he is, one phone call from Alvarez would end his career. Doc Pannell said Doc Truesort didn't wanna press charges. His lawyer told him he don't have enough evidence 'cause nothin' was stolen."

"I understand," said Ian. "It wasn't the time to call attention to the hospital lab."

"Okay. So no hard feelin's, man. We'll talk again soon." Josh got out of the BMW and started the Mazda while he waited for Miano Tse.

"One more question, Miano Tse," said Abby. "Why did you run around to the front of our car?"

"Ian might have tried to drive away. I knew he would never run me over."

Afraid to get out of the car, Abby watched from the backseat of the BMW as Miano Tse got into her Mazda. Josh stepped on the gas, and Abby saw them back out of the alley, then pivot and speed away. She started to rub her eyes and realized her cheeks were wet. She had been crying. "I think I was hysterical, Ian."

"So was I."

"Can we trust them?" Abby asked.

"What choice do we have? Miano Tse and Josh apparently know a lot more than we do," Ian said, slipping the BMW into gear. He drove through the cobblestoned alley. They didn't see the Lexus.

"*Everybody* seems to know a lot more than we do," said Abby, "and I'm getting pretty damn tired of that."

"Me too. Since Barkley had a legitimate appointment, Martha probably has info on him in her Rolodex—maybe more than just contact numbers. Try chatting with her about him—see what you can find out."

"Good idea," said Abby. "And let's also ask to meet with everyone Fred works with at Hughler who might be involved in this project. See who they are, what they have to say, and what lies they tell. It would show us how much or how little they really know."

"Fine," said Ian. "I'm not going to our storage bin tonight. It's getting late, and they close at nine. We can drop off the stuff on our way to work tomorrow, when there's less chance of being followed."

"Oh, Ian . . . " Abby sighed unhappily. "I thought we were safe once The Oxman was dead, but I guess my dad is right: there are a lot more thieves out there in some shape or form."

"Yeah. I wonder if my uneasiness today was my extrasensory perception warning me," Ian said. "I was just getting bad vibes."

"Maybe. You were making sure all the doors were locked." Abby sighed again. "I guess we still have to remain alert."

Chapter

14

ON MONDAY, SEPTEMBER 17, A WEEK after Abby and Ian's frightening encounter with Royce Barkley, Fred met with Ian, Abby, Cory, and Miano Tse in Hughler Hospital's oncology lab. Cory had played a hunch that it wouldn't hurt to bolster public relations between Fred and the hospital CEO, Harry Wimpler, and secure his support for their research. So Cory had suggested a luncheon at the hospital, with a tour for the entire research team, and Fred had agreed.

"First time I've been in your hospital lab, Fred. It's better equipped than I thought," Abby lied.

"Glad you could come over. We like showing off this place. Some of the gear I bought myself."

"At this point we don't even know what belongs to Fred and what is the hospital's," Cory said.

"Martha's reserved the VIP conference room for us," said Fred. "She's ordered a variety of foods buffet style, and she will join us for lunch. Bob Pannell and CEO Harry Wimpler will be there too. I thought it would be helpful for all of you to get to know one another better."

Fred and Cory led Abby, Ian, and Miano Tse through the labyrinth of corridors and elevator banks to a lengthy, elegant hallway unlike any other in the hospital. Mahogany paneling gleamed along the lower six feet of the walls, crowned by a strip of mahogany molding intricately carved with oak leaves and acorns.

From there to the high ceiling, the wood was complemented by cream-colored stucco.

The research team's footsteps echoed on the parquet floor as they walked past the mahogany doors of the executive suites. At the end of the hall, Cory swung open the double doors of the conference room. There the lounge chairs and oak tables were massive and repeated the same motif of oak leaves and acorns carved on the legs of the furniture.

Ian was amazed. "It's old California. Where are the conquistadores?"

Cory ran his hand through his grayish-red hair and smiled with pleasure. "Thought you'd like it. Not everyone gets to use this room. Fortunately, Fred is respected around here." Cory introduced Harry Wimpler to Ian and Abby.

The luncheon was cordial, with the usual pleasantries and casual conversations about pets, gardening, sports, and so on. Ian talked with Harry, telling him about his father-in-law's medical volunteer work. Neither Fred nor Cory mentioned anything about their research. They sat back and enjoyed listening to the conversations around them. Martha chatted with Abby and Miano Tse about Louella, who continued to be healthy and happy, enjoying her life in Paris.

Harry Wimpler complimented Abby and Ian on their interest in helping Fred with his experiments. He described how valuable Fred and Cory had been to Hughler Hospital over many years, both by working directly with patients and by studying various cancers in the oncology lab. Bob listened and added that Fred had instituted the bone-marrow bank at the hospital.

Bob, Harry, and Martha left after lunch. Once the good-byes and see-you-soons were said, Fred and his research team remained at the conference table for a brief business meeting. They reviewed the projects they were working on and scheduled the follow-up research assignments among themselves.

Fred was pleased with each scientist's intellect and perseverance. "Ian," he asked, "can you handle all the requests these people will have throughout their experiments?"

Ian laughed. "Sure. It isn't as hard as it sounds."

When they were in the elevator alone, Ian asked Abby, "Why do you think Wimpler was there?"

"Politics, I suspect. He wants to keep Fred happy, and maybe vice versa. You think Wimpler may know more than we realize?"

"Hmmm. Maybe," said Abby as she got off the elevator.

"What could Fred possibly have told a pharma company to get them to invest all that money in his research? Where could the five hundred thou have come from?" asked Ian.

"I'm not sure. Maybe my dad? He's very generous."

"Or could it be a *grant* from a pharma company? Wimpler might've recommended Fred's research for one."

"I just don't know, Ian. Perhaps it was Dad *and* Wimpler. It looks like we've got the funds to move forward. That's all I care about."

"Let's talk to Miano Tse, then. She may know something," Ian said. "You know what else I'd like to ask her? Why the hell Dr. Pannell from the ER is involved in Fred's project."

"I overheard her say she was going to the hospital oncology lab with Cory. He wanted to show her some of the hospital's equipment."

By asking a few Hughler Hospital employees for directions to the oncology lab, Abby and Ian found Miano Tse in the hallway just outside its door.

"Need to talk to you, Miano Tse," Abby said. "Privately."

Miano Tse smiled. "Okay. Cory locked up the lab and left a few minutes ago. Let's find a quiet place outside." The three of them walked down the hallway till they found an exit door that didn't say ALARM WILL SOUND. Miano Tse pushed open the door, and they found themselves in the stony parking lot near a corner of the building. A maintenance shed hid them from view. "This looks good. Nobody will hear us or see us," she said.

"With this stench, nobody would want to come near us," Ian complained. "We're next to the incinerator."

Abby laughed and leaned against the brick wall, hoping to

look nonchalant. Then she turned to Miano Tse. "Our discussion after lunch was worthwhile. Not much was said at the luncheon, though. Do you know what's going on here, Miano Tse?" she asked.

"Big tsunami over some bone marrow. I don't know why or how or anything. I tried to speak to you before the meeting, but I couldn't."

"About the bone marrow?" Abby asked. "Bob mentioned it."

"No, don't know much about that," Miano Tse said. "But Josh wants to introduce you to some of his neighbors. He thinks you might be able to help them. Maybe you could come to the farmers' market early Saturday morning, for a community meeting. Bring a basket for fruits and vegetables. Dr. Pannell will be there."

"Sure, sure, we'll come. But what is this community meeting about?" Ian asked her. "And where does Dr. Pannell fit in? How come he was with us today?"

"He hardly said a word. He's chief in the ER, right?" Abby said, standing erect now.

"Assistant chief. But he helps find patients for Fred's research," Miano Tse said.

"That doesn't make sense, Miano Tse," said Ian. "There are plenty of HIV/AIDS patients around, in all walks of life. Fred would just have to advertise to find them for the research project."

"I guess Dr. Pannell sees a lot of HIV/AIDS patients at the ER," said Abby. "He must refer them to Fred to learn the risks of the experiment and sign up for it properly. Do the patients get paid to be in it?"

"I never heard about that," said Miano Tse, "but they must get free meds and treatment, because none of them could afford it. We get paid to find the right kind of patients—"

"Who's 'we'?" asked Ian, baffled.

"Me, Josh, and Ghanna," answered Miano Tse, glancing nervously back and forth between Ian's and Abby's faces. "The docs pay us to find and screen patients. They showed us exactly what symptoms to look for. But the main thing is, the patients have to be street people. No family. Nobody to care much or sue if anything goes wrong."

"Oh my God," said Abby slowly. "Please tell me you're kidding, Miano Tse."

"No. I'm not kidding you, Abby." Miano Tse stepped back. "I thought I was doing a good thing, helping find sick people so the doctor could heal them. He paid us to find them. In our own way, we helped with his research. You and Ian are just helping in a different way." She dropped her head to her chest and blurted out, "You've never been street people. You've never been poor."

Abby paused and glanced at Ian before she said, "You're right, Miano Tse. Ian and I are privileged. But don't hold that against us. Use it."

"Miano Tse," said Ian, "all the patients should've received a full explanation of the process so they understood what the research entails for them. Then they should've signed a form agreeing to be part of an experiment despite the risks. It's not ethical otherwise."

"Oh, Dr. Truesort probably had them sign something. It was just easier and cheaper to use the street people."

"And maybe to get the glory," Ian muttered, shaking his head.

All of them were silent for a moment.

"If Fred did what you say to get tissue samples," said Ian, "that could be considered unethical. A good lawyer could probably call it charity and get him off, but nobody would hire him again. As for the rest of us"—Ian stared straight ahead—"I just don't know."

"All three of us may lose our jobs if a lawsuit comes out of this, Miano Tse," Abby pointed out.

"Perhaps we're too far down the food chain to get in trouble, Abby," said Ian. "And we may come up with a viable cure for AIDS. Who can tell? Now, who'll we meet at the market on Saturday?"

Miano Tse slowly looked up. She spat out, "People who help each other."

In spite of the sharp answer, Ian said calmly, "You can tell Josh we'll be there."

Abby put her arm around Miano Tse's shoulder. "I'm sorry I upset you." She bent down and kissed Miano Tse on the top of her head.

Ian and Abby went home after their talk with Miano Tse. There was little conversation between them. Both were pondering what they had just discussed.

Abby broke the silence. "I'm shocked that Fred would be so unethical. Good thing we found out about it."

"Yes. That conversation must've been an unpleasant surprise for Miano Tse too, since she hadn't meant to do anything wrong."

"What do you think we should do now, Ian? Do you want to stay with Fred's project or resign?"

"We've both put so much time and effort into our research. I hate to be part of anything shady, but I hate to quit now."

"We're so close to a breakthrough! I can just feel it. Fred's been unscrupulous, but I think we should stick with it. If we succeed, it'll help millions of people."

"That's true," said Ian.

"I won't tell Dad where Fred's been getting his patients until our research is sold. For now, let's find out what's on the minds of Josh and his friends."

"Sure. We could learn a lot Saturday," Ian noted. "Try to get better acquainted with Dr. Pannell too."

Saturday morning, despite dressing in sandals and battered jeans, Ian and Abby still looked too posh. Ian carried a large basket for produce, and Abby was wearing her backpack.

Miano Tse waved to them from the other side of the throng. They wriggled their way through the shoppers, bumping into shopping bags and baby strollers as they maneuvered to Miano Tse's side. "Assam said we could meet at the back of his shop. I'll go in first. You follow me a little later," said Miano Tse. "You stick out in this crowd. It's less conspicuous this way. We want to keep this project private for a while until we have a business plan."

So Abby and Ian walked on. They bartered for a pound of green beans and half a bushel of McIntosh apples to share at the meeting. After examining the bolts of cloth in the dusty window—Scottish wool plaid, cotton printed with palm trees—they sauntered into Assam's shop, formerly The Oxman's. Assam smiled, bowed quickly, and pointed to a door at the rear of the shop. His wife, Sakina, her glossy black hair pulled into a neat bun, looked up from her cutting table as they passed. She acknowledged them with a smile as she measured cloth for a customer.

Ian closed the door to maintain some privacy. When he and Abby entered the smaller room at the back, they saw Miano Tse and Josh perched on top of a Persian-style rug thrown across a stack of bolts of cloth. Alvarez, Asunta, Sally, and Lefty had also found seats on piles of rugs or bolts of fabric. Dr. Pannell sat on a roll of carpet, where Ian and Abby joined him. Ghanna sat on the only chair, leaning back against the wall with the front chair legs aloft. He held a filled ashtray in one hand and a cigarette in the other. "I'm not a chain smoker," he told the newcomers; "it just look that way."

Josh stood up. "Ghanna, you remember Abby and Ian from that meetin' over at Doc Truesort's."

Ian put down the basket of apples to shake Ghanna's hand.

Ghanna leaned forward, forcing the front legs of his chair to the floor with a thud that startled the ashes out of the tray in a gray puff. He jabbed the cigarette into his mouth in order to thrust out his right hand. "Pleased to see ya again. Pleased to see ya both," he said as he pumped Ian's and Abby's hands. "Josh and Miano Tse wanted me to talk to you and tell you what we got planned."

"Okay, Ghanna," Ian said. "Let me put this basket of apples in the center of our circle here. Thought we might need a snack."

"Thanks for the apples, Ian. That was nice of ya," said Josh. All of them helped themselves to apples during the conversation that followed, tossing the cores into the wastebasket in the corner.

Ghanna began telling the story of Dr. Truesort's research from the beginning. Others in the room joined the narrative to fill in the parts they knew best: how Fred had started off with an idea he hoped could help millions of people while bringing himself fame and fortune; how he had asked Bob Pannell to help him find patients, and Bob had asked Josh, who had then asked Ghanna and Miano Tse.

Ian and Abby learned more than they had ever known about Lee's decline and how much he had meant to Josh. They heard how Vincent's recovery had inspired the neighborhood but had attracted The Oxman's interest. And they learned more about other patients, such as Midgin and Camilla.

"So many sad stories," murmured Abby.

"But there's ways to make more happy stories 'round this neighborhood," said Ghanna. "Now, we ain't no city planners, no board of trustees, but this is what we figure. If Doc Truesort makes any money off this AIDS research, he oughtta throw us a piece of the action and keep the rest for himself."

"You think he'd do that, though?" asked Ian skeptically. "From what I've seen, he probably thinks he's paid you well enough already."

"Awww, he could give us a big bonus and still have a bundle left over," said Ghanna. "Rich dude like that, house like that—what he want more money for? He could retire. Eat good. Go fishin', swimmin', and golfin' and have a bottle of red wine every day."

The others laughed at this image of a lifestyle for Fred.

Josh said, "Well, even if Doc Truesort keeps it all, we still got ideas about improvin' life around here. We want a good clinic for adults and kids, right here in this neighborhood, where everyone can get preventive medical care and get their teeth fixed and everythin'. All the wellness clinics are too far away. Ask the doc here. He knows. The hospital ER is all most people got, an' they wait till they're real sick."

"He's right about that," Dr. Pannell agreed. "I could keep a whole staff of family-medicine docs busy. I'm lucky if I can find one pediatrician at the hospital who will come into the ER to help. They're afraid they'll be overwhelmed with cases."

"We also need a detox center," suggested Vincent. "Big-time. Until we clean up the drug problem, we'll never get out of the cesspool. I know all about that." There were nods of agreement.

"All these ideas sound great," said Abby, "but Hughler City already has a lot of social services. Wouldn't it make more sense to help staff them? Provide them with more equipment and pay some good people a decent salary to run them. I'm happy with that. What's the point of starting at the beginning if you've already got facilities available? Why reinvent the wheel?"

"It'll never work," Josh said. "Gotta be nearby."

Ghanna nodded in agreement. "Too many people 'round here ain't got cars," he explained. "You ever try ridin' a bus to the clinic way over past the city center? You can wait half an hour before the bus even show up, an' druggies checkin' you out the whole time. You gonna do that with a sick kid? Nope. You just give your kid aspirin an' hope he gets better, an' if he don't, ya take him to the ER."

"If a full medical and dental clinic and a detox facility are musts around here," said Dr. Pannell, "I'll do all I can to get them going. Staffing, equipment, lab, you name it. I've got a lot of favors I can call in."

Josh turned to the group and said, "I'm sure he does. He's the best doc in the hospital."

"We need something else nearby, too," said Asunta. "A good, affordable day-care center for our kids, with healthy food for them. The closest day-care centers are miles from here. Many aren't open when working moms from this neighborhood can get there, drop off their kids, and still get to work on time on the bus, you know? Me and my friends talk about it all the time."

Josh said, "Good idea, Asunta."

"Maybe a day-care center could even be right near the new health clinic, you think? And people from around here like Sally could get jobs there, too," said Asunta. "She helps me a lot of the time with Ramiero."

Sally smiled, pleased with the compliment.

Dr. Pannell said, "If we put together a good business plan and start speaking to the right people, all this is possible. And if you *really* want to plan ahead, you should start thinking now about training more medical personnel from your neighborhood for jobs in the future. I know about some good scholarship programs available."

Ian asked, "What about the business side? We need to figure out how to finance all this."

"Yeah," said Ghanna, "we better make sure we got the money before we go spendin' it."

"I don't think we'd better count on a windfall from Fred," continued Ian. "But I know one bank with low-interest start-up loans for businesses that benefit the community. What we are planning would fit right into that category. Let me get some information for you, and we can discuss this with one of the bank's loan officers. Who knows? It'll be an uphill battle, what with the city's recent budget cuts and all, but we may even find some venture capital out there."

"How about you, Lefty? You're a businessman. You too, Assam. You willing to help us?"

"I'll talk to my banker too," Assam offered.

"Yeah. Maybe you get dressed nice in one of them classy suits you made," Ghanna suggested, "and talk to a banker down in the center city. Assam tailors his own suits," he told the group proudly. "He's not just a Persian rug dealer."

Lefty said, "It'll take several years to accomplish what you're talking about. You gotta plan carefully. Start with the easiest parts first, and when you can afford it, take the next step."

Assam told the group, "Lefty is right. Make a list of what you want and arrange the projects in order. You know, which should come first. If you want a local day-care center for the children of working moms, see what the possibilities are. You gotta learn about everything on your list. Maybe there's a house up for sale here in this neighborhood. You look it over. Does it need a lot of repairs? What's the asking price? Things like that you have to do."

"I'll go with you if you want," Ian said to Assam. "Social services are important, but you also need a decent place to buy healthy food year-round, and not just produce. This whole farmers' market area could be transformed. We could attract some new vendors and fill up some of these empty storefronts. Get people employed right here in this neighborhood. Let's start by cleaning up this store. Assam, you would get more business if—well, if it were better lighted and not so dusty."

"The Oxman didn't care about nothin' like that when the store was his," said Josh. "Vendors stopped coming to this area. Scared away by the crime. Assam told me that right after the sting, the cops impounded all the drugs stored in the basement. Needed a truck just to haul all that stuff away." He chuckled.

Ghanna explained to Ian and Abby, "Doc Pannell here also wants us to work with the cops an' clean out drugs an' crime. He's pushin' beyond the limit, asking us to work with them cops. They almost the natural enemy—predators. Sorry, Doc," said Ghanna frankly, "can't see that happenin'."

"But now that The Oxman's gone," said Josh, "we gotta make our move an' take back our neighborhood before some new drug lord takes over, ya know? We need a citizens' patrol. Place gets cleaned up nice, and it's ripe for vandalizin'. Maybe we start with a citizens' organization, which will oversee the patrol. Alvarez, you're in security. How about you and me organize that?"

"Glad to," said Alvarez.

"Very good idea," said Dr. Pannell. "Once people buy into it, they protect it. My father practices business law in Trenton. I'm sure he'll help set up the citizens' organization. And I bet my brother will help build the clinic. He's a mechanical engineer."

"Great!" Abby said. "My dad knows a lot of professionals who work pro bono for charities. I'll ask him for recommendations if you need more help. And"—she glanced at Ian—"I can also ask my dad about putting up collateral for an initial loan. He's often generous with worthy causes. Ian and I will donate something too."

There was a pause and then Miano Tse started clapping. Sakina briefly peeked into the back room. Quickly Assam told her that they had just learned some very good news. Sakina smiled, closed the door, and returned to the front of the store to help a customer.

"As for the clinic," added Ian, "you'll need plans—you know, drawings to show what you propose. Then you have to go before the city planning board and pass inspection."

"I've been thinking about a career in architecture. Let me work on that," Josh said, watching Miano Tse's proud smile.

"You've got it," Dr. Pannell said, who saw the smile spread across Josh's face too. "My staff can tell you how a good clinic should be laid out. Many of them have experience working in well-planned spaces and poorly planned ones. Consult plenty of ER workers before you draw up the layout."

"I bet Étoile would give me good advice," Josh agreed. "She's worked in so many kinds of hospitals—in Vietnam, even. I'll ask everyone else, too."

"How come she didn't come to the meeting, Doc?" Josh asked.

"I needed her in the ER. I'll brief her when I get back."

"Abby, I wonder if Cory would be interested in helping somehow," said Ian.

"Maybe Cory would join us if we could gain his confidence," Abby suggested. "Ian, let's see what we can do about that."

"I don't think he would want to get involved with us," said Miano Tse.

"Well," said Bob, "we've discussed lots of good ideas—too many to tackle all at once. This will be a long-term project. Everyone who works on it will have to be dedicated to its success," he warned.

"You want dedicated? You got it," said Ghanna. "We're stuck in this here neighborhood, so we gotta make the best of it."

"Thank you for your hospitality, Assam," said Ian. "Let's meet regularly and report on what we've accomplished." They all exchanged contact information and agreed on a date for the next meeting.

"But before we leave," said Abby to the group, "I need to do something very important." She told them briefly about being chased by Royce Barkley on the way home from Fred's lab almost two weeks earlier, and another time weeks before that. "If Josh and Miano Tse hadn't followed us and scared him away, who knows what might've happened? He had us blocked in a narrow alley." Turning toward Miano Tse and Josh, Abby added, "I was too upset that night to thank you properly." She got up and hugged each of them.

"You're welcome, Abby," said Miano Tse. "You're a good person. You too, Ian."

"Glad to do it for ya," added Josh. "Anytime." Then he, Ghanna, and Alvarez quickly explained how Barkley had broken into Dr. Truesort's hospital lab in July.

"So if any of ya see a curly-haired white dude hangin' out in a blue Lexus, let one of us know, okay?" said Josh. "Alvarez can show ya pictures of him from the surveillance cameras."

"So anyway," said Abby, "you can see why Ian and I need to take unusual security measures. I'm too deeply involved in Fred's project to turn back. I've bet Ian's and my whole future on this research. No one is going to steal what we have found. Ian, please give me my backpack."

"You sure you want to do this, Ab?"

"Positive," she answered. "Ghanna, where do you live?"

"Hughler Street. 'Cross from the hospital."

"Please take this backpack and hide it where God himself will not be able to find it. Do not tell *anyone* where it is. When we're ready for it, we'll let you know."

Miano Tse stared at the backpack. "That's the one you had the night Royce . . . No wonder you were scared."

"Yes, I was," said Abby.

The people who had attended the meeting left Assam's shop in inconspicuous ones and twos, as they had arrived. Abby and Ian stayed a little while, browsing through Assam's rugs and fabrics.

Bob Pannell put a hand on Abby's shoulder and said quietly, "I'd like a quick word with you and Ian outside, if you have a minute."

"Sure," said Abby. "We're parked half a block down the street to the left. See you out there shortly."

Ten minutes later, Ian put the remaining apples in the trunk of the car, along with the beans and a small rug Assam had insisted on giving them. "Ab, are you crazy, giving them your research?" he murmured to her. "They live by stealing."

"Somebody had to show some faith, trust—call it what you will."

Bob joined them a minute later, and the three took a brisk walk to a quiet vest-pocket park on a street a few blocks from the farmers' market. Abby and Ian sat on a park bench. Bob stood and faced them, leaning against a tree. Ian asked Bob, "Do you think Fred would contribute to this project? You work with him, but do you trust him?"

"I did in the beginning," Bob answered. "I thought he knew something. He thought so, too. He just doesn't want to admit defeat. This thing has spun out of control for him."

"Yeah," said Ian, "we've been getting that impression too. Believe me, his theory is looking good so far. I guess we need to run some more experiments to get the full picture."

"It could go in his favor. I certainly hope so," Bob said. "But I want to talk to you about your conversation with Miano Tse after the luncheon on Monday. She told me you were upset, and I understand why. I want to assure you that I've been informing each patient privately about the clinical processes of Fred's research. I've explained to each of them the potential benefits and risks of what they will experience, such as chemotherapy, blood tests, and bone-marrow transplants. I even caught up with the first few patients who had not been informed."

"This is good news, Bob," said Abby with a sigh of relief. "I was led to believe that no one had taken care of this."

Bob acknowledged her comment with a nod and continued, "Once I'm sure each patient understands what's involved, I ask them to sign a proper legal consent form, and I've kept all the forms on file. The patients know about the medical risks, but most of them are desperate and view this as their last hope. Some have walked away when they realized the dangers involved."

"Thank you for handling the patients' consent forms, Bob," said Ian.

"You two are not part of anything unethical," Bob stressed. "Fred didn't want to be bothered with the paperwork, claiming it might be an avenue for some unscrupulous individual to gain the right to learn what you researchers had discovered. You may have noticed that Fred can be stubborn."

Ian raised an eyebrow and glanced at Abby, who smirked and nodded.

"Once he makes a decision," continued Bob, "he will not change it even when negative evidence is presented. As I told Josh, sometimes you have to protect people from themselves."

"How does Cory feel about these issues?" Abby asked.

"He told me he argued with Fred about the ethical problems but got nowhere. Cory claimed he didn't have the time to do it himself. He was glad I'd taken over that responsibility, especially since I'm experienced in relating to this population in the ER."

A broad smile spread across Abby's face. "Whew. This is a big relief."

Ian shook Bob's hand. Abby gave him a hug.

The following Monday, Cory walked into the main lab, where Abby was working at her desk. "Still analyzing, Abby?" he asked.

"Uh-huh. You want to help?"

"Okay. What can I do for you?" Glancing through the window of the clean room, Cory could see Ian at his workstation and Miano Tse prepping samples.

"See if you can get some photos of the specimens as a reference point before we start experimenting," she suggested. "That is, if you have the time. I thought you'd be working over at the hospital today."

"Nope, I've got all the time in the world," Cory said, clasping and unclasping his hands. "Fred's been called before the hospital ethics committee. Figured I'd see what I can do over here."

"Ethics committee?" Abby echoed, looking at him intently. "That's pretty serious, isn't it?"

"Yeah, but—"

"Exactly what's he being accused of?" Abby interrupted.

"Don't worry; it has nothing to do with you or Ian and Miano Tse. Besides, Wimpler will get Fred off," Cory assured her.

Miano Tse and Ian came out of the clean room. "Couldn't help but overhear. What has nothing to do with us?" Ian asked.

"I was telling Abby, Wimpler will get Fred through the ethics-committee inquiry. No problem."

"What's in question? Why are they talking to him?" Ian asked.

Cory studied them. Abby had moved away from her desk and was standing very still, focusing on him, waiting for an answer. Ian had pushed his eyeglasses up on his forehead, where his furrowed brow held them in place. His hands clenched the chair in front of him so tightly that his knuckles were white. Miano Tse sat on the edge of Abby's desk and silently slipped her hand into Abby's. Their tension was palpable.

Damn, Cory thought, *they've been out of the loop. Fred never told them about using Patsy's bone marrow for Vincent. I'd better explain.*

Cory moved a few steps closer to them. He began, "Uh . . . the truth . . . Well, the truth is . . . Uh . . . It's about Patsy Willington."

"Who the hell is Patsy Willington? And what the hell does she have to do with us?" Ian snapped out the questions.

Cory sighed. "Sit down. It's a long story. . . ."

Ian sat on an old lab stool. Abby sat on the edge of her desk and invited Miano Tse to sit on the chair next to her. Cory dragged a wooden desk chair over and sat in front of them. He continued, "She was a cancer patient of Fred's. She died. Now her parents are suing Fred because they think he used her backup bone marrow to save someone else while their daughter was in remission."

"Did he?" Abby asked in a hushed voice.

"Yes. It's what we believe contributed significantly to Vincent's recovery. If Patsy hadn't become sick again, Fred would've gotten away with it."

"Fred's been hiding this all along?" Abby asked in disbelief.

"Yeah. I'm afraid we both have." Cory interlocked his fingers and dropped his head. "I'm truly sorry. From now on I'll be sure to keep all of you informed."

Abby slid down from the desk. With her hands on her hips, she stood in front of Cory, saying, "How could you take such a risk? How could you deceive us? What will happen to all our hard work?" The words tumbled out of her mouth in an angry staccato.

"I got caught up in Fred's wave of enthusiasm even though I fully knew that some of his actions were blatantly shameful. I apologize to all three of you."

"Jesus," Ian said. "We came here believing that you were ethical. Does Abby's dad, Dr. Zelban, know this?"

"No."

"How about Wimpler? What's he know?" Abby asked.

"He knows."

"Why did he let this happen, then?" Abby demanded.

"Wimpler found out only after the fact; he never would've given permission. When he did find out, Fred appealed to his ego. Of course, at that point Fred really thought he was onto something big; he made Wimpler feel honored to be part of groundbreaking research. The bone-marrow transplants are an essential part of Fred's research procedure, as he clearly explained to Wimpler. You know, Wimpler's a former priest who thinks he can still save the world."

"Yeah? So how is he going to save Fred?" Ian asked sardonically.

"Wimpler personally covered up the tracks of the missing marrow already. He just has to keep his mouth shut. You know how the game's played, Abby. Wimpler has to cover his own ass. The ethics committee won't want to tar and feather one of their esteemed doctors, let alone the CEO. It'd make them look bad."

"Won't the committee, and the hospital, look even worse if no scapegoat is found?" asked Ian.

"Not necessarily," said Cory, "if the committee finds no wrongdoing. Fred did discuss the situation with Patsy. Of course he never told her that he had deliberately given her marrow to someone else; he just claimed it had been misplaced, and he would have to find a compatible donor—which he soon did. He could have harvested more of her own marrow, cleansed it, and given it back to her, but he didn't want to for two reasons: her body might not have been able to withstand another harvest, and her current bone marrow was not as effective as she needed."

"That's logical enough, I suppose," Ian said.

"But if Patsy had her original, healthier bone marrow, she might still be with us?" asked Abby.

"It's possible," said Cory, "but I seriously doubt she would have made it. She was pretty far gone at her last checkup. The other donor's marrow we gave her was reasonably close to her own, though it did require a larger dose of immunosuppressant, which put her body under additional stress. Her original, healthy marrow might have bought her a couple of months. That's all. Instead it did save another patient's life."

Ian asked, "So nobody thought Patsy was about to die? What brought about the abrupt change in her health?"

"We don't know. Fred and I were shocked when we found that she had deteriorated so rapidly. Up till then her four-month checkups with Fred had been good, and she hadn't complained of anything. Originally she was vigorous and athletic, with an effervescent personality. Fred felt she was healthy enough to donate bone marrow for our research. His renown as an oncologist was legendary, and I trusted his diagnosis."

"Ironic, isn't it?" mused Abby. "Donating marrow to the bone-marrow bank is supposed to be insurance, like giving your own blood before you have surgery. But it didn't work for Patsy. It just put her at greater risk because Fred stole something that might have saved her life."

"That's right," admitted Cory.

"Maybe Fred will get what he deserves," Ian said in disgust.

"Does Dr. Pannell know about this, too?" Miano Tse asked.

"I'm not sure," said Cory.

After an awkward pause, Abby asked, "You really believe Wimpler can persuade them?"

"Sure. Patsy did consult another oncologist, but he doesn't have privileges here anymore. Didn't want to do the dirty work you get at an inner-city hospital," Cory said.

"So where does this leave us?" asked Miano Tse. "Will we be considered unethical too?"

"No," said Cory. "Miano Tse, Fred decided to give Patsy's bone marrow to Vincent late last fall, quite a few months before you started working here. Abby and Ian, although you were here at the time, you weren't involved either."

"That's right," said Ian. "We didn't know anything about this until you told us ten minutes ago."

"Exactly," said Cory. "All three of you were doing preliminary work on the genetics of survivors, which isn't an easy task. Although I worked with you on that area of research occasionally, Fred and I were the *only* ones involved with treating the patients in the HIV/cancer study. Certainly none of you had any idea where the bone marrow had come from; you only knew that it helped Vincent's recovery."

"The results were remarkable," said Abby.

"Both Fred and I have scrupulously documented every step in the HIV/cancer research," Cory continued, "so that we would eventually have enough evidence to prove to a pharma company that our proposal had merit—"

"But how will the marketing of your work be received if your success was arrived at by unethical means?" Ian interrupted.

"I plan to be up front about it," said Cory. "The demand for HIV meds may overshadow any questionable ethics. In any case, Fred's and my careful records show conclusively that none of you were involved in the bone-marrow scandal. I swear I will vouch for you in court if it ever comes to that."

"Thank you, Cory," said Abby gratefully, and the others added their thanks.

Cory smiled. "You're welcome. It's possible that one or more of you may be asked to testify before the ethics committee, or in court, about Fred's decision to give Patsy Willington's bone marrow to Vincent. Just tell the truth: that you knew nothing about it until today and that the marrow helped save Vincent's life."

"Since Fred hasn't exactly been keeping us in the loop," said Ian, one eyebrow raised sarcastically, "is there any other news you can tell us? Has he sold any research to a pharmaceutical house without letting us know?"

"No, nothing's been sold, though Fred did try. I'm sure he would have told all of us if any sale went through. Someone did recently make a sizable investment in our work, but it turned out to be private money."

"Whose?" Ian wanted to know.

"I'm not at liberty to say," said Cory.

"Or you don't know," Ian retorted.

"I do know, but our benefactor wants to stay anonymous. Fred still has a long way to go before he can develop his cancer-cell research into a marketable treatment for AIDS. He's now realized that he needs a more complete, integrated package before he can go public, and meanwhile, he needs money."

"Thank goodness for that five hundred thousand dollars," said Abby. "By the way, I think I know where it came from. My dad."

"Well, since you've guessed . . . ," Cory said awkwardly.

"Nice of him to buy me a lab—but I'm doing the research without any help from him. He doesn't own my brains," Abby declared.

"In any case, you and Fred expect the rest of us to develop something marketable," Ian said.

Cory nodded. "Abby, you're the lead researcher on this project besides Fred. All of us will be glad to help you."

"Yes," said Miano Tse. "You've taught me so much."

"Well," said Ian, "Abby and I have spent too much time and expertise to give up now. What about you? Are you abandoning Fred's ship?"

"I'm no Boy Scout. Actually"—Cory sighed heavily and ran his hand through his hair—"I'm looking at this research from a very personal level. My daughter has AIDS. I figure you three may have the answers soon. She needs them *now*. Fred might just consume valuable time until he got the highest bidder. Meanwhile, patients may die. I'd like to give Nora a chance."

There was another awkward pause. "Does Fred know this?" Ian asked.

"No. It's the real reason why I agreed to work with him, though. I've been asked to appear before the ethics committee. They're interviewing individually those they think may be involved. I was asked to come in Saturday. I agreed, of course, but it means I won't get to visit my daughter. Sunday is out. It's too much driving for me in one day. I like to be in the lab promptly on Monday morning."

"Where is she now?" Miano Tse asked.

"She still lives in upstate New York, with her mother. I see Nora at least twice a month, usually more. She used to drive here to see me. Now she's too weak, so I go see her. It's hard going inside my former home. My wife and I have never resolved our differences. Here's my daughter's picture." Cory pulled a photograph from his wallet. "High school. Ten years ago now."

"Very lovely young lady," Abby said. "She has your red hair."

Ian looked over Abby's shoulder. "You must be very proud of her. If she's ever able to get down this way, maybe she'd like to see what you're researching. Her dad is working to save her life. How cool is that?"

Cory's jaw dropped open for a moment. He responded in a

husky whisper, "I never thought of it quite that way. Nora might like that."

All four of them became quiet. Cory took off his glasses and wiped his eyes with his fingers. Abby gave him some tissues. Ian patted his arm, repeating, "It's okay, Cory. It's okay."

At last, in a hushed voice, Cory said, "Sorry. Afraid I become too emotional when I confront my daughter's illness. I apologize. I probably appeared cold when I discussed Patsy's death, but it was either that or fall apart. I don't blame her parents for suing."

Ian told him, "Don't express regret for being human, Cory."

Cory mumbled, "Thanks, Ian."

Abby added, "How about both of you coming to our condo tonight, where we can continue this conversation?"

"Not me, but thanks anyway," said Miano Tse. "Josh and I are going out to dinner and a movie tonight. I'd love to another time."

"We'll be sure to invite you some other night soon," said Abby.

"Okay, great. See ya," Miano Tse called as she left.

"How about you, Cory?" asked Ian.

"I don't have anything planned. I'd be happy to join you."

"We'll have Chinese takeout. It's my best recipe," Abby joked.

Ian raised his glass of wine that evening. "Glad you could join us tonight, Cory."

"You're the first guest we've had in our new home. Welcome." Abby sipped her wine. "It makes me realize how busy we are. We do go to concerts in New York City with friends, but we have dinner with them at a nearby restaurant. They think New Jersey is too far away." Abby laughed.

"Pleased to be here. Your condo is designed efficiently, and you've obviously put a lot of thought into furnishing and decorating it. I can see why you are happy here," Cory commented.

"Thank you," said Ian. "We like the location, too: near the lab, the shops, the highways, and New York City," Ian said.

"You make a good team. I'm glad both of you feel that your research is moving forward," Cory added.

"Yes, absolutely," Abby said. "But we've also started working on a project of social and economic concern."

"At the farmers' market this past Saturday, Abby and I met with Dr. Pannell and some of the people he's contacted in the neighborhood," Ian said.

"You mean Josh and Miano Tse?" Cory asked.

"Yes, and an old man named Ghanna," Ian said.

"Miano Tse's mentioned him a few times at the lab," said Cory. "I met Josh and Ghanna during that planning meeting at Fred's, just before the sting."

"Yes, that's right," said Ian. "Ghanna seems to be some sort of a leader for their neighborhood."

Abby said, "Ghanna explained how they supplied Dr. Pannell with HIV/AIDS patients for cash."

"Ghanna and his friends played major roles in helping the cops get The Oxman off the streets, putting themselves at risk," added Ian.

"Yes, I was impressed by that during the sting," Cory said.

"At any rate," Ian said, "they feel they've risked a great deal and deserve to be a part of our team."

"I don't know what you're talking about," Cory said. "They want to share in the *profits*?"

"Indirectly and directly. They need a full-service health clinic with hours convenient for working moms, plus a children's day-care center," Abby said.

"We already have several health clinics and day-care centers in Hughler City."

"I looked into them," Abby answered. "You go to one place for pediatric care, another place for adult care, another place for detox, another place for dentistry, and so on. Most are open only during regular business hours. That's it—or after hours by appointment. These people don't have cars, and some don't have phones either. Have you ever tried to take a sick kid on a bus? They use the pay phone at Lefty's or the one at the convenience store. How can they call for an appointment or to see if the doctor is in? It's a lot easier to just walk over to the hospital ER."

"I take your point," Cory conceded.

"Ian suggested finding a bank with low interest rates for local businesses," Abby continued. "Dr. Pannell hopes we can set up a clinic that would include dentistry. He knows a lot of doctors and dentists he thinks will help us."

"He runs a dental clinic in the ER with volunteer dentists already," Cory said. "It's really the family doctor's office most days, from what I've seen."

"We agreed in principle to set up a nonprofit citizens' organization with a startup loan from us," Abby continued. "I've asked my dad. He'll help too. He often supports charitable medicine. Ian's offered to go with Assam, who now has a shop near the farmers' market, to inquire about loans for disadvantaged areas."

"You're crazy. Truesort Research isn't close to becoming profitable. Even if we were, you're still crazy." Cory took a big gulp of his wine. "Did they believe you?"

"They believed her, all right," Ian said. "If you agree to help us, we want you to know you'd be working for a salary like the rest of us. Our plan is simple. We'll set up a small research firm with the money we earn on the AIDS research project. A percentage of the profit will go back to the community. We welcome any volunteers who have something to contribute. Bob Pannell's father may help; he practices business law in Trenton. Also Bob's brother, who's a mechanical engineer. Abby's dad will refer other professionals who work pro bono for charities."

Abby added, "Did we mention that we met at the back of Assam Sadur's cloth shop? Someone told me it used to be The Oxman's. Perfect irony." She laughed.

"You're bleedin' dreamers. God save me." Cory stabbed at his chicken and snow peas with a chopstick. "Idealism and Chinese, what a double entrée! I'm a pragmatist. Whatever works is for me. Abby, do you have a fork?" Then he laughed. "Okay, what do you want me to do? Fred is going to be focused on the ethic committee's requests, his lawyer's advice, and how he can keep his head above water."

"It's that time-consuming?" Abby asked.

"Yes, he'll leave the hard work up to you. Just keep him informed, preferably by speaking to him face-to-face. Martha can help you schedule a meeting. Fred doesn't like anything in writing. He's afraid memos and emails can fall into the wrong hands," Cory advised.

"That's a good suggestion," Ian replied.

Cory added, "But I'm pretty sure I can contribute more. Like I told you a while ago at Fred's lab, I've done some microscopic imaging of viruses. You were onto something when we were working with CD4+ T cells. Remember we called Fred back to look at it? He merely glanced at it and left."

"I was hurt by that," Abby admitted. "We were looking at Louella's immune cells, which defy the HIV. They may have some important chemical property we can use. The light microscopes here at the lab have shown us that something unusual is going on with these cells, but we aren't sure exactly what it is."

"I wish Kingencorp would get back to us," said Ian. "We need their scanning electron microscope; can't take this experiment to the next level without it."

"Another thing, Cory. Do you know anything about a sales rep named Royce Barkley?" asked Abby.

"Yeah. He was from Sirgentec Pharmaceuticals. I remember he met with Fred and me back in July; he was interested in our research. But then he broke into the hospital oncology lab about a week later. Wanted to buy some bone marrow, apparently for the black market. Fred was furious! Of course the deal was off."

"We just heard about that at the meeting on Saturday," said Ian. "Did he get any bone marrow?"

"According to Fred, he just ran off down the hall," Cory answered. "Haven't seen him since, but I'll let you know if he ever shows up. It does prove how much we need security, doesn't it? I'm glad Fred's invested in first-rate security for the private lab."

"Yes," said Ian, and Abby nodded.

"Well, I'd better go," said Cory. "Thanks for the meal. You're a good cook, Abby," he joked.

Abby laughed. "Chinese takeout is my specialty."

Cory took her hand in his left and Ian's in his right. "Seriously, I'm pleased to have a real opportunity like this. My hopes have been dashed so many times."

Abby gave him a big hug.

Early the following Tuesday evening, after Miano Tse and Cory had left, Abby finished organizing her research.

"Here's the latest backup version of my work." Abby handed Ian a flash drive.

"Where's the second backup?" Ian asked.

Abby pointed to her head. "Here. Right here. I know what I changed and why."

"Then what did you give Ghanna?"

"Real stuff," answered Abby. "It's several generations removed from this, though. I know what I gave Ghanna. I've been over it a thousand times. Don't worry."

"He still may screw us."

"Somehow I don't think so. He didn't strike me as the type. For once in his life, Ghanna would like to do something grand, be noticed, and get some praise. Like Fred, in a way, but Ghanna's playing it straight." Abby walked across the lab and opened a file drawer. "I'd like to hide my handwritten notes too," she continued. "I've filled several notebooks."

"Why do you use those goddamn notebooks, anyway?"

"It's a nuisance to go back and forth to the computer. It really is great backup. I hate to discard them. I suppose we could, since we have duplicate information on a flash drive, but I really worked from these notes too. And—well, like I say, it's good to have in case there's a malfunction."

"Or an earthquake," added Ian wryly.

Abby laughed. "Don't exaggerate. We're in New Jersey, Ian. More likely they'd be destroyed by a flood."

"How about the storage unit? Throw them in with some of the junk we've stuffed in there," he suggested.

"I could, couldn't I? It's climate controlled. I'll wrap them in old newspapers and put them in that wooden box with the crazy lamp Aunt Millie gave us. Then we'll be all set."

"Perfect," said Ian. "One look at that old gargoyle and any thief would run."

"Aunt Millie is not a gargoyle."

"I was referring to the lamp, but on second thought . . ."

Ian dodged a mouse pad.

part SEVEN

Triumph and Terror

Chapter 15

THURSDAY MORNING AT FRED'S lab, Abby hung up the phone and yelled, "Ian, Cory, Miano Tse, start packing your gear! Kingencorp just called, and we're due over there at one o'clock, to use the electron microscope! They had a cancellation and can squeeze us in! Isn't that terrific? I was so excited, I forgot to ask for directions, but never mind; Kingencorp is somewhere out on Route 46. I'll just use my GPS. The secretary there told me our time allotment may be limited; it's really just a favor to Dad. But they are even supplying us with a researcher skilled in the use of a scanning electron microscope! His name is Emile. We ask for him when we arrive. He'll help us prepare our samples and everything! I've watched others work with these microscopes and occasionally helped a little, but I've never had much instruction."

"Cool! Really cool, but calm down, Ab." Ian began loading up his backpack.

Abby tossed a blank bound book into it. According to standard procedure for scientific research, she wanted to have Emile sign off with date and time, acknowledging her handwritten results of the experiments. That way, if another research team made a similar discovery almost simultaneously, it could be proved officially who had priority—who had made the breakthrough first.

"I wish Louella could be there too," Abby said. "It's her immune system we'll be studying."

"Me too, Abby." Cory started checking his slides and packing some specimens. "I worked with a scanning electron microscope a few years back. Now I'll get a chance to use it again."

$$\sim\!\!\wedge\!\!\wedge\!\!\circ$$

That afternoon Emile welcomed Abby, Ian, Miano Tse, and Cory at the door and led them to the lab. "Put your specimens here for the time being. Don't be concerned. I realize those specimens are valuable. I will lock the lab, and I am the only one with a key. Come on over to the conference room. You can explain what your research involves more comfortably there."

Everyone admired the plush surroundings of that room. The team from Fred's lab had already eaten lunch, but they helped themselves to coffee, tea, and cookies. Emile asked Abby if she was Dr. Charles Zelban's daughter. She smiled and said yes, then introduced her colleagues while she distributed copies of the proposal she had outlined. Emile listened intently as Abby described their work and reviewed her proposal. "In general," she concluded, "we need the scanning electron microscope to see what happens to the chemicals of the immune-system cells when the HIV attempts to invade them."

"And you want to compare the patients who have AIDS with those who test positive for HIV but do not become ill," said Emile, looking up from Abby's brief proposal. "You'll be analyzing immune systems that resist HIV to see if you can ultimately duplicate their properties, with the result of obtaining a medicine that will help those whose bodies cannot fight off the HIV."

Abby nodded. "That's right."

Emile continued, "You know there are some other researchers working on similar theories."

"Yes," Abby said, "we are aware of that."

"However, many have given up on the search for a cure. Now that we have medicine that holds the virus at bay, the research for a cure has diminished."

Ian added, "We realize we are looking at a minuscule part of a complicated problem. Still, we feel that anything we can contribute is worthwhile."

"Just thought I should warn you." Emile stood up, shaking his head at what he thought was an overly optimistic, altruistic attitude. "Glad to do whatever I can to help."

"Thank you," Miano Tse said. "We worked with Dr. Fred Truesort's patients. "Our research is partially based on his ideas."

"Will he be here?" Emile asked.

"Unfortunately not," Miano Tse responded.

Abby explained, "We are using tissue from a carrier who has never suffered from AIDS even though she has had HIV in her system for years. Dr. Truesort has monitored her since 1985. At first it was thought that she might be a survivor. However, by examining how her immune system reacted to HIV, we saw that her CD4+ T cells resist the HIV's attack. I'm sure the superior resolution of your electron microscope will allow us to see in detail *why* and *how* these cells are such good warriors. We'll find out for sure whether a mutation is involved."

Ian added, "We've found that the subject's cells contain a rare protein that might be the result of a mutation. Miano Tse and I searched protein sequences globally but found none like it. We suspect that this protein may play a role in the subject's resistance to HIV, but we need confirmation."

"You've come to the right place," Emile stated with confidence.

"Emile, I was told our time may be limited. Do you think we will have enough hours to accomplish what we have outlined?" Abby asked.

"Your work is valuable. You will be allotted all the time you need," Emile emphasized. "Abby, it's up to you and your fellow researchers to decide if you are making progress and should continue. If not, then go back to your own lab. I can't make that decision for you. Anyhow, I've been instructed by the board that you folks have top priority."

"Okay. And would you be willing to sign my results, which I will enter into this bound book of blank pages, for confirmation and priority?" Abby put the book on the table.

"Certainly I would."

"Great!" said Abby. "How soon can we get started?"

"Right now. Follow me."

Emile opened the lab door wide and said, "Here we are." The electron microscope with its ancillary gear almost filled the clean room. One wall in the remaining space outside the clean room was lined with micrographs: images similar to photographs but taken with the scanning electron microscope. They included pictures of blood cells, hair cells, a section of a fern leaf, and a hypodermic needle.

Emile gave the researchers a mini tour of the equipment through the window of the clean room. He pointed out several components of the scanning electronic microscope, or SEM: the console with its keyboard and electronic controls, the stage or platform for the specimens, and the monitors that provide the visuals. "That large vertical column you see at the top of the microscope contains a device called an electron gun," he explained. "It emits a beam of electrons, which are used both to magnify and to illuminate the specimen."

"This is so much more sophisticated than the microscopes in our lab. I'm glad we have you to guide us, Emile," Miano Tse remarked.

"As you know, the scanning electron microscope is superb for medical research," continued Emile. "Researchers can magnify samples thousands of times more than they can with an optical microscope. The SEM's images are far superior with excellent resolution. In fact, you can actually watch chemical reactions taking place! All this is because electrons have wavelengths about a hundred thousand times shorter than those of visible light."

Emile led everyone to the foyer attached to the clean room, where they all went through the air shower and put on sterile white caps (resembling shower caps with elastic around the bottom to keep them tight), booties over their shoes, sterile gloves, and lab coats over their street clothes. Then Abby, Ian, Cory and Miano Tse gathered around Emile in a semicircle to watch him prepare the specimens for Friday.

Emile promised to set up the specimens himself because they had to be prepared carefully to survive the vacuum inside the microscope. He showed how he sliced the specimens of frozen tissue very thinly with an instrument called a microtome so that he did not harm the specimens themselves. Each specimen would require careful preparation to ensure that any foreign particles were removed. Miano Tse helped with that process. She had checked specimens before to make sure they were clean when she worked with the light microscopes. With her fine dexterity and Emile's guidance, she caught on to this new method very quickly.

Emile told the group, "For you to study DNA, the tissue sample must be very small so you can distinguish its parts. I like to study proteins under an environmental cell: a chamber where I can increase the humidity slightly and protect the sample from the full vacuum. These steps create an environment similar to that of the protein's natural surroundings, which will give you more time to study it. Next I attach the environmental cell onto the scope."

Miano Tse said, "This is fascinating." Emile smiled at her and continued, "Because the specimens you have are not metal, they will not conduct the electrons. You must cover the specimen with a thin layer of gold to make it conductive."

Emile showed Abby how to apply the gold to the specimens, and she coated several of them herself. She was glad to learn this skill because she realized she would have to be able to do this once Emile left.

"The electron gun at the top of the column will be shooting electrons down through various lenses and other apparatus to your specimen, which we will put on the viewing platform," Emile explained. "Let me show you."

Emile placed a microscope grid (which looked like a sieve) across the specimen stage. Next he put the sample across the grid and left it there. "The tissue sample is so sticky, it usually remains in place," Emile said. "Now look. You can study the DNA in the sample."

Cory looked at the monitor. "Excellent image! Can you show us how to move the sample around on the grid to look at other parts? It's been a while since I worked with this stuff."

"Sure," Emile answered. "And if a piece breaks off and gets into the vacuum, no problem: it's too tiny to do any harm. Electrons may kill the sample. If so, just move on to another area on the same grid, or get a new one."

"What a beautiful picture! I can't wait to work with this," Miano Tse said as she stared at the monitor.

"I agree," Abby said.

Ian said, "Wow, we should've come to you sooner, Emile. Okay if I stream the SEM images to my workstation back at our private lab?"

"Sure," Emile replied. "Let's set it up right now."

Cory added, "And could we run this experiment for twenty-four hours and add a readout of time and date? We might get a lot more activity with a longer test, and timing of the interactions is critical."

"Absolutely," said Emile. "It's a good way to get plenty of data."

Cory helped Emile and Ian set up the equipment that would continuously stream the images of cell activity to his workstation at Truesort Research. "I'm glad you understand how this streaming transmission works, Ian. I sure don't," Cory admitted.

"It's pretty amazing," Ian said.

Once the images were being streamed back to Fred's private lab, all the researchers gathered around to stare at the monitors, mesmerized by the interaction of the HIV and CD4+ T cells from Louella's immune system. Now, for the first time, they could actually *see* the HIV attempt to attack her cells and repeatedly fail.

"The HIV's not attaching! *That's* why it can't infect the cells!" announced Miano Tse.

They stood in awe as they realized the import of the images, then broke into a cheer. Abby and Ian now knew there was no doubt. The mutation they'd strongly suspected in Louella's DNA was there, and now they could prove it.

Ian said with a grin, "Just as we hoped, Louella's genes did her a big favor."

"Christ, Abby and Ian, you've got it." Cory's voice rasped with excitement.

"Louella's immune system has got it," Abby whispered. "This is the *first* step toward a real cure. Oh my God, this is it, everybody!

We've done it! We've actually found our first clue to solving the HIV mystery."

Ian laughed, gave Abby a hug, and said, "Looks like all the time I spent studying protein sequences has finally paid off. We've reached a crucial milestone."

"Terrific, Miano Tse!" said Emile. "Wonderful, Ian!"

"Next we've got to analyze *why*," said Cory. "Once we know precisely what chemical reactions are involved with that protein you discovered, Ian, we should be able to develop a drug that imitates them."

"Yes," agreed Miano Tse: "a true remedy that attacks and stops the HIV before it can invade immune cells and cause AIDS."

Emile shook everyone's hand and gave Abby a hug. "As soon as you're finished making notes in your bound book, I'll be glad to sign it."

Fifteen minutes later, Abby handed Emile her book, where she'd written a concise description of what they'd just discovered. "Thanks for signing it for me, Emile. I'll keep you informed and let you know our progress."

"My pleasure, Abby," he answered, handing the signed book back to her. "I'm leaving now, but I'll be back around nine thirty tomorrow morning. If you want to stay overnight to keep an eye on your experiment, just tell Security. You're welcome to call me if you have any questions. Here's my card with my cell number. If any of you want to come back for further work with the SEM, let me know, and I'll arrange it in the schedule."

"Great!" said Abby. "Thanks so much." All of them thanked Emile, and then he left the lab.

"Let's take shifts," said Cory. "Eight hours each. No way should we leave this going without someone here to protect it. I'll stay and keep a close eye on the reactions, make sure everything is okay. You three can figure out who wants to relieve me in eight hours. Who knows: the HIV may attach to the CD4+ T cells yet."

"Let's see: we have a little more to do. Abby and I will leave around five, and I'll come back at one in the morning. Abby and Miano Tse will return at eight. Will the guard here let us back in?" Ian asked.

"I'll let Security know we're working through the night," Abby said. "Dad told me to deal with Morton because he won't give us a hard time."

"Cory, what should we tell Fred?" Ian asked.

"Just that we think we're onto something."

"Yeah," Ian agreed. "Don't say too much. After twenty-four hours we'll be certain. Don't raise his hopes now."

"How about Dr. Zelban?" Cory asked.

"Nothing. As with Fred," Ian said. "Abby, okay with you?"

"Yeah, sure." A minute later she closed her cell phone. "Morton said it was good we called. He'll ask for two types of ID, just as he did when we arrived."

"Good. But once we leave here," Cory asked, "where can we keep our work where it'll *really* be safe, just in case any competitors hear about this discovery? Ever since I heard about that guy breaking into the hospital lab, I've been scared."

"We four would be at the top of the search list," Ian said.

"How about Dr. Pannell?" Abby asked. "He could help us if someone tried to steal our work. He's even a Green Beret."

"Yes, good idea," Ian agreed. "Pannell could help."

Cory shook his head.

"Why not?" Abby asked.

"Well—he's worked with the street people. . . ." Cory suddenly noticed Miano Tse calmly staring at him, and he felt ashamed. "Uhh—maybe he's okay," Cory said. "Yeah, sure, let's use him. He has put his career on the line for us."

"Good. Should we show him the video?" Ian asked. "I can run one if you want."

"Let's see how he reacts," Abby said.

"Does he know how to get here?" Cory asked. "It's almost four o'clock. You can call the ER."

"I'll call him, Cory. He should still be there even though his shift supposedly ended at four o'clock," Miano Tse said, looking at her watch. "Doc Pannell never gets away on time."

The Kingencorp guard searched Dr. Pannell's briefcase and escorted him to the lab. Then, back at the building's entrance, the guard dialed a long-distance number. "Hello? Morton here, Kingencorp Security," he said quietly. "Remember you asked me to let you know if anything unusual was happening?"

"Oh . . . Yes, Morton, yes. What's going on?"

"They're working overnight. Yeah. Thought you would wanna know."

"Good, Morton. Thanks for the information. Just keep me posted. I'll certainly make it worth your while. Bye for now."

$$\sim\!\!\!\sqrt{\vphantom{l}}\!\!\sim\!\circ$$

Dr. Pannell walked into the lab briskly, but as he read the faces there, his pace slowed. He stopped five feet from them. "What happened? Is something wrong?" he asked softly. "You're so quiet."

Abby smiled. "Everything is right as right can be."

Cory walked a few steps closer to Dr. Pannell. "It's so right, we need your help."

"We've solved an important aspect of the HIV/AIDS puzzle," Abby said softly. Her lips pinched together. Her eyes welled up with tears. "I can hardly believe it myself, but we have the proof," she whispered.

Dr. Pannell smiled and then looked at Ian quizzically. "Is she okay?"

"She's fine. Just exhausted," Ian said.

"I'm really happy, Bob," said Abby. "Look, Ian has the reaction up on the monitor. It's one of our experiments."

Dr. Pannell watched intently while Ian ran the video slowly a second time. Abby explained to Dr. Pannell what was happening on the screen.

Dr. Pannell enthusiastically congratulated them all. "I know how hard you've worked. Now all our efforts have been rewarded."

"Not quite," Abby warned. "How can we keep this miracle safe?"

"I've streamed the video to my workstation over at Fred's lab," Ian told Bob, "and I can easily make more duplicates there."

"So will you need to take anything from here?" Bob asked. "Do you need the actual samples as well as their computer images?"

"We'd like to take some of the extra components we didn't use back to Fred's lab. They're the basis we work from for this experiment," Ian explained.

"How many guards have they got? Just Morton?" Bob said.

"That's all we've seen. You think he'd let us take our samples back out?" Cory asked. "Or would he think we were stealing Kingencorp property mixed with ours, like the gold for coating specimens?"

"Maybe. He did check my briefcase very carefully when I arrived. Bribery might be the simplest way, but that confirms you have something to hide."

"What did the Green Berets do?" Ian asked.

"In situations like this we created a diversion," Bob said. "It's a tried-and-true method."

The researchers accepted Cory's offer to stay the night. He went to the conference room for some coffee and cookies to fortify himself during his long shift, along with some trail mix he'd stashed in his pocket when they left for Kingencorp.

While he was gone, Bob, Abby, and Ian used the time to plan what Bob called a nonchalant escape. Abby would be in front of Ian and Bob, carrying her big pocketbook. Ian and Bob would follow about eight feet behind her. Ian had his briefcase and the same specimen carrier he'd brought in the beginning, still with some of the original specimens not used in the experiment. Bob carried his own briefcase.

As planned, first Abby chatted with Morton. When Ian and Bob were approximately three feet away, Abby's pocketbook slipped out of her hand, its contents sliding all over the gray and white ceramic tile. Abby knelt down to retrieve her belongings, apologizing as she gathered her pocket calendar, her keys, two tubes of lipstick, and an eyeglass case that slid a couple of feet away, along with her cell phone and a hairbrush. Morton looked down at her with a scowl. Bob stood next to him, set his briefcase close to Morton's feet, winked at Abby, and began helping her.

Suddenly Morton realized that Ian was pushing the heavy exterior door open with the specimen carrier. He yelled at Ian and tried to run after him. All he really did was fall over Bob's briefcase. Bob stood and helped Morton to his feet, holding him firmly by the shoulder. He told Morton, "I'm a doctor. Are you all right?" Morton pulled away and leaned against the wall for support as he rubbed his shin. Abby continued to gather up the rest of the contents of her pocketbook, then stood and snapped it closed. Bob apologized to Morton, saying he should not have put his briefcase so close to Morton's feet. Bob and Abby exited the building, leaving a bewildered security guard.

Abby and Ian returned the specimens to their own workspace in Fred's private lab. They reasoned that any thief would have to know exactly what to do with these specimens to understand and use a viable process. They knew they needed a lot of Louella's tissue to do thorough action and reaction analyses by the immune cells and the HIV.

On the way home, they stopped by their rented storage bin, opened the box with Aunt Millie's lamp, and hid the written log and the bound book with Emile's signature establishing priority.

Now that one of her hypotheses had been confirmed, Abby was more cheerful and energized, yet simultaneously relaxed. She and her colleagues knew they were on the right path. All of them were working to isolate the properties of Louella's CD4+ T cells and specific strain of HIV. Already one component in the cell chemistry had been identified as a probable player in Louella's immunity; the pieces of the puzzle were beginning to fit. Even Fred was less worried about money, since the research results could soon be sold to a pharma company.

So Wednesday night, two weeks after their first session at Kingencorp, Abby actually left Fred's lab at five thirty, assured that the research was moving forward successfully. She walked through the supermarket, selecting ripe plums and pears, then cubes of beef for stew, along with parsnips, carrots, fresh mushrooms, and Vidalia onions. Finally she put milk and eggs into her cart and moved to the side of the aisle to answer her cell.

"Hi, Dad. Fine. I'm grocery shopping. Ian and I have actually started cooking. He's becoming an excellent chef. No, lately we haven't had as many experiments extending till eleven at night. Now *all* of us are concentrating on Louella's immune system; her mutation holds the key. It's so exciting to watch this theory develop, Dad! We're on the verge of a truly marketable breakthrough in the field. Amazing, huh, after all this work? The electron microscope gave us a giant leap forward; thanks again for making those arrangements with Kingencorp.

"Mm-hmm. You'd like us to come up for a few days? You think Ian and I should get away? Sure, sure. It was very restful last time, Dad. For the weekend? We'd love to! The Weather Channel says it's going to be hot in New Jersey: Indian summer. The leaves are starting to turn here. It must be beautiful up there. Ian will have a chance to see fall foliage in its prime. How about if we come up tomorrow night—Thursday? We could leave directly from the lab around six and stay until Monday morning. Okay, great. I'll confirm it with Ian and call you back. Can you be there, too? No? That's too bad. Oh, another conference. In Chicago? We'll miss you, but good luck at the conference. Bye. I love you, too. Don't work too hard. Thanks for the invite."

On her way home, Abby drove past three blocks of old mansions—some of them vacant and run-down, a few still intact with well-trimmed lawns. She passed the city's impressive mosque, then turned into the drive of her condo building with its row of individual garages on the basement level. After pressing the automatic garage-door opener, she parked the BMW carefully, steering around Ian's motorcycle. Abby then pushed the button to close and lock the outer door, pulled the groceries out of the front passenger seat, and headed to the smaller door leading to the interior hallway. *Love this place. Don't even have to go outside in bad weather.* She punched in the access code to enter the building, waved at the surveillance camera as she stepped into the elevator, and rode to the fifth floor at the top.

When Abby walked into their condo, Ian grabbed the grocery bags out of her arms. "I probably shouldn't have bought this. Just talked to Dad and made plans to relax in Connecticut this weekend. Take Friday off."

"And you read my mind." Ian put both bags on the counter, twirled Abby around, and pushed her toward the door. "Don't change your mind. Let's leave now."

"But the food—"

"Freeze the meat. Everything else will keep in the fridge."

"My clothes, my lab experiments. I told him we'd leave Thursday night. It's only Wednesday."

"Yeah, you're right. It *is* only Wednesday. I was hoping you wouldn't notice," Ian teased. "How about leaving early tomorrow morning? We can check on the experiments first thing, then go directly from the lab. I'll make dinner. You pack what you want to take with you and avoid the last-minute rush."

"Okay, I guess we could do that—just check everything quickly in the morning and then take off. You know, Dad rarely calls me. He doesn't mean to neglect me or anything; he's just so busy. Maybe I sounded weary the last time I called him. He hardly ever calls me, let alone calls to tell me I need a break. That's really awesome!" Abby began searching for her suitcase at the back of the bedroom closet.

"Oh, I thought you called him."

"No. You know, I think I'll take a copy of our wedding picture with us," Abby replied from the depth of the closet. "He won't be there . . . has another conference this weekend in Chicago. But I'm going to take the photo and prop it up on the mantel anyhow. He's not as sentimental as Mom was, but I think he'll be okay with it. At least that way he'll see it eventually, put it in whatever kind of frame he wants. I doubt Dad will be at our condo anytime soon."

"Too bad your mom couldn't see you."

"She did, Ian. She was looking down from heaven. You don't mind driving to Connecticut, or do you want me to?" Abby began pulling open bureau drawers.

"I'll drive; you navigate."

"Okay. Let's pack the car now," said Abby. "Tomorrow we can leave right from the lab."

"It'll be great to have that big house to ourselves," Ian said.

"Should we take the latest experiment data with us, or stop by the storage unit?" Abby asked him.

"You think you'll have anything new?"

"Don't know for sure. I'm reviewing the electron-microscope work."

"Already put into storage what you did today," said Ian.

"Good. I'll probably just finish up my review tomorrow and then get rid of it. Won't want to start anything new until next week. You want to stay until Monday?"

"Can't," Ian answered. "Have some equipment being delivered. Want to be sure it's okay."

"Okay. I'll call Dad, tell him our revised schedule: leaving from the lab early tomorrow, staying until Sunday afternoon, not Monday as I told him before. Maybe he can get away early and visit with us for a couple of hours on Sunday morning. Doubt it, though."

"Okay, Ab. Sounds good," said Ian, putting the groceries away after all. "We can make a nice beef stew when we come back."

Chapter

16

"IN CASE YOU HADN'T NOTICED, ABBY, today is Thursday. Wake up. Ab, wake up." Ian reached over in bed and kissed Abby's neck. "Come on, sweetheart. Let's go in early. Check on our experiments and take off by ten. Come on."

Abby stared blankly at him. Gradually her eyes brightened. "What time is it?"

"Seven. Come on, Ab."

"You're worse than a little boy going to camp for the first time."

"I'm anxious to have a totally relaxed wife all to myself. Throw something on. We'll have Martha pick up breakfast for us and bring it to the lab."

Abby swung her legs over the side of the bed and sat slumped with her head in her hands. "Ian, I just can't."

"Can't what?"

"Can't move. I ache all over. I think I've got the flu. Even my fingernails ache."

"You of all people should know that's impossible."

Abby suddenly bolted for the bathroom.

"Damn! So much for a long weekend in the country," Ian said to himself. His shoulders slouched, and his fists punched against the pillows. "Ab," he yelled at the closed bathroom door, "are you all right?"

He heard the toilet flush. The door opened slowly. "I'm okay, but I feel like hell. I've got an elevated temp. I ache, and I just vomited." Abby held a couple of aspirin. "I know, 'Take two aspirin and call me in the morning.' Maybe some dry toast and weak tea." Abby sat on the bed, looking at the aspirin in the palm of her hand. "I don't think I can hold down the aspirin yet. I'm so sorry, Ian. I wanted to get away as much as you did. Now look at me—or maybe you'd better not. I'm a mess." Abby leaned back against the pillows. "I'll rest a little while."

Disappointed, Ian nodded and left the bedroom.

Soon he tiptoed back in and placed a snack tray with toast and tea on the bedside table. Abby woke up and stared at the tray. "Abby, tell you what. You eat and drink this slowly. A pot of tea's on the kitchen counter. I'll go to the lab on my motorcycle and leave you the car. Maybe you'll feel well enough to go to Connecticut in an hour or two."

"Oh, I hope so. But, Ian, click off the program you're running at Fred's lab that's filming the reactions."

"Okay. Don't worry, backup copies of everything important are in the storage bin or with Ghanna."

"And most of it is right in this aching head of mine." Abby groaned.

"Here's your cell phone in case you need something. I've got my laptop in my backpack in case I need it. And you know what? Just to keep you from working like the obsessive researcher you are, I'm also taking *your* laptop to the lab, to make sure you'll rest."

"Not much chance of my working this morning," she answered.

"See if you can get some sleep. When you wake up, give me a call, and we'll decide what to do. Don't be upset. There are many weekends in our future. If you're well enough to go, or if you need me for anything, I'll come home. Otherwise I'll continue working. Drink your tea," he told her as he closed the bedroom door.

Abby sipped the tea and nibbled on the toast, and decided to swallow the two aspirin after all. Soon she gave up trying to eat anything, dropped her head back on the pillows, and fell into a deep sleep.

Suddenly she heard a crash and the snapping of broken wood. Abby sat up. "Is that you, Ian?" she called. She pushed away the blankets and slowly stood up. Her alarm clock was blinking sequential red numbers. She looked at her watch, which was on the bedside table. *I've slept four hours. It's eleven thirty.* "Ian, hold on. Wait. What's happening? We've had a power failure. Is there a storm?" she yelled. But a glance out the bedroom window told her it was a sunny day.

Abby wrapped and tied her bathrobe around herself, picked up her cell phone, and walked toward the living room. *Maybe the lock doesn't—*

Then she stared in horror. The door panel was splintered. Trembling, she backed away. A plaid-coated shoulder pushed through the opening, ripping the door from its hinges.

"Hi, lady. 'Fraid it ain't Ian. It's j-just me and my brainy friend here. I'm the muscle, h-he's the brain. Good team, huh? He finally p-paid me an old debt, six hundred fifty bucks, so we're—"

"Shut *up*, idiot!" said another man, pushing past the first one into the living room. He wore a brown tweed jacket over a yellow turtleneck shirt and khaki trousers. Abby backed away from both of them.

She glared at the second man as her mind wheeled around, searching for answers. "Why are you here? What do you want? Who are you?"

The first man laughed. "Royce and me been p-planning this—"

Royce! There can't be many—

"I said shut *up*, William!" Royce demanded. "Your empty head is showing." He lunged toward Abby and wrenched the cell phone out of her hand. Then he turned it off and shoved it into his pocket.

Abby moved backward again, closer to the kitchen. "I'd like to hear more from your empty head, William," Abby said, still looking at Royce. "How about some tea while we talk over this intrusion?"

Royce looked at her. "You're one cool chick. You know that?"

"William, prop up the door. Anyone in the building might think there was a break-in," Abby ordered.

"You're not in charge here. I am," Royce told her. He walked toward the kitchen counter. "We checked. Nobody's here. Besides, we've cased this place for weeks. Everyone, absolutely everyone, has left for work by now—except you. They'll probably complain that the power to run elevators and refrigerators is down when they return from work tonight. All the automatic access codes have been erased. We've done a thorough job. So, sure, we have time for tea. And William here doesn't have to fix the door. Our problem is that we couldn't get into Truesort's private lab—some asshole installed a brand-new, state-of-the-art security system over there—and we didn't find anything in your car. Thought both you and Ian decided to ride on the motorcycle this beautiful morning and leave the neatly packed BMW for later."

Abby scrutinized Royce. "So you are *Royce Barkley*."

"Of course. If you had left like you were supposed to, you wouldn't have met me. But since you're lounging around at home today, we can work with you in person."

"Yeah?" said Abby. "I'm home because I have the flu. You're welcome to my germs if you want them."

"Don't try to be funny," continued Royce. "You're a smart girl; I'm sure you have some backup outside the lab. So tell us where you've hidden your research: laptops, CDs, flash drives, printouts, anything we can use. That way we won't have to trash this trendy condo, and you can go back to bed."

"There is nothing. Not. A. Thing. I, too, have more brain than muscle."

Abby turned her back to Royce and heated a cup of tea in the microwave. She grabbed a towel from the counter to get the steaming cup when it was ready. Royce stepped closer to her. He smelled like onions. Abby's body went stiff. He yanked her head back by her hair. Abby pulled away and threw the cupful of hot tea into his face. The cup crashed onto the floor.

"*Aaaaaarrgh!* You little *BITCH!*"

Royce dragged her with him as he ran for the kitchen sink. He turned on the faucet with his free hand and ran cold water over his scorched skin, shrieking a stream of epithets as he splashed water on his cheek.

Abby wrenched away from his weakened grasp. Her nausea had returned, and she ran for the bathroom.

She heard Royce say, "You're going to regret this, you whore! You're lucky I'm not shoving your head right down that toilet."

Abby tried to slam and lock the bathroom door, but Royce's foot was already in the way. She just barely had time to finish vomiting and flush before he yanked her to her feet and dragged her into the living room.

Meanwhile, William had made himself at home on the sofa. Abby could see the handle of a gun poking out of his pocket. William was kicking his strong leg up and down, looking at Royce's dripping face. *Guess she showed you that time, Mr. Know-It-All,* he thought with a smirk.

"Get over here, William," ordered Royce. "Bind her hands to one of those columns between the living room and the dining room." William gripped Abby's hands behind her back and began to lash them with her bathrobe tie, winding it tightly around the column and her waist.

"Now, you search the bedroom," Royce told William. "I'll do the living room." Unable to break free, Abby watched Royce and William search: dumping all the clothing on the floor, slashing upholstery and pulling down curtains, forcing up loose floor tiles with a hinge from the broken door. They pulled food from kitchen shelves, dumped drawers of dish towels and silverware onto the table. They even moved the refrigerator forward but found only an half-inch layer of dust and a lost pearl earring.

Royce kept watching Abby. Her facial expression never changed; she stood as still as a statue. Her body language did not give away any hiding spot. She stared out the window, praying: *God, help me.*

"All right," said Royce at last. "Since we're not finding anything here, we're going to take you for a little ride. Maybe you'll decide to talk. Untie her, William. Get dressed, Abby. Like you're going to work. Don't try to escape. If you do . . . well, you're smart. You know you'll be shot. Go on into your bedroom. Hurry up. Leave the door ajar."

Abby laughed at him. "If you kill me, your search will end, unless you know how to clone my brain. Are we taking my car or yours?" She feigned sarcasm to hide her fear—fear of torture.

She went into the bedroom and stood by the bed with her back toward the door, blocking the men's view of what was in front of her: the hard-wired phone on the nightstand. Instantly she grabbed it, and— *Thank God, a dial tone! They forgot to disconnect it!* She had just punched in Ian's number when her right arm was pulled around behind her waist and shoved up toward her shoulder blade. "Not so fast, babe. Give me the phone *now*," Royce commanded. Wordlessly Abby extended the handset toward him with her left hand.

"Hello? Hello, Ab, what's the matter?" they heard Ian ask.

"Your wife is fine, Ian. We just stopped by for a little visit. I'm an old friend of the family," Royce said, confident that he'd be gone before Ian could get to the condo. Abby watched Royce hang up and cut the phone's wire. "William, you *bastard!*" yelled Royce. "What kind of fool are you to leave the phone intact?"

Abby thought, *Ian has caller ID. He knows the call was from our condo. God, help Ian too.*

—ᴧᴧᴧ∘

At Fred's lab, Ian was still saying into the phone, "Abby, are you all right? Are you feeling worse? I'll come over right now," but the line went dead. Ian dashed over to Miano Tse's lab bench. "Miano Tse, something's wrong! Something's going on with Abby! I've got to get right over to the condo. Glad nobody else is here but you. Just got a weird call from some guy on our hard-wired phone. Don't want to go to the police under the circumstances—"

"Take a deep breath, Ian," Miano Tse advised.

"Call Josh. Let him know, but you stay here, like nothing's happening. Don't panic. Abby is smart. I'll call you as soon as I know anything." He ran out the lab door, pulling on his motorcycle helmet as he went.

Miano Tse immediately called Josh's cell and told him what was going on. Josh was just as alarmed as she was. "Miano Tse, you gotta stop Ian from going back to the condo alone. You understand? Too dangerous. I'll get there as quick as I can and see if I can bring Ghanna and Doc Pannell and Alvarez, too. Okay? Bye."

"Ian, Ian!" Miano Tse grabbed her pocketbook and ran to the parking lot, but Ian was already zooming down the street. So she jumped into her green Mazda and chased him down the street at eighty miles per hour, honking her horn. *Please let me not get stopped for speeding,* she thought. *At least it isn't rush hour.*

Miano Tse slowed to a stop about ten feet in front of Ian, compelling him to halt, then called to him through her open window.

Ian slowed his motorcycle. "Miano Tse, what the hell are you doing? This better be good, or—"

"Josh says he's calling Ghanna. Ghanna's going to get Alvarez and Doc Pannell to help. Josh says don't go into the condo alone; it's too risky. Whoever broke in is after you, too—"

"I don't care," yelled Ian. "I've got to help Abby!"

"You listen to me, Ian. You can't help her if they get you too. Josh will meet you at the mosque parking lot near your condo as soon as he can, and he'll bring help. You wait for him!"

"Then tell him to hurry," Ian yelled back.

"Josh will slip out of the ER somehow. Ghanna will keep you posted," Miano Tse called back. "I'll stay at the lab and tell Ghanna I spoke to you. Bye." Miano Tse waved and drove back to Fred's lab.

When Abby came out of the bedroom a few minutes later, dressed in jeans, a sweater, and sneakers, Royce immediately retied her hands behind her back. Then he gave her pocketbook to William. "Here, macho man, hold on to this. It goes with your outfit."

William rolled his eyes at Royce's jibe but took the pocketbook and rifled through it. "Oooh, this'll come in handy," he said. As they went through the doorway, William slung the pocketbook over his shoulder, then balanced the door back on its hinges.

"Looks like a simple break-in. Very amateurish," Royce said. "The door will fall off the moment someone touches it."

"It won't look amateurish when they find out you were able to dismantle the security system and erase all the access codes," said Abby. "You are really a very accomplished thief."

"Thanks," said Royce, smiling with pride. "William dropped me off here and went to park his car. By the time he came back, I'd disabled your building's entire security system."

"I'm truly impressed," said Abby. "Do you do safes too?" But Royce declined to answer.

The three of them walked through the empty hallway, past the disabled elevator, and down the staircase to the garage.

"You better use the c-car in the garage," said William. "She might escape if you wait for me to get my car where I parked it at that old mansion down the street."

Royce only grunted. "You just want to drive a BMW. Not now. I'm in the driver's seat for this ride."

When they arrived at Abby's car, out of habit she started heading toward the driver's side. "No. Not so fast, bitch," said William. "You sit in the front on the passenger's seat. And remember, I've got you covered from the rear."

Abby walked calmly around the back of her car, stepping over the heap of belongings that had been so neatly packed in it the night before. She eased into the passenger's seat with grace, although her hands were tied behind her back.

"H-here you are, then," William said with unexpected courtesy, placing her pocketbook on her lap.

Royce put Abby's seat belt on and fastened a sleeper's mask over her eyes. "Always use this when I fly. Never thought it would come in handy when I'm on the ground. You'll look like you're just getting a little rest. Stop smiling, William, and get that pile of junk out of the way so I can back up."

Abby felt the car jolt as Royce put it in reverse. He obviously did not know how to drive a stick-shift car. The car traveled in uneven jerks and stalled out. Royce had William retie Abby's mask since the motion jostled it loose. At last Royce managed to put the car into third gear, and the BMW finally accelerated normally. He drove down Adams Avenue and took the curving highway ramp onto Route 46 West. From there he proceeded toward the complex intersection with Routes 80 and 23.

$$-\wedge\!\!\!\!\wedge\!\!\!\!\!\Gamma\!\!\!\!\sim_\circ$$

Ian raced to the mosque parking lot only five minutes too late to see his car lurch down the street. He waited there for ten agonizing minutes, which seemed more like ten centuries. When Josh still had not arrived, Ian decided to check out the condo building from the outside.

He saw that his garage door was wide open and the BMW was missing. Suitcases and clothing were thrown all over the garage floor like garbage. *The car's been stolen! Is Abby upstairs or kidnapped in the car? Jesus! I've got to find her!* Ian phoned Ghanna and quickly described what he'd seen. "If she's in the BMW, it can't be far away. That phone call was only ten minutes ago. I'm leaving the mosque to hunt for my car. Oh, hold on—wait. Here's Josh now. No, don't call the cops yet," Ian told Ghanna.

Abby could tell that the car was traveling at highway speed, but she had no idea in what direction. After about half an hour, she felt the car slow down, pull off the highway, go around a few slow curves, and stop.

Royce played the courteous husband. "Wake up, my dear. We're here." He removed her mask.

Abby blinked and pretended to awaken. She could see that Royce had parked at the back of some motel. The parking lot opened onto a side street that fed into a highway she could not identify. She glimpsed an unfamiliar mall on the other side of the highway. "Behave yourself and maybe we'll untie your hands," Royce muttered to her before opening the car door.

Abby watched him walk the few yards to the outside door of room 18 and open it with a key, leaving her and William in the car. William held the revolver to her temple.

"Just wanted you to remember my little friend here. H-he's wearing a silencer now. Yep, all dressed for the occasion. Y-ya can walk into the motel room like the fine lady ya are."

Abby glanced right and left by moving only her eyes, hoping someone had seen William's gun, but there were only empty cars.

Royce returned and opened the passenger door. He took the knots out of the bathrobe tie that lashed Abby's hands behind her back. "There you go, bitch," he said softly in her ear. Abby winced as the circulation returned to her fingers. Royce asked mockingly, "Oh, finally learning what a little pain is like, huh?" He wrapped his arm firmly around her waist and walked her into the motel room. William followed, carrying Abby's pocketbook again. Once they were inside with the door shut, Royce repeatedly slapped Abby's face from the right and the left, his torso swinging from side to side with the momentum of his arms.

Abby did not cry out. She focused on the wall. She did not even murmur. She recoiled into herself and began to relax as her mom had taught her. *Never would Mom have thought her pain-relaxation technique would be used like this. I bet she was thinking of childbirth, hoped I'd have kids someday and make her a grandmother.*

Then Royce stopped and abruptly sat down. "That's to teach you who's boss," he said.

Abby continued to focus on the wall, but she did hear a muffled thump at her feet as something fell. She watched Royce while she slowly moved her head from side to side, checking her mouth and teeth, fingering her sore face. Then she moved her head up and down in a nodding motion. That's when she saw her cell phone.

"I'll remember who's boss from now on," she said to Royce, gazing directly at him as she quietly pushed the cell with her foot, letting it slip under the fringe of the bedspread. She turned to William, who still stood just inside the closed door. "Like William does." She saw him grimace before he glanced away. *I must look terrible. I sicken him.* "I have to use the bathroom," she announced, and walked to it as calmly as if these thugs were family.

Abby looked at her reddened face and began putting on cold, wet washcloths to soothe her cheeks. She looked at her hands, letting warm water run over them. Lest her captors think she had escaped out of the one-square-foot window, she went back out into the bedroom and sat on the only chair, hoping for an opportunity to retrieve her cell phone.

"Let's order pizza," she said. "The clock radio on the night table says it's already after one. Are you hungry?"

"Yeah, I could go for some pizza," said William.

"There's a menu from a local pizzeria on the bureau. I see you brought my purse from the car. If you left me any money or credit cards, I'll buy. You can get the tip." Abby used the same noncommittal tone. She had discovered that an unperturbed demeanor worked with these animals. *No. Animals are kinder than this.*

"Take Abby's pocketbook, William," Royce ordered.

William gave her the pocketbook. "From what I s-saw before, you can pay for the tip too."

Abby took out her wallet with a shrug. "Order whatever you want. But please get me some aspirin from the front desk, and a Coke. Here's a credit card." Abby put her pocketbook down on the phone table between the two king-size beds. Only one looked as though it had been slept in.

While the two men checked through various choices on the menu and debated what to order—fried shrimp, chicken wings, salami sandwiches, cheese and sausage pizzas—Abby quietly eased the cell phone out of its hiding place with her foot. She casually bent over, retied her shoelace, and picked up the phone when a glance confirmed that the men weren't looking, then put it in the front pocket of her jeans. She slipped into the bathroom to get another cold, wet washcloth for her face, pulled her sweater out over the cell phone, and returned to the chair, then moved it closer to the bed so she could rest her legs on it.

Abby asked William to turn on the TV for her. Without comment he switched it on, gave her the remote, and returned to circling the menu choices he planned to eat. Royce promptly called in their order.

After watching TV for a while, William limped over to Abby and leaned against the chair. "I'm the one with the b-bad leg," he announced. "Let me sit there."

Abby got up, putting the wet washcloth under the edge of the bedspread. "I'll show you something, William." She directed William to put the chair upside down on the lower half of the bed that had not been slept in, so that the upper edge of the chair's back and the front edge of its seat rested on the mattress. The chair's back and legs tilted toward the ceiling at a forty-five-degree angle.

Then she laid a large pillow and a blanket on top of the chair's back, so that it formed a padded, sloping surface. Finally she propped several more pillows up against the bed's headboard. "Okay," she told William, "lie down. Put your legs up on the chair, with your knees straight, and rest your head on the pillows. That's it. Isn't that relaxing?"

"Yeah, very n-nice," William admitted.

"It's the best way to rest with your legs higher than your head. I use it all the time. If you want to sit up more, you can just move closer to the headboard and lean on it."

A cry of "Pizza! Pizza delivery!" soon interrupted William's rest.

"We're coming. Shut the hell up!" called Royce. He grabbed Abby's pocketbook off the phone table and dumped the contents onto one of the beds. Then he picked up Abby's wallet, ignoring the credit card she'd gotten out, and grabbed all the bills, shoving most of them into his pocket. "How much do we owe you?" He opened the door a crack and peeked out.

"Fifty-two thirty. Want me to carry the boxes in for you, sir?"

"Just leave them here at the door." Royce pulled a crumpled hundred-dollar bill out of his pocket and extended it through the slit of the slightly opened door. "Keep the change."

"Thank you, sir!" crowed the deliveryman, obviously delighted.

Royce closed the door. Once he heard the delivery car drive away, he opened the door wide enough to bring in the food and drinks. Then he set them on the table before quickly closing and locking the door behind him.

Royce stared at William. "Thanks for answering the door. You think you're an invalid or something. But you probably would've looked straight at him. He'd probably remember you."

"Yeah. And you just wasted almost fifty bucks."

"Didn't want that bastard seeing in here. Don't you have any sense? I've always got to do the thinking for both of us. I couldn't sign the receipt for Abby's credit card. Had to use cash. Besides, cash is harder to trace."

"Here's your aspirin and Coke, Abby," said William. "You want some pizza? We got chicken too."

"Thanks. Maybe a little chicken. I'm not quite as nauseous."

William rolled off the bed, leaving the chair and pillows in place. "That felt good on my legs," he commented. "Thanks, Abby. Gonna try it at home." He helped himself to the food he wanted and sat on the edge of the bed to eat.

Abby sipped her Coke slowly, hoping it would soothe her stomach. She still ached all over, more from the beating than the flu. The men ate hurriedly. William slurped, chewed, and burped his way through the pepperoni and cheese, the chicken wings, and the soda. *They must not be planning to stay here long,* Abby realized. *I wonder what's next?*

"Clean up, William. You eat like a slob. Time we were leaving before anyone finds us here," Royce said, getting to his feet. "I'll tie up Abby. Throw the garbage in the Dumpster in the corner of the parking lot. Get the duct tape out of my trunk and bring my car over to the door."

He parked his own car here? thought Abby uneasily. *It'll be harder for the cops to trace; they'll be looking for mine. And duct tape . . . not good.*

William pulled up next to room 18, tossed Royce the keys, then turned to Abby. "Good thing you did put that washcloth on your face before," he told her. "You don't look so beat-up; less suspicious that way."

"I'll put it back in the bathroom," she answered, picking it up from the floor just under the bedspread. Once in the bathroom, Abby tried to text Ian for help. When Royce banged on the door, she pretended to be vomiting. She called Ian on her cell, flushing the toilet at the same time to cover her voice—but, to her enormous frustration, she saw that her phone wasn't getting any signal. *This building must be constructed with steel!* Abby turned off the phone and returned it to her pocket. *It might ring after we leave.*

When Abby came out of the bathroom, Royce grabbed her arms and bound her hands in front of her with the duct tape. "Good, you're grimacing. Be glad I'm not putting this tape over your mouth." He kicked her butt. "Get the hell over to the door, lame-ass," he said, laughing as she stumbled. He looked into the bathroom and the closet, then around the room. "Damn, William left a pizza box. Aahh, it probably doesn't matter. Chair on the bed looks funny, but who cares. I doubt anyone will do much detective work. We're leaving your BMW here. We're ready to go in my car. William is waiting outside, but I'll drive."

Abby had a quick glance at the car. It was a dark Honda . . . and past it, at the far end of the parking lot, she glimpsed Royce's baby-blue Lexus. The sight brought back the terrifying car chases through Hughler City, and her heart sank with horror.

William honked the horn and yelled, "Hurry up. It's already two fifteen. We gotta get moving."

Since Royce couldn't reach William and yell at him to shut up, in his frustration he grabbed Abby by the shoulders, jerked her forward, and kicked her legs as she staggered, banging her forehead on the motel-room door. Numbed by dread, she felt Royce's beating as though it were a nightmare.

Fortunately William clambered out of the driver's seat as fast as his limp would permit to open the back door for her. He helped Abby to a sitting position in the backseat while Royce slammed the door to room 18 and strode around to the driver's seat of the Honda. William said softly to Abby, "It's h-hard to keep your balance with that asshole—um, sorry, lady—tying your hands in front of you."

Royce scowled at William from the driver's seat. "Shove her hair out of her eyes and prop her up straighter than that. She shouldn't attract any attention."

William was surprisingly gentle as he helped Abby sit up straighter and smoothed her hair as best he could.

"Get the fuck up here," Royce growled. "We've got to get her out of here!"

Abby stretched her hands out in front of her, resting them on her knees. She did not want William to discover her cell phone tucked in the front pocket of her jeans. She didn't even want to think about what Royce would do if he knew she had it, but he seemed to have forgotten all about it. "B-before my accident I was going to be a d-dentist," William told her.

"That's nice, William," said Royce sarcastically. "You fool, Abby isn't interested in you. Now get your ass up here or you're next. This isn't a beauty pageant."

William patted Abby's arm softly, slammed the rear door, and went to the front passenger's seat. "Where're we headed?"

"You know, William, while you were taking care of Abby back there, I had a brilliant idea. See that gigantic shopping mall with the entrance right across the highway? The Mall for All?"

"Yeah. Hey, look, that's probably the place that brought us the p-pizza. Didn't take them long. You know, it advertises chicken too.

They must be the ones. This motel ain't got nothin' but vendin' machines."

"Will you *shut* your *trap*? Try listening for a change. We're going to park over by those trees. I have my cell. I have my laptop. We can conduct our negotiations right there. I want to add ransom to the bill."

Royce glanced in the rearview mirror. "Even Abby knows it's a good plan. So good, she might never finish her research. Wonder what her daddy's going to say?"

"Fine. Call him," she said.

Then, turning to Abby, Royce continued, "For a scientist, you're pretty stupid, aren't you? You still don't get it, sweetheart. Your daddy *hired* us."

Abby stared at him, desperately trying to look calm. *No. It can't be true.* "I don't believe you," she finally stated with more confidence than she felt. "You're just bluffing."

Royce and William only laughed.

"My father is a highly respected doctor who would never associate with criminals like you," insisted Abby.

"Oh, but he *does* associate with me," said Royce. "It's been going on for months now, hasn't it, William?" He pulled a cell phone from the front-seat divider compartment and showed Abby that her father's number was already stored there.

"So?" said Abby. "Just because you know his phone number doesn't mean you know *him*. Plenty of people have it."

"But he told us you were leaving for Connecticut this morning, so it'd be the perfect day for us to stop by," said Royce. "How else would we know that?"

"Yeah," added William. "We were just gonna go into your condo and tell him what we found. But then you hadda st-stay home this morning and ruin the whole plan."

"Not really," said Royce. "Now we're entitled to some ransom money. We'll still share the research profits with your daddy, as he planned, but the ransom he pays to save your life is just for us, huh, William?" Royce laughed at his extraordinary luck. "How much do you think you're worth, Abby?" he asked.

Oh my God, is it possible? If they knew about Connecticut . . .

"Who told you about Connecticut?" Abby asked with a hushed voice.

Royce said, "Now you're finally catching on, aren't you? So you'd better do what your daddy says, little girl, and give us your documentation—the real stuff. No games, no bullshit! We want your printouts, flash drives, notes, CDs showing those cell experiments—whatever you've got—so we can all save our asses. Your life is on the line, Abby, and so is my career. An awful lot of people will still be very sick without your help. All Daddy and I want is a little bit of the action."

William giggled. "And a lot of the m-money."

Abby moaned and stared out the car window, hoping she wouldn't break into tears. Royce started the car, left the motel parking lot, and drove a few miles to the nearest U-turn, then entered the shopping mall lot. He paused and decided to pull into a perfect parking space: at the edge of the lot, with a group of trees on one side and a large recycling truck on the other. It would be difficult for anyone to see into the car from the sides or the back, but from the front he had a panoramic view of the mall parking lot. He was parked near the last store in the mall, MexTex Tacos.

"My father would never hire anyone to steal my research—his own daughter!" said Abby. "You're crazy," she added.

"But that's exactly why he did it: he figured you'd never suspect him," retorted Royce.

"Then let me speak to my father. I want to hear him tell me to surrender the research," Abby said firmly.

—⌁—

While Ian was burning with impatience and looking at the mess in his garage, Josh and Alvarez had been speeding across the city in Josh's Ford. "Thanks for the ride, Josh," said Alvarez.

"No problem, man! We need your special skills today."

"Is Doc Pannell coming too?" Alvarez asked.

"Yeah. It's his day off, but Ghanna's phonin' his pager and his cell."

"What if the doc's not home?"

"Nah, he'll be home, all right. Before he left the ER yesterday, he said he was gonna relax today, get caught up on a little shut-eye. Don't worry, he'd never let us down." Josh rounded the corner and pulled into the mosque parking lot. "Good! Ian's still here. I was afraid he'd go upstairs alone."

Ian immediately ran up to Josh's car. "Thanks for coming, you guys."

"Glad to help, Ian. Which building is it?" Alvarez asked while they rushed across the parking lot to the street.

"Yellow one"—Ian pointed—"over there on the corner. New building. C'mon, this way through our garage. That's how they broke in. It's a mess, but that can wait. Gotta see if Abby's upstairs! God, she'd better be okay!"

The door from the garage into the ground-floor hallway was ajar, and the three of them hurried through. The hallway was completely dark, so Alvarez took the flashlight from his belt. "Here's the electrical box and the security camera. No lights, no elevator means no working generator. Look, Ian. Everything is down. What floor do you live on?"

"Top—fifth floor." Ian turned and raced up the stairs frantically. Josh and Alvarez were right behind him.

The place was tomb quiet. Only their footsteps made any sound. "Look at that door," said Alvarez. "It's been broken down. Some idiot balanced it on its hinges."

Ian shoved it aside and rushed through the rooms, trying to believe he would find his wife unharmed or a note telling him where she was. As he realized she was gone, Ian's head and shoulders sagged. Gradually he took in the full reality of the situation. He wandered aimlessly, shocked by the devastation of their home.

Josh hugged him. "I'm sorry, man."

Alvarez put his arm across Ian's shoulders. "Truly sorry—truly sorry, Ian."

Man, look at this place! Josh thought, staring around him at all the dumped belongings and ruined furniture. "What a wreck! These guys were pigs, worse than druggies!" he murmured to himself.

Alvarez checked the closets, the bathroom, the bedroom. "They were looking for something and probably were disappointed," he stated grimly, glancing at Ian.

"Who knows what they wanted?" Ian said, picking some clothes off the floor and tossing them on what was left of the sofa.

Josh walked into the kitchen. "Look. Spilled tea and a smashed cup on the floor. Somebody stepped in the spilled tea. Think it was Abby?"

Ian picked up Abby's loafer out of the mess and placed it against the footprint. "The print is bigger than Abby's foot, Josh. Looks like a man's print."

"It's strange," said Alvarez. "Nobody heard anything, nobody reported anything to the cops, 'cause they aren't here. How come?"

"The building's still lookin' for tenants," Ian said. "A few other families moved in recently, but everybody's gone all day. Working. And most of the mansions along here are abandoned."

"Nobody can afford to live like that anymore," said Josh.

Ian explained, "Abby didn't feel well this morning. I left the car for her so she could come to the lab later if she felt better. We packed the car last night to go to Connecticut this weekend. Did she drive out somewhere, maybe before the break-in?" he asked hopefully.

"No, Ian," said Josh gently. "Wish I could believe that, but I don't."

"She'd take her purse," said Ian, looking around. "I don't see it here."

"Nope, me neither," Josh agreed.

"But if Abby had left *before* the break-in, your garage wouldn't be a mess," added Alvarez. "Plus, why would any intruder call you at the lab? No, she was here when they broke in. And if Abby managed to escape *afterward*, she would call you as soon as possible to let you know she's okay."

Ian kicked a torn chair across the room. "It's been at least forty-five minutes since she tried to phone me. I keep trying to call, but her cell must be off. Oh my God, she's been kidnapped in our car! Better call the police." Ian's realization hit him like a clap of thunder.

"Not in this city, you don't. You know how corrupt and inefficient Mouski's cops are; you saw what happened that night we took down The Oxman. Besides, we got Al here. He's worth more than the city's whole friggin' force," Josh exaggerated.

"C'mon, Ian. Let's go back downstairs to your garage," Alvarez suggested.

On the way to the staircase, he shone his flashlight around them. "Look: none of the other condo doors on this floor have been touched. Evidently whoever broke in wanted you two specifically." He shook his head. Ian cursed under his breath as they descended the dark stairs.

"Ian, what kinda car you drive?" asked Alvarez, looking at tire marks on the garage floor. "A stick shift?"

"Yeah. 2006 BMW. Silver. California plates. Stick shift's easier on gas."

"Looks like they made a right turn onto Adams Avenue, probably heading for the ramp onto 46 West," said Alvarez. "The driver doesn't know how to shift. Look here. Big tire marks when he reversed it. And again when he shifted to first, then to second and finally into third. He also accelerated too much and had to slam on the brakes in the drive as he entered traffic. Seen this kinda thing before."

"Abby knows how to drive that car. She couldn't have been driving. I just came along Adams from the lab. Didn't see anything suspicious."

"You might've missed them by just a few minutes," Alvarez pointed out.

Josh answered his cell phone. "Ghanna just called. Doc Pannell will be here in a few minutes."

"Good," said Alvarez. "Hey, look up at the exterior garage door. It's intact, Ian. They must've used a computer program that goes through all possible combinations of digits and letters to get the high-frequency access code. All they hadda do was sit in their car, maybe fifteen minutes to an hour depending on how complicated the code was. Then—bingo, they're in."

Ian groaned and said softly, "I'll never forgive myself. Should've installed my own security devices. Me, of all people, relying on somebody else! I could have protec—"

"Don't beat yourself up, Ian," interrupted Josh, laying his hand on Ian's arm. "No time for regrets. We gotta go find Abby."

"You're right, we do," said Ian, pulling himself together. "Till Dr. Pannell gets here, figure out what you can from the mess they made. I still want to search for Abby myself."

Dr. Pannell screeched to a halt in the condo parking lot and jumped out of his car. "Ghanna told me to get over here quick because Abby's in deep trouble. What the hell is going on?" he asked, looking at the empty suitcases and clothes tossed around.

"Looks like the bastards who did this have kidnapped Abby," said Alvarez.

"Christ!" exclaimed Dr. Pannell.

"Let's plan a search strategy," said Alvarez. "Ian, you take 46 East to Route 3. We'll take 46 West to the merge with 23 and 80. Those three highways are like a plate of spaghetti out there. We can't search all the possibilities—the thugs could take off in any direction. Call Ghanna with your positions and any other information. He's our communications coordinator."

"But first, Ian," added Dr. Pannell, "call the state police. I've dealt with them on occasion. Unlike our local police, they're not persuaded by bribes, and if necessary, they can post alerts on the overhead highway signs. Tell them your car is stolen, describe it, and give them your ID information. *Nothing more.* If Abby's been kidnapped, any revelation about her might make matters worse, since the people who took her probably are after the research. If the press gets hold of that, you could be damned. Sorry to speak to you this way, Ian, but I am concerned about your wife's safety, and yours," he said emphatically.

"I understand," said Ian. "I'll try to cope and keep cool. Where do you think they'd hide out?"

"Good question," said Josh. "Maybe some cheap motel—you know."

"All right. I'll keep an eye out for anyplace that looks likely."

"Great. Don't forget to keep Ghanna posted," said Alvarez. *"Let's go find her!"*

After calling the state police, Ian shook hands with his three friends. Then he hopped onto his motorcycle and sped away, praying that Abby would soon be found unharmed.

Dr. Pannell, Josh, and Alvarez stood silently, watching Ian leave. Then Alvarez pointed to something in the mess of open suitcases and clothing in the garage. It was an unframed wedding photo of Ian and Abby, and someone had stepped on it.

"That footprint is bigger than the one we saw upstairs, Josh. Different kind of tread, too. It's valuable evidence. Don't touch anything."

"Course not, man," Josh said impatiently.

"I think I can photograph this wedding-day image with my cell and at least get their faces—without laying a hand on the original," Alvarez said. He clicked the photo and then passed his cell phone over to Josh and Dr. Pannell.

"This is pretty good, Al. What're ya gonna do with it?" Josh asked.

"Show it to anyone who might've seen Abby."

"You're a good detective, Al," Dr. Pannell commented.

"Doc, you wanna come with us?" Alvarez urged.

"Yeah," Dr. Pannell said. "But let me drive. My car's faster."

"Bring your piece?"

"Yes, just in case. I had a feeling something was really wrong."

"I brought mine too—hope I won't need it," Josh said.

Alvarez looked at his friend with surprise. "I never knew you had a gun, Josh."

Josh laughed. "Of course I have a gun! How d'ya think I've lived this long in this city?"

"I've got my handcuffs too," Alvarez added. "Lucky I left right from work. When I'm on duty, I always have them clipped to my belt."

"Great. Let's go," said Josh.

"Brought these too." Doc Pannell handed Josh high-powered binoculars. "Left them in the trunk after I went hiking last weekend with some friends. But this time they're for finding Abby, our top researcher."

"And her 2006 silver BMW with California plates," added Alvarez. The three piled into Dr. Pannell's Camry and quickly drove off.

—⌐ᵔⱼᵔ—ₒ

As they sped along Route 46 West, Alvarez said, "The way I see it is we're lookin' for at least two people, probably both men. And because the thieves defeated the access code with a computer program, I wonder if this is the same fucker that got into Truesort's hospital lab?"

"Could well be," Dr. Pannell answered as he merged into the left lane.

"That guy knew his way around the surveillance cameras in the hospital—avoided being seen by using the hallways where none were installed. Whether it's the same guy or someone else, he's smart," Alvarez admitted.

Dr. Pannell turned into the driveways of boardinghouses, luxury motels with canopied entrances, and many motels. The three men developed a procedure. Alvarez looked around the lobby and went to the registration desk to ask if the woman in the photo had checked in. Dr. Pannell drove slowly around the parking lots to see if he recognized the BMW or any other vehicles. Josh meandered through as many hallways as he could slip into, then sat in the reception area as if waiting for a friend.

After they'd been searching for about an hour and forty-five minutes, Alvarez's cell phone rang. "Hi, Ian. Seen anything yet? No, we haven't either. Nah, don't go any farther east. Go north on 21 and take some back roads up to 80 West, and explore some of the exits off of it. We'll do 23 North for you." He put the phone back in his pocket.

"There's our next stop," said Josh. "Keep to the right, Doc: the Kellsley Motel. Looks too clean, but a BMW would blend in." Dr. Pannell drove off the highway onto a side street and turned left into the motel parking lot in order to circle around the entire building.

"Will you look at that?" Alvarez whispered. "There it is. They wanted to be found."

"You think this is a trap?" Josh asked. "It's too easy."

"Probably left. Switched cars." Dr. Pannell got out, put on surgical gloves, and opened the BMW. "It's not locked. Found the keys under the mat. May have some prints. Nobody wiped it down, from what I can see. The police may want to check it to be sure. Josh, report in to Ian and Ghanna, and the state police too. Oh, and tell Ian to bring another set of keys. The ones under the mat may have the thief's fingerprints," Dr. Pannell said as he put the keys carefully into the glove compartment.

Alvarez merely glanced at the car. "Let's look around the motel room right in front of the BMW." He slid his credit card into the lock, and the door swung open.

Dr. Pannell noticed a pizza box in the garbage. "Wondered why this place smelled so good. Here's a receipt, too, with today's date and this room number. Call 'em up, Josh. Here's the phone number right here on the box. Find out who ordered it and what time it was delivered. Maybe they're still nearby."

Dr. Pannell walked around the outside and returned to the room. "They would be fairly inconspicuous here. Abby could be moved into this room easily without anyone noticing."

"Yeah, I agree," Alvarez answered. "Maid hasn't cleaned up the room yet, so whoever was here must not have checked out today. But no suitcases, no toothbrushes on the sink, no laundry or clothing hangin' in the closet. Obviously they weren't plannin' to stay here for long. From the footprints back at the condo, we know at least two people were involved. I bet one of them stayed in this room last night but not the other. One bed looks like it was slept in and somebody tried to smooth out the covers. The other, with the pillows and chair on it, still has the bedspread pretty much intact, but someone sat on the edge. Bathroom's clean, but a couple of washcloths are really wet."

"I see what you mean," Doc Pannell said, looking at the beds. "What do you think of that chair and stuff on top of the bed? Weird, huh?" Then he went outside to consider the clues they had found and what they meant.

Meanwhile, Josh had called the pizzeria. "They delivered pizza, chicken, and sodas at one forty-three this afternoon," he reported.

"The guy who delivered the food said the man tipped him almost forty-eight bucks."

Alvarez raised his eyebrows. "Probably Abby's money," he said.

The roar of a motorcycle along with men's voices summoned Josh and Alvarez outside. "You found it." Ian pulled off his helmet and parked his motorcycle. "Thanks," he said, shaking the state trooper's hand.

"Don't thank me. Thank your friend here. He actually found the car before I did."

Dr. Pannell nodded. "Glad to help," he said. Ian shook the doctor's hand too.

"Just need some ID, Mr. Lightfoot," the policeman explained. "Doesn't look like there's any damage. Must've taken it for a joyride and then driven away in a different car. Happy to help," he said. He took a quick look at Ian's ID and started to return to his car.

"Just a minute," Dr. Pannell called. "Just a minute, Officer. We'd like to find out who did this."

"They're long gone by now," the policeman said as he got into his car. "What can you possibly give me to go on? You're just lucky you got the car back in good shape. Have a nice day." He drove out of the parking lot, joined the highway traffic, and sped out of sight.

While he watched the police car disappear, Josh's jaw dropped in amazement. "Didn't know they treat white folks like that, too."

"He's okay, Josh. Anyway, he's a state trooper. I didn't tell them about Abby," Ian said with a heavy sigh.

"So now what?" Josh asked. "How the hell we gonna find the thieves' car?"

"You're going to call the county sheriff," Dr. Pannell said. "Remember, you suggested him when we were going after The Oxman?" he told Josh.

"I didn't meet him under too favorable a circumstance. Maybe you—"

"We can't stand around here playing diplomat," Alvarez scolded him. Dr. Pannell, Ian, and Josh took the hint and followed Alvarez into the motel room.

"I'll ask the motel clerk the license-plate number for the guests in room 18, plus any other details about their car," Alvarez said. "And while I'm at it, I'll ask the clerk for the sheriff's name and phone number. Usually it's on the emergency phone listings."

"Then *you* can call the sheriff, Doc. He'll listen to you," Josh quickly added. "Maybe Ian can help ya."

As Ian walked into room 18, he couldn't restrain an excited cry. "Abby was definitely here, Al! See that chair upside down with the blanket padding the back? See the pillows propped up at the headboard? That's how Abby rests when she's been on her feet a lot."

"Good, Ian, good," said Alvarez. "I'm going to the front desk to see if I can find out anything more. You three wait here."

Alvarez returned to the room about ten minutes later and told the group what he had learned. "The front-desk clerk said the two men in 18 arrived last night in a blue Lexus, said they'd be checking out tomorrow. This morning one of them returned in a different car, an old black Honda Civic. The manager wondered why they brought two cars, so she got the Honda's license-plate number too. Anyway, when they arrived last night, the two men asked for a room around back on the ground floor, away from the noise of the traffic. Besides, one of them was handicapped; he limped."

Dr. Pannell and Josh stared at each other. "Are you thinkin' what I'm thinkin'?" Josh asked.

"William!" they exclaimed simultaneously.

"Who's William?" asked Ian.

"William *Meddlebach*?" Alvarez asked.

"Yup, the hospital snitch," Josh explained. "The hospital people hired him 'cause they wanna look like do-gooders. He keeps an eye on things and cleans up, mostly outside."

"He hangs out in the parking garage," added Dr. Pannell. "A little strange."

A puzzle piece suddenly clicked into place in Alvarez's mind. "Doc, Josh—I just realized something. It's circumstantial evidence, but suppose William and Royce Barkley are in on this together. You think they might've been partners in July too—breaking into the hospital lab? William would've been *just* the person to tell Royce how to avoid the security cameras."

"Made to order," Josh agreed. "Let's catch up with 'em and find out."

"Gave William some painkillers for his leg once," said Dr. Pannell. "Bet he was the one who used that chair, Ian."

"But Abby's the one who set it up that way," said Ian. "Maybe she's all right if they allowed her to do that."

Dr. Pannell nodded. "We can't count on it, but it's a hopeful sign. I'm about to call the county sheriff from the parking lot. It's deserted out there, and my cell will get better reception. Ian, why don't you come with me? I'm sure the sheriff will want to question you—and your father-in-law too, just in case he has any helpful information. If Abby's kidnappers demand ransom—"

"Do you think they will?" asked Ian.

"They might," said Dr. Pannell. "Dr. Zelban is a wealthy man. But the sheriff can help manage the situation safely. You know your father-in-law's phone number?"

"Yeah," said Ian. "Here's one of his business cards, and I'm writing his cell on the back. But he's leaving for a conference in Chicago. I think Abby said he's flying out of Newark Airport this afternoon, since he had a meeting in Manhattan this morning."

"Okay, let's pass along that info."

Josh and Alvarez gave Dr. Pannell descriptions of Royce from the security tapes back in July. Alvarez also handed him a note with the sheriff's name and phone number as well as the license numbers of the Honda and Lexus.

"Sheriff Zachary Van Nisen, huh?" asked Dr. Pannell.

"Yeah, that's him," said Josh. "Couldn't quite remember the name."

"Thanks, Al," Dr. Pannell said. "Okay, Ian, come on out into the parking lot. Let's call him."

A few minutes later they returned to the room to report back to the others. "A sheriff's deputy is on his way over," said Ian. "He's going to comb this room for clues and keep his eye on a certain blue Lexus—"

"But where is the Lexus?" asked Alvarez, dumbfounded.

"I just noticed it in a corner of the motel lot. The hood was cold, so it must not have been used this afternoon," Dr. Pannell said with a smile.

Josh whistled admiringly.

"Nice goin', Doc!" said Alvarez.

"And that's not all," Dr. Pannell continued. "Sheriff Van Nisen has already issued an alert for the old black Honda Civic throughout several counties; I gave him that plate number and descriptions of Royce and William. The sheriff will also try to track down Dr. Zelban before he leaves for Chicago."

"I talked with him too, answered some questions," added Ian. "I emphasized that this investigation must be done quietly and not involve the general public." Ian got on his motorcycle and called back to the others, "I'll explore the side roads around here, since those guys and Abby were in the area recently. Call me if you find anything!" He zoomed away.

"Hey, here's another idea," said Josh. "Maybe Miano Tse can email the sheriff's office a photo of Royce Barkley. We been watchin' him for a while." When Dr. Pannell nodded his approval, Josh updated Ghanna, who arranged for Miano Tse to pick up Royce's photo, scan it at Fred's private lab, and email it to the sheriff as a confidential attachment.

"Time we got on the road again too," said Dr. Pannell. "It's already three fifteen." He closed the door of room 18 and walked briskly toward his Camry, followed by Josh and Alvarez.

Josh pulled the binoculars out from under the front passenger's seat and got in the car. Alvarez sat in the back.

Dr. Pannell asked his two cohorts, "Which way would you go with Abby from here? You guys seem to know more about them than I do."

"North, probably north. More isolated," Alvarez said. "Just get back onto 23."

"Okay. I told the county sheriff's office what I was driving."

Dr. Pannell reached into his pocket and handed his cell phone to Alvarez. "Here, you take this for now."

"Okay, Doc. How come you told him what you're drivin'?" Alvarez asked.

"Take a look at us, Al. Josh here is peering through binoculars, and he doesn't look like the bird-watching type. You're sitting in the backseat with your security uniform on. I'm the only one who looks plain."

"See what ya mean," said Josh, smiling.

Dr. Pannell drove onto the highway just as his phone rang. Alvarez clicked it on. "Hi, Sheriff Van Nisen. Yes, he's here. He's gonna pull over so he can talk to ya."

Dr. Pannell learned that two of the sheriff's deputies had already arrived at Newark Airport and would try to apprehend Dr. Zelban before he boarded his plane. "Great! Good luck, Sheriff. For now, I'm on Route 23, driving north into Morris County, with two good men helping me. I'll keep you posted about any change in plans. Right. Thanks again." Then he clicked off his phone and pulled back onto the highway.

"You know him from before?" Josh asked.

"No. But we found out today that we're both Green Berets, and Green Beret men are all brothers."

"We're comin' to a divided highway. I'll watch on the other side. You keep watchin' nearby," Josh told Alvarez. "Binoculars aren't much good at this speed. Just use your naked eye."

Alvarez kept staring at the gas stations, farm stands, and the parking lots of the strip malls but saw nothing unusual. "We might as well turn around and go south. Nothing much up this way," he concluded. "Besides, sooner or later, somebody has to come back for the Lexus."

Dr. Pannell agreed and took a U-turn to return to the motel. They wanted to speak to the sheriff's deputies and find out if the Lexus was still there.

Ten minutes later, as they passed the mall across from the Kellsley Motel, Josh suddenly yelled, "William! I see him! William, down there in the parking lot. Doc, Al—look!"

Dr. Pannell pulled over inconspicuously and ordered, "Give me the binoculars. Yeah, that's William, just getting out of the black Honda. He's in a plaid sports jacket. That's gotta be them, in that secluded parking spot."

"Fortunately not entirely secluded from the highway," Alvarez said, looking through the binoculars.

"Who'd ever think those two lame-asses would stay right near the motel?" Josh asked. "I didn't figure them for that."

Dr. Pannell laughed. "None of us did, Josh. Probably learned their lesson from the terrorists. Figured it would be hard for us to move on them if they're in such a public space. Counted on our fear of collateral damage."

"They played a great game of musical cars, too," said Alvarez.

Josh pulled out his cell phone. "Ian, it's Josh. I spotted 'em. Yeah. They're in a black Honda Civic in the parking lot at The Mall for All. Where are you?"

"Route 23 North, almost at the motel," Ian answered. "I can see the traffic light at the corner of the motel parking area."

"Great! You're almost here. The black Honda is parked at the south end of the mall, near MexTex Tacos. Even with binoculars, I can't make out exactly who's in the car or the numbers on the license plates. Don't go near it yourself, Ian. They could be armed."

"Okay. Want me to call the sheriff? Get him to bring his deputies now, Josh?" Ian said, trying to keep calm.

Josh conferred briefly with Dr. Pannell.

"Nope, take 'em down," the doctor answered. "Hold 'em and then call in the deputies. We're already here; they're not. Too much risk of these guys getting away. I see a parking spot four aisles over. That's where Al and I will be. Tell Ian to take the northern entrance into the mall, park his bike a few aisles north of MexTex Tacos, and walk casually to my Camry."

Ian agreed. "But this better be the right Honda," he cautioned. Ian eased his motorcycle back onto the highway, then at top speed weaved his way through the traffic toward the mall.

"He'd better not ride like a maniac," muttered Dr. Pannell. "Poor guy, he's too overwrought to have reliable judgment."

"Doc," Alvarez pointed out, "when we drive down into the parking lot, we're gonna lose sight of William. How about if Josh stays up here at the bus stop by the mall entrance, where he'll have a better view?"

"Good idea!" said Dr. Pannell. "Here's the bus stop, Josh. Just watch William and keep us posted, okay?"

"No problem, Doc," said Josh, getting out of the Camry. "Now we got work to do. Let's rescue Abby and catch a pair of thugs!"

Chapter 17

*T*HE MALL FOR ALL was in a small valley encircled by a ridge forming a natural bowl. The highway that ran past the motel was on the level of the ridge top. Entrance and exit drives led into a road lower on the sloping terrain that circled the entire mall; another two-lane road went across the center, providing shoppers entry to the parking aisles and sidewalk space along the storefronts. Many stores—including the pizzeria William had noticed—had been added on the ridge itself as the mall gained in popularity.

A few minutes before Josh noticed him, William had announced to Royce, "Think I'll do a little shoppin'. Won't need this." He shoved his gun into the glove compartment. "Never had a c-credit card before. I bet you have lotsa credit, huh, Abby? This'll be fun. Thanks for the shoppin' spree," he went on, thinking he could pass for a relative with permission to use her card. "Okay with you, Royce? Might as well make use of the time till dear ole Dad comes. Or are you gonna p-persuade the lady to talk without waitin' for him? Anyways, I'm outta here." William got out of the car and limped across the parking lot, glancing at the stores' window displays. The red Camry at the traffic light, waiting to enter the mall, was the furthest thing from his mind.

When William left, Royce knocked Abby down across the backseat and attempted to rape her. Abby kneed him in the groin repeatedly to protect herself. Finally Royce managed to crawl onto her stomach and press his mouth on hers until her lips were bleeding. Royce raised himself up, repulsed by the blood. Abby didn't speak. Instead, with a burst of sheer strength, she suddenly raised her head enough to butt Royce's chin, breaking four of his front teeth. He could see her eyes narrow with the success of revenge. She thought, *I hope you catch my flu.*

Royce, humiliated, slapped her across the face, yelling, "You bitch! Just wait till later. I'll take you to a lake north of here. I know just the spot. If you don't do what I say, I'll drown you. Nah, that would be too easy. Maybe you could do a bullet dance while I shoot at your feet. Your only hope now is the ransom. If I get enough from your dad, you may be okay. If not . . ." Royce shrugged his shoulders and told Abby, "I'll leave that up to your imagination."

Then he returned to the driver's seat, confident that no one could hear him yell at Abby or see his unsuccessful attempt to rape her. Royce looked at the guns in the glove compartment as he held a wad of tissues over his chin. He hesitated and thought, *No, I've gone far enough for now. I'll just increase the ransom.*

Abby gradually wriggled into a sitting position. She pushed with her feet and managed to bend her knees so she could sit and look out. There was very little to see. *If only someone can find me,* she thought. *How can I let anyone know where I am when my hands are tied?*

⎍⎔⎍₀

Ian rode into the mall. He circled around the shoppers, cruised past MexTex Tacos, and parked. He didn't want to go directly to Dr. Pannell's car. *If I could just find Abby by myself,* he mused while searching along aisles of parked cars near a recycling truck. Ian finally gave up and got into the front passenger seat of Dr. Pannell's Camry, where Josh had been sitting until he got out at the bus stop.

⎍⎔⎍₀

Josh phoned Alvarez from the bus stop. "William's headin' to the stores up this way. Should I nab him?"

"Can you get him before he gets into the store?" Alvarez asked. "We're just driving into the parking lot now, below you. If not, wait until he comes out and is a good fifty feet away from the storefront. I see him. Don't see the black Honda from here, but we already know exactly where it is. We'll be cautious. We don't want William to recognize us and warn Royce. You just mosey up to William from behind. Nice and casual-like. Put your gun in his ribs, but keep it covered under your shirt. You know what I'm sayin'. Surprise him."

"Yeah, gotcha," Josh answered. "I'll frisk him too."

"Josh, he's turned around. He's walkin' away from the store like he forgot somethin'. Can you still see William from the ridge up there?"

"Yup, still see him. He's walking toward a maroon SUV."

"Right, I see it. Keep in back of him as you move in. Hide behind that maroon SUV, then grab him and hold on to him. We're gonna park as close to it as possible. Then just hustle him into our car. He'll sing like a druggie in withdrawal."

Dr. Pannell's eyebrows went up as he watched Josh run across the street from the bus-stop shelter, leaping over hoods of cars waiting at the traffic light. Keeping hidden from William, Josh sprinted down the hill into the mall parking lot. He turned right into the aisle closest to the maroon SUV and crouched behind it.

"Wow! Did you see that guy run? No wonder he stayed ahead of the law." Dr. Pannell was flabbergasted.

"He thinks he's runnin' hurdles," Alvarez said with a grin. "He was the high-school track hero, ya know. Hear the cheers. The shoppers loved it. It was a great distraction. He ran less than a minute to get to the SUV."

If this is his definition of nonchalant, what would he do if we asked him to show off? Dr. Pannell wondered.

"He doesn't always take advice," said Alvarez. "But you gotta admit he caught up with William pretty fast."

"He's already disappeared. Where'd he go?" asked Dr. Pannell.

"By the maroon SUV, like I told him," Alvarez said.

"I'll help Josh," Ian said, and ran toward the SUV. When he was a few steps behind William, Ian silently followed him, blocking William's path to escape.

William was limping along, head down, studying the signature on Abby's credit card.

"Excuse me, sir." Josh leaned over him from the roof of the maroon SUV. He grabbed the credit card and slid to the ground. "You see a black Honda Civic? I lost my car in this here big parkin' lot with so many people cheerin' me on."

Shaking, William stared at Josh. "No need to be scared, William. You know me, your old friend Josh. Just gotta frisk ya. Good. You ain't got no gun. Where you headed? Goin' in or goin' out? Let Ian and me give you a lift."

Josh smiled at his play on words as he and Ian carried William toward Dr. Pannell's red Camry. Josh's gun remained in his pocket.

Alvarez ordered Dr. Pannell, "Drive over near the SUV. We'll put William in the backseat. Hope nobody sees them carrying him."

"They're right in plain sight. Let's hope nobody does anything about it," Dr. Pannell said, annoyed.

Ian helped Josh push while Alvarez pulled William onto the backseat of the Camry.

"Good goin', Josh," Alvarez said, pushing William up so he could sit in the middle between Josh and himself.

William realized that he was trembling with fear. He was stuck between two strong men.

Dr. Pannell said, "Hey, Al, if you want to tie up William, there's some heavy twine under the seat somewhere. I was using it for packages the other day."

Alvarez looked at the twine and decided to use handcuffs instead. *Not doing his feet. Too painful with that lame leg. Anyhow, he can't get far.*

Now that William was secured in the backseat, Ian got out and just stood by the crowded car for a few minutes, anxiously surveying the scene and looking through the binoculars for the Honda or any suspicious-looking accomplices. When he got back into the car, Ian switched places with Josh and took a turn guarding William in the backseat, along with Alvarez, while Josh moved to the front. Dr. Pannell drove around the rear of the stores and parked behind a delivery truck. "We don't have much time before the county sheriff arrives, William, so tell us everything."

William quivered. His mouth moved soundlessly.

"We'll make it easy for you," Alvarez said. "Where's Abby?"

William pointed in the direction of the recycling truck.

"Is she in that black Honda Civic?" Alvarez continued.

William nodded. "It's R-royce's car, see, not mine. He's in there with her."

"Royce? Royce Barkley?" Alvarez asked.

"Uh-huh," William said, looking down at his feet.

"Thought so," said Alvarez. "Does he have a gun?"

"Yeah," William said. "We both do. We keep 'em in the glove compartment. I even have a s-silencer on mine," he bragged.

Josh asked, "Is Abby—?"

Dr. Pannell interrupted. "Enough of these questions. We're going to drive over there." He started the car and drove to the front of the stores.

"Josh, you drive. Don't think Royce will know my car, but it really doesn't matter at this point. Al and I are getting out," Dr. Pannell said. He pulled a couple of maps, directions to a state park, and a flashlight out of the glove compartment; next he pulled his low-caliber gun with a silencer out amid the remaining paraphernalia. Noticing William cringe, Doc Pannell added, "You're not the target, William. Relax. Al's my backup. We're going to use the trees for cover to shoot the driver's-side tires on the Honda. If we're lucky, we'll do the same thing to the passenger side. I figure no one will hear the shots. It'll slow down or even stop the Honda—make it useless for a getaway. Maybe he'll run for it. Who knows?"

"Man, is that cool; it's really awesome," Josh said, laughing.

"To make sure you're not recognized, Josh, you'll have to drive counterclockwise once you get on the road that circles the entire mall. Park behind the trees. We'll be looking for you there."

"Got it." Josh hopped into the driver's seat as soon as Dr. Pannell slipped out.

Using the parked cars as cover, Alvarez and Dr. Pannell maneuvered toward the Honda. Josh drove around the parking lot and slowed down so Ian could join him to watch for Abby and search for the Honda.

"God, I hope she's all right!" Ian said, rubbing his palms together. "I can't wait to get my hands on that bastard!"

William looked up slowly and eyed Ian. "I t-tried to help her. She's okay. Royce was p-pretty mad and was mean to her. It wasn't s-supposed to happen this way. Saw Royce get in the backseat of the Honda."

"What *was* supposed to happen?" Ian turned and lunged toward William, seizing him by the shoulder.

Josh leaned over the seat, grabbed Ian's arm, and held his wrist in a bone-crunching grip midair. "Don't. He'll just clam up if you do. Try to stay cool, man." He dropped Ian's arm and continued driving.

William rolled his body across the backseat, trying to look for the Honda from the back window. It was not in view. *Royce ain't gonna hear me. We gotta collect that ransom money.* Without looking at either Josh or Ian, William began to speak in a monotone. "The condo was s-supposed to be empty, nobody home. I've been w-watchin' it all week. Abby's dad s-said you and Abby were—"

"WHAT?" Ian interrupted the monologue. "Her *DAD?* What does he have to do with this?"

"I was *trying* to tell you," said William. "He said you and Abby were going to his country house for the weekend, so it'd be easy to g-get in and take the research he wan—"

"Who hired you, Royce or Abby's dad?" Ian broke in again.

"Royce hired me. Dr. Z-zelban hired Royce."

"That greedy, evil bastard! How can he steal from his own daughter and put her life in danger?"

"There they go." William pointed to Dr. Pannell and Alvarez. Then abruptly he began to yell to Royce in the black Honda a hundred feet away. "Watch out! Royce, watch—"

Josh just laughed. "He's not gonna hear ya, William. Too far away, and under the circumstances I'm sure Royce would have his windows closed."

"Yeah, but somebody near us might hear," Ian said, clapping his hand over William's mouth. "Josh, stop the car. See what Dr. Pannell's got in the trunk. Might have some duct tape. Hurry, this son of a bitch is strong." Ian grappled with William to control him.

Josh popped the trunk and opened the kit of auto tools, then a satchel of medical supplies. He grabbed the sterile packs of gauze and some tape as he listened to the continuing struggle between Ian and William in the backseat.

"Hold his head still, Josh. Let me push the gauze into his mouth. Then we can tape it."

As Josh let go, William bit him. Josh yowled and slugged William across the offending mouth, but Ian stopped the fight. "Now who couldn't keep his cool?" he admonished Josh.

Josh shrugged, returned to the driver's seat, and began easing the Camry toward the Honda. Now William was whimpering in pain in the backseat. Ian sat next to him and gave a running commentary, trying to contain his anxiety: "I swear I'll *kill* that bastard! How could he expose her to this? But I'm not really surprised. I had a feeling something wasn't right with him. I just didn't know what it was."

Ian, becoming edgy with William's whimpering, told William he would take off the tape if William promised not to yell. William nodded, so Ian pulled the gauze out of William's mouth.

William cleaned his mouth with the remaining gauze and began to talk again, happy to be the center of attention. "Royce hit her and she d-didn't even cry," he said.

"Royce doesn't know Abby. Chas doesn't know his daughter very well, either," Ian said with disgust. "She'll take the research information to the grave rather than give it up now."

"Doc Pannell is calling. Find out what he's learned," said Josh, handing his cell phone to Ian.

Ian listened carefully, occasionally nodding. "Okay, I'll tell Josh. Al with you? Good. They did? Great! Bob, please call the sheriff again and tell him William says Chas hired Royce. Unbelievable! That's right. They'll want to look into that very carefully when they question him. Thanks, bye," Ian said, and handed the phone back to Josh.

"Okay, here is what's happening, Josh. Doc Pannell called the sheriff again and explained our situation. The sheriff said it was too much for us to handle by ourselves. We are to stay back and wait. That means no shooting tires," Ian explained emphatically.

"Damn," said Josh. "I wanted to see that."

"Nope, gotta do what the sheriff says," said Ian. "The best news is, they already have Chas; picked him up at the airport—the bastard!"

"All *right!*" said Josh.

"By calling his secretary and an airline rep, they confirmed his travel plans. They're going to bring him over after they talk to him. Now they can find out whether William here was telling the truth," Ian said.

Thanks to his limo driver and the promise of a substantial tip, Dr. Zelban had breezed through the traffic, arriving at Newark Liberty Airport in time to check his suitcase and start through security when he heard someone shouting his name. He turned and saw a policeman running toward him, holding up his badge with his right hand while shoving the crowd of passengers out of his way with his left.

"This man has a serious problem at home," the policeman explained to the security officer, taking hold of the doctor's elbow and guiding him out of the queue to a relatively quiet corner of the waiting area.

Silently Dr. Zelban sat and stared at the policeman. *Oh my God, this can't be related to Royce, can it? What went wrong? How'd they find me?* he asked himself apprehensively.

Less than a minute later, two sheriff's deputies strode up to Dr. Zelban. They displayed their badges, introduced themselves as Donald Krainer and Newman Frion, and escorted Dr. Zelban to their car. Deputy Krainer drove; Deputy Frion sat next to the doctor in the backseat. As they pulled out of the airport's vast concentric network of parking lots, Dr. Zelban asked, "What's this all about, gentlemen? Do you realize you've made me miss my flight to an important medical conference? I already checked my luggage through."

"Worry about all that later. Your daughter has been kidnapped," Deputy Krainer said bluntly. "Sheriff Van Nisen wants to question you, just in case you have any information that might help her."

No! No, it can't be. "Oh my God! Are you sure? Are you sure it's my daughter?"

Deputy Frion held up a copy of the photo of Abby and Ian on their wedding day, which one of the sheriff's detectives had obtained from the couple's garage and given to the deputies. "Unfortunately, yes. Any idea who might've done this, or why?"

"None whatsoever," Dr. Zelban said, shaking his head as he tried to cope with this unbelievable event. "Let me think."

"Anyone approach you for ransom?"

"Of course not," Dr. Zelban said, glowering at Deputy Frion. "Who would *dare* threaten her? Whoever did this ought to be—"

Just then Dr. Zelban's cell phone rang, and he answered the call. Deputy Frion watched the doctor's face slowly turn ashen. "Look," Dr. Zelban said in a hushed, tense voice, "I'm taking care of an emergency now. Talk to you later. Don't do *anything* till you hear back from me, understand?" He groaned, turned off his cell, and shoved it into his pocket. At last Dr. Zelban accepted the fact that Abby had been kidnapped.

"Who was that?" Deputy Frion asked.

"Just an incompetent intern," muttered Dr. Zelban.

"I see," Deputy Frion responded. Actually he thought, *Probably the kidnapper, but why won't this guy admit it?*

They rode without speaking for a while. Hoping to find some useful information, Deputy Krainer said, "My wife's birthday is tomorrow, and I haven't decided what to get for her. You ever have that problem, Doctor?"

"Not anymore. I'm a widower," Dr. Zelban said wistfully.

"Oh, sorry, very sorry." After a brief pause, Deputy Krainer asked, "Any other kids besides your daughter?"

"Yes, a son, Steven. Lives in California."

"Would he have any idea who would try to harm his sister?"

"No more than I would," Dr. Zelban said in an agitated tone. "Wait a minute. Unfortunately, my son is addicted to gambling. Maybe he owes some money. It would be a large sum if they were bothering to come to the East Coast to collect," he reasoned.

"Might be that. But then we'll have to work with the California cops to solve that crime." Deputy Krainer continued, "Do you know anyone in California? Ever live out there yourself?"

"I have professional associates all over the country, including California," said Dr. Zelban, "but I've never lived there. Abby and Ian did until recently, though."

Hmm, interesting. I'll note that in the file, Deputy Frion thought.

As they pulled into the parking area of the sheriff's head-quarters, Deputy Frion told Dr. Zelban, "I apologize, Doctor, but we'll have to keep your cell phone temporarily. It may help our investigation."

"But I need it for professional reasons," protested Dr. Zelban. "My colleagues, my patients—"

"Sorry, Doctor. You'll get it back soon enough. What's the password?"

"Symbiosis, typed in as numbers."

"Okay, wise guy, spell it for me. I'm sure I won't be able to read your handwriting," Deputy Frion said, jotting down the password in his notebook.

"All right then," said Dr. Zelban, handing over his phone. "But you won't find anything there." *Gotta stay calm, gotta seem cooperative. Hopefully they won't bother looking too hard. Most of my calls are to other first-rate doctors anyway!*

When they walked into the building, Deputy Frion gave Dr. Zelban's phone and password to Sheriff Van Nisen and spoke privately to him about the doctor's strange behavior during his phone call in the car.

Sheriff Van Nisen took the phone into a back room and handed it to one of his detectives. "Check out Dr. Zelban's cell, Brad," he said. "Text me within ten minutes about the last few days of calls and text messages sent and received. By tomorrow I want a complete analysis of all information on the cell, along with recorded backups."

The detective nodded and got to work.

Then Sheriff Van Nisen returned to Dr. Zelban and the two deputies who had brought him in. "We're leaving immediately for the local mall, where your daughter's kidnappers are trapped by law-abiding citizens," he announced. "Dr. Zelban, you will come with me in my unmarked car. Newman, you can drive us."

"Sure, Zach."

"I've already told the local police force we're going to do a lockdown and alerted the mall management. Three marked cars should be enough since the local police will be there," Sheriff Van Nisen reasoned. "I've dispatched a couple of our squad cars to the mall to control the exits near our rendezvous position; they're already en route. Don, you take another squad car to check anything suspicious."

"Okay, Sheriff. We'll take different routes; less conspicuous that way."

"Good," the sheriff agreed. "Get there as quickly as you can without sirens."

"Impressive, Sheriff. We need more leaders like you," Dr. Zelban said, attempting to gain favor.

"We must proceed very carefully to ensure your daughter's safety," continued the sheriff, ignoring the doctor's comment. "You may be able to help us negotiate with the kidnappers."

"Of course. I'll be glad to help in any way I can," said Dr. Zelban. "I'd give anything—*anything!*—to get her back safely. She'd better be okay." *That's it: I'm the loving father, the innocent blackmail victim. Who would ever suspect an exemplary doctor of anything else?*

—∿╫⊸—

Royce was alarmed when a dark-green Chrysler 300 parked about four feet in front of his Honda. *Damn! What the HELL is that guy doing?* Royce beeped his horn, but the Chrysler didn't move.

Maybe I can back up and go around him. He revved his engine and shifted into reverse, but in his panic he crashed into the yard-high retaining wall behind him with a loud, scraping *bang*. "GODDAMN IT!" he bellowed, shifting into drive and trying to swerve to the left. The car lurched forward but halted abruptly, tires squealing against the curb beside him. Even if he could have made it over the curb, there were too many trees just beyond it—and the huge recycling truck still loomed on his right. Royce returned the Honda to its original parking spot, with a few feet on each side of the car.

Crap! Horrible place to park! Why didn't I think of this before? There's gotta be a way to—

Oh my God! That's not some idiot shopper. Look at the hat the guy is wearing. It's the SHERIFF!

Abby's eyes revealed her amusement at Royce's dilemma. *At last I've been found!* she thought. *Oh, thank God! Ian must've called the police. Thank you, Ian, thank you! But hurry, Sheriff: deliver me from this maniac! Watch out—he has two guns hidden in his glove compartment, and now he's trapped and desperate.* Abby put her bound hands over her face and slid lower in the seat. *Ian, if you're anywhere nearby, please, please be careful!* she thought, filled with hatred and fear, yet keeping her faith in Ian.

Sheriff Van Nisen called the mall management to summon the driver of the recycling truck and tell him to come immediately. The sheriff wanted to protect innocent citizens, and the truck would be a good barrier to keep away the curious. When the truck driver arrived, eating a taco, the sheriff explained to him that a kidnapper and his hostage were in the Honda, and asked him to drive his rig into the space now occupied by the Chrysler, to block in the Honda from the front. As the driver did so, the sheriff moved his car out of the truck's way and parked beside the Honda instead.

Royce was trapped on all four sides.

From the backseat of Dr. Pannell's red Camry, Ian said to Josh, "The sheriff's deputies and the stores' security guards are closing off the exits and entrance drives. And nobody is going into or out of the stores. Security is blocking all the doors. Al and the doctor want you to pick them up, Josh. Here they come, over by that jeep. They can handle William. I'm going to get Abby."

"But I want some of the action," Josh said as he watched Ian disappear behind a tan Acura. He saw Ian spring into the back of a

4x4 pickup parked in the last row of cars. Josh slowly drove nearer to MexTex Tacos, blocking Ian from the stores' view. *The security guards may mistake him for the enemy. How come Royce doesn't make a run for it? Scared, probably, holdin' Abby hostage.*

The 4x4 faced the sheriff's car from about forty feet away. Ian could see his father-in-law in it but couldn't see Royce or Abby now that the recycling truck was in front of the Honda. Ian decided to go through the stand of trees and approach Royce's car from the back. After sneaking through the parking lot, darting from behind one car to the next, Ian reached the trees and crept between them till he was about fifteen feet diagonally behind the Honda's left tail-light. He could see the very top of Abby's head and glimpses of Royce in front of her at the wheel, apparently pounding his fists on the dashboard. *Beat the dashboard all you want,* Ian thought, *but leave my lady alone.* Ian blew her an unseen kiss as tears of joy rolled down his cheeks.

Ian saw Dr. Zelban leave the sheriff's Chrysler with a deputy, who barked in a deep bass voice: "I'm Deputy Krainer. Unlock your doors and roll down your windows! Sheriff's orders!"

Deputy Krainer remained standing a few yards from the passenger side of the car, because the sheriff was uncertain what Royce's reaction would be. The deputy also turned on his iPhone's recording app and put the phone back in his pocket.

Ian heard the door locks click and saw the windows roll down before Dr. Zelban got into the backseat on the passenger side of the Honda, right next to Abby. *Damn bastard.* Then the door slammed shut.

They know the deputy can hear them, thought Ian. *Will they be careful what they say?*

But Royce was beyond caution or reason. He turned his head and screamed hoarsely at Dr. Zelban, "You got William and me into this mess, you GODDAMNED BASTARD! 'What the hell, let those two lowlifes figure a way out. *I'm* Dr. Charles Zelban. *I'm* an untouchable.' Is that it?"

"How DARE you?" yelled Dr. Zelban, his face nearly purple with rage. "How could you kidnap my daughter and then have the audacity to demand ransom from me? You vile, inhuman—"

"Oh, shut up, Mr. Arrogant! You're going down with William and me. No way are you going to squirm out of this one. Remember, you *hired* me," Royce shouted at Dr. Zelban.

"I never hired you to do *this*!" Dr. Zelban yelled back at Royce, gesturing toward Abby. "Just look at my daughter! She looks like she was run over by a truck! How could you be so cruel? Don't you know torture doesn't work? You should rot in prison for the rest of your life!"

"You started it all, you goddamned motherfucker. 'Just look around and find Abby's research,' you said. 'It'll be easy,' you said. You got me to do the dirty work, tailing Abby and Ian all over the place, because you were too busy being a rich, important doctor. 'Don't drive that old, beat-up Honda. Drive your blue Lexus,' you said. 'It'll look less suspicious.' Well, why didn't you search for the stuff yourself? You're her *father*." Royce took a quick look at Abby. "But from what I see here, she'll never be your daughter anymore," he added as he turned back to the wheel.

Deputy Krainer and Ian saw how Abby turned away from her father. When Dr. Zelban reached out to touch her shoulder, she refused to look at him. She turned again but looked ahead, avoiding any eye contact with her father.

"I'm so sorry, Abby. I never thought you would be harmed. I know what I did was wrong. I hope someday you will find it in your heart to forgive me," he said, and kissed her gently on her cheek. Abby sat as if she were a stone statue.

With fists clenched, Ian waited for Sheriff Van Nisen to make a move. The sheriff said something into his cell—Ian thought it sounded like "Thanks, Brad. I thought so." Then the sheriff strolled over to the driver's side of the Honda, followed by Deputy Krainer. The sheriff turned to ask the deputy, "You got the whole thing recorded, Don?"

"Yup, every word" was the deputy's answer. "Pretty damning evidence, too."

Ian slowly let out his breath. He watched Sheriff Van Nisen receive Royce's license and registration. Suddenly the sheriff opened the car door, grabbed Royce's collar, and yelled, "Come out and put your hands up! You are under arrest for breaking and entering, for kidnapping this woman and holding her hostage, and—I suspect from her appearance—assault, battery, and attempted rape."

Royce stumbled out. Deputy Krainer frisked him against the car while Sheriff Van Nisen read him his rights. Then the deputy handcuffed Royce and cautioned him, "You should be more careful about what you say on the phone. You're going to stand right over there, next to that squad car, till my colleague takes some photos of you." Three burly local policemen, who had been summoned by the sheriff, escorted Royce around the recycling truck to one of the county sheriff's marked cars nearby.

Ian heard the sheriff yell again: "You stay in the car, Dr. Zelban." But the doctor struggled to get out despite the sheriff's warning. He had one foot on the macadam when Ian catapulted through the trees and pounced on his father-in-law, pulling him past the open car door, spinning him around and forcing him backward with a barrage of furious punches to his chest, finally pinning him beside the smelly recycling truck.

"Enough!" the sheriff yelled, and pulled Ian off Dr. Zelban. "Stop! Keep your hands off him. You may already have given him a broken rib or two," the sheriff added sarcastically.

"Good!" said Ian. "He deserves it after what he did to my wife—his own daughter!" But Ian did step back as the sheriff had asked.

Ian watched the sheriff handcuff Dr. Zelban. "You are under arrest as a co-conspirator in a kidnapping, which is a federal offense," said Sheriff Van Nisen. Then he read the doctor his rights.

Dr. Zelban shouted, "But I never meant for this to happen! Abby, I never meant to put you in danger! I didn't think you'd be home! You must believe me!"

"Tell it to the jury," said Sheriff Van Nisen coldly. "If you entered a conspiracy to commit one crime, the law holds you liable for additional crimes arising out of that conspiracy, even if committed by the other co-conspirators and not you. You shouldn't have hired these men to break into your daughter's condo without thinking about what might happen if she was home at the time."

Deputy Krainer and two local policemen marched Dr. Zelban toward the marked car. The sheriff smiled at Ian. "You're Abby's husband, huh? Well, I don't blame you for hating that guy, but you still can't attack someone that way, buddy. Instead, say hello to your wife. Looks like she's okay. I'm sure she's glad to see you."

Ian helped Abby struggle out of the backseat onto the parking lot. She still had to be photographed with her hands taped, as part of the evidence to be used in court. Abby was glad to be standing after long hours sitting in one position. She was a little wobbly, so Ian put his arm around her shoulder to support her.

Sheriff Van Nisen came over to speak to them. "You're both wondering why I let Dr. Zelban sit in the car with Abby before arresting him, I'm sure. Two reasons: first, he was arrogant enough to think he wouldn't be arrested, so he wouldn't try to escape; second, I wanted him to see his daughter's injuries and how defenseless she was with her taped hands. He caused it all."

Ian spotted the red Camry slowly coming toward them. "Sheriff, my friends Josh, Alvarez, and Dr. Pannell are in that red Camry. They need to speak to you," he said.

When the Camry pulled up, Josh rolled down the window and called, "Here's another accomplice, Sheriff," pointing to William in the backseat. "He and Royce got concealed weapons in the glove compartment of the Honda."

Sheriff Van Nisen gave Dr. Pannell a questioning look. "Yeah, he helped Royce here," Dr. Pannell said from the front passenger seat, corroborating Josh's accusation. "Told us about it while we were waiting for you in the car."

The sheriff arrested William as a third co-conspirator and read him his rights. After Alvarez took off William's handcuffs and clipped them back onto his own belt, the sheriff fastened a set of his own handcuffs around William's wrists. Alvarez escorted William to join Royce and Dr. Zelban while Deputy Frion, with gloved hands, collected William's and Royce's guns from the Honda's glove compartment and put them in a ziplock bag.

Then Sheriff Van Nisen looked directly at Abby. "Did either of these two suspects harm you?"

"Yes. Royce beat me, slapped me around, and attempted to rape me; but I managed to fight him off so he wasn't successful. William never struck me, but he held me at gunpoint when they were searching the condo, and in the car."

"That's all I wanted to know for the time being. We'll talk later," the sheriff said. After getting Ian and Abby's contact information, he shook hands with Ian and told Abby he would follow up with her the next day.

Sheriff Van Nisen told everyone to wait. Initial photos had to be taken of Dr. Zelban, Abby, Royce, and William for evidence in the trial. "We'll do your images first, Abby. I realize your hands must be hurting."

Deputy Frion photographed her taped hands and swollen, bruised face. He took close-ups from several angles, proving that she had been beaten, as well as full front and back shots showing her disheveled clothing. Once Deputy Frion was finished documenting this evidence, Ian cut Abby's hands free. The other photos of Dr. Zelban, Royce, and William were done individually. All three remained in handcuffs.

Deputy Frion drove the BMW over to Ian and Abby and helped them into it. He explained, "I'll lead you to the nearest hospital. Ms. Zelban-Lightfoot, you will have to be examined as a victim of a violent crime. The results of your medical exam will be recorded and used in evidence during the trial, including photos of any injuries under your clothing. You'll need to leave your clothing for evidence as well, but the hospital will give you a clean warm-up suit to wear home. I'll stay in the hospital waiting room in case you or the staff have any questions. Once the exam is complete and the paperwork is in order, we can all go home."

"Thanks," Ian said. "It looks like Dr. Pannell wants to speak to us."

"Just tell me when you're ready to leave," the deputy said.

Dr. Pannell handed them keys to his apartment. "Your home is uninhabitable right now. After Abby's hospital exam, why don't you two stay at my place tonight. We'll talk in a couple of days. I jotted down some directions and my address. I see you have a GPS. Oh, and I'll take your motorcycle to my garage, Ian."

"Thanks, Bob," Abby said.

Ian thanked Bob also and handed him his motorcycle keys. "That'll give me some wheels while we're staying at your apartment," Ian said.

Then Abby turned and wrapped her arms around Ian in a tearful hug. "Thank God I have you," she said, laying her sore face on his chest.

Ian held her in his arms and whispered, "You've got me forever, darling." Then, anxious to leave before he ripped Dr. Zelban apart, Ian asked Deputy Frion to lead them to the hospital.

Next the remaining group learned that the sheriff needed all of them to come to his headquarters. Josh, Dr. Pannell, and Alvarez would ride in the green Chrysler with the sheriff. They were going to have an informal meeting to explain their roles in the capture of William and Royce while the details were fresh in their minds. Formal testimony for the trial would be handled later. Sheriff Van Nisen assured them that they could call their lawyers if they wanted to, or he could provide a lawyer (on call) if they preferred. He also said when the meeting was over, one of his deputies would drive them back to the mall to get their vehicles.

Dr. Zelban and William were taken to the backseat of a marked car by Deputy Krainer, who returned to the sheriff and whispered something discreetly. The sheriff told Royce: "Because you've urinated in your pants—what's wrong, you scared of being treated as badly as you treated your victim?—you will sit on the *floor* of the county deputy's vehicle and follow us."

Once Royce was squeezed into place, with William wrinkling up his nose, Sheriff Van Nisen explained to the three suspects, "Each of you can call your lawyer as soon as you get to my office. Dr. Zelban, if you would like a medical exam to make sure you're okay, I will arrange that. We need the complete story for the record and further official photos of all of you. I've given Abby Zelban-Lightfoot and her husband a few days to recuperate before I hear their testimony. She has assured me she is going to press charges."

The motorcade of witnesses, criminals, county sheriff, and deputies followed the unmarked, dark-green car out the exit onto the side road, to the salute of the patrolman who had cordoned off that entrance. The other patrolmen drove away, freeing the highway access drives. The stores' security guards opened the shop doors. Business resumed as usual—that is, with the normal consumer vigilance for bargains.

Chapter 18

WHILE ABBY AND IAN WERE TRYING to cope with her father's perfidy as they drove to the hospital, Josh was adjusting to a more positive experience. "Never been driven by no sheriff before. In the passenger seat, I mean. Pretty cool in an unmarked car. What kind of engine this got?" Josh asked as he rubbed the green plush upholstery.

The sheriff smiled. "Like this experience, Josh? Like being on the right side of the law? Right next to the driver's seat?" Josh's only answer was silence. "Eight-cylinder HEMI, Josh. Everybody comfortable back there? Warm enough?"

Dr. Pannell and Alvarez said they were comfortable. "Okay if I call my friend?" Alvarez asked.

"Sure."

"Forgot to call Ghanna. Things happened so fast." Alvarez tapped Ghanna's number. "He ain't answerin'. He never leaves his post. This ain't like Ghanna. Gotta call Asunta." After a moment he was on another call. "Yeah, honey, we're bringin' them in. Yeah, she's all right, *gracias a Dios*. Beat up a little, but nothing that won't heal. Tried to call Ghanna but only got his voice mail. Prob'ly on another call. Yeah. Would ya let him know Abby's okay? He'll be so glad. Call me back, *amor mio*. Thanks. Love you too."

The sheriff studied Alvarez in the rearview mirror. "How long have you been married, Alvarez?"

"Fifteen years."

"Any kids?"

"One boy. How about you, Sheriff?"

"Twenty years. A boy and a girl. Your wife knows this guy Ghanna?"

"Everybody down our way knows Ghanna. Just *about* everybody, anyway."

"Obviously he was a big help rounding up these criminals," the sheriff noted.

"Yeah, he coordinated all the phone calls."

"Think he would testify?"

"Probably. But I can't speak for him." Alvarez called Ghanna again, this time with success, and told him about Abby's rescue. "Ghanna, listen up. The sheriff wants you to testify. Yeah, you're hearing me right."

When the phone call ended a minute later, Alvarez reported to the sheriff, "He'll do it—but he found it very funny to be 'on the right side of the law,' like you said to Josh a few minutes ago."

"So I guessed from your end of the conversation," the sheriff said with an amused smile. "I'll need that lady Abby, too. Doc, when do you think she'll be able to talk to my detectives?"

"Couple of days, maybe sooner," answered Dr. Pannell. "I'll speak to her. This going to trial?"

"Of course. How else can we control these fraudulent bastards?"

—∿╂⊸—

That evening Abby and Ian drove toward Dr. Pannell's apartment. She wore the warm-up suit the hospital had given her. For a long time she stared silently out the window, rubbing her wrists.

"Do your wrists hurt?" Ian finally asked.

"Yes. They ache—actually, I still ache all over from the flu—but the doctor said no bones are broken," Abby answered.

"Yeah, the doctor told me about that too and gave me a copy of their findings. According to the hospital exam, your injuries aren't severe. I hope the pain relievers are helping. You really took a pounding," Ian said.

"Whenever Royce became aggravated, he would beat me. I was his whipping boy," Abby said with a moan.

"Maybe you'd rather not talk about it," Ian said, realizing his comment might have been insensitive.

"It's okay," Abby said. "It's a relief to be able to discuss it. I'm glad I didn't get a concussion. I thought I might have one, because I had a terrible headache."

After another awkward silence, she added, "Royce didn't rape me, Ian. He tried, but I just fought him off. You might say my father raped me, though, in a different way."

Ian clenched his fists tighter on the steering wheel. "Did you hear Royce ask your dad for ransom money?" he asked.

"Yeah, but before that, Royce showed me that he had my dad's cell phone number stored on his phone. I blew it off and told him a lot of people have that number. But actually, that was when doubt about my dad began seeping into my thoughts. Then Royce said something about you and me going to Connecticut this weekend. That's when I realized my dad *must* have told them that, and I knew I was done for. All I wanted was to escape somehow and be with you, Ian." Abby patted him on his shoulder.

"I used my motorcycle trying to find you. Figured it would be easier to maneuver around traffic and into sequestered areas. But in fact Bob, Josh, and Alvarez found you first."

"They were just luckier, that's all. I'm so grateful to you—to *all* of you—for searching for me! If you hadn't . . ." Her voice trailed off unsteadily.

After a brief pause, Ian said, "I was frantic. Were you scared too, Abby?"

"Of course, but I tried not to show it. The worst was when the recycling truck parked in front of us and Royce realized he was defeated. He yelled and screamed, slamming his fists on the dashboard. He really went berserk. I had no idea what he would do next—even shoot me. He was so panic-stricken, he actually peed in his pants."

"Thank God he didn't hurt you any worse when he was panicking," said Ian. "Here's something I don't understand about all this, though. Why did Royce and William assume we were gone when they broke into our condo this morning, even though they found our car in the garage?"

"Royce said they figured maybe both of us rode to the lab on your motorcycle. The weather was perfect for it," Abby replied. "Or, if you'd gone earlier on the motorcycle and left the BMW for me, I guess they felt they could overpower a woman."

"Yeah," said Ian, "maybe that's what they were thinking. How wrong they were."

"Of course, my father can be quite commanding. I'm sure he wanted information promptly. Do you think they just took his word for it that we'd already left for Connecticut? Then, when they saw the BMW, they decided to finish the job anyway, even though they must have known that at least one of us might be home. Probably me."

Ian slowed the car and pulled over to the side of the road. He turned and looked at her. "Abby," he said slowly, "I hate those two thugs, but not as much as I hate your father. What he did is unforgivable. Don't refer to him ever, in any way. From now on he must be out of our lives."

Abby hugged him. "I know. I know. We've been betrayed by the person I thought I trusted and loved. Please, let's just go," she said through her tears.

"We owe a lot to our friends, Abby. They were phenomenal. Really worked as a team."

Abby agreed. "When we start building the clinic and launching our own medical-research business, they all should be a part of it. I held on to my sanity by thinking about you, and our future plans."

"You are a strong person, my wife. We survived this."

Dr. Pannell's apartment was comfortable that evening—a secure nest after a day of fear-filled turmoil. Ian's cell phone rang soon after he and Abby arrived.

"It's Bob. He's going to stop by and make sure you're okay. Also wants to know if you need anything."

"Just some clean clothes for the next few days."

Ian hung up the phone. "The sheriff's detectives are going through the condo. Bob said our clothes are strewn all over the garage and bedroom. Some are torn to shreds or white with dust from ripped-out ceiling tiles." He grimaced with disgust. "Apparently mine survived better than yours, so Ingrid is sending over some things for you. She's about your size. Tomorrow I can buy anything else you might need."

"*Ingrid?* Fred's wife? How'd she find out about all this?"

"Bob filled in Fred and Ingrid on the details. They're shocked. Fred insisted that Bob stay with them and let us stay here until we decide what to do."

"If their shock is genuine," Abby said, "at least they weren't in on the scheme."

"Apparently Miano Tse's wall of silence cracked. People wanted to know where we were and why. Everyone's been frantic: Cory, Miano Tse, Martha. I told them you didn't want any company for a day or two."

"You're right. I need some quiet time," Abby agreed.

"Bob will bring the clothes over himself. He has only one key—he will have two made for us. Oh, and your brother called the lab early this afternoon, looking for you. At that time Martha told him you were on your way to Connecticut."

"I'm too beat to deal with Steven. And I know you probably don't want to deal with anyone in my family. Just leave him a message. Tell him I'm all right and I'll call him sometime next week."

"What if he answers?"

"Steven won't. But even if he does, tell him the same thing. Since Mom died, the only times he ever called me were when he wanted me to help him persuade Dad to give him some money. Let's see. That's three times in nine years. Yeah, he's due. It's been about three years since I heard from him. It's a lot of money; otherwise he would be forced to call more often. Probably has to pay off a gambling debt."

Abby took a shower and wrapped herself in an old white terry-cloth bathrobe she found in the closet. "For a bachelor, he's pretty neat," she told Ian, who just waved his hand in acknowledgment.

As she was drying her hair, the phone rang again. "Bob is in the lobby," Ian reported to Abby.

"Tell him to come up," she said, wrapping the terry-cloth bathrobe around herself more tightly. She sat on the big recliner by the television with her legs elevated and an afghan over her. As soon as Ian opened the door, Abby smelled food.

Bob was carrying a large insulated bag in his right hand and a long plastic bag of clothing for Abby and Ian draped over his left arm. "Miano Tse wants you to try her lasagna and her egg-drop soup."

"That was nice of her," said Abby. "She didn't have to go to so much trouble."

"The lasagna was frozen," Bob answered. "She told me she cooks on Saturdays and freezes everything so she doesn't have to cook during the week. She defrosted this in the microwave for you, but it may need a little more thawing. Her lasagna is excellent. I had some before I came over."

Ian took the lasagna and soup and put them on the kitchen counter until the oven was warmed.

"I stopped by your garage after the police were finished and packed a few more items, especially for Ian. None of us wear his size. They're in my car."

"Yeah, I never got any hand-me-downs. Thanks, Bob, thanks."

"Had too much to carry—I'll give them to you when I leave. They survived better than Abby's. There's a laundry area in the basement here you can use if you want."

"Maybe tomorrow we'll do that," Abby said. "Thanks."

Bob walked over to Abby and kissed her on the top of her head. "You sure you're okay? William said Royce kicked you and slapped your face. I see you have swelling and contusions on both cheeks."

He rocked back and forth on his feet as he spoke. The plump bag of clothing over his arm swayed in rhythm, along with a pair of slip-ons dangling from his hand. Mentally he was singing one of his ludicrous songs.

Abby answered, "Guess you've had a lot of experience with this sort of thing in the ER. But no, Bob, I got a thorough exam at the hospital, and they said I'm okay. I really don't think I need any further medical attention. And honest, Royce didn't rape me."

Ian put the lasagna into the oven to finish thawing and the soup on the stove to simmer, and then he joined Abby and Bob. "Abby," Ian said, "even though Royce didn't rape you, you are the victim of a serious crime. Kidnapping is a federal offense, you know. You've got to press charges, get him and William behind bars."

"I agree with Ian. You should press charges, Abby," Bob added.

"Of course I'll press charges," declared Abby. "Those two creeps wrecked our condo and attempted to rob us. They kidnapped me at gunpoint. Royce physically abused me. Actually, he did try to rape me when William left the car, even though he was expecting Dad."

"Royce probably wasn't thinking rationally or he felt he had plenty of time," Bob said. "So sorry you went through all this, Abby." After a short pause he added, "I hope you also press charges against your father."

Abby sighed and continued, "Yes, I will, even though it'll be really painful. His greed and lust for power and prestige were the triggers that set this entire debacle into motion."

"Ian, this must be terrible for you, too," Bob said. "When you love someone as deeply as you love Abby, you wish you could suffer instead of her. Your wife is a strong person, mentally and physically. She's come through brutality and vindictiveness and managed to remain reasonably calm."

Ian nodded. He was beyond speech. He sat on the couch next to Abby. She sighed again and put her hands in his, then commented, "Several times, when Royce became violent—which usually was when he was frustrated—William tried to intervene. In fact, I think William was coming back to the car to protect me from Royce's attempt to rape me. William had glanced back and could have seen that the front seats were empty. He might even have watched Royce get out of the driver's seat and get into the back. I saw William turning back just before Royce pushed me down across the backseat."

"That's about when Josh grabbed William. Yeah, he was heading back like he forgot something," Bob remembered.

Ian gently dropped Abby's hands and left her side to get up and walk around the room. He kept clenching and unclenching his fists as he listened. "I'd love to work that Royce guy over. He'd be a raw piece of meat."

"Josh said you came pretty close to roughing up William, and we all saw you punching your father-in-law. Don't fall into that pit, Ian. You were lucky Van Nisen let you off this time. Stay away from any revenge," Bob insisted.

"Even with Abby's dad?"

"*Especially* with Abby's dad. He's the real culprit, but with his money and his connections, he may just get a slap on the wrist. Believe me, anything you do or say can—and will—be used against you. You know as well as I that husbands are always prime suspects. Any lawyer will use that. Don't give them the chance."

Ian stopped pacing, stared at Bob, and said in a hushed voice, "You can't believe I would ever hurt Abby?"

Dr. Pannell walked over to Ian and put his arm on his shoulder. "I know that, Ian. I know that. Everybody knows it. We've seen you two together. I just want you to be cautious because I care about you. Now, come on. We can have our supper. Let's see how good a cook Miano Tse is."

By Monday morning Abby and Ian were continuing their research at Kingencorp, along with Cory and Miano Tse. Emile was working at another lab and would arrive in the afternoon.

"It's not a fluke!" yelled Abby triumphantly. "The results are replicated!"

"We did it, Ab! All of us did it!" said Ian with a huge grin at all three of his colleagues.

Abby said, "The chemical reactions are revealing themselves one by one, and soon we'll know *exactly* why the HIV can't attach itself to Louella's CD4+ T cells. Cory, you tell Fred. You're the closest to him." She danced around the lab, pushing the numbers of Fred's private line as she moved.

Cory grabbed the phone. "He's not answering," he told Abby. Then he left a message: "Fred, give us a call at Kingencorp. We have some news."

"I haven't seen him in a few weeks. Is he all right?" Ian asked.

"I saw him in the parking lot at our lab the other morning. He just waved and drove away," Miano Tse said.

"Haven't you heard?" asked Cory.

"Heard what?" asked Miano Tse.

"Looks like Patsy Willington's parents are going to win the case against him."

Abby stopped dancing midhop. "You mean . . ."

Cory glanced uneasily from Abby to Miano Tse to Ian before he answered, "I mean it looks like he is going to have to do time."

"Cory, what happened?" Ian asked. "I thought the hospital administrator—what's-his-name, Wimpler—was supposed to support him."

"Patsy had seen another oncologist, Dr. Quintel, for a second opinion. Quintel testified against Fred, and his evidence was pretty damning."

"What a mess," said Abby. "Where the hell does that leave us?"

"I'd say you are okay. Louella, Vincent, and the other patients whose samples you worked with—all of them did sign consent forms; Bob made sure of that. Maybe he knew what was going to happen. At any rate, Martha's got the forms in her file. Martha and I were both called in to witness the signatures."

"Wish you'd told us about Fred sooner," said Abby. "But that explains why we haven't seen him." Her cell rang. "It's Fred, and he wants to talk to you, Cory."

"Hi, Fred. Yeah. At Kingencorp. Yeah, we've made the breakthrough. Yes! It's been replicated! It's the first step in the cure. What? Oh! I'm sorry to hear that. Do you want to talk to her? Okay. Here's Abby."

"Congratulations, Abby," said Fred. "You're the lead researcher now. Put your name first on the research papers."

"Are you *sure*?"

"Yes."

"Thank you, Fred."

"I'm afraid I will be of no use to you. My career is over. The sentencing is tomorrow, but it doesn't matter which way it goes.

My professional reputation is coated with mud. I'm sure you can find someone who will be able to guide you through the rest of the research."

Maybe Emile, Abby thought.

"I'm so sorry, Fred. Absolutely, we'll keep in touch, keep you posted on the project. Yes, Emile has been very helpful. Um . . . you'll be missed. Sure, I'll explain it to everyone. Good-bye."

Abby looked from Cory to Ian to Miano Tse and back again, shaking her head. "Sometimes Fred has been very difficult to work with, but this—this I *never* expected!"

"Me neither," said Ian.

Abby continued, "I remember that initial staff meeting, when he angrily insisted that his name must come first on all research papers. I thought he was so arrogant. Now he told me to put my name first instead."

Cory said, "That means your name appears first on the peer review papers and all publications thereafter."

"He didn't mention my kidnapping, though—or ask if I'm okay."

Ian said, "He does know about it. Bear in mind, Bob spoke to him and Ingrid. They sent over clothes for you. He's got a lot on his mind now, Abby. Give the guy a break."

"When your world turns upside down, you feel very peculiar. Maybe it was too painful for him to discuss our success with you, Abby," Miano Tse suggested.

Abby looked at her colleagues and became conscious of their concern for her. Suddenly she realized something: "Fred trusted my dad, too," she said. "Dad's blatant betrayal must have been very hard for Fred, not just for me."

$$\sim\!\!\wedge\!\!\upharpoonright\!\!\sim_\circ$$

Monday afternoon Judge Culmantski confided to Fred's lawyer, "Dr. Truesort operated on my wife. In fact, he was the only doctor in this area who knew how to treat her cancer. We had consulted many doctors, with extremely limited success. I trust Fred. He can go home on his own recognizance. Just make sure he is back in the courtroom at nine o'clock tomorrow morning. The jury should reach a verdict tomorrow."

Dr. Quintel watched Dr. Truesort go down the granite courthouse steps. *That'll teach you, you arrogant son of a bitch. We got you this time.*

Dr. Truesort stared straight ahead, neither recognizing nor speaking to anyone. His whole being was turned inward. The shock of losing his case left him babbling incoherently in whispered murmurs only he could hear. His body slumped. His arms hung limply at his sides. He lifted his feet carefully as he plodded in an exaggerated stride, like a drunk trying to maintain his balance. *The jury is still out, but no way can I win.*

—⅄⼁ᄂ₀

"What are you doing home so early, Fred?" Ingrid gave him a hug. She looked into his eyes. "What's wrong?"

Fred froze. "I . . . I'm . . . finished. Quintel and Wimpler went against me. The Willingtons are going to win the lawsuit. My license, my privileges, my practice: all stripped away." Fred spoke like an android.

"What lawsuit?"

"I lied to you, Ingrid. I wasn't going to the hospital these last few weeks. I, uh, I was going to court."

"But you've had medical lawsuits before. You've always won."

Pacing back and forth in the living room, Fred haltingly explained how he'd been sure he was on the verge of a great medical discovery, how he'd illegally used Patsy's bone marrow for another patient, how Patsy had consulted Dr. Quintel and later died. "Quintel had them throw the book at me. The jurors looked at me like I was slime."

"But you've always, always won," Ingrid cried out. "We can sell this house and its contents. We could move to southern France."

"Ingrid, try to understand: my career is over. My savings are gone. I spent everything on the goddamn research. Nothing's left. Nothing. Our house belongs to the bank. My stocks and bonds have been sold."

Ingrid stepped back, held Fred at arm's length, and stared at him. "You—so careless! How *could* you? What happened?"

"Chas . . . he hired some thugs to spy on our project. One of them was posing as a sales rep, but a week later I found the bastard searching my hospital lab. Our hush-hush research endeavor almost became public knowledge."

"*Chas* did that to you?"

"Yes, Ingrid. And—I might as well tell you—remember when the police shot that man in our backyard?"

Ingrid shuddered. "How could I forget a horrible thing like that?"

"He wasn't just some burglar. He was a drug lord trying to kidnap Vincent and blackmail me."

"Oh my God, Fred! Why weren't you honest with me?"

"I didn't want to scare you. It was all so ugly—I wanted to shield you. Hoped the danger was over after that, but things kept going downhill. Chas had the thugs search Abby's condo. He wanted to steal our research, but all he'll get is a jail sentence."

"Chas did that to *Abby*? That's the real reason Abby needed clothes? It wasn't some random druggies? Why didn't you tell me? Why?"

"I knew how much all this would upset you. Just couldn't bring myself to do it. I told Abby to put her name first on the research papers. That means it was her idea that worked, which is true. She's the lead researcher."

Ingrid's hands dropped to her sides. They were like weights at the ends of her limp arms. In a whisper she soothed, "Come on, Fred. Let's take a walk out back." She took Fred's hand and led him out the patio door as though she were guiding a child.

They strolled like ghosts around the rose beds, whose bushes were now carefully wrapped in burlap to protect them during the winter. They continued down to the river path, where they watched the sunset turning the sky orange behind the silhouetted trees and gazed out at the rushing river. Fred kissed Ingrid and smiled. "Go see if dinner is ready. I'll be along in a minute." He rubbed her cheek.

Ingrid smiled and began to walk up to the veranda when she heard a splash. "No . . . *no, Fred,* NO!" She ran back to the riverbank. Fred's arms were flailing, his body twisting in the swift current. "NO, GOD, NO!" she screamed as she waded out toward him. She fell sobbing into the current, gasping, and grabbing at Fred.

No one saw them drown in the rapid swirl of the river.

Epilogue: A New Community

*I*T WAS NOW MAY 2011, and the Truesorts had been dead three and a half years. Fred would never know how fortuitous it had been for him to hire professionals who would be responsible leaders. Now, through dedication and hard work, a whole neighborhood was changing from a slum to a vibrant, safe, sought-after community. Fred would have been pleased. At last his dream to do something outstanding had been fulfilled.

Abby Zelban-Lightfoot, Ian Lightfoot, and Cory Maxwell had benefited from selling their research to a renowned pharmaceutical house. Bob Pannell had received 20 percent of the profits, as Fred had promised in his original contract. Bob had also acquired a substantial sum by finding the right patients for Fred's research.

The success of these four people became the foundation for significant renewal and renovation of the entire neighborhood. Their leadership rested not only on the health center they had financed or the private pharma research company Abby and Ian had established, but on the motivation these engendered for dozens of people around them.

Abby and Ian had employed Miano Tse, who used the bonus she received from the research sale to get a BS in chemistry. She became a bona fide medical research chemist.

Cory's daughter, Nora, with the help of the medicine her dad had worked on and the money he earned from it, was now well enough to graduate with a BS in chemistry also and have a career as a histology technician in Abby and Ian's lab. As Miano Tse had told Martha when Nora was hired, "Nora and I are accustomed to working together. Often we would study at my apartment. It is nearer to the college than her home is."

"I would help Miano Tse with some of the English jargon common to chemistry. She would help me with the experiments," Nora added.

"Dr. Fred would be so pleased," Martha said with a smile. She also had joined Abby and Ian's staff as office manager.

Cory, although retired, became a freelance consultant hired by Abby and Ian, and sometimes by Bob at the health-clinic lab, doing the usual analyses needed at any city hospital.

The group of people who had first conferred years ago at Assam's shop about revitalizing the neighborhood had formed a committee and remained devoted to their cause. Ian, Lefty, and Assam had worked with a local bank to gain a loan for the project. The committee members had agreed by consensus to place Bob in charge of the building project. He had hired a local firm, Hughler City Architects Inc., to replace the crumbling warehouse with a modern health clinic. They had moved forward with building a new health center and renovating a cozy home nearby for the local preschool population. Both facilities would be managed by one organization.

Ghanna's knowledge of who was trustworthy became a good guide for Bob. Wherever possible, Bob hired the skilled population in the vicinity, such as construction workers, plumbers, electricians, interior designers, and capable landscapers—along with Miano Tse's former junkyard crew, whose members had junk removal experience and were adept at carrying away much of the construction debris.

"This building is their own. These workers may need it themselves someday," Bob would point out when onlookers wondered why those building the health clinic were so dedicated. There were neither long delays nor shoddy workmanship.

Next the health-center committee formed a subcommittee to recruit medical personnel, which hired a consultant to research possible candidates to employ and carefully reviewed the consultant's recommendations. The recruitment subcommittee was cochaired by Judge Culmantski and Bob Pannell. Nora, Abby, Ian, Martha, and Miano Tse were members at large. They had begun the staffing process for medical and nonmedical positions.

Bob had been promoted to chief of the Hughler Hospital emergency room. He donated the money he received from Truesort Research to add a wing to the health clinic for psychological care, plus a long-term alcohol and drug-abuse facility. His contribution included the staffing of this ward. "Every city needs to have this kind of care available," he'd said to Harry Wimpler, who had instantly agreed.

Harry had survived the ethical debacle of *Willington v. Truesort* since he was not directly involved in the bone-marrow switch. It was just a bump in his career path. He became a reasonably successful CEO adept at avoiding controversy.

Bob had helped Josh apply for a scholarship at a nearby technical institute that offered a five-year architecture program. Josh had one and a half years left till graduation day. Now he was getting hands-on work developing blueprints for the health clinic and creating a model display of its buildings and surrounding grounds. After receiving his architecture degree he would still need three years' internship required for professional licensure.

Cory had bought a home in the suburbs of Hughler City for himself and his daughter. He often went to hear Vincent and Nora when they entertained at Lefty's and other bars and clubs around the city.

Lefty had finally gotten his tin ceiling painted and even refurbished the furniture. Vincent and Nora had brought in more customers. The fact that many drug addicts were gone from his neighborhood boosted Lefty's income too.

Ghanna had enjoyed watching the health clinic go up. He abandoned his little park and rode his power wheelchair over to the construction site, with his boom box tucked neatly into a basket attached to its side. Ghanna played music for the workers and became their sidewalk superintendent.

Abby and Ian's lab was only two blocks away from the health-center site. Miano Tse would pack sandwiches and a thermos of iced tea to join Josh—now her fiancé—and Ghanna for lunch. Josh was gaining practical instruction working at the clinic building site along with theoretical knowledge in the classroom.

At the end of the day Sally or Ramiero, now eleven, would escort Ghanna back to his apartment. One time Ramiero had told Ghanna and Sally, "I'm glad The Oxman can't hurt us anymore. My dad told me about that night. He said I'm old enough to understand now, but he made me promise not to tell my mom."

Ghanna had answered, "Your father is a brave man, Ramiero."

Alvarez was also an ambitious man, able to establish his own small business while he continued to work for the security company used by Hughler Hospital. Alvarez asked Sheriff Van Nisen if he had any suggestions and advice on installing electronic safety and security devices in the new health clinic; he also asked the sheriff to recommend any recruits since the county had downsized its force recently.

Alvarez wanted the electricians to plan and install a first-rate security system when the building was framed out but the walls and floors were not fully constructed. He figured that about eighteen security guards, in three rotating shifts, would be enough for the health clinic since they would be using state-of-the-art electronic devices, ready for whatever the future could bring.

When the construction work was at a point to house the security equipment, and the alarm system was installed, Alvarez ran a surprise trial. It worked without a glitch, so wallboard was ready to be put in place.

That same day Alvarez handed in his resignation to the security company that serviced Hughler Hospital. He sent a thank-you text message to Sheriff Van Nisen for his advice and help. Now Alvarez was on his way to starting a security-installation company of his own. He began by hiring the licensed electricians who had worked on the health center, and he had already picked up a lot of knowledge as a security guard himself. Until his new business was fully established, he earned money by taking security-guard jobs at special events, and the salary Asunta was now making could tide them over. After all, Alvarez was accustomed to taking risks. Wasn't he the man who had lured The Oxman into a trap?

As promised, Asunta did continue to receive free medical care for her cancer from one of Dr. Truesort's colleagues, who took her as a patient after Fred died. By now she had been in remission for two years. Since The Oxman was gone, she and Alvarez had decided to stay in the neighborhood after all. Asunta found a job within walking distance as a teller at a branch of a local bank. Within a year she was promoted to assistant branch manager.

William was given a light sentence since he turned state's evidence. He was given two years in prison and two years of community service.

Hughler Hospital did not hire William back. He found work with a landscaper, riding a tractor-style lawn mower in the summer, using a leaf blower in the fall, and driving a snowplow in the winter.

Royce Barkley was given fifteen years in prison without parole for breaking and entering, assault and battery, kidnapping, and attempted rape. Ever since William had been released from jail, he had visited Royce once a month and would continue to do so throughout Royce's incarceration. During all that time, William was Royce's only visitor.

Dr. Zelban, sixty years old, was sentenced to a total of twenty years in prison: ten for an attempt to pirate intellectual property and ten for being a co-conspirator in his daughter's kidnapping. This former plastic surgeon had no outstanding bills when he entered prison. As soon as he could, he gave Ian the power of attorney through his trustee, despite the anguish of his son, Steven. Later, to everyone's amazement, Dr. Zelban responded to a grant proposal from the 24/7 Health Center administration with a generous sum of $20,000 annually for twenty years, for a total of $400,000.

On Friday afternoon the whole block of the 24/7 Health Center was being closed to all vehicles. Early the next morning, two ambulances would be in place, one at the north entrance and one at the south. Dr. Pannell had insisted on the block closure and the ambulances for safety reasons.

Patrolman Cairnly and Chief Detective Mouski, along with the Hughler City Recreation Department, placed wooden sawhorses and orange pylons around the block to prevent any vehicles from driving into the streets surrounding the health clinic.

Posters designed by Josh had been placed throughout the neighborhood—on telephone poles and trees, and in storefronts, including Assam's cloth shop and Lefty's Bar:

Open House and Gardening Day
Volunteers Needed at 24/7 Health Center
Saturday, May 28, 2011, 9:00 a.m. to 4:00 p.m.
Free Checkups and Vaccines

The two officers walked around the health center on Friday and admired the brick building. "They must've had a barrel of money after suing them two doctors to have been able to replace a ramshackle warehouse with a modern health clinic," Chief Detective Mouski said. "You know the doc who opened up his mansion so we could nab The Oxman?"

"That was a long time ago—what, almost four years now? But yeah, I remember him. What about him?"

"Committed suicide. His wife with him. Bodies were recovered in the river downstream in the rapids about four days after, according to the coroner. Didn't you hear about it, Cairnly?"

"I heard about two bodies being pulled out of the river sometime back then, but I didn't know it was Dr. Truesort." Cairnly paused. "Why'd he do it?" he asked. "He had everything!"

"Don't really know, Cairnly," Mouski answered. "I just don't get it."

The crowd began to drift in around eight thirty on Saturday morning. Some wore burkas; others wore the broad woven straw hats common to Southeast Asian field hands. Most dressed in jeans and

T-shirts, beat-up sneakers, worn work boots, and baseball caps on backward or cotton bandannas tied around their heads. These volunteers were armed with rakes and clippers, wheelbarrows, potting soil and plants, trowels and spades. Some had garden gloves and others had bright yellow waterproof household gloves. They all hoped the gentle breeze would keep them cool all day.

Today the folks who had lobbied for a health clinic in their neighborhood were celebrating. A new brick structure was completed, replacing the old 1890s warehouse. A wrought-iron hand railing from the original building was installed on the exterior steps as a token to history. The neighborhood was becoming a safe place to live again.

Assam and his wife, Sakina, signed in volunteers at the south end of the block; Étoile and Martha were at the north end. Martha commented, "I wonder what Dr. Fred would say about this large turnout?"

"I think he would be pleased," Étoile said tactfully.

Now neighbors were meeting neighbors as they helped with the landscaping and joined in tours of their brand-new medical facility. In order to keep the tour groups small, Josh and Miano Tse divided the volunteers into groups of ten and sent them to Ramiero and Ghanna. Some prepared and planted flower beds first or planted shrubs in front of the foundation while others toured. Then the workers would switch and take their turn touring the health clinic.

With Ramiero's help, Ghanna led groups of visitors into the building, using his power wheelchair. He took them to the waiting room, where he proudly pointed out an exhibit of before-and-after photos as well as Josh's miniature model of the health clinic and its grounds.

Local men and women who had worked on the construction of the building gave tours, explaining how they had worked as a team to make the neighborhood volunteers' dreams a reality.

Dr. Pannell offered free checkups to adults and children. He also discussed first-aid processes and had an American Red Cross volunteer demonstrate CPR. A few practiced on a CPR dummy in a room in the adult ward.

In the children's ward, two pediatricians had free vaccinations on hand for children who needed them. If parents brought their children's birth certificates and a record of the children's previous vaccines, the children could be cared for immediately. If not, the parents could return the following week with written verification to get their children vaccinated.

The dental clinic was open for children and adults. The dentist helped those with immediate needs free of charge. Others made appointments.

Down the hall, Cory and Miano Tse showed a PowerPoint presentation they'd created, demonstrating how the light micro-scope magnifies blood cells. Then many tried to see the blood cells through a light microscope themselves. For most it was a first-time experience. Ramiero was fascinated by what he saw. He asked, "Can I learn to do this too?" Cory and Miano Tse assured him he could.

Visitors went into the second lab, where Ian and Abby, not to be outdone, showed how they analyzed DNA. They demonstrated with a large, three-dimensional model and discussed how impor-tant DNA is for each person. Ian also explained what bioinformat-ics was, with the actual equipment shown on a video screen. He allowed viewers, including Ramiero, to manipulate some of the gear in a truly hands-on experiment, while Abby explained, "In our research, we focus on finding innovative ways to use blood-forming stem cells in bone-marrow transplants. This technique shows great promise for healing many diseases, such as AIDS and various types of cancer, including leukemia and Hodgkin's disease."

Across the hall, Sally was inviting children and their parents to walk down the block to visit the renovated home for preschool children with all its toys. Sally had taken evening courses to become qualified to manage a preschool. Her diploma was framed and hung on the wall behind her desk. She read a few stories to the children and promised them that when they returned, there would be a swing set, a slide, and a climbing rock right outside in the backyard.

All recyclables went to Sally. She insisted on donating the money she received from Gardening Day back into the 24/7 Health Center treasury, earmarked for the preschool budget.

The cafeteria was a favorite stop on the tour. A caterer was hired for this special event. She had a breakfast station and a luncheon station, along with condiments, desserts, and a variety of sodas, teas, and coffees. And it was all free.

Television crews circled the compound, documenting the work for the evening news. Dr. Pannell allowed them inside the closed-off block. The reporters and video photographers parked their vans at the north and south entrances and proceeded from there on foot.

Reporters questioned the volunteers and the organizers. Laughter and the volunteers' close-harmony singing provided the background music to the televised report, occasionally punctuated by a shout of delight when a garden area began to look attractive or a heavy rock was rolled out of the way.

"How many have come so far?" a reporter asked Abby.

"We stopped counting at three hundred fifty. Entire families are here: babies wrapped in ponchos on their mothers' backs, tots in strollers. Some of the older kids have been taking care of the younger ones. Teenagers are helping serve the food and keep the cafeteria tables clean."

Ian added, "Dr. Pannell got fifty-two patients to visit his examining room for checkups. About half were kids. We did hope for more, but it's a start."

Vincent and Lucien, who had returned to be part of this special day, were lugging a pail of vegetative waste to the Dumpster when a TV reporter asked Vincent in sugary tones, "What brings you here today?"

The burly, shirtless Vincent wiped his hand across his sweaty forehead. "Helpin'," he answered. "Helpin' the people. That's what all the organizers did for me. Figure I can do somethin' too. Now you'll have to excuse me, ma'am." Vincent held up a dirty hypodermic needle he pulled from the debris. "Tomorrow is comin'. I gotta work so tomorrow gets here for *everyone*."

Acknowledgments

My thanks to the colleagues, family members, and friends who have guided me through the process of creating my own novel. The actual planning, research, and writing were interrupted many times as I balanced family and business responsibilities. Yet the support of family and friends never wavered.

My love and gratitude to:

> My husband, Ron Goehner, Sr., for his patience throughout and his vast knowledge of things scientific, which he readily shared with me.

> My son Ron Goehner, Jr., whose expertise in research chemistry was an irreplaceable guide.

> My son Tom Goehner, whose astute observations of humankind gave me valuable insights into people's lives.

> My daughter and fellow writer, Janet Goehner-Jacobs, for her thoughtful advice.

> My son-in-law, David Jacobs, for his expertise and continuing assistance with a poorly behaved computer program.

> My grandson, Philippe Kallagov, for graciously sharing his artistic talent and visual skill in design and photography.

My nephew John Stanzel, Esq., for giving me l

My husband's cousin Carol Schumacher J
helped with accurate descriptions of medical procedures.

My friend and fellow writer Karen Haas, for her help in finding
an editor.

Marilyn Miller Gildea, who encouraged me to work on this
project and reminded me that a mutual friend, novelist Grace
Mojtabai, might enjoy reading it.

Many thanks to:

Rosemary and Elien Young, for their insight into the pharmaceutical side of medical research.

 Marge Smith and Sonia Sellars, who volunteered to proofread
more than four hundred pages.

I am also grateful for the skill and professionalism of the team that
made this publication possible:

Saija Autrand, designer, for her outstanding ability to create
and make a blank page come alive.

Andrea Curley, who copyedited the manuscript with a wonderful awareness of detail.

Carver Washburn, for the careful work he did with his company Signs of Design.

Abigail Powers, who proofread the manuscript on short notice.

Janet Frick, for all her patient guidance throughout the writing and editing process, and for recruiting a terrific team of
additional publishing professionals. Because this was my first
novel, I needed someone who knew the publishing world, and
Janet provided much useful feedback that made this a better
book.

Discussion Questions

1. How does the setting of the novel impact the story?

2. As the story progresses, which characters change the most? For example, which ones emerge as leaders? Which make the worst mistakes? Were you surprised by the fates of any of the characters? Why or why not?

3. What are the long-term goals of some of the characters? Do those who make significant progress toward their goals have anything in common? What about those who do not?

4. The book contains many references to biochemistry and the immune system of the human body. How did you react to this information? Was some of it new to you? Did you skip over it? Were you curious enough to look up any unfamiliar terms?

5. Do you believe that unethical behavior is ever justifiable if it helps achieve an important, worthwhile goal? If so, under what circumstances?

6. Why do you think there is so much prejudice against those who have HIV/AIDS, beyond the obvious fear of contracting the disease? Do you think the stigma has lessened during the past twenty years?

7. At the end of the epilogue, Vincent tells the TV reporter, "Tomorrow is comin'. I gotta work so tomorrow gets here for *everyone*." What do you think he means?

List of Characters

Abby Zelban-Lightfoot, PhD: geneticist at Truesort Research, LLC (Fred's private lab); wife of Ian Lightfoot; daughter of Dr. Charles Zelban

Alvarez Delgado, aka **Al:** supervisor at Hughler Hospital; husband of Asunta and father of Ramiero; upstairs neighbor of Ghanna Topallo in building across from hospital

Arnold Mouski: chief detective on Hughler City's police force

Assam Sadur: shopkeeper who sells Persian rugs, odd-lot items, and sewing supplies in reclaimed warehouse; husband of Sakina

Asunta Delgado: Alvarez's wife and Ramiero's mother; upstairs neighbor of Ghanna Topallo in building across from hospital

Aunt Millie: Abby Zelban-Lightfoot's aunt; gave Ian and Abby a crazy lamp

Bob Pannell, MD: assistant chief of Hughler Hospital's emergency room

Brad: detective reporting to Zachary Van Nisen, county sheriff

Calvin: Hughler Hospital security guard reporting to Alvarez Delgado

Camilla: Fred Truesort's patient; abused wife

Carlos: Miano Tse's dependable assistant in junkyard crew

Charles Zelban, MD, aka **Chas:** renowned plastic surgeon; Abby Zelban-Lightfoot's father and Ian Lightfoot's father-in-law; does lots of charity work; went to Harvard Medical School with Fred Truesort

Chewy: Fred and Ingrid Truesort's black Doberman

Cory Maxwell, PhD: medical research chemist at Hughler Hospital, where he reports to Fred Truesort and has been his closest colleague for fifteen years; also works for Fred at Truesort Research, LLC (Fred's private lab)

Culmantski, Edward: presiding judge at *Willington v. Truesort*; husband of a patient of Fred Truesort

Culmantski, Marion: a patient of Fred Truesort; wife of Judge Edward Culmantski

Darian: young boy saved from fire by rescue dog; brother of Matthew

Donald Krainer, aka **Don:** one of the deputies of Zachary Van Nisen, county sheriff

Eade Raschieu: drug dealer and hit man for The Oxman

Emile: electron-microscope expert at Kingencorp

Étoile Chantel: supervising nurse at Hughler Hospital's emergency room

Francisco: one of Miano Tse's junkyard crew; auto mechanic

Frederick Truesort, MD, aka **Fred:** chief oncologist at Hughler Hospital; close colleague of Cory Maxwell, whom he's supervised there for fifteen years; owner of Truesort Research, LLC (private lab); husband of Ingrid Truesort

Ghanna Topallo: ex-convict; lives in apartment across from Hughler Hospital; downstairs neighbor of Alvarez, Asunta, and Ramiero Delgado

Gus: one of The Oxman's bodyguards

Harry Wimpler: new CEO of Hughler Hospital

Hero, aka **Sniffer:** retired rescue dog, now family pet; saved brothers Matthew and Darian

Ian Lightfoot: bioinformatics engineer at Truesort Research, LLC (Fred's private lab); Abby Zelban-Lightfoot's husband; Charles Zelban's son-in-law

Ingrid Truesort: Fred Truesort's wife

Jack: chief of police in Hughler City

Joe: one of The Oxman's bodyguards

Joshua King, aka **Josh:** aide in Hughler Hospital emergency room; boyfriend of Miano Tse

Kevin: emergency medical technician; experienced with dogs

Lee Ribbentrop: first AIDS patient in Fred's research project

Lefty: owns bar near Hughler Hospital

Lexi Bakov, MD: psychiatrist who works with Hughler City police

Louella Parkman: has been HIV positive for years but does not have AIDS; patient of Fred Truesort and friend of Martha Antoine

Lucien Walters: reforming drug addict and dealer

Magahali Triestane: clerk in Hughler Hospital's emergency room

Mark Calhoun: bone-marrow donor who died in car accident

Martha Antoine: Fred's secretary and office administrator; immigrant from Haiti

Matthew: young boy saved from fire by rescue dog; brother of Darian

Miano Tse: Chinese immigrant and entrepreneur; was lab technician in China; girlfriend of Josh

Michael Cairnly: rookie Hughler City police officer

Midgin: extremely ill patient

Morton: Kingencorp security guard

Newman Frion: one of the deputies of Zachary Van Nisen, county sheriff

Nora Maxwell: Cory's daughter; lives in upstate New York

Oxman, The: drug lord

Patsy Willington: one of Dr. Truesort's cancer patients

Pedro: Hughler Hospital security guard reporting to Alvarez Delgado

Ramiero Delgado: Alvarez and Asunta's young son; lives upstairs from Ghanna in building across from Hughler Hospital

Royce Barkley: interviews Fred Truesort and Cory Maxwell as a sales rep from Sirgentec Pharmaceuticals

Sakina Sadur: Assam's wife; first name means "quietude"

Sally Kenyan: homeless woman who collects aluminum cans

Schmutz: Chas's German shepherd

Steven Zelban: Abby Zelban-Lightfoot's brother; Charles Zelban's son; lives in California

Tim: technician from security company

Todd Quintel, MD: oncologist with privileges at Hughler Hospital; Patsy Willington consults him for second opinion

Vincent Monique: heroin addict, guitar player and former stand-up comic; second AIDS patient in Fred's research study

William Meddlebach: member of Hughler Hospital's maintenance crew

Willington, Mrs.: Patsy's mother

Zachary Van Nisen, aka **Zach:** county sheriff; supervises Brad (detective) and Deputies Newman Frion and Donald Krainer, among others

Zanden: one of the Hughler City detectives trailing The Oxman